...[ple]d into an era
[of film]ing [film]. His most recent novel, *Dead Men's Trousers* was a number one *Sunday Times* bestseller. Today, he has written twelve novels, four short story collections and numerous plays and screenplays. Irvine Welsh currently lives in Miami.

ALSO BY IRVINE WELSH

Fiction

Drama

Screenplay

IRVINE WELSH

Dead Men's Trousers

VINTAGE

1 3 5 7 9 10 8 6 4 2

Vintage
20 Vauxhall Bridge Road,
London SW1V 2SA

Vintage is part of the Penguin Random House group of companies
whose addresses can be found at global.penguinrandomhouse.com.

Penguin
Random House
UK

First published in the UK by Jonathan Cape in 2018
First published by Vintage in 2019

penguin.co.uk/vintage

A CIP catalogue record for this book is available from the
British Library

ISBN 9781784708436

Printed and bound in Great Britain by Clays Ltd, Elcograf S.p.A.

Penguin Random House is committed to a sustainable future for our
business, our readers and our planet. This book is made from Forest
Stewardship Council® certified paper.

for Sarah

CONTENTS

PART THREE: MAY 2016, SPORT AND ART   249

PART FOUR: JUNE 2016, BREXIT   331

Prologue
Summer 2015
Fly Boys

A disquieting rivulet of sweat trickles down my back. Nerves jangling; fucking teeth slamming together. Sitting bitch in economy class, crammed in between a fat cunt and a jumpy pissheid. Couldnae get a business seat at short notice and now my chest and breathing are constricted as I pop another Ambien and avoid the eye ay the drunkard next tae me. My troosers are too fucking tight. I can never find ones tae fit me. Ever. The thirty-twos I'm wearing now constrict, while thirty-fours hang awkwardly and look shite. Few places do my optimum thirty-three.

To distract myself, I pick up my *DJ Mag* and my shaky hands turn the pages. Too much fucking booze and ching at the Dublin gig last night. Again. Then, flying intae Heathrow, a heated exchange with Emily, the solitary female in the trio of DJs I manage. Me wanting her back in the studio tae master this demo I love, her having zero confidence in it. I pushed it and she kicked off, causing a bit ay a scene, as she sometimes does. So I left her at the airport, boarding my connecting flight tae Los Angeles.

I'm fucked, my back playing up, on the verge ay a massive panic attack and the piss artist next tae ays is rambling on, transmitting his fear through the plane. I sit scanning my mag, gasping, praying for the pills tae kick in.

Then the boy suddenly goes quiet, and I'm aware ay somebody standing over me. I lower the magazine and look up.

3

My first thought is *no*.

My second is *fuck*.

He's standing in the aisle, his airm hanging casually on the seat top, above the terrorised drunkard's heid. Those eyes. They fry my insides. Make the words I want tae speak evaporate in the desert ay ma throat.

Franco. Francis James Begbie. What the fuck?

My thoughts cascade in a fevered torrent: *It's time. Time tae concede. No tae run, because there's naewhaire tae run tae. But what can he dae, up here? Smash ays? Destroy the plane in a suicide mission, taking everybody doon wi him? It's over, for sure, but how will he take his revenge?*

He just looks at me with an even smile, and says: — Hello there, my old buddy, long time no see.

That does it, this fucking psychopath is being too reasonable no tae be ready to dae something! I spring up, scrambling over the fat cunt, him letting out a yelp as my heel skites down his leg, and I topple intae the aisle, battering my knee, but quickly scurry upright.

— Sir! an oncoming stewardess screeches, blonde hair lacquer-stiffened, as the fat fuck behind me howls something in outrage. I push past her and tear into the lavy, slamming and locking the door. Wedging my body against the flimsy barrier between me and Franco Begbie. My heart is pounding like a fucking drum as I rub my throbbing kneecap.

There's an insistent tap from outside. — Sir, are you okay in there? It's the stewardess, in a casualty-nurse voice.

Then I hear it again, this subverting, reasonable tone, a flavourless transatlantic version of the one I ken so well. — Mark, it's me … He hesitates. — … It's Frank. Are you okay in there, pal?

No longer is Frank Begbie an abstract article, some phantom generated fae harrowing memories in a chamber ay ma mind,

4

whiffling invisibly in the air around ays. He's been rendered flesh and blood in the most mundane of circumstances. He's on the other side ay this biscuit-ersed door! Yet I'm thinking about his expression. Even through those brief glances I sensed something markedly different about Franco. About more than how he's aged. Quite well, I consider, but then the last time ah saw the cunt he was laid out bleeding oan the pavement at the foot of Leith Walk, smashed by a speeding car, purely due tae his reckless pursuit ay me. That doesnae bring oot the best in anybody. Now he has me trapped in this box, six miles in the air.

— Sir! The stewardess raps again. — Are you sick?

I feel the soother of Ambien, taking my panic down a notch. *He can do nothing up here. If he kicks off they will taser the cunt and restrain him as a terrorist.*

With trembling hand, I click the door open. He stands facing me. — Frank ...

— Is this man with you? the stewardess asks Franco.

— Yes, he says, and with an air of controlled authority, — I'll look after him, and he turns tae me, in apparent concern. — You okay, buddy?

— Aye, just a wee panic attack ... thought I was gaunny be sick, I say to him, briefly nodding to the hostess. — I'm a bit of a nervous flyer. Eh, good to see you, I venture to Francis James Begbie.

The hostess warily peels away as I'm thinking, *Don't leave me*. But as well as looking tanned and lean in his white T-shirt wi a funny red wine stain on it, Franco is so unbelievably calm. He's standing there, smiling at me. Not in a nutter-keeping-his-powder-dry way, bristling wi suppressed menace, but as in *not angry*.

And tae ma utter fuckin astonishment, I realise that not only have I been waiting for this day, but now that it's arrived part ay me fuckin welcomes it. A heavy mass levitates fae ma creaky shoodirs, and I'm sick wi a terrifying, giddy liberation. It could be the Ambien. — I think I maybe owe you some money, Frank … is all I can say, as a boy squeezes past us into the bogs. There is fuck all else that will suffice.

Franco keeps his smile on me, raises an eyebrow.

Make no mistake, there's owing some cunt money, then there's ripping off a violent nutjob who's spent most ay his life in jail. Whom you've known through the grapevine has been looking for ye for donks, and who several years ago almost caught ye, brutally self-wrecking in the process. *Owing him money* doesnae even fucking begin tae cover it. And all I can dae is stand here with him, in the limited space by the lavies. Surging through the sky in this metal tube, its engines roaring around us. — Look … I know I need tae pay ye back, I say, feeling my teeth chatter. And by saying this, I not only consciously realise that *I do*, but also that this might now be possible without him fucking killing me.

Frank Begbie maintains that relaxed grin and easy bearing. Even his eyes seem serene, no at all manic or threatening. His face is mair creased, which surprises me, as they look like laughter lines. Begbie seldom displayed mirth, unless it was at the misfortune ay others, usually occasioned by his actions. His arms are still strong; tight cables of muscle spilling out fae that strangely marked T-shirt. — The interest might be pretty high. He raises a brow again.

It would be fucking astronomical! It was more than just the monetary debt. More, even, than his self-injury by running blindly in front ay a careening motor in his manic pursuit of me. There was that bond ay twisted friendship dating way, way back. It was something that I'd never be able to fathom, but come tae believe had played some part in defining me.

Before ah ripped him off for that cash.

We'd done a dodgy drug deal. I was young, and a junky, and I just needed to get the fuck away fae Leith and the quicksand I was sinking intae. That money was the ticket oot.

Now ah cannae even begin tae address what the fuck this cunt is daein on an LA flight, as I'm the one who needs tae be offering the explanations. I figure he deserves at least an attempt at a reason, so ah tell him why. Why I ripped off him, Sick Boy, Second Prize and Spud. Well, no, Spud was different. I compensated Spud, and, much later, Sick Boy, before being party to stinging that cunt for even more, in another disastrous scam. — I was ready to pay you back too, I contend, trying to keep my jaw from rattling, — but I kent ye were after ays, so I thought it best tae avoid ye. Then we had that accident … I wince, recalling him being thrown in the air by that Honda Civic, coming to rest in a crumpled heap on the tarmac. Me supporting him, as the ambulance came and he drifted into unconsciousness. At the time, I genuinely thought he was deid.

As I talk my body involuntarily tenses further in anticipation of a violent dig, but Franco just listens patiently, drawing in firm breaths ay the sterile air. A couple of times I feel he's fighting down the urge tae speak, as stewards and passengers jostle past us. When I finish my breathless spiel, he just nods. — Right.

I am flabbergasted. I would back away in disbelief if there was anywhere tae go in this narrow space we find ourselves trapped in. — Right … what do you mean by 'right'?

— I mean that I get it, he shrugs, — I understand that ye needed tae get oot. You were fucked wi drugs. I was fucked wi violence n peeve. You got that ye had to escape fae where we were, long before I ever realised it.

What the fuck?

— Well, aye, is all I can say. I ought to be terrified, but I'm no getting the vibe that I'm being set up. I can scarcely believe that it's Franco. He would never have had this mindset, or even been comfortable using those words before. — I didnae use the right escape vehicle though, Frank, I confess, both humbled and embarrassed. — I betrayed my mates. For better or worse, you, Sick Boy, Spud and Second … Simon, Danny and Rab, you were my friends.

— Ye fucked Spud by giein him the money. He was right back oan the skag. Franco breaks out his cold, bloodless expression, that one that used to set me on edge, as it was one that generally preceded violence. But now things seem different. And there was nothing I could say about Spud. It was true. That three thousand two hundred quid hadnae helped him at all. — Had ye done the same for me, you'd have probably fucked me with the drink. He lowers his voice as another stewardess passes us. — Actions seldom have their intended consequences.

— That's true, I stammer, — but it's important tae me that you know –

— Let's no talk aboot all that. He raises the palm of his hand, shaking his head, and half shutting his eyes. — Tell me where you've been, what you've been up tae.

All I can dae is comply. But I'm thinking about *his* journey as I go through my yarn. After Franco's attempted attack on me back in Edinburgh, even though I knew he was banged up, I became a very mobile DJ manager, rather than the landlocked club promoter I'd previously been. A manager is always on the move. He follows his clients all over the globe; dance music now has no frontiers, blah, blah, blah. But it was an excuse: a reason tae travel, tae keep moving. Aye, ripping off that poxy few grand delineated my life as much as his. Probably more.

Then this beautiful lassie with collar-length blonde hair comes up tae us. She has a slim, athletic build, with a long, swan-like neck, and eyes that exude a sort of tranquillity. — There you are, she says, smiling at Franco and turning tae me, urging an introduction.

What the fuck?

— This is Mark, an old friend of mine from Leith, the cunt goes, almost sounding like fucking Sick Boy impersonating Connery's Bond. — Mark, this is my wife, Melanie.

I'm giddy with shock. My sweating palm reaches into my pocket tae the comforting bottle of Ambien. This is not my auld mate and deadly nemesis, Francis James Begbie. The horrible possibility dawns on me: perhaps I've been living ma life in fear ay a man who no longer exists. I shake Melanie's soft, manicured hand. She stares at me in puzzlement. The cunt has obviously never even fuckin mentioned ays! I can't believe that *he's* moved on, tae the extent that the guy who ripped him off and caused him to be badly injured, his (ex) best mate, disnae even warrant being idly mooted tae his missus!

But Melanie confirms this when she says, in an American accent, — He never discusses his old friends, do you, honey?

— That's cause maist ay them are in jail, and you know them, he says, at last sounding a little like the Begbie I knew. Which is simultaneously scary and oddly reassuring. — I met Mel in prison, he explains. — She was an art therapist.

Something flares in my mind, a blurry face, a snatch ay conversation half heard in a noisy club through an E rush or coke rant: maybe fae my veteran DJ Carl, or some Edinburgh head in the Dam on holiday. It was something about Frank Begbie becoming a successful artist. I never gave it any credence or dominion in my consciousness. Any mention ay his name ah just tuned out. And this was the maist outlandish and improbable ay the many myths circulating aboot him.

— You don't look the jailbird type, Melanie says.

— I'm more of a prison warden-cum-social worker type.

— So what you do for a living?

— I manage DJs.

Melanie raises her eyebrows. — Would I know any?

— DJ Technonerd is my most famous.

Franco looks blank at this information, but not so Melanie. — Wow! I know his stuff. She turns to him. — Ruth went to one of his gigs in Vegas.

— Yes, we have a residency there, at the Wynn Hotel, the Surrender nightclub.

— *Steppin in, steppin out of my life, you're tearin my heart out, baby* ... Melanie hums DJ Technonerd's, or Conrad Appeldoorn's, latest hit.

— Ah ken that yin! Franco announces, sounding very Leith in his enthusiasm. He looks at me as if he's impressed. — Nice one.

— There's another name you might recognise, I venture, — mind ay Carl Ewart? N-Sign? Was big in the nineties, or maybe more the noughties? Mates wi Billy Birrell, the boxer?

— Aye ... was he no a sort ay albino guy, a buddy ay Juice Terry? Stenhoose boy?

— Aye. That's him.

— He's still DJing? Ye never hear ay him now.

— Aye, he moved into film soundtracks, but he split up with his missus, hit a bad patch, and let Hollywood doon wi a score for a big studio movie. He cannae get any mair film work, so ah'm masterminding his DJing comeback.

— How's that gaun? Franco asks, as Melanie shifts her look between us like she's watching a tennis rally.

— So-so, I admit, although shit would be better. Carl's passion for music has gone. It's aw ah can dae tae get the cunt oot ay bed and behind the decks. As soon as the gig is finished, vodka and racket takes over and I, only too often,

10

get dragged along in the slipstream. Like in Dublin last night. When I was a promoter based in Amsterdam, I used to keep fit. Karate. Ju-jitsu. I was a machine. Not any longer.

As the guy vacates the toilet, Melanie goes inside. I try tae no even think about how lovely she is, as I'm certain that Franco will read my mind. — Listen, buddy, I drop ma voice, — it's no how I thought this would play out, but we have a wee bit ay catching up to do.

— Do we?

— Aye, cause there's that issue that needs tae be resolved in your favour.

Franco looks oddly bashful, then shrugs and says, — We should swap numbers.

As we're exchanging contact details, Melanie reappears, and we return to our respective seats. I sit back down, apologising effusively to the corpulent cunt, who ignores me but wears a scandalised perma-pout, passive-aggressively rubbing his beefy thigh. I shudder in the sort ay fear and excitement I huvnae experienced for years. The nervous flying drunk looks at me in bleary, jittery empathy. Meeting Frank Begbie under those circumstances is telling me the universe has gone arse-over-tit.

I pop another Ambien, and drift off into a half-sleep, my mind restless and looping on life's themes. Thinking about how it hardens and stultifies you ...

... *the good stuff you seem tae have less time for, and you find yourself constantly drowning in the bullshit, so ye start no tae gie a fuck about other people's crap – it just overwhelms you if ye gie it the space – you kick back and watch* Pop Idol *– ironically of course, with lashings of haughty, critical disdain – and sometimes, just sometimes, it can't quite blank oot a strange overwhelming silence, and there it is, a little hiss in the background – that's the sound of your life force draining away –*

– listeeeeeennnn –

– it's the sound of you dying – you're a prisoner of your own self-confirming, self-restraining algorithms, allowing Google, Facebook, Twitter and Amazon to bind you up in psychic chains and force-feed you a crappy, one-dimensional version of yourself, which you embrace as it's the only affirmation on offer – these are your friends – these are your associates – these are your enemies – this is your life – you need chaos, an external force tae shock you oot ay your complacency – you need this because you no longer have the will or the imagination to do it yourself – when I was younger, Begbie, who has jolted himself so dramatically out ay his Leith and prison trajectory, did this for me – as bizarre as it seems, part ay me has always missed the cunt – you have to live until you die –

– so how do you live?

Later, in the airport terminal, we chat some more, waiting for our luggage tae come off the belts. I try to stretch out my lower back, as he shows me a picture on his phone of their kids, two sweet little girls. All this is profoundly disorientating. It's almost like the sensible, normal friendship we were meant tae have, rather than me constantly trying tae find ways to deactivate his violence. He tells ays aboot his forthcoming art exhibition, inviting me along, enjoying the incredulity on my coupon that I cannae even try tae hide as my tartan wheeler bag inches towards me. — Aye, I know, he graciously concedes, — it's a funny auld life, Rents.

— You can say that again.

Franco. A fucking art exhibition! Ye couldnae make that shit up!

So I watch him leave the LAX arrivals lounge with his young wife. She's smart and cool and they are obviously in love. It's a big step-up from what's-her-name, back in the day. Grabbing a bottle of water from the vending machine, I slip another Ambien down, heading for the car hire with the unsettling sense that the universe is badly aligned. If somebody told me there and then that Hibs were going to win the Scottish Cup next season, I'd have almost fucking well believed them. The shaming, bitter truth of it: I'm jealous of the cunt, a creative artist with a gorgeous bird. I cannae stop thinking: *That was meant to be me.*

Part One

December 2015

Another Neoliberal Christmas

1

RENTON – THE
TRAVELLING MAN

A rash ay sweat beads are forming on Frank Begbie's forehead. I am trying no tae stare. He's just come intae the air-conditioned building fae the heat outside, and his system's adjusting. Pits ays in mind ay when we first met. It was warm then n aw. Or maybe no. We start idealising shit as we get older. It actually *wasn't* at primary school, as I had often recounted. That tale seemed tae have slid intae that weird overstuffed volume between fact and folklore, where a lot ay Begbie stories ended up. No, it was before that: at the ice-cream van outside the Fort, probably on a Sunday. He was cairrying a big blue Tupperware bowl.

I had no long started school, and recognised Begbie from there. He was the year above me then, but that would change. I stood behind him in the queue, a bright sun in our eyes, bursting oot fae gaps between the blackened tenements. *He seems a good boy*, I thought, watching him dutifully hand the bowl over to the ice-cream man. — It's for eftir dinner, he said with a big smile, on noting me observing proceedings. I recall that this impressed me greatly at the time; ah'd never seen a kid entrusted to get a bowl filled in that way. My ma just gave us tinned Plumbrose cream with our sliced peaches or pears.

Then, when I got my cone, he had stalled and was waiting for me. We walked back doon the street thegither, talking about Hibs and our bikes. We were fleet-footed, especially him, speed-walking and bursting into a trot, mindful of the melting ice cream. (So it *was* a hot day.) I headed to the towering council flats at Fort House; he veered across the road to a sooty tenement. *Auld Reekie* was just that back then, before stone cleaning removed the industrial grime. — See ye, he waved at me.

I saluted back. Yes, he *did* seem a good boy. But later on, I would learn different. I always told a story of how ah was seated next to him at secondary school, as if this penance was imposed on me. But it wasn't. We sat thegither because we were already friends.

Now I cannae quite believe I'm here in Santa Monica, California, living this kind of life. Especially when Franco Begbie is sitting across the table from me, with Melanie, in this nice restaurant on 3rd Street. We are both light years away from that ice-cream van in Leith. I'm with Vicky, who works in film sales, but hails originally from Salisbury, England. We met on a dating website. It's our fourth outing and we huvnae fucked yet. After our third would probably have been the time. We're not bairns. Now I sense we've let it slide too long and are a bit tentative in each other's company, wondering: is this going anywhere? I thought I was being cool; truth is that she's a lovely woman and I'm aching to be with her.

So it's tough being roond Franco and Melanie; such a bright, bronzed and healthy couple. Franco, twenty years older than her, almost seems a match for this fit, tanned, blonde Californian. They are easy and languid in each other's company; a touch ay hand on thigh here, a sneaky wee peck on cheek there, a meaningful glance and exchange of conspiratorial smiles everywhere.

Lovers are cunts. They rub your face in it without meaning to. And that's what I've had from Frank Begbie since that

18

fucking insane day on the plane last summer. We did stay in touch, and have met up a few times. But never just us: always with Melanie, and sometimes whatever company I bring along. Strangely, this is at Franco's instigation. Whenever we arrange a get-together for just the two of us, so I can discuss paying him back, he always finds a reason to cancel. Now here we are in Santa Monica, with Christmas looming. He'll be here for the festive period, in the sun, while I'll be in Leith, with my old man. Ironically able to relax, now that the guy sitting opposite me, who I thought would never leave the old port, or only for a prison cell, is no longer a threat.

The food is good and the company is pleasant and chilled out. So I should be at peace. But I'm no. Vicky, Melanie and I split a bottle ay white wine. I crave a second but stay silent. Franco doesnae drink any more. I keep saying that tae myself in disbelief: *Franco doesnae drink any more*. And when it's time tae leave and head tae the apartment in the Uber with Vicky, who lives close by in Venice, I'm again pondering the implications of his transformation, and where it's left me. I'm far from a strict temperance guy, chance would be a fine thing, but I've done enough NA meetings over the years tae ken that no paying him back just isnae a valid psychological option for ays. When I do compensate him – and I realise that I must, not just for him but for me – it'll be gone, that fucking huge burden. That need to run will be forever extinguished. I can see more of Alex, maybe rebuild some kind of a relationship with Katrin, my ex. I can perhaps make a proper go ay it with Vicky here, see where it takes us. And all I need to do is tae pey this cunt off. I know exactly how much I owe him at today's money. Fifteen thousand four hundred and twenty quid: that's how much three thousand two hundred pounds is worth now. And that's small beer compared tae what I owe Sick Boy.

But I've also been putting money aside for him and Second Prize. Franco, though, is more pressing.

In the back of the Uber, Vicky's hand fastens around my own. She has big paws for a woman of around five-six; they're almost the same size as mine. — What are you thinking about? Work?

— Got it, I lie glumly. — I've those gigs at Christmas and New Year in Europe. But at least I'll get back home tae spend time with the old boy.

— Wish I was going home, she says. — Especially as my sister's making it back from Africa. But it takes too much time out of my leave. So it'll be Christmas with some expats ... again, she groans in exasperation.

Now would be the time to say it: *I wish I were spending Christmas here with you.* It would be a simple, honest statement. However, meeting Franco has once again discombobulated me, and the moment passes. But there are other opportunites. As we reach my building I ask Vicky if she wants to come up for a nightcap. She smiles tightly. — Sure.

We get upstairs and into the apartment. The air is thick and stale and hot. I hit the air con and it creaks and whistles into action. I pour two glasses ay red wine and slump down on the small couch, suddenly tired after all my travelling. My DJ Emily says that everything happens for a reason. It's her mantra. I never buy into all that cosmic forces shite. But now I'm thinking: *What if she's right?* What if I was meant to run into Franco, in order to pay him back? Unburden myself? Move on? After all, that's what he's done, and I'm the one who's fucking stuck.

Vicky has sat down on the couch beside me. She stretches out like a cat, then slips off her shoes and pulls her tanned legs up, smoothing down her skirt. I feel blood flowing from brain to baws. She's thirty-seven and has had a proper life, from what I can gather. Been messed around by a couple of

20

wankers, broken a few saps' hearts. Now she has a fire in her eye and set tae her jaw that says: *Time to get serious. Shit or get off the pot.*

— You think it's time we, eh, took this to the next level? I ask.

Her eyes are slitty and alert as she touches the sun-bleached brunette-blonde hair scrapped right back off her forehead. — Oh, I think so, she says in a voice that is meant to be sexy and is.

We're both relieved tae get the first shag out the road. Already beyond excellent, it'll only kick on from here. It always fascinates me how, when you fancy somebody, they often look even better with no clothes on than you imagine. But the next day, she leaves early for work, and I have to get on a plane tae Barcelona. It's for a gig that isnae important in itself, but at a club night promoted by a guy who does the Sonar Festival there. Our participation in that was sealed by agreeing to do this Christmas show. Who knows when Victoria and I will hook up again. But I travel happy and with a bit to think about, and maybe something to come back for. And that's been a long time in happening.

So here I am, flying east, the dreaded east. Business class is essential for this one. I should lie flat but the stewardess offers a nice French wine from their selection, and before I know it I'm shit-faced at altitude again. All I'm thinking about is getting some coke. I settle for an Ambien.

Yes, it has gotten obnoxiously trendy. Aye, money has ruined it. For sure, it's been colonised by cosmopolitan fuckers high on solvency and low on personality, their mirthless laughter from the bars and cafes echoing down its narrow streets. But for all those caveats, the simple fact remains intact: if you don't like Barcelona, you're a cunt, and totally lost tae humanity.

I know I still have some kind of pulse, cause I love it. Even when I'm fighting tae keep my eyes open, and shutting them jaunts me back into the hell of the sweaty nightclub I've either just left or am heading to. I have a constant four-four beat pounding in my brain, despite the cab driver playing tinny Latin music. I stumble out the taxi, almost falling over with fatigue. I pull my roller-wheeled case out the back, and struggle intae my hotel. The check-in is swift but seems like an age. I feel myself letting the air out my lungs in a long sigh to hurry the clerk up. I'm shiteing it in case one ay my DJs or the promoter walks in right now and wants *to talk*. The plastic strip that gains me entry to my room is issued. Some notes about the Wi-Fi and breakfast. I get intae the lift. The blinking green light in the lock tells me the key works, *thank fuck*. I'm inside. On my bed.

For how long I'm out I don't know. But the room phone wakes me with loud burps. My mind journeys with each one; the pause long enough to give me hope I've just heard the last of them. Then … it's Conrad. My most high-maintenance client has arrived. I push my bones vertical.

I'm wishing I was in LA or Amsterdam, I don't care, watching *Pop Idol*, Vicky perhaps tucked into my side, but I'm a shuddering mass of jet lag and ching in this Barcelona hotel, feeling my IQ almost satisfyingly slip away as my heartbeat pumps up. I'm in the bar with Carl, Conrad and Miguel, a promoter at Nitsa, the club we're playing. Fortunately, he's one of the good guys. Emily enters and refuses to join us, pointedly standing at the bar, playing with her phone. She's making a statement, one that compels me to rise and go to her.

— You get those wankers in your little boys' club sorted out, why not me?

No much in my job disturbs me. Certainly setting up a DJ with prostitutes doesn't even twinge my moral compass these days. But when the DJ is a young woman, who is seeking the company of another young woman, it's outside both my skill set and comfort zone. — Look, Emily –

— Call me DJ Night Vision!

How do you react when a young lassie with wavy dark hair, a beauty-spot mole on her chin and big swimming-pool eyes looks at you as if she indeed does have night vision? She once told me that her mother was of gypsy stock. That surprised me as I've met her dad, Mickey, who seems pure English Defence League. I can see why that one didn't last. Her title has become a big thing with her, since she heard me calling Carl N-Sign and Conrad Technonerd. — Look, DJ Night Vision, you're a beautiful woman. Any guy, I correct myself, — I mean girl, or *person*, in their right mind, would want tae sleep with you. But you shagging a lipsticked-and-stiletto-heeled hooker will depress the fuck out of me, as I crash in the next room alone with a good book. Then it'll do the same tae you, as you'll have tae lie tae Starr.

Emily's girlfriend Starr is a tall, gorgeous, raven-haired medical student. Not the sort of lassie that gets cheated on, you'd think, but nobody is too beautiful to suffer that fate. Carl's ex, Helena, is a stunner, but it didn't stop this weird-looking albino cunt from Stenhoose banging anything that smiled at him. Emily sweeps her hair oot ay her eyes and rocks back on her heels, looking over at the boys. Carl is animated, gesticulating, arguing with Miguel: his voice high, fuelled by powder. I hope tae fuck the cunt isnae burning this gig down. Conrad watches in detached semi-amusement, cramming some complimentary nuts intae his face. Emily turns back to me, her voice harsh and low. — Do you care about me, Mark?

— Of course I do, babe, you're like a daughter to me, I say, a little blithely.

— Yeah, one that makes you money instead of one you have to pay college fees for, right?

Emily Baker, Night Vision, doesn't actually make me that much money. With a few notable exceptions, female DJs don't do that well. Back when I had the club, I booked Lisa Loud, Connie Lush, Marina Van Rooy, Daisy, Princess Julia and Nancy Noise, but for every one of them there were scores who were still worth booking but who weren't. Female DJs more often than not have great taste and play the cool, righteous house music I like. But they generally aren't as obsessive-compulsive as male ones. In short, they have lives. Even those who don't are still tough to break, as the industry is extremely sexist. If they ain't lookers, they don't get taken seriously, ignored by the promoters. If they are lookers, they don't get taken seriously, cruised by the promoters.

I'm not going to mention the track or the studio though, that will set Emily off; it's great but she lacks confidence in it and I cannae give anybody lessons in how tae live. I have more hassles with my DJs than I do with my own kid, the difference being that I try harder tae make a difference with them. When I tell people what I do for a living, the daft cunts actually see it as glamorous. Is it fuck! My name is Mark Renton and I'm a Scotsman who lives between Holland and America. Most ay ma life is spent in hotels, airports and on phones and email. I have around $24,000 in an account at Citibank in the USA, and €157,000 in the ABN AMRO in the Netherlands, and £328 in the Clydesdale Bank in Scotland. If I'm no in a hotel, my head rests on a pillow in a flat overlooking a canal in Amsterdam or a balcony-less condominium in Santa Monica, a good half-hour walk from the ocean. It's better than being on the dole, stacking shelves in a supermarket, walking some rich cunt's dug, or cleaning some slavering fucker's arse, but that's about it. It's only in the last three years I've started making serious money, since Conrad has broken big.

We've caned it a little at the hotel and get taxied to the club. Conrad seldom does coke or E but smokes a ton of weed and eats like a beer-titted horse. He's also narcoleptic and has fallen into his customary deep sleep in the anteroom off the green room, which is a busy space, full of DJs' managers, journos and hangers-on. I head to the bar with Miguel to talk business, and when I go to check on my superstar DJ around forty minutes later, something isn't quite right.

He's still under, lying on his side, his arms folded, but ... there's something attached to his forehead.

It's ... it's a fucking dildo!

I pull gently on it, but it seems stuck fast. Conrad's lids dance but remain closed, as he gives out a low growl. I let go.

Fuck! Which cunt ...?

Carl! He's in the DJ booth. I head back to the green room, where Miguel is conversing with Emily, who is about to go on. — Who the fuck ... In there, his heid, I point, as Miguel moves through to investigate while Emily shrugs blankly. — Carl ... That cunt ...

I charge out to the booth as Carl is finishing up for an unenthusiastic audience, on a quarter-full floor. Emily appears at my shoulder, ready to replace him.

— C'mere, ya cunt. I grab his wrist.

— What the fuck –

I'm pulling him out the booth, through the green room and into the anteroom, pointing at the still power-napping, dildo-heided Dutchman. — Did you do that?

Miguel is in attendance, looking at us with startled wide eyes. Carl laughs, and slaps the Catalan promoter on the back. Miguel chuckles nervously and raises his hands. — I saw nothing!

— Looks like one more complex management problem for you to resolve, bro, Carl grins. — I'm heading out onto the dance floor. There was a sultry wee honey I kept making eye contact with. She could be getting rode. So don't wait up. He punches my airm, then shakes Conrad's shoulder. — Wake up, ya dickheided Dutch dope!

Conrad doesn't open his eyes. He just shifts onto his back, the cock pointing upwards. Carl departs, leaving me to sort this fucking mess out. I turn to Miguel. — How the fuck do you remove superglue?

— I do not know, he confesses.

This isn't good. I always feel that I'm on the verge of losing Conrad. Big management agencies have been sniffing around. His head will be turned. It happened with Ivan, the Belgian DJ I broke big, and the cunt jumped ship as soon as the royalties started flowing in. I can't afford Conrad to do the same, although I scent the inevitability.

Watching him slumber, I pull out my Apple Mac and batter through some emails. He's still under when I check my watch; Emily is coming to the end of her set soon, so I shake him. — Buddy, time to rock.

He blinks awake. His eyes roll into his head as his peripheral vision sees something loom above them. He touches his forehead. Grabs at the dick. It hurts. — Ow ... what is this?

— Some cunt ... probably Ewart, fucking around, I tell him, trying to make light of it. Miguel is over. The sound engineer shouts that Conrad is due on.

— Tell Night Vision to hold the fort, I say, pulling on the dildo. It looks like it's growing out his head.

26

Miguel looks on in mounting perturbation, his tones sepulchral. — He will have to go to the hospital to get it removed!

My touch isn't that deft, as Conrad lets out a howl. — Stop! What the fuck are you doing?

— Sorry about this. After your set, bud, we go straight to casualty.

Conrad sits bolt upright, storms over to the wall mirror. — What ... His fingers pull at the phallus and he yelps out in pain. — WHO DID THIS? WHERE IS EWART?

— Pussy hunt, mate, I advance timidly.

Conrad is gingerly probing and pulling at the cock with his doughy fingers. — This is not a joke! I cannot go on like this! They will laugh at me!

— You have to play, warns Miguel, — we have an arrangement. Sonar. It is in the contract.

— Conny, I beg him, — help us out here!

— I cannot! I need this off me! He tugs at it again and screams out, his face contorted in pain.

I stand behind him, my hands on his big shoulders. — Don't, it'll take your skin off ... Please, bud, go out, I implore. — Own it. Make it your joke.

Conrad swivels round, breaking my grip, panting like a pressure cooker, looking at me in pure, earnest execration. But he's off, led by the big cock, and he steps out behind the decks to cheers and the flashing of camera phones. Fair play to the fat lad, he rolls his head and lets the dick flop around, to feverish screams from the floor.

Emily stands back and giggles through her fingers. — It's funny, Mark.

— It's not fucking funny at all, I declare, but I'm laughing too. — I'll never hear the end of this. He will make me pay with my blood, sweat and tears. I was relying on him to help me elevate you and Carl, but he's no going to play nice now!

— Everything happens for a reason!

Like fuck it does. I have to hand it to Conrad though: he sidelines his petulance. On the chorus of his hit 'Flying High' with the refrain *Sexy, sexy baby*, he faux wanks the cock to great cheers, roaring into the mike, — I luff house muzik! It is the ultimate headfuck!

It's a monster gig, but when it's over Conrad's understandably back in the strop big time. We get him to the hospital where they apply a solution to loosen and remove the dildo quite easily. He still isn't happy, as a nurse sponges the excess glue off his forehead. — Your friend Ewart, trying to build his comeback on my reputation. There is no way! I am laughing stock! It is all over social media! He shows me Twitter on his phone. The hashtag #dickhead has been well used.

The next morning sees the familiar shaky rise for another flight, this time to Edinburgh. A favourable article I find while netsurfing lifts my spirits. It's by an influential dance-music journalist who was at the gig. I show Conrad, who reads, his eyes bulging and a wheezy purr insinuating from deep within.

A lot of the modern DJs are humourless bores, dull tech-heads with zero personality. You certainly can't slot Technonerd into that box. Not only did he play a blistering set in Barcelona's Nitsa, shining in comparison to the stodgy veteran N-Sign who preceded him, he also displayed great levity, hitting the box sporting a dangling penis, swinging from his forehead!

— See? You fuckin owned that shit, I say with a passion only partly contrived, — *and* you owned that fuckin crowd. It was a flawless display of dance-music entertainment, the humour and wit matching the tunes and –

— I did. Conrad punches his big tits and turns across the aisle to Carl. — And I owned his tired old has-been ass!

Carl turns his head into the window, doghouse hung-over, and lets out a groan.

Conrad leans into me, and says earnestly, — You say flawless performance ... this was the word you used, *flawless*. But this implies, does it not, that it was purely technical? It was contrived, and it lacked soul. This is what you mean, yes?

Fuck sake, what kind ay a life is this tae lead ...? — No, mate, it had soul brimming out of every pore. And it wasn't contrived, it was the polar fucking opposite. How could it be contrived, I point over at the now slumbering Ewart, — when this cunt did that to you? It forced you to dig deep, I slap his chest, — and you fucking came up with the goods. Proud as fuck of you, bud, I say, watching his face for a reaction.

A satisfied nod tells me things are okay. — In Edinburgh, the Scottish pussy is good, yes?

— The city boasts the most stunningly beautiful women in the world, I tell him. — There's a place called Standard Life; mate, you do not want to know.

His brow arches in intrigue. — The Standard Life. This is a club?

— More a state of mind.

When we land, I scrutinise the emails, the texts, fire off some in return, round up the DJs, check into another hotel like a zombie. Get the DJs to bed, get some sleep myself, then stroll down Leith Walk in the murky cold, biting after the Californian sun, and even the Catalan one. But bold in my strides for the first time in decades, not caring about bumping into Begbie any more.

Perversely, some stretches of the old boulevard of broken dreams are not too dissimilar from parts of the Barcelona I

29

just left: old pubs tarted up, students everywhere, rip-off flats like cheap false teeth in the gap sites between tenements, cool cafes, eateries of every type and cusine. Those sit comfortingly alongside pockets of the familiar: a vaguely recognised tab-puffing bam outside the Alhambra strangely reassuring as he gives me the snidey eye.

Down to Dad's gaff by the river. I stayed here for a couple of years after we moved from the Fort, but it never felt like home. You know you've turned intae a cunt with nae life, whose fetid arsehole is owned by late capitalism, when times like this feel an imposition and you cannae stop checking your phone for emails and texts. I'm with my dad, my sister-in-law Sharon, and my niece Marina and her infant twin boys Earl and Wyatt, who look indentical but have different personalities. Sharon has packed on the beef. Everybody in Scotland seems fatter now. As she fingers an earring, she expresses guilt about them staying in the spare rooms, while I'm in a hotel. I tell her it's no hardship for me, as my dodgy back demands a specialist mattress. I explain that the hotel room is a business expense; my DJs have gigs in the city. Working-class people seldom get that the wealthy generally eat, sleep and travel well at their expense again, through tax deductables. I'm not exactly rich, but I've blagged my way into the system, onto the steerage class of the gravy train that bulldozes the poor. I pay more tax registered in Holland than I would in the USA, but better gieing it to the Dutch to build dams than the Yanks to build bombs.

After the meal prepared by Sharon and Marina, we're kicking back in the cosy cramp of this small room, and the drinks slip down nicely. My old boy still has a decent posture to him, broad-shouldered, if a little bent over, not too much muscle wastage in evidence. He's at the time of life where nothing at all surprises. His politics have drifted towards the right, in a moany auld cunt nostalgia way, rather than intrinsically hardcore reactionary, but still a sad state of affairs for an old union man, and indicative of bigger existential distress. That leakage of hope, of vision and passion for a better world, and its replacement by a hollow rage, is a sure sign that you're slowly dying. But at least he lived: it would be the worst thing on earth to have those politics at an early age, to be born with that essential part of you already dead. A sad gleam in his eye indicates he's holding on to a melancholy thought. — I mind of your dad, he says to Marina, referencing my brother Billy, the father she never saw.

— He's off, Marina laughs, but she likes to hear about Billy. Even I do. Over the years I've learned tae recast him as a loyal, steadfast big brother, rather than the violent, bullying squaddie that for a good while dominated ma perception ay him. It was only later that I realised that both were complementary states ay being. However, death often serves to bring somebody's good qualities to the fore.

— I mind after he was killed, Dad says, his voice breaking as he turns tae me, — your ma looked oot the windae. He'd just been hame on leave and had gone back that weekend. His clathes were still hingin oot tae dry; everything except his jeans, his Levi's. Somebody, some scabby bastard, he half laughs, half scowls, still hurting after all those years, — had swiped them off the line.

— Those were his favourite jeans. I feel a tight grin stretch my face, looking at Sharon. — He fancied himself a bit in them, like that model ponce in the advert who took them off in the launderette and put them in the washer dryer. Became famous.

— Nick Kamen! Sharon squeals with delight.
— Who's that? Marina asks.
— You'll no ken, before your time.

31

Dad looks at us, perhaps a bit miffed at our frivolous intrusion. — It fair set Cathy off that even his favourite jeans had gone. She ran upstairs tae his room, and laid aw his clothes oot oan his bed. Wouldnae let them go for months. I took them tae the charity shop one day, and she broke down when she found out they were gone. He starts bubbling and Marina grabs his hand. — She never quite forgave me for that.

— Enough, ya auld Weedgie radge, I say to him, — of course she forgave ye!

He forces a smile. As the convo moves on to Billy's funeral, Sharon and I share a guilty glance. It's bizarre tae think that I was shagging her in the toilet after that grim event, while Marina, sitting comforting ma faither with her own kids, was unborn inside her. I would now have to class that one as bad behaviour.

Dad turns tae me, tones heavy with accusation. — It would have been nice tae have seen the wee man.

— Alex, well, that just wisnae gaunny happen, I muse out loud.

— How *is* Alex, Mark? Marina asks.

She's never got to know her wee cousin so well. Again, that's my fault.

— He should be here, he's as much a part ay this family as any ay us, my dad growls in contention, his square-go-then-ya-cunt expression on. But he cannae add tae ma considerable hurt on this issue.

— Dad, Sharon gently reprimands. She calls him that more than I do, even though she's the daughter-in-law, and with more justification.

— So how's the jet-setting life, Mark? Marina changes the subject. — You seeing anybody?

— Mind you ain business, nosy! Sharon says.

32

— I never kiss and tell, I say, feeling wonderfully schoolboy bashful as I think ay Vicky, and switch the tone myself, nodding at my old man. — Did I tell you that I'm pally with Frank Begbie again?

— Heard he did awright wi this art stuff, Dad says. — Ower in California now, they say. Wise move. There's nothing here for him but enemies.

2

POLICE HARASSMENT

It's a nice enough little house, he concedes. That Mediterranean burnished-antique look many Santa Barbara homes have, with its Spanish colonial-style architecture, the red-tiled roof and whitewashed courtyard, covered in climbing bougainvillea. It has steadily gotten hotter, the breeze coming off the ocean having faded as the overhead sun stings the back of his neck, the roof down on the convertible. What burns Harry more, though, is being on a stakeout without a badge. That tight omnipresent ball of acid in his gut, despite his over-the-counter drugstore shit, waiting to rise and blister his oesophagus. Suspended, pending investigation. *What the fuck did that actually mean? When were those IA assholes actually going to investigate?* Harry has been swinging by the Francises' deserted home in this quiet cul-de-sac in Santa Barbara for months now, worried that the killer Melanie lived with has done something to her and their kids, just as he most certainly had with those drifters Santiago and Coover.

It isn't a bad spot for surveillance: a tapering street, on a turn-off from a highway and close to a narrow intersection, then a slip road onto the freeway. They probably thought they were being smart when they picked it. Harry smirks to himself, wet hand leaving a damp trace on the leather wheel he's been tightly gripping, although the car is long stationary. *Close to downtown, accessible to the freeway.*

Assholes.

For a while his only sighting has been the couple from next door. They have a dog, one of those big Jap bastards. Sometimes Melanie's mom – he remembers her from his high-school days, a looker like her bitch of a daughter – swings by to pick up the mail. Now she's an older woman, her blonde hair fading to ash-grey, with complementary silver-rimmed specs. Is she still fuckable at a push? Hell, yeah, Harry would spring to giving the old girl a taste of dick. But she's not his target. Not her, nor the two little grandchildren Melanie and the killer have given her, whom she's now looking after.

It's felt like an age but it must have been only a few days, and suddenly, one late afternoon, Melanie is back. The car pulls up and there they are. Her little daughters, the oldest not that much younger than Melanie herself was when he first met her ... and there he is ... that monster she married.

Harry rubs the bristle on his face, adjusts the rear-view mirror to see anything that might approach from the bend behind him, in the quiet, tree-lined street. To think he looked up to Melanie, thought of her as strong, smart and good. But he was wrong; she's weak, deluded by a sense of her own self-righteous liberal bullshit, easy prey for that animal. Harry can imagine him, with that weird gravelly voice of his, giving her that jailbird hustle, that born-on-the-wrong-side-of-the tracks BS. But maybe she's just blind. And if that's the case, then it's Harry's duty to make her see straight.

He watches the old Paddy motherfucker helping their two daughters out of the station wagon, into the home. The way his evil eyes look back, scanning the street. Scum, scum, scum. *Oh, Mel, what are you fucking doing?* She worked with the killer in that Irish jailhouse – or was it Scotch? – what the fuck was the difference? – where he first conned her. She knew then he was a killer! Did she really expect him to change? Why can't she see through him?

Those two bums; no sign of Coover, the water and fish probably doing their work on his body right now. Forget him. But the other one, Santiago, found snagged onto the oil platform, though with his pulped face and the gunshot wound still easily detectable. The bullet extracted, bagged and tagged in the evidence room. It could be traced, to a still-missing weapon. But he is no longer on the case (on *any* case), and nobody else freaking cares.

Then Melanie appears again: wearing a blue hoodie, sneakers and shorts. Is she going for a run? No. She gets into the car. Alone. Harry takes his chance, waits till she drives past, then pulls out and follows, tracking her all the way to the mall. This is good. It's public; she won't suspect his motives.

He follows her inside, slipping past her, before stopping and doubling back, so that he accidentally-on-purpose runs right into her. On seeing his approach and widening smile of recognition, she pointedly looks the other way. This is bad. Even after everything that has happened, and with that drunken phone call, he didn't expect such a blatant snub. He has to say something. — Melanie, he pleads, stepping in front of her, his palms turned outwards, — I need to apologise. I made a terrible mistake.

She stops. Looks at him warily, her arms folded across her chest. — Fine. Now that's the end of it.

Harry nods slowly. He knows what will fly with her. — I've been in rehab for alcohol addiction, and I'm attending meetings regularly. It's important for me to make amends. Can I buy you a coffee? Please? It would mean a lot to me. His tone's pleading and emotional. *Liberals liked to hear that people are basically good and trying to be better. Why shouldn't I make the same play on her as that criminal psycho asshole she married?*

Melanie flicks her hair back, sighs and gestures wearily to the food court. They head over, finding seats at the Starbucks, close to the counter. As Harry joins the line and orders two skinny lattes, Melanie starts talking on her phone. His ears prick. Is she talking about him? No, it sounds like harmless banalities, dispatched to a friend. *Yes, we're back … The kids are fine … Yes, Jim too. I think it did us both good to get away. Last year was all about reconnecting with family … Sicily was wonderful. The food – I need to hit the gym, big time.*

Harry lowers the coffees to the table, slides one across to her as he gets into the seat opposite. Melanie picks up her cup, takes a tentative sip, mumbles some thanks. Her phone sits on the table in front of her. He has to broach this carefully. She'll still have the recording made of his message from last summer, when he was drunk, stupid and weak. That cunning monster she married would see to that. But Melanie had to know that she's hitched to a psychotic killer. And Harry will prove it. He will show that Jim Francis murdered those two men.

At first they talk blandly of old college and high-school days, and mutual acquaintances. It's going smoothly, Harry reckons, straight from the cop's interpersonal playbook. *Establish normality. Build trust.* And it seems like it's working. Hell, Harry even draws a smile out of Melanie, through recounting a tale of one of their buddies. It excites him, as it has always done. It allows him to glimpse possibilities. So he talks about himself a little. How Mom didn't last long after Dad passed, kind of just gave up. How he inherited that lovely old house up in the woods. It's a bit isolated, but he doesn't mind that. But then something goes wrong. The part

37

of him that so desperately still wants her to be with him, in that house, it suddenly emerges, and Harry jumps topic too quickly. Can't hold back. Can't stop the cop in him coming out. — You're in serious trouble, Melanie. He shakes his head in tense gravity. — Jim is not the man you think he is!

Melanie rolls her eyes and picks up her phone, putting it back in her bag. She looks at him evenly, speaking in a slow, deliberate tone. — Keep the fuck away from us. From me, my husband and our children. Her voice rises, to pull nearby patrons into referencing the drama. — You've been warned!

Harry draws in a breath, shocked at the depth of her loathing. — I've been suspended from the department. I've lost everything, but I'm never going to let him hurt you!

— Jim isn't hurting me, you are! I'm telling you, if you approach me again, I'm making a formal complaint, through an attorney, and giving your department a copy of the tape, and Melanie rises, swinging her bag over her shoulder. — Now stay away from my family!

Harry pouts, his bottom lip involuntarily trembling, but then he turns away, facing two women who have been eavesdropping. — Ladies, he says in a slow, sardonic seethe of acknowledgement, before sipping at the latte. He looks forlornly at the lipstick mark around the rim of the other cup. It seems to belong to a ghost he has been chasing most of his life. Sure enough, by the time he turns back, Melanie has gone, vanished into the throng of shoppers. Harry can scarcely believe that she was ever sitting so close to him.

When Melanie returns home she finds Jim in the kitchen, making a sandwich. It is an elaborate, layered effort, involving lean turkey breast, avocado slices, tomatoes and Swiss cheese. Her husband's ability to immerse himself so fully in the most

38

mundane of tasks, as well as the most complex, never fails to amaze her. The still intensity he brings to everything. Through the window, she sees the girls playing in the yard with the new puppy, which is out of sight, but Melanie can hear its excited barking. Jim looks at up her, cracking a smile. It slides south as he quickly senses that something is wrong.

— What's up, honey?

She extends her arms and grips the countertop, leaning back to stretch the tension out of her. — Harry. I ran into him at the mall. I suspect he engineered it. He was apologetic and sensible at first, so I had a coffee with him at Starbucks. Then he started coming out with that same delusional bullshit about you killing those two guys on the beach! I threatened him with the tape and he backed off.

Jim hauls in a deep breath. — If this happens again we might have to take action. Get ourselves a lawyer and file a harassment suit against him.

— Jim, you're a resident alien and a convicted felon. Melanie looks glumly at him. — The authorities don't know a lot about that part of your life.

— Those two guys, I blew up their van ...

— If all this comes out, you could be deported.

— To Scotland? Jim suddenly laughs. — Ah don't know if I could handle the girls growing up talking like me!

— Jim ...

Jim Francis steps forward, filling the space between him and Melanie, taking his wife in his arms. Over her shoulder he can see their daughters playing with Sauzee, the recently acquired French bulldog. — Shhh, it's okay, he coos, as much to himself as to her. — We'll sort it all out. Let's just enjoy Christmas.

Christmas in the sun, Jim thinks, then considers Edinburgh and lets a phantom chill race up his spine.

3

TINDER IS THE NIGHT

Euan McCorkindale examines himself in the bathroom mirror. He prefers what he sees when he removes his glasses, this act sending his features into a satisfying blur. Fifty years. A half-century. Where had it all gone? He replaces the spectacles to contemplate an increasingly skull-like head, apexed by a silver buzz-cut bristle. Euan then looks down at his bare feet, pink plates on the heated black-tiled floor. It is what he does, in the same way others study their faces. How many pairs of feet has he seen in his life? Thousands. Perhaps even hundreds of thousands. Flat, twisted, broken, fractured, crushed, burned, scarred, pitted and infected. But not his own: those have lasted better than the rest of him.

Moving through from the en suite bathroom, Euan dresses quickly, nagged by a mild envy of his still-sleeping wife. Carlotta has the best part of a decade of youthful advantage on him and is handling middle age well. She bloated in her mid-thirties, and Euan was secretly looking forward to her gaining some of her mother's upholstery; he likes women who tend towards the plump. But then a dedicated diet-and-gym regime seemed to make Carlotta go backwards in time: not only approximating her youthful self, but in some ways even surpassing it. She never had muscles like that when they first got together, and yoga has given her a suppleness and range of motion previously beyond her. Now Euan is experiencing the acute return of a withering sensation, which he hoped

40

age would completely vanquish: that he's massively punching above his weight in this relationship.

Euan, however, is a devoted husband and father who has spent his married life happily indulging his wife and son. This is especially the case around Christmas. He loves Carlotta's Italian social extravagance and wouldn't have wished his own austere background on anybody. A birthday that fell on Christmas Eve, in a Wee Free family – it was a recipe for privation and neglect. But Euan's enjoyment of the festive period is generally ring-fenced around Carlotta and Ross. His bonhomie tends to dissipate when others are brought into the mix, and tomorrow he is expected to host Christmas dinner for her family. Carlotta's mother Evita, her sister Louisa, Lou's husband Gerry and kids: they are all fine. It's her brother, Simon, who runs a dubious-sounding escort agency in London, whom he isn't so sure about.

Thankfully, Ross and Simon's son Ben seem to get on. It's just as well. Simon has seldom been around the last two days. After arriving from London with the young man, he unceremoniously dumped poor Ben on them, and took off. It wasn't on, really. No wonder Ben is such a quiet young chap.

He finds Ross down in the kitchen, still in his pyjamas and dressing gown, sat at the table, playing a game on his iPad. — Morning, son.

— Morning, Dad. Ross looks up, bottom lip protruding. *No 'Happy birthday'. Ah well.* It's obvious that his son has something on else his mind.

— Where's Ben?

— Still asleep.

— Everything okay with you guys?

His son pulls a face Euan can't interpret, and snaps his iPad shut. — Aye … it's just that … Then Ross suddenly explodes, — I'm never gaunny get a girlfriend! I'll be a virgin till I die!

Euan cringes. *Oh God, he's sharing a bedroom with Ben. He's a nice lad, but he's older and he's still the son of Simon.* — Has Ben been teasing you about girls?

— It's no Ben. It's everybody at school! They've all got girlfriends!

— Son, you're fifteen. There's still time.

Ross's eyes at first widen in horror then narrow into slits, as he contemplates his father. It isn't a comfortable expression for Euan to witness. It seems to say: *you can either be a god or a joke depending on how you answer this next question.* — How old were you when … the boy hesitates, — when you first done it with a girl?

Fuck. Euan feels something hard and blunt strike him inside. — I really don't think that's the sort of question you ask your father … he nervously offers. — Ross, look –

— How old?! his son commands, in real distress.

Euan regards Ross. The boy often seems the same tousle-headed little rogue of old. However, a certain ranginess and rash of spots, as well as a more sullen demeanour, testify to puberty's ongoing assault, and therefore the inevitability of this conversation in some form. But Euan grimly assumed that today's boys and girls would be watching extreme pornography online and hooking up on social media sites, doing despicable things to each other, then filming and posting the grotesque and humiliating results. He anticipated dealing with the psychological problems of post-capitalist abundance, yet here he is, confronted with traditional scarcity. He clears his throat. — Well, son, those were different times … How can he tell the boy that school sex was out of bounds in his village, as it would invariably have meant shagging a blood relative? (Not that this stopped some of them!) That he was

42

twenty-two and at university by the time he enjoyed full congress with a woman? That Ross's mother, Carlotta – then eighteen to his twenty-five and infinitely more experienced – was only his second lover? — I was fifteen, son. He opts to embellish an incident where he got the tit from a cousin's visiting friend into an episode of penetrative, mind-blowing, no-holds-barred sex. This isn't such a difficult step as this masturbatory bejewelling has taken place countless times in his imagination. — I remember it like yesterday, as it was around this time, a few days after my birthday, he says, pleased that he's got in the reminder. — So don't worry, you're still a young chap. He ruffles the boy's hair. — Time is on your side, trooper.

— Thanks, Dad, Ross sniffs, mildly reassured. — And happy birthday, by the way.

With that Ross runs back upstairs to his room. No sooner has he departed than Euan hears a key in the front-door lock. Moving out to the hallway to investigate, he witnesses his brother-in-law creeping in. Simon's eyes are wild, rather than bleary, with his shock of grey-black hair, shaved at the sides, sprouting from a still-angular face, all cheekbones and wedged chin. So he's stayed out again, hasn't used the spare room they made up for him. It's ludicrous: he's worse than a teenager. — You're in, Euan, Simon David Williamson says with puckish enthusiasm, instantly disarming Euan by pushing both a card and a bottle of champagne into his hands. — Happy five-zero, buddy boy! Where's kid sis? Still in the Maggie Thatcher?

— She has a lot to do for tomorrow, so I expect she'll lie in, Euan declares, heading back to the kitchen, lowering the champagne to the marble worktop and opening the card. It features a cartoon depicting a wily, sophisticated man, dressed like an orchestra conductor, holding a baton, and linking arms with a young buxom woman on each side, both of whom hold violins. The caption: THE OLDER THE FIDDLE, THE BETTER THE TUNE, SO GET YOURSELF FIDDLING ABOUT REAL SOON! HAPPY 50TH BIRTHDAY!

Simon, his gaze burningly intense, drinks in Euan's study of his offering. Euan looks up at his brother-in-law and house guest, feeling himself surprisingly moved. — Thanks, Simon … It's nice somebody remembered … My birthday tends to get forgotten in all the Christmas hullaballoo.

— You were born one day before that daft hippy on the cross, Simon nods, — I mind of that.

— Well, it's appreciated. So what did you get up to last night?

Simon Williamson's face screws up as he reads a text message that has jumped onto his screen. — It's what I didn't get up to that seems to be the problem, he snorts. — Some women, mature women, will not take no for an answer. Life's crazy casualties … Otherwise, old acquaintances. You need to keep in touch; it's only good manners, Simon insists, popping the champagne, the cork smacking the ceiling, as he pours the bubbling elixir into two flutes he's taken from the glass display unit. — If somebody gives you champagne in a plastic vessel … no class. Here's a story that will interest you, professionally speaking, he snaps in a way that permits no dissent from this contention. — I was in Miami Beach last month, at one of those hotels where they strictly adhere to glass. That's Florida, you aren't allowed to do anything there unless it's potentially hazardous to others; guns in waistbands, cigarettes in bars, drugs that make you cannibalise strangers. Of course, I love it. I was ogling some poolside lovelies, cavorting in their skimpy wee two-pieces, when a bit of drunken horseplay resulted in the breaking of a glass. One of the said lovelies stood on the shards. As her blood plumed in the blue water at the edge of the pool, to the consternation of all in the vicinity, I was straight over, taking a leaf out of your book and doing my 'I'm a doctor' thing. I demanded that the staff brought me bandages and plasters. As they were swiftly procured, I wrapped the girl's foot and helped escort her back to her room, reassuring her that although it didn't need stitches, it would be best if she lay down for a bit. He breaks off his tale to hand Euan a glass, and toasts him. — Happy birthday!

— Cheers, Simon. Euan takes a drink, enjoying the fizz and rush of the alcohol. — Was it bleeding heavily? If so –

— Aye, Simon continues, — the poor lassie was a bit worried that the blood was seeping through the bandages, but I told her that it would soon clot.

— Well, not necessarily –

But Simon is allowing no interruptions. — Of course she started asking about the Connery accent and how I became a doctor. Obviously, I was giving it the old chat, inspired by you, buddy. I was even telling her the difference between a podiatrist and a foot surgeon, for fuck sakes!

Euan can't help but feel the balm seep into his ego.

— To cut a beautifully long story crassly short, his brother-in-law's large eyes blaze as he necks the remains of the flute, urging Euan to do the same before topping them up, — soon we were riding away. I'm on top, banging her senseless. In response to Euan's raised brows, he helpfully adds, — Young thing, fit as a butcher's dug, on holiday fae South Carolina. But when we're done, I'm concerned to note that the bed is covered in blood, and the poor poolside lovely, on also noting this, starts going into shock. I told her we'd best call an ambulance in order to be safe rather than sorry.

— God … it might have been the lateral plantar, or perhaps one of the dorsal metatarsals –

— Anyway, the ambulance arrived post-haste and they took her away and kept her in overnight. Just as well I was off the next morning!

Simon continues his tales of his recent Florida holiday, every one of which seems to Euan to involve sex with different women. He stands and listens patiently, drinking his glass of champagne. By the end of the bottle, he feels satisfyingly heady.

— We should slip out for a beer, Simon suggests. — My mother will be round soon and I'll get the usual shit from her about where my life is going, and we'll just be under Carra's feet as she prepares the meal. Italian women and kitchens, you know the drill.

— What about Ben? You haven't really seen much of him since you've been up here.

Simon Williamson rolls his eyes in contempt. — That lad is spoiled tae fuck by her side: rich, Tory, Surrey, cock-sucking, hound-wanking, House of Lords- and monarchy-worshipping paedophile bastards. I'm taking him to the Hibs–Raith game at New Year. Yes, he'll pine for the Emirates, but the boy needs to experience the real world, and we're in the hospitality suite, so it's not like I'm exactly throwing him in at the deep end … Anyway … He makes a drinking gesture. — El peevo?

Euan is swayed by Simon's logic. Down the years stories about his brother-in-law have abounded, but as Simon lives in London, they have never done anything as a duo. It would be nice to get out for an hour or so. Perhaps if they bonded a little it would make for a more pleasant Christmas. — The Colinton Dell Inn has a really nice guest ale from –

— Fuck the Colinton Dell Inn and its guest ales all the way up their petit bourgeois rectums, Simon says, eyes up from fiddling around on his phone. — A cab is on its way *right now* to whisk us into town.

A couple of minutes later they emerge into brisk and squally weather and climb into a hackney cab, driven by a loud, brash man, his hair a mop of corkscrew curls. He and Simon, whom he calls Sick Boy, seem to be arguing about the merits of two dating sites. — Slider's the best, the driver, whom Simon refers to as Terry, argues. — Nae fuckin aboot, jist get right doon tae it!

— Bullshit. Tinder rules. You need at least the veneer of the romance. The intrigue of seduction is the best part of the whole enterprise. The hump at the end of it is just simple bag emptying. The process of allurement and inveigling *always* provides the bulk of the magic. Not that I generally use Tinder for sexual purposes, it's more of a recruitment tool for the agency. You know, I'm thinking of opening a branch of Colleagues in Manchester. Well, with the BBC now in Salford ... Simon has his phone out and is skimming through what appears to Euan to be headshots of women, and mainly young ones.

— What ... that's a phone dating application?

— What a shite name for an escort agency, Terry contends, as the taxi rumbles towards the city centre.

— Is it *fuck* a shite name, Simon protests to Terry, ignoring Euan. — It's not a *hoors'* agency, Terry, it's designed for the business professional. Anybody can get sex now. This is about surface, image: businesspersons wanting to make the right impression. Nothing says success like having bright and gorgeous associates. Thirty-two per cent of our girls are MBAs.

— Mooth Before Erse? Ah should hope so!

— Masters in business administration. At Colleagues we like them to be able to talk business as well as get down to it. It's all about sophistication.

— Aye, but they still ride them. That's hoorin tae me, ay.

47

— That's for the girls to negotiate, Simon says impatiently, looking at his app. — We take our fee as an agency and get client feedback to ensure the girls maintain the standards we expect. Enough of this, though, he gruffly declares, — on to affairs festive. His eyes scan the screen. — Three prospects in the Counting House: two young things and a seasoned pro that looks good value. Simon sticks the headshot of a pouty brunette in front of Euan. — Would you? Assuming, of course, you were single?

— I don't – well, I suppose –

— You'd fuckin ride it raw, mate, Terry sings from the front seat. — It's the wey wir hard-wired. Guaranteed. Ah'm only gaun by Richard Attenborough. That cunt's been aw ower this fuckin planet, watched everything that moves n analysed its cowpin behaviour. Scientific. He taps his head. — Trust in Dickie.

Simon is looking at another incoming text message. — Hunting the women you want, avoiding the ones you don't, it's such a drag … He glances up at the back of Terry's head as they roll over the North Bridge into Princes Street. — And it's *David* Attenborough, ya fucking docile mutation. *Richard* was the cunt that died. The actor. Humped Judy Geeson after strangling her in *10 Rillington Place*. Mind, kenning you, ye probably did mean Richard, Simon asserts, setting off a round of laughing and bickering with Terry, which to Euan's ears is both pointless and obscene.

They fight their way to the bar of a George Street pub packed with festive revellers. Christmas songs of the seventies and eighties blast out. As Euan gets the drinks in, Terry immediately hooks up with a woman whom, Simon explains, he arranged to meet on Slider. In truculent entitlement he manoeuvres elbow room at the bar, Euan deploying polite

48

diligence to attain the same result, as Terry vanishes with his consort. — And that's it? He's off with her? Euan asks.

— Yes, done deal. He'll probably bang her in the back of the taxi. Simon holds up his glass. — Happy birthday!

Sure enough, Terry returns fifteen minutes later, a smile etched on his face. His companions are only halfway through their beers. — Mission accomplished, he winks. — Slide it in, slide it oot, git thum frothin at the mooth.

With their hard-won advantageous position at the bar, Euan anticipates another round, but Simon, checking his phone, suggests they move to an establishment down the street.

Outside, the cold is starting to bite. Euan is relieved that they don't wander too far down Hanover Street before Simon leads their descent into a basement space. As his brother-in-law hits the bar, Euan turns to a yawning Terry. — Are you and Simon old friends?

— Kent Sick Boy for years. He's Leith, ah'm Stenhoose, but we eywis goat on. Baith shaggers, baith Hibbies, ah suppose.

— Yes, he's taking Ben to Easter Road at New Year.

— You follow the fitba, bud?

— I do, but I don't really support any team. On my island, passions weren't highly aroused.

— Keep aw that for the cowpin, mate, right? Country birds ur meant tae be game as fuck. Suppose thaire's nowt else tae dae but, ay-no, mate?

Euan can only force an awkward nod, but his blushes are saved as Simon returns from the bar, carrying incongruously summery-looking drinks. He steers them over to a relatively quiet spot close to the toilets. — Time for a sneaky wee guzzle of the most vile cocktail ever. If you can knock this back in a oner, you are *fucking men*, he declares, thrusting beverages that look like pina coladas at Terry and Euan.

— Fuck … it's Christmas but, ay, Terry says, holding his nose and knocking his back. Simon shadows him.

Euan sips at his drink. Despite the pineapple, coconut and lemonade, it has a rank but metallic bite to it; there is something bitter and evil at its centre. — What is this?

— My own special recipe. Designed for your birthday! Drink, drink, drain your glass; raise your glass high! Simon commands in song.

Euan gives a well-it-is-my-birthday-and-it-is-Christmas-Eve shrug and swallows it back. Whatever abominable concoction lies in the fabric of the cocktail, it's easier to down it in one.

Simon eyes are diverted from the phone's screen to look over to a woman wearing a green top, who is scanning the bar. — That one's probably been on the prowl in the same spot since I rogered her last Christmas!

Terry swiftly looks across. He puts on a David Attenborough voice: — If the beast is at its watering hole, it's about to get its hole watered … and he sweeps back his corkscrew mane, winks at the woman and heads over to her.

Euan and Simon watch him in action. When the woman starts giggling at some comment, her hand reaching to her hair, they know the deal has been sealed. To Euan, Simon's rapacious eyes scrutinise Terry as much as his new companion. — Terry is phenomenally effective. With a *certain type* of woman, he spits out bitterly.

His reaction makes Euan uncomfortable, and inclined to change the subject. — You were up last Christmas to see your mum?

— Yes … Ah ha, he says, his busy index finger flicking through an on-screen catalogue of girls' faces, most of whom seem to be in their twenties, — a Ghost of Christmas Tinder Present!

— I can see why it would be a powerful dating tool, Euan says nervously. He is suddenly aware of nausea in the pit of his stomach, followed by a tingling in his arms and chest. He feels warm and he is sweating. After a brief panic clashes with this excitement, he succumbs to a strange glow coming over him, like a golden cloak of levity has been lowered onto his shoulders.

— Euan, you can download this app in seconds, Simon urges. — Seriously. Or I'm happy to shop around on your behalf, and he casts his eye over a group of women, compelling Euan to follow.

— I can't! I'm married … he says wistfully, thinking of Carlotta, — to your sister!

— Jesus fuck, am I in the wrong century, or what? Simon snaps. — Let's enjoy the benefits of neoliberalism before it goes tits-up, finally detonating this wretched planet from under our feet. We have a perfect synthesis of the very best of the free market and socialism, right here on our phones! It's the answer to the greatest problem of all time – the loneliness and misery caused by not getting your hole at Christmas – and it's free!

— But I love Carlotta! Euan shouts in triumph.

His brother-in-law rolls his eyes in exasperation. — What's love got to do, got to do with it, he sings, then explains in a forced patience: — In today's marketplace, sex is a commodity like any other.

— I'm not in today's marketplace, and I don't want to be, Euan says, feeling his jaw starting to grind. His mouth is dry. He needs water.

— How quaintly Protestant. Johnny Knox would be proud. I am fortunate to be blessed with the papist's slate-wiping gift of confession, which I cheerfully deploy once every few years.

Euan dabs his sweaty forehead with a hanky, sucks in some air. The Christmas tree lights and the glow of tinsel are particularly vivid. — I feel pretty buzzed after the champers and that vile-tasting short ... What was it ...? That lambswool jumper of yours, he touches Simon's forearm, — it feels so soft.

— Of course. I spiked the cocktail with MDMA powder.

— You what ... I don't do drugs, I've never done drugs ...

— Well, you're doing them now. So kick back, relax and enjoy.

As Euan sucks in air and pushes his melting bones into a seat at a suddenly vacated table, Terry, who has been chatting to the woman in the green top, storms over to Simon, all lit up. — Did you pit E in that drink? Turnin ays intae a fuckin lesbo, ya sabotaging cunt! Ah'm away tae the bogs tae hit the ching n take the love oot ay this mix n git the fuckin shaggin back in. Fuckin clart! And he shakes his curls and heads to the toilets.

WHOOSH!

Euan is rising up through himself in an unabating ascent. It is good. He thinks of his father and that rapturous high the old man seemed to get from prayer and song on Sundays. He considers Carlotta and how much he loves her. He doesn't tell her often enough. He shows it, but doesn't say the words. Not nearly enough. He has to phone her now.

He moots this to Simon. — Bad idea. Tell her straight or not at all. She'll just think it's the drug talking. Which it is.

— No it's not!

— Tell her tomorrow then: at the Christmas dinner table. In front of us all.

— I will, Euan states emphatically, then he starts to tell Simon about Ross, and then his own sexual experiences. Or lack of.

52

— Ecstasy is a truth drug, Simon says. — I thought it was time we got to know each other. All these years we've been in the same family, yet we've barely spoken.

— Yes, we've certainly never had a time like this ...

Simon prods his brother-in-law's chest. The action isn't aggressive or intrusive to Euan, it feels quite bromantic. — You need to experience different women, Simon's head swivels across the bar, iPhone finally sliding into his pocket, — or the resentment will eventually destroy your marriage.

— No it won't.

— Yes it will. We are nothing but consumers now: of sex, drugs, war, guns, clothes, TV shows. He waves his hand in grandiose derision. — Look at this crowd of miserable cretins, pretending to have fun.

Euan checks out the revellers. There is a kind of desperation about it all. A bunch of young lads in Christmas jumpers are swaggering in superficial bonhomie, but waiting for the one drink that will pit them violently against some strangers, or, failing that, each other. A group of office girls are comforting a morbidly obese colleague, who is bubbling in tears. Sitting a little apart, two others chuckle in a vicious, conspiratorial glee at her distress. A barman, lower lip hanging and eyes dulled in clinical depression, sets about the joyless task of collecting the glasses that appear on the tables like baby rabbits in a spring meadow. All this to an unceasing medley of Christmas pop hits from the seventies and eighties which have become such staple fare every Yuletide that they have people mumbling the words under their breath, like discharged military combat victims of post-traumatic stress.

It is in such an environment that Simon David Williamson increasingly warms to his theme. — We have to keep on going till the train hits the buffers; then we shelve the insanity and neurosis and build a better world. But we can't do that until this paradigm comes to a natural end. So for now we simply go with neoliberalism as an economic and social system, and pursue those addictions relentlessly. We have no choice in the matter. Marx was wrong about capitalism being replaced by a wealthy, educated, workers' democracy; it's being replaced by an impoverished, tech-savvy, shaggers' republic.

Enthralled and horrified by Simon's bleak dystopia, Euan shakes his head in agitation. — But there has to be choice, he protests, as Roy Wood once again reiterates his wish that it could be Christmas every day, — there has to be *doing the right thing*.

— Increasingly not. Simon Williamson tosses his head back, running his hand through black and silver locks. — Doing the right thing is now for the loser, the mug, the victim. *That* is how the world has changed. He takes a pen and small notebook out of his pocket and draws a diagram on a blank page.

Before 35 Years of Neoliberalism: -

CUNT		HUMAN BEING		MUG

After 35 years of Neoliberalism:

CUNT		HUMAN BEING		MUG

— The only real choices are proscribed, slightly different versions of the wrong thing, basically picking an alternative route to the same overriding hell. Jesus, these poodirs are total fucking old-school … Simon says, wiping some sweat from his brow. — Still, he lets his saucer eyes swivel to Euan, — it's not all bad, then he turns and stares at a girl, who is standing a few feet away with a friend. He holds

up his phone. She stares back and laughs before coming over, introducing herself as Jill, and presenting her cheek for, and receiving, a dignified peck from the rising Simon. As she converses with his brother-in-law, Euan is enchanted to find his misgivings peeling away. Jill is nothing like the desperate online daters of his imagination. She is young, confident, good-looking and obviously smart. Her friend, roughly the same age, but a little bit plumper, looks at him.
— I'm Katy.

— Hi, Katy, I'm Euan. Are you, em, a Tinder person too?

Katy seems to evaluate him for a second, before responding. 'My Girl' by Madness comes on the jukebox. Euan thinks of Carlotta. — I use it occasionally, but it can get dispiriting. Most people are just looking for sex. Fair enough. We all have our needs. But it's sometimes too much. Do you use the app?

— No. I'm married.

Katy raises her brows. She touches his arm, looking at him in enervated leniency. — Good for you, she sings, but in a detached manner. Then she spots somebody and flutters across the bar. Euan is staggered to experience a deep sense of loss at her departure, which is assuaged by the notion that everything is okay.

A slender blonde woman, probably in her thirties, Euan fancies, has entered the bar and is staring at Simon. She is striking, with almost translucent skin and haunting, luminous blue eyes. On meeting her stare, his brother-in-law sighs loudly. A Ghost of Christmas Tinder Past, and he apologises to Jill, and heads over to address the incomer. Jill and Euan watch in silence as they exchange some words, which Euan senses are heated, before Simon heads back to them. He jostles Jill and Euan over to an empty table.

To Euan's surprise, the blonde woman joins them, a glass of white wine in her hand, never taking her eyes off Simon.

He is preoccupied, canoodling with Jill. It's at that point Euan thinks that the woman might be older than he first thought; her skin is flawless, but her eyes carry a weight of experience.

She turns to Euan, still looking at Simon. — Well, *he* obviously isn't going to introduce us. I'm Marianne.

Euan extends his hand, glancing over at his brother-in-law whose fingers now caress Jill's dark-stockinged thigh, as her tongue goes into his ear.

And Euan is looking at Marianne, who watches the scene in sheer loathing. Yes, he considers, she might even be close to his age, but there is something majestic about her. All the flaws of ageing, the lines, the bags, the crow's feet, seem to have been airbrushed from her. He wonders if it could be the drug. All he sees is the essence of this strikingly beautiful woman. — Euan, he introduces himself. — Have you known Simon long?

— For years. Since I was in my teens. I'd say twenty per cent a blessing, eighty per cent a curse, she informs him in a monotone voice. To his ear, it straddles scheme and suburb.

— Wow. In what sense? he asks, moving closer to her, and looking at Simon.

— He's a menace to lassies, Marianne says matter-of-factly. — He makes them fall for him, and then he just uses them.

— But … you're still here, in his company.

— Then I'm still in his control, she laughs joylessly, then bitterly lashes out and kicks Simon's shin. — Bastard.

— What? Simon breaks his grip on Jill to glare at her. — Are you fucking mental? Calm doon!

— Fucking bastard. Marianne kicks out again, then, looking at the younger woman, acidly scoffs, — You poor wee fucking cow. He's an old cunt now. I least I was conned by a young, exciting guy, and she rises and throws the contents of her wine glass over him.

Simon Williamson sits immobile, wine dripping from his face, as the oohs and aahs of the nearby drinkers reverberate. Euan fishes out his hanky and passes it to his brother-in-law. — Go after her, Simon urges him, nodding at the departing Marianne. — Talk to her. Been stalking me for weeks, knowing I'd be up from London for Christmas. She resents that she's no longer young, but it happens to us all. I mean, get the fuck over yourself, he intones in a rising plea to the bar, before turning to Jill. — Repeat after me: I will never turn into my mother!

— I will *never* turn into my mother, Jill says emphatically.

— Attagirl. Simon appreciatively grapples her knee. — It's all a state of mind. You obviously have the big-match temperament.

— I'm ticklish, Jill chuckles and pushes his hand away, before asking, — Do you think I could work for Colleagues? I've no got an MBA but I've an HND in Management Studies fae Napier and I just need another four credits to get it made up tae a BA.

— If BA stands for beautiful arse — and I think in your case it does — then it seems to me that you have all the essential attributes! Though all potential partners, as we call them, are subject to the most rigorous and searching interview procedures, he purrs.

Euan is done with Simon's company. Perversely, his brother-in-law probably meant well in his own twisted way, but he has filled him full of drugs, and attempted to get him to cheat on his wife, the man's own sister! He hesitates for a second, before rising to follow Marianne. In the event, she has only got as far as the bar, where she stands, holding her bag as if waiting on somebody. — Are you okay?

— I'm *fine*, Marianne says, the second word hissing out.

— Are you …?

— I'm waiting on a cab. She waves her phone, the motion seeming to precipitate its ringing. — Here we go.

— Ehm, if you don't mind me asking, which way are you going? I'm going to bow out too.

— Liberton, Marianne responds in a vague tone, tucking her hair behind one ear. — Any good?

— Yes. Great.

In the back of the cab, the relative heat gives Euan another set of E-rushes. They head up the Bridges towards the Commonwealth Pool. It isn't *that* far from his house. But he can't go home in this state.

She picks up on his agitation. — Are you okay?

— Not really. Simon spiked my drink with MDMA powder. It was apparently his idea of a big festive joke. I'm not used to drugs … these days, he feels the need to add, worried that she'll find him a little straight and dull. He suddenly glances at her feet; small, dainty and strapped into heels. — You have very beautiful feet.

— Kinky that way, are you?

— No, but perhaps a little obsessed. I'm a foot doctor, a podiatrist, he explains, as they pass his employ at the Royal Infirmary.

Jill has gone to the toilet with Katy to do some powder, leaving Simon the opportunity to get back on Tinder. However, he sees Terry advancing towards him. — Where have you been?

— Took that yin in the green toap roond tae Thistle Street Lane in the cab. Thanks tae your daft wee MDMA ah jist chowed at her fanny till she went bananas. Didnae even ram it. Now she wants tae see ays again, the lot. Thinks ah'm like that aw the time. Telt her tae git the fuck oot ay ma cab!

58

— You're a gentleman, Tez.

— N ah saw your brar-in-law, that Euan cunt, sneakin oaf wi that Marianne bird, Terry declares, his eyes dancing in front of Simon. — How come ah nivir rattled that yin back in the day? Fit as.

— Knobbed her aw weys fir years. First her faither threatened me, then her fucking husband. Obviously I was still banging her when she got married, and at her instigation. But I was a gent. I told her I found it inherently ungracious breaching a pussy bequeathed to another chap, so I always jacksie-rammed her eftir that. Taught her how to orgasm on anal, the lot.

— Gap oan the CV for lean Lawson, n thaire's no many ay thaim, he says, put out. — Cunt, if she wis that much ay an imposition, ye should've slipped me her phone number, ah'd have got ye oaf her mind. Or mibbe that's what ye wir feart, ay!

— That. Will. Be. The. Fucking. Day.

— Shoatie, Terry glances at the two young women returning from the toilet, — here's the fanny back: time fir the fuckin charm offensive!

The first to rise in the McCorkindale household on Christmas Day is Simon Williamson. He hasn't been able to sleep, as is always the case when he's done loads of alcohol or drugs. He regards this wanton consumption as a weakness, but as it's Christmas, and pretty much a rarity for him these days, he resists beating himself up about it. Euan soon joins him in the kitchen, still looking a little blitzed from the night before. – That was some stuff, he gasps, his voice low. — That powder. I couldn't sleep.

— Ha! Welcome to my world. Try doing some ching and base on top of it, like me –

— You are on your own! I had to get back to Carlotta. Luckily she's a heavy sleeper. I lay awake beside her the entire night, all sweating and stiff like a drug addict!

— On that note, how was Marianne? Did you go to hers?

Euan seems to think about lying, before realising the futility of it. — Yes, I really needed to get myself together before going home. I had an interesting chat with her. She's a very complicated woman.

Simon Williamson raises a solitary brow. — The untrained eye would certainly see it that way.

— What do you mean?

— She's not complicated at all. Complicated is good. Complicated is interesting. She's neither.

— Well, she seemed that way to me.

— A damaged simpleton can appear *complicated* because their personal behaviour is erratic and they have no impulse control. But that is not good. Damaged simpletons are merely exasperating and tiresome. I told her several fucking *decades* ago that she'd gotten obsessed with me and that I wanted nothing more to do with her. But no, she kept coming back, demanding to see me. The spoiled daddy's girl used to getting everything she wants. Simon Williamson stares brutally at his brother-in-law. — Her faither, first gauny kill ays for riding her, then gauny kill ays for no riding her! He shiver-shrugs, as if literally casting off a chilling cloak of injustice. — The entire family is a bunch ay controlling nutters.

— Keep it down, Euan shushes him, as he hears the toilet flush from a bathroom upstairs.

Simon nods and drops his voice. — So muggins here kept dutifully slamming it up her, with, I hasten to add, increasing reluctance. In her defence it has to be said that she's a terrific ride, though I have to take some credit for that: she flourished under my selfless tutelage. Then, when she vanished over a decade ago, I thought: *good riddance*. But I genuinely hoped she had found *happiness*. He says the word in a French accent, making it sound like *a penis*. — But no, the dopey prick who took her on board, he's seen the light. *Voilà*, she's back in my face, hassling me by text, castigating me for chasing minge that is a) younger, and b) not her. He shrugs. — So what about you, did you give her the message?

— Don't be ridiculous, Euan splutters. Whoever had used the upstairs bathroom seemed to go back to bed. — I went to her place to compose myself and let that MDMA you gave me wear off. Thankfully, Carlotta was fast asleep when I got in. She wasn't charmed when she briefly stirred this morning, but she was, in her words, 'glad we'd bonded'.

Suddenly there is activity. Ross comes down the stairs, with Ben following. — Here's the gadges! Simon announces. – Merry Christmas, you handsome young bucks! A pair of heartbreakers, huh, Euan? That vintage Italian-Scots genetic and cultural combination: it devastates the girls. Leaves them senseless, heaving wreckages.

His son and nephew look at him, both deeply embarrassed by his proclamation, and each more than a little doubtful.

— Anyway, I'm going to check out some morning telly, Simon declares. — In fact I'm not going to move from that couch until it's time for my Christmas dinner. This is breakfast, and he unwraps the gold foil and bites the ear off a Lindt chocolate teddy bear, pointing to the heart on its chest. – Take that, ya Jambo bastard, and he decants to the living room.

Carlotta comes downstairs and starts on the meal preparations. Euan wants to help but his wife insists she has it all planned and that he should sit down with Simon and the boys and watch TV. Ross and Ben are less than enthralled at the prospect and retreat upstairs, while Euan complies, to

61

find Simon enjoying an Innis & Gunn lager with the chocolate teddy, watching a rerun of *White Christmas*.

— A little early, Euan says, looking at the tin of beer.

— It's Christmas, for fuck sake. And this lager is amazing. Who would have thought that the Scots could produce the best lager in the world? It's what I would imagine Sleeping Beauty's sweet douched-out fanny to taste like!

This extreme sexualisation of everything, Euan ponders, *does he ever stop?* Then he considers that it might not be a bad idea to have a couple of beers. Still woozy from the MDMA, they might provide a covering excuse for his lassitude. Fortunately, Carlotta seems too caught up in the Christmas dinner preparations to notice. Euan can hear his wife singing, the Eurythmics 'Thorn in My Side', melodic and sweet. He feels his heart swelling in his chest.

His mother-in-law and sister-in-law arrive, with Louisa's husband and three children, all between the ages of seventeen and twenty-four. The house is busy and presents are swapped and unwrapped. Ross and Ben receive identical PS4s, and immediately head upstairs to download a favoured game from the Internet.

The Innis & Gunn lager is settling nicely into Euan, producing a satisfying, mellow cheer. He vaguely thinks something is off-kilter about his son as Ross suddenly reappears in the hallway, cornering Carlotta as she goes into the kitchen, urging his busy mother to follow him upstairs.

He cranes his neck over the back of the settee to watch them and is about to speak, when Simon shakes his arm, and mother and son ascend the stairs behind them. — I love this bit when Crosby makes that speech to Rosemary Clooney about the knight falling off his silver charger … he says, tears welling in his eyes. — That's the story of my life with women, and he chokes, as if something is breaking in his chest.

Euan observes this in mounting unease. Simon appears to be absolutely genuine in his sentiments. It dawns on him that his brother-in-law is so dangerous to women due to his ability to totally immerse in, and believe, those self-cast fantasy roles.

Eventually, they are shouted through to the dining area at the rear of the kitchen for the meal. Photographs are taken with an air of ceremony. Simon Williamson snaps the family, then, individually, his mother Evita, who looks vacant, Carlotta, Louisa, Gerry and kids, Ben, a sullen Ross, and even Euan. Throughout this process, both Simon and Euan feel a strange tension in the air, but they're now hungry and looking through mild intoxication's fug, as they take their seats. Carlotta is whispering urgently to her mother and sister. Mindful of the weight of the Christmas dinner, she has prepared a light starter; small prawn cocktails, with a minimal lemon-based dressing, sit on the table.

Euan sits back appreciatively, and is about to speak, when he sees the tears streaming down his wife's cheeks. Clutching her mother's hand, she doesn't meet his concerned eyes. And Evita is looking daggers right at him. Instinctively, he and Simon glance at each other in puzzlement.

Before Euan can say anything, his son stands up and slaps him hard across the face. — You're a fuckin dirty old bastard! Ross points at Carlotta. — That's my mum!

Euan can't react, or even open his mouth, as his eyes go to his wife. Carlotta is now sobbing in heavy despair, her shoulders shaking. — You should be ashamed of yourself, Louisa screeches at him, as Evita curses in Italian.

The overwhelming sense that the world is crumbling to dust sucks every piece of energy and, indeed, sentience out of Euan.

And then Ross turns on his iPad, holding it up to his shocked father's face. There he is, yesterday, with that

Marianne woman, and they are naked, on her bed, and he is pushing his cock into her lubed-up arsehole, as he strokes her clitoris. She is coaching him through her groans, telling him what to do. And then he looks, in trauma, at his brother-in-law, realising that the words coming out of her mouth are really Simon David Williamson's.

It flashes through his mind in a storm, as the faces gape in shock and disgust at him: Marianne has emailed him the tape they made. It must have gone to the family iCloud. Ross has accessed it by accident when trying to download the video game for his PlayStation 4. Now they are all watching it, as a family, literally over their Christmas dinner; Euan's first ever drug-induced infidelity. His sister-in-law and her husband glare in disgust. His mother-in-law is crossing herself. Simon, genuinely shocked, looks at him in a phantom admiration. But in his son and wife, Euan can sense nothing on their shattered and wrecked faces but a deep, uncomprehending betrayal.

Euan McCorkindale can find no words. But he is speaking them, obscenely and deliciously, on the screen, which Ross grips with outstretched arms, firmly, unbendingly, in front of him.

It is Carlotta who finds her voice. — You are fucking out of here. You are fuckin oot ay here right now, and she points to the door.

Euan rises, with his head bowed. He is mortified in the sense of almost turned to actual stone by his shock, beyond even embarrassment. His limbs are heavy and his ears ring, as a rock the size of a black hole fills his stomach and chest cavity. Looking to the door, which seems so far away, he feels himself move towards it. He doesn't know where he is going and it is only instinct that makes him pick up his coat from its hook in the vestibule, as he leaves his family home, quite possibly forever.

Closing the door behind him and stepping out into the cold, gloomy streets, all he can think of is that Christmas will never be the same again. But his hand goes to the iPhone, and plucks it out of his pocket. Euan McCorkindale doesn't google hotel accommodation. Instead he hits the Tinder icon, the application he downloaded after leaving Marianne's in crippling, joyous guilt, in the wee small hours of Christmas Day morning. Already, his cold fingers are quickly scrolling a new future.

4

SPUD – HERE'S TO YOU, MR FORRESTER

A soft Sqezy-boatil heartbreak whine leaks ootay the wee gadge. He needs tae git a trim likesay, ye kin barely see they sparkly wee eyes through yon fur. — Freezin the auld hee-haws oaf here, Toto. Ah'm sorry aboot this, pal, but wi you bein likesay a West Highland terrier, you've goat the fur coat, man, ah tells ma boy, curled up at ma feet. Ah feel ehs neb, it's stane cauld awright, but that's meant tae be a sign ay canine health. Sometimes ah feel pure bad though, man, like ah'm one ay they gadges thit only gits a dug as an accessory for ma beggin pitch, a sympathy gambit, likesay. N they see Toto n say, — Spud, ah thoat you wir intae cats, man, n ah say, — Aw animals, likesay. N ah tell ye but, it's pure done ays nae herm huvin Toto. For the beg, n that, ay. People hate tae see animals suffer.

— Bit that wisnae the reason ah goat ye, Toto, it wis mair fir the companionship, ay, pal, ah goes tae um. Ah ken animals cannae make oot what yir sayin, bit they kin detect the vibe, man, they wee bits ay negative body lingo ye gie oot whin yir voice or even think they bad thoats. It's how the world's sick, man: that media run by the corporations, spreadin that virus ay bad vibes. That Rupert Murdoch cat in that *Sun*. Every time ah see a headline in that paper ah just go: aw, man. Ah dinnae like subjectin Toto tae that sortay deal. It's true but, ye need a wee four-legged buddy tae go through life wi, now that aw the two-legged yins have aw waltzed oaf intae the sunset, ken?

The beg's gaun no too bad but, the festive period is eywis decent. Cats aw fill ay good cheer n booze, and wi the weather bein that cauld, it sort ay turns aw they indifferent herts, ken?

So ah'm happy wi ma twelve quid sixty-two pence bounty. Four hours in the cauld, still below minimum wage, even if ye do git peyed fir jist standin aroond. It's funny, but whin ye start the John Greig, ye pit oan that coupon: that sad, baleful pus that screams 'help ays' tae the world. By the end ay the mooch, whin the cauld has crept intae yir bones, ye dinnae need tae fake it any mair. So ah'm aboot tae pack up whin ah realise thaire's a figure standin ower ays. Likesay lingerin, no makin any attempt tae chip a coin intae the auld styrofoam. Ah pure dinnae want tae look up, cause sometimes ye git a radge or a wideo giein ye hassle. But ah hears the friendly tone, — Awright, Spud, so ah raises ma heid.

Man, it's Mikey Forrester starin doon at ays. — Mikey! How goes? ah asks. Cause ah've goat tae say that Mikey boy seems a wee bit doon at heel n aw, wearin a tatty fleece, jeans n trainers. Ah'm kinday surprised, man. The last time ah seen him, the Forrester gadge seemed tae be daein well; aw tin flutes n long coats fae wannabe gangster central.

— Good, Spud, Forrester goes, but ye kin sortay tell the cat's tryin tae summon as much enthusiasm as he kin, ken? — Ah've got a wee bit ay graft, if yir interested. Involves good food and travel. Fancy a pint?

Ah'm aw lugs in this situ, man. — You'll have tae be the cat in chair, like, Mikey. Ah'm a bit short ay the hirey's gadgie, ah tells a wee fib. Cannae afford tae use that twelve quid oan beer, man: thaire's beans n toast fir me n dug food fir Toto tae come ootay yon haul.

— I gathered that.

— They let ye in wi dugs in that place ower the street there, ah points tae the pub.

Mikey nods and we head ower the cobblestanes intae that awfay welcome howf. Ken whin the heat jist blasts oot? Ye cannae beat that, man, even though it's like the maist miserable time for a wee while, while the body pure adjusts. It's like that fulum ah saw once whin they wir in space n hud tae wrap up in likesay tinfoil n jump fae one ship tae another, wi nae suits oan or nowt. Even jist a few seconds ay that cauld. It's the decompression time. Git they hands n taes warmed up. It helps wi Toto curlin up oan ma feet as Mikey shouts up two pints ay San Miguel lager.

When eh sets thum doon oan the table, eh goes, — I've gone intae a wee partnership wi Victor Syme, then eh adds in a low voice, — Vic's back, like.

Ah'm pure no sae keen oan this gig now, man, cause Syme's well kent as a bad cat, n ah dinnae think it'll be Mikey that's runnin the show here. So the wee alarm in ma heid's gaun: aw-aw, aw-aw …

— Thaire's decent spondoolays in this, and it's a piece ay pish.

But, well, let the cat ootline the deal but, man. Does nae herm tae listen tae what the boy's goat tae say, ay. — Is thaire any chance ay a wee poppy advance oan the fee fir this joab, man? Things been a bit slow, likesay.

— I'm sure we kin work something oot. No want tae hear my proposition first but?

— Eh, aye, ah goes, suppin mair ay the pint. But ah'm awready jumpin aheid ay masel, thinkin thit things are lookin up but, n it's aboot time the boy Murphy caught a wee brek.

Everybody else, even the maist marginalised kittens in the basket, seems tae huv left ays behind. Boot in the hee-haws fir the auld self-esteem, man. No kiddin ye. But tae be wanted again, for anything, it feels barry.

So the Forrester felly is tellin ays that aw ah need tae dae is pick up a wee package and droap it oaf. If ah wis tae git a cash advance ootay Mikey, thaire's mibbe some new troosers, n a pair ay trainers wi some tread oan thum oot ay it. Ah dinnae ken aboot Mikey but; likesay whether the dude is trustworthy or no. Goat tae dae the fieldwork here, man.

— The delivery but, it's no collies, man, is it? ah asks um.

— Cause ah'm no like one ay they drug smugglers, no way, Jose.

Mikey shakes that shaved dome, then runs a hand ower it. It's like eh tries tae copy aw they gangsters, the likes ay Fat Tyrone n that. — Ah swear, bud, it's nowt like that, the Forrest Fire explains. — Aw ye need tae dae is fly tae Istanbul and a boy'll pick ye up at the airport and gie ye a boax tae take tae Berlin oan the train. You git the package thaire, ye gie it tae another boy. Under nae circumstances, and the cat looks awfay, awfay serious, — dae ye try n open the boax.

— Sortay like that fulum, *The Transporter*?

— Exactly.

— But, eh, what *is* in it, likesay?

Mikey gies ays a grim smile. Looks around, lowers ehs voice, leans intae ays. — A kidney, Spud. A human kidney: for a life-saving operation.

Uh-oh. Ah'm no sure aboot this, man. — What? Is that no illegal, smuggling body parts, like the invasion ay the bodysnatchers n aw that?

Mikey shakes ehs heid again. — This is aw kosher, buddy boy. We've goat a certificate for it, the lot. Ye cannae open the boax cause it's aw sealed n sterile, wi the kidney packed in ice or some frozen cauld chemical that isnae ice but works like ice.

— It isnae ice?

— Naw, but it works like ice. Like what they've invented tae replace ice.

— Replace ice ... Whoa, man, no sae sure aboot that. Ice is pure natural like, well, it's usually made artificially in fridges like, but in its natural state in the polar regions –

Mikey waves ehs hand n shakes ehs heid. — Naw, Spud. No in likes ay drinks n that, eh laughs, hudin up his pint.

— But it works better freezin organs.

— Keeps thum tip-top till auld transplant, likesay?

— Bang on the money! Ye open the boax n the cunt starts tae deteriorate n it's fuckin useless, ay?

— But the transportation ay this, man, is it no a bit dodgy?

— Well, ye cannae take it through airport security, but ye kin git it oan trains easy enough. A boy meets ye wi it at the Istanbul airport and you just jump oan the train tae Berlin. Another gadge picks it up, you bounce tae the airport in a Joe Baxi n head hame, five hundred bar richer. N that's eftir ah front ye another five hundred bar right now. Cannae say fairer than that.

Five hundred bar ... right now ... — Whaes kidney is it?

— A doner's.

— Like some deid gadgie's?

— Aye ... well, no necessarily, cause ye can live fine wi just one, Mikey says, then goes aw thoughtful. — It might be somebody daein this for one ay thair family. Ah dinnae ken. Ah'm no gaunny say tae Vic Syme ... n eh looks at ays n droaps ehs voice, — ah'm no gaunny say tae the boy that runs the saunas, where's this came fae and where's it gaun? Ma motto is ask nae questions n yi'll git telt nae lies. Here's aw the paperwork, eh sais n passes ays a certificate.

It looks like something ye could git oaf that Internet, likesay download, so ah suppose that makes it sortay official enough. — It's goat tae be snide though ... Vic Syme, likesay ... ah goes. Dinnae ken the boy but that jungle cat has the rep ay bein a sabre-toothed killer.

— Well, mate, there's ey gaunny be risks, n it's obviously black-market goods, it'll be some private clinic daein the op, aye. But the job's yours if ye want it, Mikey sais. — Aw ah kin say is that they've been daein a lot ay this sortay stuff and thuv no hud any bother yet, n eh pits an envelope stuffed wi readies oan the table.

Ah think aboot this, a wee adventure, and lit's face *el factos*, thaire's nowt else doon fir ays. — No sayin nowt against naebody, Mikey, but ur they people, likesay Vic Syme, ur they trustworthy, ken? Ah'm no wantin in if naebody is trustworthy.

— Spud, you ken me, Mikey shrugs.

N it's true, cause ah've sort ay kent um for years. N eh's no ey been trustworthy ehsel, but ah've no either. Mibbe he's changed n aw. Ye huv tae gie folks the benefit ay the doubt. He's giein me a second chance, so ah've goat tae gie him yin. Ah've nowt tae lose. — Aye, sound, n ah reaches ower n takes the envelope, like that boy in *Mission: Impossible*, the wee gadgie in Hollywood that wis in *Top Gun* wi the barry bird wi the great hair that ye nivir hear nowt aboot now. The tape or whatever's inside disnae self-destruct but, so it's aw good! — Ah wisnae tryin tae be wide, or cast any aspersions, Mikey, that wis jist me daein ma due diligence, ken?

— Nae offence taken, bud. Goat tae keep the heid screwed oan. Ah'd be much mair nervous giein the joab tae some daftie that wisnae askin they sort ay questions. Gies ays confidence that ah've picked the right boy for the mission!

N eh pure yazed the word *mission*, which makes ays feel barry. We clink glesses. — Aye, man, ah'll dae it awright.

71

— Great, kent ah could count oan ye, ma auld mucker, Mikey goes. — N Spud, try n tidy yirsel up a wee bit, ay, mate?

Ah ken that Mikey's no bein wide, eh jist doesnae want ays likesay standin oot gaun through Checkpoint Charlie or wherever it is. — Wi this dosh, the answer tae that is basically, aye, catboy.

5

RENTON – CLIENT CONFIDENTIALITY

I love dance music, but draw the line at DJs: pish situation tae be in when you're a manager ay them. It never used tae be like that – some DJs were fuck-ups, aye, but most weren't, they were just people who loved clubs and dance music. That changed when those entitled straight-peg millennial cunts took ower – a very general rule of thumb, and aye, exceptions abound but: the more money they get paid, the mair ay a prick the DJ is. So as I made poppy, I worked with mair grandiose, vainglorious arse-holes, then, after I built his career, one ay the fuckers sacked me – Ivan – long-haired, silent Belgian cunt – it happens – it's no a hard-luck story, ah've done okay, jist an illustration that you need a thick fucking skin in this game. I have to get those DJ cunts out their fucking beds in the afternoon, procure them drugs fae scumbag promoters, sometimes pull them oot ay the fuckin jail, and even mair galling, argue the toss with corporate lackeys about publishing royalties. But the worst ay it: I have tae try tae get the bastards laid – this is no always as easy as it soundzzzz –

Lying on my bed in a truly sybaritic penthouse suite in this Vegas hotel. It's divided into two bedrooms, each with a marble bathroom, and a large living room with a luxury kitchen and an ornate fireplace. Of course, it's on account and a tax write-off, but I'm so jet-lagged after this Edinburgh–London–Amsterdam–Barcelona–LA–Vegas travelthon that I scarcely know where the fuck I am or what I'm meant to be doing, in fact I'm unable to grab hud ay a single thought. Despite having slid *just one solitary* Ambien (and a Vallie) down the hatch, this fucking laughing gas they pump intae the room, tae keep ye at the tables doonstairs twenty-four/seven, ensures sleep remains beyond ays. All I can dae now is lie back and catch up on *Game of Thrones*. Then a rap on my door, and I pull my carcass off the bed and let Conrad in. The Technonerd felly comes right tae the point. — I cannot sleep now, and I will not later in the morning in Los Angeles. I need to be with a woman!

— Fine. I freeze the image on the screen, and sit up, my head woozy. Dinnae ken if I buy Jon Snow coming back from the dead, but that's a straightforward task compared tae mine. Conrad was a leanish young Dutch boy just two years ago. Then he started spunking a fair chunk ay his new-found wealth on food, and the cunt isnae that discerning. What's sadder than a young millionaire ordering the limo tae pull up ootside a fuckin McDonald's? When you're the daft cunt that has tae go in and buy the shit that's sending his cash cow tae type 2 diabetes. He literally cannae stoap eating. It's aw tae dae wi the munchies, cause eh smokes tons ay weed. Now, at twenty-two, the cunt is a wheezing tub ay lard. I can feel my ain arteries furring just by standin next tae him.

— But the woman has to be dark-haired, Conrad's round, entitled baby-face insists, the whistle of his Dutch voice exacerbated by the thin gasp ay burgeoning respiratory disease. — And she has to have medium-sized breasts; they cannot be small, but they must not be too heavy and pendulous. No implants. And lips that are full, but natural –

I cut him off. — Conny, you've obviously been wanking off tae porn. Just cut tae the chase and show me the adult entertainment performer who is blessed tae be the object of this superstar DJ's desire.

He looks briefly at me as if irony is something he *almost* gets, and pulls out his phone. Fortunately, the porn star has a website *and* does escort services, *and* is based in LA. If I can deliver her it saves me spending fucking years in a futile search for a lassie that *looks like* her. When you're doing this *on behalf of somebody else*, it's the most spirit-crushing employment imaginable. It will cost a pretty penny but that sad little twat is the one bringing in the cash, which makes me just about the most pathetic cunt in Christendom. — If you want this yin, it'll have to wait till the wee small hours of the morning, when we get back to LA. If your needs are immediate, there's an agency here in Vegas I can call –

— Fuck those tacky Vegas bitches, they just see money, he snaps.

— Well, that tends tae come with the territory. Like prostitution, ken? At least Conny, being Dutch, gets it when I say ken. In Dutch the verb *kenen* is also 'to know'.

— But it is no good if they cannot act with sophistication.

Of course he's right; the most successful hoors are those who dinnae act like they are. That's why the high-end escorts get top dollar: it's the emotional labour they excel at. Conrad believes Vegas is too replete wi one-off out-ay-towners, rather than repeat business. He looks crabbily at me, opening a packet ay crisps fae my well-stocked kitchen area. His suite is next door and he's probably already cleaned oot its contents as well as hammered room service. — Set me up with this Brandi girl tonight, he says, grabbing a PowerBar as he leaves.

It takes ays twenty minutes to get in touch and conclude the deal, even wi the usual 'client confidentiality' speech thrown in. The woman is very cool and businesslike, dispensing wi the breathless baby-doll tones once ah tell her I'm working on behalf ay some other cunt. I then call Conrad. — She'll be waiting at the Standard around 4 a.m., when we get back to LA.

I hit the hay and believe that I'm actually about to drift off, when the cunt is back hammering at my door again. — I still cannot sleep.

— Here ... I go to my drawer and pull out some Ambien. — Take two ay these. I drop the wee browny-orange pills intae an upturned duvet-like hand. I don't feel good about doing this. I'm trying to sack those bastards myself, so it's a bit naughty passing them on.

— Okay ... and why am I staying at the Standard? I like the Chateau Marmont, he moans.

Too fucking bad: I have a discount deal with the Standard. — Fully booked, bud, I lie, knowing he's too lazy tae check, — and besides, the honeys, the Glen Hoddles and the Hollywood starlets all party at the Standard these days. It's hot again.

— West Hollywood or Downtown?

— The West Hollywood one.

Conrad's doughy fingers rip open a packet of gum. He offers me a stick. I decline. — They say the downtown Standard is more awesome. He opens two gums and crams them into his mouth.

— I'd dispute that. Downtown gets the arty crowd, but West Hollywood is certainly better for the Gary Busey. I check his face for signs ay understanding. He smiles, starting tae get the rhyming slang. — And most of our business is around there. You don't want tae be stuck in motors on choked freeways. Ye ken how you get in cars wi the motion sickness.

As he sulks in compliance, I feel like my dad must have on family outings; North Berwick, Kinghorn and Coldingham. Those stone beach picnics, under dull, cloudy skies in a

76

freezing cauld wind. *Not too much ay that ice cream, it'll make ye sick.* No wonder we became fucking drug addicts. Never mind deindustrialisation: sugar and biting-cold wind played their part.

Conrad leaves again – the Ambien must have relaxed him – and there are nae mair interruptions. I drift off intae a fucking weird kip where all my life's confusions are given the Salvador Dali remix, whirling around in my head. When I wake up I'm more exhausted than ever. I lie in bed most ay the day, sending emails on my laptop, and avoiding phone calls.

In the evening I've booked a bunch of us in for dinner at the Wing Lei, the wonderful fine-dining Chinese joint at the Wynn Hotel. It's one ay my favourite spots. With its warm and lavish but somehow sedate gold furnishings and lush gardens, it does what the very best places in Vegas do: make ye forget you're in Vegas. It's also the first Chinese restaurant in America tae be awarded a Michelin star. In addition tae Conrad and Emily, who I aim tae have supporting him here eventually, though not tonight, we have Jensen, a hanger-on mate ay my superstar DJ. He's an annoying buck-toothed wee cunt with a black fringe that hangs in his eyes, but strangely useful tae have around as he distracts Conrad fae hassling ays. Mitch, the promoter, is also present. Carl, as usual, who is opening, hasn't shown up yet. It was a major endeavour on my part tae convince Conrad no tae remove him fae the bill after the dickhead incident.

And now my two other guests arrive. Francis James Begbie and his wife Melanie have driven to Vegas in a hire car, making a big desert road trip out of it, a diversionary night in Palm Springs thrown in. Like lovers do. They can fly back with us on the rented jet, which takes less than an hour. Some cunts say *private* jet. It's a *rented* jet ride and tax-deductible. Again, propaganda designed to intimidate and inspire awe in the masses. I don't know of any star musician who is silly enough to run a private jet. Just hire one when you need it.

Melanie has her hair pinned up and wears a stylish mauve-coloured party dress. Franco sports a white shirt and black jeans. His hair is number-two short. Once we'd only sit down tae grease in some grubby Leith cafe together, nursing brutal hangovers. Now good food is a vice we share and our meets are always in a nice restaurant. After introducing them to everyone, I run a proposition past him. — Listen, this Edinburgh exhibition you've got in May; how do you fancy us putting a party on? I can get my DJs tae play there. Carl Ewart will love it, I offer, wondering where the fuck he is, again checking my phone for messages, as a waiter delivers sizzling ribs on two platters. Desperate bullets of sweat shoot from Conrad as the dish is laid in the centre of the table, far fae his clammy grasp. — What about it, Frank?

As Franco hesitates, Melanie intervenes. — Oh, that sounds great!

— Nah. No wanting any fuss, ay? Frank Begbie shakes his head. — Back over there, right in, right out, he says, as I catch Conrad lunging for glory, literally pushing Jensen aside to get at the goods.

— It's no bother, Franco. Least I can do, I say, glancing doon the table tae marvel at my superstar DJ. He's filled his plate up and is working hard on a pile of ribs and barbecue sauce, while absent-mindedly chatting tae Emily. Fuck me, I'm sure I heard the words 'track' and 'studio'.

— C'mon, Jim! Melanie urges.

— Okay, Franco smiles, — but it's against ma better judgement.

— Oh, and another thing, I drop my voice, bending in close to him, — I have that money for you.

Franco falls silent for a few long seconds. — It's cool, mate. We're sound, he emphasises. — Just nice tae see ye again, out here in America, daein so well. He takes in the stylised opulence ay the restaurant. — Life is weird, ay?

I can only agree wi that contention, but as I prepare tae get back onto the cash theme, Carl arrives, gaunt-faced, and wearing a Stetson and shades. He's with this woman, late twenties, blonde hair with crimson tendrils, sly eyes, whom he introduces as Chanel Hemmingworth, a journalist on a dance-music website. — She's doing a piece on me.

He briefly chats to Franco about Juice Terry, Billy Birrell and some other old names, before heading to the other end of the table to join Chanel. Conrad looks at him in a forced disdain. As Carl displays classic coked-upness, eating very little and ranting, Conrad is eavesdropping desperately. I'm trying to blank out his bullshit but in a conversation lull I catch a sleazy, cruisy, — I'm addicted to women but also allergic to them, so that's a bad mix.

Chanel Hemmingworth stays cool; she's obviously been in this situ before.

Checking my watch, I shout for the tab, settle up, and herd those unruly cats doon tae the club. Forget procuring sexual services: *this* is the hardest part ay the job. Vegas clubs have shitloads of security, so we have tae go through a labyrinth of basement corridors, even being diverted through a sweaty, fully-staffed kitchen (that a superstar DJ is treated to such indignities annoys Conrad, while the sizzling food preparations torment him), before we get tae the premier VIP box, located behind the DJ booth wi its decks and mixing desk. Carl's been dragging his flight case ay records wi him, perspiring like a Thatcher Cabinet minister wi the education portfolio up for grabs, and looking dangerously red. When we arrive, he makes straight for the giant bottle ay iced voddy clocked by a sexy hostess, who pre-emptively fixes him a drink. As Carl takes his refreshment and slips into the DJ booth and Conrad scans the crowd, I offer everybody earplugs. Melanie accepts; Emily and Franco don't. — It gets loud, I warn, placing mine lightly in. — I'm not losing my hearing for a fucking DJ. You shouldn't risk yours.

— Go on, Jim, Melanie urges.

Franco reluctantly takes the plugs. — I've never really been yin for dance music.

— You still a Rod Stewart fan?

— Aye, still dinnae mind a bit ay Rod, but have ye heard Guns N' Roses' *Chinese Democracy*?

— Wisnae too keen. It's no a real Guns N' Roses album, it doesnae have Slash oan the guitar.

— Aye, but the boy who plays guitar is fuckin better than Slash, he says, suddenly sounding like Begbie again, before inserting the plugs to eradicate any objections I might make.

Carl is a bit fucked and his hour warm-up set, spinning old vinyl on record decks that naebody has used for a decade or more, doesnae go doon that well. I always phone ahead to tell them to dig out old-school Technics turntables as the cunt still insists on spinning vinyl. They think it's a joke at first, then they generally curse me tae fuck. Some flat refuse: albino Luddite intransigence has cost us bookings. And it's not as if anybody here gives a fuck about his deep-house music. The Vegas weekend shagger crowd craves only the big names in EDM. They sit at their tables getting loaded on peeve, and hit the floor en masse when Conrad waddles intae the booth tae replace Carl. The star's gig is pretty damn good if ye like that sort ay seedy table-service pseudo-prostitution deal, which I dinnae. Tae me, the brand ay jumpy cut-up EDM shit Conrad has adopted – lucratively, so I cannae criticise him – is a fucking misnomer. It's totally undanceable, but the brostep frat-boy crowd and the husband-hunting suburban bimbettes lap him up.

Chanel, the journo, seems to have absconded, so Carl sits drinking steadily, making heavy-handed passes at the hostess. He's pretty fucked off. His heart wisnae in that gig. In order tae gie the lassie, whae's just daein her job, some respite fae his predatory attentions, I pull him aside and try tae say reassuring things. — Vegas will never be acid house.

— What the fuck am I doing here, then? he shouts as Conrad cuts up some more pop hits tae a dangerously rammed and intoxicated dance floor.

— Making money. Getting your name back out there.

Carl took the split with his missus Helena very hard. I got him this gig supporting Technonerd, which neither of them is happy about. But it's Surrender at the Wynn, one ay the best nightclubs in the USA. So the term 'ungrateful cunt' resonates in my head a little.

Surrender is opulence personified, and we are making a fortune, but as usual, it's no enough. It's never enough. Not for Carl, and not for Conrad, who after the gig, is singing the same old tune as we have a drink before making our way tae the airport. — Why do I not get a residency in XS? Guetta has one in XS!

XS is the Wynn's other nightclub, which is even bigger and more opulent than Surrender. It's bigger and more opulent than *anywhere*, an ancient Roman palace of vice and decadence. — Because Guetta's Guetta and you're Conrad Technonerd, I snap in tetchy exhaustion, climbing down in face of his pout. — Next year you'll be up with him, mate. Let's just enjoy that express elevator ride to superstardom.

— So next year we will play in XS?

Jesus fuck. Greedy fat cunt. — We'll see, buddy boy. But the prognosis is good.

— There is a girl ... I said that I would take her and her friend back to LA. He nods over to a storm of sexy in the form of two lassies, all tans, hair, teeth, eyes, breasts and legs, who have managed to slip past security into our box.

Fucksticks. It means I have tae arrange passes, documentation and insurance for these sleazy-but-hot youngbloods who have targeted the fat Dutch boy. *And* I've already set the gluttonous cunt up wi an expensive hooker back at the Standard. I hope they all like the taste ay pussy and polder plug. We get into the minibus. Carl is pished, slumped in the very back seat and shouting about coke. At least Emily is quiet; she's talking to Melanie.

— It must be so shit to know that you are finished as a DJ, Conrad shouts back to Carl, as Jensen chuckles and the two girls gasp in fake admiration.

— Fuck off, dickhead. Play some music, and he pulls out his phone, showing pictures of Conrad with the dildo attached.

I roll my eyes as the storm of squabbling builds. Franco turns to me, nods behind us. — However much you make, you deserve it, having to babysit them!

I learned fae babysitting the master; trying tae have a night oot withoot you cutting some cunt's heid off. — I keep telling myself that, I say.

The private airfield is adjacent to McCarron, and thus a short hop from the Strip. I'm on the phone the rest of the way, trying tae arrange clearance for the two lassies, one of whom Conrad is sweatily pawing, while Jensen is hanging on Emily's every word as she pontificates about her influences, no realising that he has zero chance. Carl has fallen intae silence. I dinnae like seeing him in that frame ay mind. We get into the jet and are LA-bound with minimum fuss. Melanie is impressed, and so is Franco. He keeps looking at me with that *you flash cunt* expression of disbelief.

— It's a tax write-off against expenses, I stress. — Uncle Sam pays us to fuck up the environment, so we can get to our beds without having tae spend another sleepless night as high as kites in an oxygenated Vegas hotel room.

— Aye, right, Franco says doubtfully.

Although it's a short flight, I'm jittery without the Ambien, and feel my mitt sweaty on the yellow container in my pocket. We land at the private airport in Santa Monica, where I say goodbye to Franco and Melanie, who are getting picked up by obviously loyal friends at this hour. Emily has hooked up with her party pals and Carl has a couple of sleazy druggies meet him and vanishes into the dark LA morning. I'm about tae get Conrad, Jensen and the girls intae a taxi and myself intae an Uber, but he's having nane ay it. — You must come with me to the Standard, to make sure that the bitch whore you hired shows up, he commands, pushing a Hershey bar he got from the vending machine into his clammy pus.

My Santa Monica pad is ten fucking minutes away. I'm beyond exhausted and my jaw rattles as I think ay that bed. No a particularly great structure, but boasting a very expensive mattress. West Hollywood is around thirty minutes away, even in the clear roads at this time of day, and the same back. But he's the talent. This fat, obnoxious, spoiled misogynistic little prick who calls women 'hoes' and 'bitches' because he's a stupid rich white kid, trying to imitate some dumb black rapper twat he once met at a hip-hop conference: *he* is the fucking talent.

— Okay, I say, feeling my soul wither a wee bit mair.

I zone out at the front by the driver, trying tae block out Conrad's charmless patter, and the fake, sycophantic laughter of Jensen and the girls. I'm already looking forward tae getting back tae Edinburgh for the New Year. I'll even kip on the dodgy mattress in my old boy's spare room. But then I think of Victoria, and realise that LA has its charms.

Thankfully, when we get to the Standard, the escort, Brandi, is waiting, and she's pretty cool. Conrad vanishes with her and both ay the girls, shutting a miserable Jensen out ay the party. But he has a room, paid for by Citadel Productions, to be later charged to their client Conrad Appeldoorn as a management expense. I take an Uber back tae Santa Monica and my bed. I try to get to sleep, craving that fluttering comma induced by two Ambien and half a bottle ay Night Nurse. I resist, in spite of my eyes snapping open at intervals and devouring the ceiling in creeping dread. When sleep comes it's in the dreamscape of a theatre stage, where I seem to be taking part in a Noël Cowardesque play, with a monocled and smoking-jacketed Franco, and a ballgown-wearing Vicky/ Melanie mixture.

My apartment in Santa Monica is in a dreary complex on the corner of a block. The orange paint covering the exterior walls has been diluted to save money, tapering out from brash and showy, to a meagre, insipid covering, pallid as it bends into the side street. On the plus side, it has a communal rooftop sundeck, with a pool rarely used by anybody other than two chain-smoking French queens. In the mornings, as I call the afternoons – I tend tae operate on DJ hours – I like tae sit up here with my laptop and dae emails and deal with calls. Up comes one I've been avoiding, a promoter back in Amsterdam. The poor cunt is so persistent that I have tae take it. Fucking time zones. — Des! We've been playing phone tag!

— We need Carl at ADE, Mark. He has relevance. Carl Ewart *is* acid house. Yes, that movable feast we know and love has fallen on hard times. But it *will* be back. Next year is the thirty-year anniversary of Ibiza '87. We need N-Sign in that booth and on top form.

I'm silent in the face ay his rigmarole. It's a heartbreaker when somebody is bringing their A-game and you ken that you're still gaunny disappoint them.

— Mark?

I look at the blinding sun, screwing up my eyes. Should have put on sunblock. I consider hanging up or telling Des I cannae hear him. — We can't do ADE, mate. We booked another gig in Barça.

— You bastard. You promised me at Fabric that you'd be at ADE!

I was coked. Never make promises on drugs. — I said we'd try. The Barça gig is a good stage for Carl, Des, we couldnae pass it up. They gave us the Sonar slots this year. Can't disappoint them.

— But you can disappoint *us*, right?

— Des, I'm sorry, mate. You know the score.

— Mark ...

— Yes, Des?

— You're a cunt.

— I'm not going to fight you on that one, Des. I stand up, walk over to the parapet and look across at the freeway traffic, moving slowly towards the beach. Up ahead, the rumbling ay a new metro train on the downtown Santa Monica stop, at last connecting the beach towns with LA and Hollywood. There was a time when I'd have been excited about that; now I realise I haven't even been on it, and tae ma horror, I can't think ay when I'd need tae. Instead I'll charge around in rental cars on choked freeways, looking for parking validation in hotel and office underground lots. Fuck sake.

— Wise move, Mark. Fuck you, you double-crossing motherfucker! If you knew the hassle I had to get your washed-up druggie homeboy on that fucking bill!

— C'mon, Des, let's take it down a notch.

He sighs. — Fair enough, but fuck you anyway.

— I love you, Des.

— Yeah, sure you do, he says and hangs up.

I *do* feel like an absolute cunt, but as soon as ah acknowledge this, it just fades away. Back in the day, I never had that much ay a thick skin, even though ah pretended tae. Then, suddenly, it was just there. Like ah was a fuckin Tony Stark whae'd invented a psychic Iron Man suit. The upside ay developing that armour is the obvious one: fuck all bothers ye that much. The downer? Well, it's like antidepressants. You dinnae get the lows, but ye sure as fuck miss the euphoria ay the highs.

The last few days have been so disorientating. Travel, time zones, sleep deprivation. I seem to be on the phone constantly, without making any inroads. Muchteld in the office back in Amsterdam, calling in various states ay alarm about it all. All this pish about online banking: it disnae work so smoothly when you're between countries. Ah've spent most ay the eftirnoon talking tae ma bank in Holland, the ABN AMRO, to get them tae transfer money intae ma Citibank account here in the USA. Of course, trying tae withdraw cash is still a fucking hassle because … just fucking banks.

As is trying to withdraw fae Ambien. My eyeballs feel full of grit and my pulse trashes in them. Thankfully Vicky helps, coming round and dragging me tae bed. She tells me no more pills, just sex. After we make love I fall intae the deepest sleep I've had in months. In the morning, I'm delighted tae find that she's stayed over. It feels great tae wake up with her. Even though it's criminally early for me, I feel rested for the first time in ages. She even talks me into going for a run down the beachfront. Although she's taking it easy, I'm struggling tae keep up, sweat surging and lungs burning. I dig in, pride at no being perceived as a past-it cunt propelling ays on. Afterwards we get some brunch then go back tae the apartment and bed. As Vicky stretches out, a big yawn, her sun-bleached locks sprawling over my pillow, it hits me through my ain exhaustion that I've no been this happy as I am at this precise moment in years.

In the evening we head tae Franco's exhibition, or 'Jim Francis' as he now professionally styles himself. I suggest we take the metro. At first she looks doubtful, then agrees, and we glide in jocular relaxation towards downtown LA. Vicky is wearing a knockout glittering black dress and pumps, her hair pinned up. I feel an exalted, lucky bastard.

The gallery is in a single-floored warehouse conversion about fifteen minutes' walk from Pershing Square in a neighbourhood full of cool street art. We chat to Melanie, with whom Vicky has already struck up a fine rapport. Although Vicky is English and shorter, there is a galling similarity in the way they talk and move. It seems bizarre that Franco and I can have similar tastes in women. Wearing chinos and a V-necked T-shirt, he stands a bit apart from everyone. He still gives off something that makes strangers reticent about approaching him, but it's now more of a weary aloofness than naked aggression. Melanie provides the charm, excusing herself as she greets some more visitors, who are probably potential buyers.

We head over to Franco who welcomes Vicky and myself warmly. I haven't told her his backstory (and mine) other than he was a bit rough and ready in the bad old days, doing some jail time before discovering art. As he chats to her about a painting depicting the crucifixion of Cameron, Miliband and Clegg, I look over at a grinning, charismatic wee guy with dark hair, who is being fussed over by an entourage. — Is that Chuck Ponce?

Franco nods, and Vicky remarks, — I'm working on the overseas sale of his latest film for Paramount. Not that I've met him!

The enthusiastic, slightly autistic star beams at Jim Francis, the artist formerly known as Begbie, and rushes over to us. Vicky and I get a nod and a cheesy smile, before he focuses on Franco. — Jimbo! My man! Long time no see!

— Yes it is, Franco concedes, his face immobile.

— I need a head! I need you to give me head, bro, he laughs. Franco remains stoical. — Charmaine, my ex … he drops his voice, as Vicky excuses herself and heads for the restroom, and I pretend to look at the art hung on walls and mounted on plinths. I pick up that Ponce is obviously trying tae get Franco tae dae a head ay Charmaine Garrity, his ex-wife and fellow Hollywood star. I grab a gless ay red wine fae a server's tray and inch closer, hearing him urge, — Help a brother out, dude.

— I did already. *The Hunter Strikes*, mind?

— Yeah, man, pity about that movie. I had real problems with the accent. But you've been doing great work, and I want an original Jim Francis!

— Shut up, I hear Franco say, as I look at the crucifixion painting, — I like these sort ay commissions to be confidential.

— You got it, bro. How do I get in touch?

— Give me your digits and I'll get in touch with you, Franco goes. I'm looking at Cameron's greetin baw pus. It's pretty good, as is Miliband, hapless and nerdy, but that looks fuck all like Clegg.

— Sure thing, pal, Ponce beams, reciting his number as Franco keys it into his phone. — You ain't still sore at me, huh, dude?

— No. Not in the slightest, Franco replies.

Ponce play-punches him on the shoulder. — Cool. Get in touch, bro! Name your price. I gotta have one while I can still afford you!

As the grinning Chuck leaves, heading back to his crew, tracked aw the wey by Franco, I slip back ower to the artist's side. — So you're big mates with Hollywood idols and rock stars?

— Naw, he says, looking at me soberly, — they urnae your friends.

Vicky returns from the restroom – I hate myself for calling the lavy that – but is intercepted by Melanie and they start talking to two other women. I take my chance, delving into my bag and thrusting an envelope at Franco. — Here it is, buddy.

— Naw ... naw ... yir awright, mate. He pushes it away like I'm trying to gie him dog shit.

— It's yours, bud. The money at today's value. It comes tae fifteen thousand four hundred and twenty quid sterling. We can quibble on the method ay calculation –

— I dinnae need it. He shakes his head. — You have tae let go ay the past.

— This is *me* doing that right now, Franco. I hold out the envelope — Take it, please.

Suddenly this guy wi black-framed glasses, whom I'm assuming is his agent, rushes across tae us. He's obviously excited and says to Franco, — Sam DeLita has just bought a piece for two hundred thousand dollars! The Oliver Harbison head!

— Tidy, Begbie says, completely unmoved, as he scans the crowd. — Axl Rose no here?

— I'm not sure, the guy says, puzzled at the crushing anticlimax, — I'll check. Rumours abound, and he looks at

89

me. Franco reluctantly introduces us. — This is my agent, Martin. This is Mark, a pal from the old country.

— Pleased to meet you, Mark. Martin shakes my hand firmly. — I'll catch you guys later. There's a room that needs worked!

As Martin heads off, Franco says, — See? I've got everything I want, mate. There's nothing you can dae for me. So keep yir money.

— But you'd be helping me oot if ye took it. *You* could do something for *me*.

Franco's head turns slowly in the negative. He looks across the room, nods and smiles at some people. — Listen, you ripped me off and I forgive you, he says, his voice low. He waves at a swankily dressed couple, and the guy salutes back. It's another actor cunt that was in a film I saw recently on a plane, but I cannae think ay the boy's name or the movie. — The bad choices I made would have happened anyway, that was just where I was at that point in ma life. He gives me a wee smile. — But I've let go ay the past.

— Aye, and I want tae n aw, I tell him, fighting doon ma exasperation.

— Delighted for you, he says, not that sardonically, — but you have to find your own way, ma auld buddy. The last time you tried to dae that ah was a fucking vehicle for ye. He pauses, and the old coldness fuses intae his eyes.

It sears my insides. — Franco, I'm sorry, man, I –

— I'm no gaun there again. This time it has tae be a solo gig, and suddenly eh smiles and punches me *softly* on the airm, almost in a parody ay the auld Begbie. It hits ays: *this cunt is taking the pish*.

— Fuck sake … this is perverse! I'm offering ye money here, Frank! Money that's yours!

— It's no mine, it came fae a drug deal, he says, poker-faced. Then his hand is on my elbow, guiding me ower tae

90

a painting ay Jimmy Savile, unknown in America, lying battered tae a pulp outside the Alhambra Bar. Savile's eyes have been torn out and blood from his genitals stains his white tracksuit groin like dark red piss. Underneath it bears the title:

THIS IS HOW WE DEAL WITH NONCES IN LEITH
(2014, oil on canvas)

He points tae a rid dot on it, indicating that a sale has been made. — *This* is mine. I used tae fuck up people's faces and get jailed. Now I dae it and get paid.

I'm looking aroond, scanning the portraits and cast heids that he's produced. I have tae say it, even though ah confess that ah don't know much about art: this is the biggest pile ay shite I've seen in ma fuckin life. He's totally gaming those thick, spoiled rich fuckers, whae probably think it's cool tae collect the works ay this savage jailbird. Fair play tae the cunt, but fuck sake, casting somebody's face and then mutilating it: that's no fucking art. Ah observe the occupants ay the gallery, shuffling fae one exhibit tae the next, eyes screwed up, pointing, discussing. Tanned men and women with bodies honed in gyms, decorated wi nice clathes, impeccably groomed, stinking ay top cologne, perfume and wealth. — Do you know where *their* money comes fae? Drug trafficking? Human trafficking, for fuck sake! A few people in a proximate group turn roond in response tae ma raised voice. Fae the corner ay ma eye, a security guard cranes his neck. — You must have a charity you like, something ah can gie it tae?

— Quiet, bud. Franco now looks like he's really enjoying this. — You're embarrassing yourself.

I feel incredulity warp my face. — Now I've been told by *you* tae stop making a cunt ay masel in public: game, set and match! Now gies ays the name ay your favourite charity, Franco, for fuck sake!

— I dinnae believe in charity, Mark. And call me Jim, please.

— What *do* you believe in? So I have to gie fifteen and a bit grand tae Hibs?

— I believe in looking after my ain, mate. He nods at his postcard Californian blonde wife, as the speakers suddenly rumble and Martin the agent guy gets tae the front ay the house.

Vicky rejoins me. — All good? she asks. — What's that? She points to the envelope in my hand.

I put it back in the bag and zip it up. — Trying to give Frank something I owe him, but he won't take it.

— Well, I must say, it all looks very exciting cloak-and-dagger stuff. Does it come from an illicit drug deal?

Franco turns and I cannae look the cunt in the eye because I suspect neither ay us would be able tae keep a straight face. — We only deal in Provi cheques in Leith, I tell her.

As I glance back at Franco, there's a sound ay fingers hitting the mike, causing a static crackle, hushing the crowd intae silence. Martin the agent clears his throat. — Thank you for coming along. Now I'd like to introduce the director of this gallery and great patron of the arts of the City of Los Angeles, Sebastian Villiers.

A white-heided, rid-couponed, country-club cunt, whae looks like every American politician I've ever seen, gets up and starts talking utter shite aboot Begbie. About how his 'work' is the best thing since sliced breid. I cannae listen tae this pish! All I can think ay is getting Vicky home. I thought I was saturated with sex after this afternoon. No fucking way. I look at her, and her raunchy smile tells me she's thinking the same. As we slope away, a DJ starts playing funk, and

Franco and Melanie are dancing smoothly tae that Peter Brown track 'Do You Wanna Get Funky with Me'.

Fuck me. That cunt. Dancing. And the fucker has moves. Is that really fucking Francis Begbie? Maybe it's me. Maybe my Begbie beliefs are inculcated from another era. Maybe I just need tae let go ay aw that shite, like *Jim Francis* evidently has.

6

SICK BOY – IN SEARCH OF EUAN MCCORKINDALE

Drink and drugs are a whippersnapper's game: there is little worse than a hangover or an E comedown after you hit fifty. Even under the licence of Christmas, you just feel weak and stupid, as the facts have to be faced: the meagre, diminishing returns of fun to be squeezed out in no way justifiy the subsequent extended horror show.

So I'm half submerged in this comfy couch, in front of the big flat screen and blazing coal fire in the McCorkindale home, a pot of tea by my side. I'm channel hopping, trying tae keep in a positive frame of mind. I can see Ben, outside in the garden, talking into his mobile phone, all big smiles. I decide that I'll hang around here a few days longer, once I get him packed off south, after the Hibs–Raith encounter. I was set against Scottish independence, believing that we'd totally fuck it up. Now I'm changing my mind: the vibe and confidence in the city suggests we'd cope better than the shit-show down south. I'm thinking of calling Jill, speculating about an Edinburgh Colleagues, maybe identifying some more raw recruits and licking them intae shape!

I'm distracted by Carlotta, man-marking her darling brother, literally looming *right over* me. Obviously on her agenda: a missing hubby, the disgraced man of this formerly esteemed household. Carlotta isn't going to move, or speak, and I don't know how long I can keep pretending she isn't staring at the top of my head. It's been her MO since she was a kid. Always knew how tae use the power of brooding, silent outrage to increase the air pressure. I elect tae cashie it oot. — Hi, sis. Just trying to decide on my viewing. There's ... I pick up the handset, hit the guide button and read the screen, — 'an enchanting romantic comedy starring Audrey Tautou' that isn't *Amélie* –

— You find Euan! You find ma husband! I look up and she's glaring at me. Her voice set in that controlled, precise way of hers.

I turn to her and spread my palms. — Sis, I really can't take volume right now ... which is the wrong thing tae say as her eyes burn with murderous Latin passion. — He'll show up when he's go—

— FIND HIM!

What could be worse than walking those cold streets in that dead zone between Christmas and New Year? Staying here and enduring that banshee wail. I cough out my agreement and she heads off, her feet thumping up the wooden stairs. I'm putting on my coat in the hallway, with scarf and hat, as Ross comes through with a silent stare that commands a response. That laddie is perhaps his mother's son.

— How's Pitch and Toss? And what's cuz Benito up to outside? Lady shenanigans, no doubt.

Then I realise that this little fucker is only balling his fists at me as if he wants a square go! — Mum said that you set Dad up with that woman, his high voice bleats.

Saucy mare, her! And cheeky little cunt, too! Well, the smart wee fucker is going head-to-head with the big boys now. I fix him in an even gaze, and lower my voice. — Maybe the blame was yours though, buddy, and I watch his mouth flap open in disbelief. — Maybe you made Euan want to prove himself, with you going on about being too much ay a pussy virgin tae git yir hole.

— What … How did you … Who said –

— You may wish tae factor that into your calculations. I flick my scarf over my shoulder and start buttoning my coat up.

His eyes blink rapidly in concert with his trembling lips. – You shouldnae … You don't … He tries to run away, but I reach out and grab his arm. — Get off me!

— Go on, run to Mamma, I sneer. That stops his struggle in its tracks. — That'll work, if your quest in life is to stay a virgin forever. That'll ensure you achieve your goal, awright.

Ross's head is hung low. It's as if he's looking at the imaginary Minecraft world he's set up on the floor.

— Lift your head up, I tell him. — Be a man, for fuck sake.

He physically struggles to do this. — But … but … but …

I assist him, wrenching his chin north. Forcing him to look into my eyes. — You can't get your hole. Fine. I get it. I understand how important it is, and I release my grasp ay his face. I note his chin dips a bit but his eyes remain set on mine. — Your mother won't help you get laid, Ross. Your father … well, come on, I tell him, feeling a little disloyal. But nobody asked Euan to fuck Marianne or for them to get fruity with the video camera. *That horny hoor … her sluttish adventurism is suddenly exciting to me. I should have ridden her, not that prick …* — But *I* will, I tell him, watching his eyes suddenly bulge. — If you want it.

Yes, even through his despondency, something in those lamps has ignited! — You … you'd do that for me?

— Of course I will. I punch his airm. — Blood is thicker than water. I want you to have a full sex life, tae be able to talk tae women and enjoy congress with them, and I pull him into the alcove by the front door, lowering my voice. — I don't want to see you wasting your teen years on guilty masturbation, choking whenever a girl you fancy steps into the room, I explain, enjoying the shade of Jambo maroon his coupon is bursting out into. — I had a great friend, Danny Murphy, his name was; he never got any action, I wistfully recount. — So the boy grew up wrong. I don't want any ay that nonsense for you, good buddy.

I feel my blandishments move him, but he's still suspicious. — What's it to you? Why do you want to help?

— Well, I have one considerable advantage over your mum and dad.

— What?

— I don't see you as a daft wee bairn. To me you're a normal young guy who is just trying tae make his way in life, and I realise that this is the most important thing in your world right now.

— It is! Ross squeals in gratitude. — I'm glad somebody understands!

I nod upstairs, urging him to lower his voice by dropping mine. — Well, naturally I do. Have you any idea what I do for a living?

Ross swivels his head to check the coast is still clear. Then he faces me, sucking in his bottom lip. — I've heard Mum and Dad talk about it. It's like an escort agency.

— Exactly. I'm in the business of hooking up lonely and frustrated people with desirable members of the opposite sex. It's *what I do*.

— You could –

Again, I take my voice down a notch, and nod up the wooden staircase. — Shh … Yes I could, I hiss. I can hear Carlotta thrashing around in rage, slamming doors too hard, stamping across the sanded floors. I gaze out to the garden where Ben is ending his call, doubtless ready to come in and hit me for cash. The kid is a money-guzzling machine. I blame the Surreyites and their careless indulgence of him, or, perhaps more realistically, their planned humiliation of one Simon David Williamson; forcing me to compete in a game I can never win. — What you need is an experienced woman to guide you through this cherry loss.

Ross looks at me in horror. — But I fancy –

I cut him off. — I know who you fancy; some feisty, pixie-faced wee heartbreaker at school, who struts around well aware that she's a playground supermodel. But to hunt that sort of game you need the tools, and I ain't just talking about that cannon in your troosers, which I'm hoping is a Williamson 9.5 rather than a McCorkindale 5.5, if you get my drift.

The kid's pained face tells me it's closer to the latter.

— No, buddy, you need the confidence that experience gives you: social as well as sexual. That's what Prof Unc Si from Shaggers University offers. Now think it through. And tell your mother fuck all. This is a bros' thing. Promise?

— Right ... Thanks, Uncle Simon, he squeaks in gratitude, bumping my proffered fist.

Just then, Ben appears at his shoulder, looking a little smug, but still shooting us a what-the-fuck stare.

— Benito the bandito! I'm trying to talk your *piccolo cugino*, Pitch and Toss here, and I place an arm around the shoodirs of the spotty boy, — into joining us at the ER hozzy.

— The ER hozzy ... Ben says in his lazy, posh, suburban Home Counties accent ... *My God, he's one of them. My son is one of them.* — Is that something to do with Uncle Euan?

— No! ER as in *Easter Road*, hozzy as in *hospitality*. For the match of the season against the mighty Raith Rovers!

— Yeah, cool, Ben says, massively underwhelmed, but coming to some animation on noting that I'm attired in a coat and scarf. — Where are you going?

— A wee message for your auntie.

— Are you going to find Dad? Ross bleats. — I want tae come!

— Not possible, pal of mine, I contend as I hear thumping steps down the stairs.

— Ross! Carlotta barks from the doorway. — You'll stay here with your cousin!

Ross has that what-the-fuck-have-I-done-wrong expression of hangdog bemusement.

I tip him a wee wink, which seems to console him a little. This is as opportune a time as any to make good my escape. Enough of all the family shite! This festive blight on the calendar is a headfuck, and thank Christ (literally) that it's only once a year.

So I head out on my dispiriting search. The frosty bite of winter tingles my face, as the street lamps blink into an insipid glow. The daylight hours here are so fleeting it's almost more of an insult inserting such meagre, murky grey slithers of shit into the total darkness. Funny, but in my younger days, I always wanted out of this city. London offered a bigger canvas. Now, unaccountably, I feel a perverse loyalty towards it. I even contemplate taking a stroll down Leith Walk, but that would only serve to invite crushing despondency. The one thing worse than hearing the words: SICK BOY YA CUNT, WHAIRE HUV YOU BEEN HIDIN YIRSEL? – delivered at maximum volume across a filthy pub – would be not hearing them at all. I set course away from town, towards the Royal Infirmary, Euan's place of work. When I get to the reception desk, they phone personnel in response to my enquiry, before informing me, — Dr McCorkindale is on leave until the 6th of January.

So I get the bus back into town. It's fuckin nippy alright; my coupon is stinging with the cold air and my lips are cracking over. I head into a Boots tae buy some lip balm and condoms.

As he's not a lost waif, there's no sense in trawling the bus or train stations, so I opt to hang around the hotel lobbies. At least they're warm. Euan has dosh but is too much of a penny-pinching Calvinist wanker to splash out on the Balmoral or the Caledonian. It will be a functional, clean budget chain, so I hit a few and loiter; they're full of sales and marketing cumsplats, but no sightings of disgraced Colinton podiatrists.

Applying the same logic, I doubt Euan would have gone to a high-class escort agency. I'm betting he's been slumming it in the saunas, loving the thrill of the transaction, and part of him excited at the potential humiliation of being rumbled by a work colleague. Yes, I reckon he subconsciously craves all this drama. I hit a couple of the Mary Tyler Moore hooses, one at the top end of Leith and the other in the New Town, showing the Christmas photo I took of Euan on my phone, without exciting any signs of recognition.

I find those tacky premises and their grubby clientele dispiriting. This place in the East New Town is like a shabby government office of the eighties. With its bland reception area, you feel as if you are here to get your passport stamped rather than your pipes cleaned. I head outside, about to call it a day and return empty-handed to face Carlotta's wrath, when I hear somebody emerging behind me. Then a voice urges, — Hi, mate, hud on a minute.

I turn to face what can only be described as a total fuckin radge. His eyes, slitty but burning with a focused intent, announce him as big trouble. He wears an expensive-looking suit, but it somehow seems scabby on him, as if it's gotten damp from him *actually wearing it in a sauna*. I know who he is; he's the psycho cunt that runs some of these establishments, and whom Terry once did some work for. This isn't good. When a stranger refers to you as 'mate' in that tone of voice, it never is.

— You've been gaun roond the saunas, asking about a boy?

— Aye. I take the initiative and show him the picture on my phone.

— Well, if you're playing detective and no going tae the bizzies, it cannae be kosher, this bastard says. God forged this cunt's pus when He was sat constipated on the toilet seat and thinking of the word 'snide'. Not the Creator's best work, it must be said.

— The boy's a bit ay a sex case, I explain. — His missus is ma sister, and she caught him playing away fae hame. Chucked him oot. Now she wants him back. I thought he might have been hooring, is all.

All the time this cunt's slanty, malicious, sweetie-wife eyes are going from the screen to my coupon. Then he suddenly says, — Ah ken you! Sick Boy, they called ye!

They presumably being his fellow retarded idiots, ones also created from the grunting congress of mongol siblings. — Ha ... no heard that one for a while.

— Ayyye ... you punt aboot doon in London now. Wi Leo, and the Greek cunt, what's-his-name ...

My heart skips a wee beat. This product of retard *kinshafting* has a long reach, and with fellow insect-brained fuckers not programmed to compromise their mechanical goals. If he's mobbed up with them, there is no hiding place and it means I'm duty-bound to assist. — Andreas ... Yes, Leo, great lads. But that's all in the past. These days I run a respectable dating agency. We have an application –

— You're a Leith boy, he accuses, — used tae run wi Franco Begbie.

101

— Aye, I concede. I hate the way these cretins use the term 'run', their pathetic gangster pish vexes me, and I can't believe I'm hearing *Begbie's* name now; that violent psychopathic cunt who conned his way out of jail on some bullshit art ticket. This nightmare grows bleaker by the second. It's dark and cold and I'm hung-over and I crave that couch. Even Carlotta's verbal assault and iciness must beat being in the uncomfortable proximity ay this fucker. Now the wind is whipping freezing fucking rain into my face.

— Well, ah dinnae care who you are, ye dinnae come intae ma premises and poke yir neb in. Got that?

— Well, I wisnae really. As I explained, I was looking for my brother-in-law. He's a surgeon and he –

The next thing I know is the wind is battered oot ay ays by a jackknifing blow tae ma guts … I can barely breathe, as I reach out and grab the railing. There are people walking by in the rain, some at a bus stop, others smoking outside a pub. Not one of the cunts has even noticed this prick's assault on me!

I look up at his pitiless eyes. — Ah'll take that phone, he gestures tae the mobby in my hand.

— Ma phone … what the fuck …?

— Dinnae make ays say it again.

I hand it over, hating myself, but trying to catch my breath. The options of running away or striking back are beyond me at this point in time, and probably any. This cunt is a killer.

He casually types his number into my phone, and calls up his own, letting it ring. He hands it back to me. — We have each other's contact info now. So ah'll let you ken if this boy shows up. Meantime, you keep the fuck oot ay my premises, unless invited by *moi*. Right?

— Right. I feel my breath coming back. — Thanks … appreciated. I'm thinking to myself: *If this cunt has any hoors worth thieving, they will all be working for me at an Edinburgh*

102

Colleagues, while he'll be wearing that famous maroon jersey as he's getting rogered daily on the beasts' wing at Saughton. I will make that happen.

— Okay, I'm Victor, by the way, Victor Syme, this cunt says, now scarier than ever with his gossiping fishwife tones and his hand on my shoulder. — Ah'll let ye ken if I hear anything about this ... he plays with the word, — ... this *surgeon* felly. And I'm sorry aboot the wee dig, but thaire's a lot ay wide cunts aboot, n ye huv tae draw a wee line in the sand, he grins. — But if ye ken the likes ay Leo, and, of course, Frank Begbie, then that's okay wi me.

I'm happy to depart this cunt's company, although I only get round the corner before a text from him comes in.

I won't forget. Vic S.

It's replete with a smiley emoticon, which has never looked so sinister.

I find a grotty cafe and sit down, trying tae compose myself over a cup ay tea. This fucking town! I have to get out of here. And fuck Scottish independence: in no time at all we would be a gangster state run by scum like this cunt Syme! It's true: you never escape old associations, no matter how tenuous you believe them to be. On that note, I'm straight on to Juice Terry. — Tezza. What's the story with this Victor Syme cunt? Heard you did some work for him.

— Cannae talk right now, buddy boy. Where are ye?

— Broughton Street, I tell him. He must have some cunt in the back ay his cab.

— Be there in five minutes. Where aboots?

— See ye in the Basement Bar.

I retreat to the Basement, settling into the comfy seats towards the rear of the bar with two bottles of lager.

Terry is as good as his word, and swings in. Unfortunately, he leaves me waiting for such a long time while he chats to a barmaid that I have to phone him. He rolls his eyes and heads across. — You're a cock-blocking bastard, Williamson. Seriously.

— This is important, bud. Victor Syme, I urge.

— Aye … he wis away in Spain. Terry takes a glug of lager. — The bizzies wir pittin heat oan um, but eh came back last year, Mr Fuckin Untouchable. Does that no say grass tae you? It sais it tae me.

I refuse to get enmeshed in pathetic local gangster politics. — How do you ken him?

Fae the school. Fuckin nowt in they days, we aw used tae caw um the Poof, that wis ehs nickname. Every cunt battered the wee creep back then; eh wis a late developer. Now eh thinks eh's Mr Big cause ay Tyrone bein deid –

— Tyrone? Potted heid? This was news to me. Tyrone had been around since I was a boy. — So what happened tae the fat man?

— Burnt tae death in a fire in his hoose. He hud some war wi the young team. One ay them got done doon Leith Docks. A lot ay people are thinkin the Poof took advantage and moved in oan thum baith: Tyrone and the young gadge. Rumour is eh's connected; goat Police Scotland, East Europeans, cunts in London and Manchester aw owin um tons ay favours, or so they say, ay? Might be shite, might no. But ah ken one thing, the cunt wis oan the lam in Spain cause the polis wir lookin for him in connection wi the disappearance ay this bird that worked in the saunas. Cowped it masel, but as a mates' thing, nivir peyed for it. Terry looks at me in sombre insistence.

— I've no doubt that you could charm a prostitute into sleeping with you without a cash transaction, Terry. But you said Syme was on the run?

— Cunt hud fuck all gaun for um. He wis oot the sauna game, hidin in Spain. Then eh jist waltzes back ower like nowt's happened. Terry looks around. Lowers his voice. — Thinks ah'm at his beck n call. 'A wee favour, Terry mate ...' and he does a passable imitation of Syme's snidey tones. — But he'll git his, Terry says in empty belligerence. — Cunt's a heidcase, keep away fae um, he warns. — Anyway, how did yir Christmas turn oot? Usual borin family stuff?

— You ken how it goes, I tell him, thinking of that cretinous brother-in-law and his imbecile son, the bother their blood-filled cocks and bloodless brains are causing me, and I idly pick up a discarded magazine on a chair. It shows an image of the actress Keira Knightley, half naked and in a sultry pose, advertising perfume.

— Fuckin ride yon, Terry announces.

— Knightley, I muse.

— Aw fuckin ooirs if she wis game.

We chat for a while, and Terry drops me off in the cab at Carlotta's. It's so pitch black I can't believe that it's only just after 8 p.m., it feels like two in the morning. I see Ben, once more in the garden, on the phone, illuminated by a trip light. Probably talking to some bird; he tells me fuck all, which I totally admire. Of course, the fact that I'm without Euan is enough tae send Carlotta into another rage. I tell her I checked the hospital and the hotels, omitting the saunas. It seems to calm her down a bit, before another bolt of fury suddenly sears her. — What did you say to Ross?

— Nothing, I protest, rubbing my gut, still tender as I lower myself onto the couch, considering that Syme might actually be able to do me a favour. Sometimes radges need to be assimilated – the Borg in *Star Trek* strategy – rather than opposed or ignored. The pain brings back a memory of being bullied by Begbie at school, before I became friends with Renton, who was his best mate. This was purely in order to get that psycho cunt off my back. My head is spinning.

Carlotta's eyes are batty. — Just urged the wee man to try and learn a lesson from Euan. Where is he? I see Ben out there –

— At Louisa's, she spits, then these lamps narrow. — A lesson fae Euan? What the fuck do you mean?

I don't know what baked beans that spineless little twat has spilled, but he's going to get some shit back from me, via his beloved mammy. — Look, what Ross saw was quite traumatising, I concede, — but perhaps not as much as it should have been.

Carlotta's looking at me with the big Eyetie peepers both of us inherited from Mamma, firing on full tilt. Poor Louisa: she got the old boy's vicious, furtive Jockoid slits. — What are ye trying tae say?

— He's my nephew and I love him, so I don't want to grass him up, but I have good reason to believe that Ross has been watching extreme pornography.

— What?! Ross? Pornography? Online?

Oh, sis! After all those years, still making schoolgirl errors: the mistake of admitting the possibility. When defenders back off, keep running at them, twisting and turning like a squat Argentinian. Think Lionel. Think Diego. — Furthermore, I believe Euan discovered this and it unhinged him a little. Being a lad from the country and sexually inexperienced before he hooked up with you –

— Wait! Euan told you this?

— Well, in a blokish roundabout sort of way, yes, but it was more that I deduced it. No names were dropped or details offered, but I kind ay worked out it was a Taylor Swift–Michael Gove courtship with you guys, I smile. — Vamp–nerd scenario.

That teases a confirming bitter-sweet smile out of her.

— I think he was vulnerable, turning fifty n all, and that crazy harridan Marianne took advantage of the situation tae

106

get at *me*, by hurting the one thing I care about, I look at her with all the intensity I can summon, — family.

Carra shakes her head. She's heard versions of this over the years. — I don't believe you, she says, her voice rising. — So all this mess is my son's fault?

— No. It's society's fault. It's the pace of technological change, I advance, but I now have a sense of her shepherding the ball harmlessly out of play for a goal kick. If I can just get a leg in ... — But Ross was its conduit in inflicting pain on this family. Our social mores haven't developed to keep pace with the Internet, the digital revolution, the iPad and the Cloud, thus our cognitive dissonance.

Carlotta takes a step back. Looks at me as if I'm a dangerous specimen on the wrong side of the zoological bars. — You are a total fucking bastard, she gasps. — You wreck people's lives tae gie yirsel cheap thrills!

The younger Williamson lassie cannot be written off on the counter ... — Look, sis, let's not point fingers. It does naebody any good.

She steps forward, and I think she's going to punch me. Instead she shakes her fists like maracas. — It's always let's no point fingers when it's you that's tae blame!

I have to pull something out of the hat here. Attack is usually the best form of defence. — I'm forever taking stock of my life, especially at this very reflective time of year. Am I blameless? No, very far from it. I fold my arms across my chest. Carlotta has never gotten physically violent before, but these are uncharted emotional waters. I decide to amp it up. — But please, dinnae fuckin gies it that this is aw ma fault, I say, getting into outrage mode. — Dinnae hit ays wi that pish, that old let's-exonerate-everybody-but-Simon approach. As a tactic it must have prima facie appeal, but it's disingenuous and waaay too convenient. The moon is not made of green cheese!

Carra's eyes are like a Rottweiler's balls. — What are you fuckin talkin about?! Do you even live in the same fuckin world as the rest ay us?! Her breathing is thin and she's having palpitations.

I go to embrace her. — Carra ... *la mia sorellina* ...

She pushes me back, both her palms slapping into my chest. — MA HUSBAND IS MISSING AND MA SON IS IN PIECES, and now her fists pound me. One hits the spot below the ribcage where Syme's well-placed thug-blow struck, and I stumble. — BECAUSE AY YOU! YOU FIND HIM! YOU BRING HIM BACK!

— Chill, sis, I'm on it, and I pick up my phone and look at my calls list and my text from Vic with the emoticon.

Then Carlotta, compulsively checking emails on her own phone, starts to suddenly shriek. — AH DINNAE BELIEVE IT! She looks at me, in shock. — It's fae Euan ...

— That's good, I knew he'd eventually come to his senses and get in touch.

— But he's ... he says he's in FUCKIN THAILAND!

Just then, a text from Syme jumps in.

No word from the surgeon boy?

I groan out loud, and we both say at the same time, — What the fuck are we going to do?

Then Ben comes in from the back, contentment scored on his face. I don't know how much he's heard of our little shouting match, but he seems laconic about it.

— I know that look of love, I tease, as Carlotta removes herself forcibly from the room. — Who's the lucky lady?

— I'm not a kiss-and-tell sort. The boy gives me a bashful smile. All of a sudden, I protectively want him back in Surrey, away from all the shit that's going on around me.

7

RENTON – SICK BOY PAYBACK

It's a clear, crisp day, as I look out onto the Royal Mile. My cup twitches and rattles as I lower it tae my saucer, like I've a nervous disease. I cannae keep jumping on long-haul flights, the jet lag is destructive. I've sacked the Ambien, Xanax and Vallies but I barely trust myself tae sugar this tea. I cannae go on like this.

It was tough leaving Vicky. We've amped it up; both now that hungry, excited, stupid way ye are when ye meet somebody you're really into. I think I might have fallen in love at some point; perhaps when I said that I'll never forgive the Muslim extremists for 9/11, because it made it so much harder to move drugs around, and consequently made my life as a DJ manager mair difficult. She looked at me sadly and said that her cousin had worked in the World Trade Center and died in the terrorist attack. I gasped in horror and coughed out apologies, before she laughed and told me she was winding me up. Hard no tae love a lassie like that.

Now she's in LA and I'm in a cafe in cauld and frosty Edinburgh. People walk past, bleary. Global commercialism has compelled the Scots tae pretend tae like Christmas, but we're genetically programmed tae rebel against it. Ah come oot in a rash if I'm stuck in a hoose wi family for more than two days. New Year is more our natural speed. Not that I'm looking out the windae too much, because the view inside isnae so bad. Marianne always was a very good-looking girl, a pouty, superior, willowy blonde; athletic-slim, with ersecheeks like a superhero's biceps. She had the world at her feet, but was burdened by a fatal flaw: she was besotted with Sick Boy. Of course the cunt ruined her life. But she'll probably ken where he is or be able tae find him. I got her number through Amy Temperley, a mutual friend fae Leith, and we hook up at this cafe on the Royal Mile.

My initial thought: fuck me, Marianne has aged spectacularly well. Those Scando-Scot genes don't bloat and her skin has remained excellent. She's guarded at first. No wonder. I'm fucking guarded too. I ripped Sick Boy off for a lot more than that three-point-two grand, which I paid him back during the porno-flick era. That repayment was just a set-up, tae dae him out ay sixty grand, back in 1998, which is about ninety-one grand now. But I only did this because he tried tae steer Begbie onto ays as revenge for initially ripping him off. And I also snaffled the masters of the pornographic film we made. It's complicated. — So you want to pay him this money back? Marianne says doubtfully. — After all this time?

Ah think she's aboot tae tell ays tae fuck off, so I add, — I just want tae let go ay the past and move on.

A light clicks on behind her eyes. — Didn't you try Facebook?

— I'm not on social media myself, but ah did have a look. Couldnae find him.

She scrolls on her phone, and hands me it. — He's not under his own name. This is his escort agency.

The Facebook page links tae a website. The Colleagues. com mix of nudge-nudge, wink-wink innuendo, coupled wi a corporate eighties business-speak, replete wi motivational poster sloganeering, give ays absolutely zero fuckin doubt that the copy was written personally by him. — Sick Bo— Simon, he runs this escort agency?

110

— Aye, Marianne says, taking her phone back and checking it.

In spite ay myself, ah feel a warm glow in my chest, followed by a surge ay excitement. The dynamic between Sick Boy and me always veered towards the destructive, but it was seldom boring. I'm inexplicably chuffed tae get the details. Marianne then says, wi a certain impatience, — Do you want to get a proper drink?

Did I want to get a proper drink? I'm thinking about Vicky. But what are we? Is the connection all in ma mind? I don't even know whether she would be hurt and offended if I slept with somebody else, or laugh in my face for being so ridiculous. I hear my treacherous words slide out: — We can go back tae my hotel if ye fancy it.

Marianne says nothing but she gets up. We head out, and walk side by side, down Victoria Terrace, her heels gunfiring across the Grassmarket cobblestones. We pass a pub that has probably changed its name a million times, but I recall that bands used to play there in my youth.

Ripping off Sick Boy was the other reason (as well as being the cause of Begbie's injury) that I left running a club to manage DJs. My first client, Ivan, I put everything into. Then, as soon as he broke big, a manager with even fewer scruples and a bigger Rolodex poached him. It was an important lesson, and I showed I had learned it when I saw Conrad play in a Rotterdam club. He was being sort of looked after by his friend's older brother. I quickly realised that the cunt was a prodigy. He could do any kind ay dance music. I talked tae him and ascertained that he wouldnae consider it beneath him to try and make pop hits. Those would make me the kind of money where I could pay off big debts quite easily. And now they have.

Of course I dinnae want tae gie that hard-earned money tae Sick Boy! But if I'm consistent wi this rehabilitation and

111

personal atonement plan, I need to see him right as well. And Second Prize, who refused payment back then. He got religion and nobody's heard from him. Like Franco, he's due his fifteen grand. But it's fucking Sick Boy who is gaunny totally wipe ays oot wi his big chunk. So I deserve some compensation.

When we get tae the hotel, I make the pretence of indicating the bar, but Marianne abruptly says, — Let's go to your room.

I can't fucking do this, and yet I have tae do it. It's *Marianne*. I recall her as a teenager; feisty and contemptuous ay me, impossibly beautiful and sexy as she hung from a lecherous Sick Boy's arm. I had zero chance with her back then, but now she's offering herself tae me on a plate. Maybe it's all part ay the process; maybe ye need tae exorcise past demons before you can move on.

We take the lift and get tae the room. I'm embarrassed because the bed hasn't been made yet and there's a dusky smell. Ah cannae recall if ah shot my load or no last night. I never wank these days, as ah enjoy such vivid wet dreams in the waking hours. There's also a miserable lonely ennui with masturbation after you've shot your duff in a hotel room, something that bothers you mair as ye get aulder. I switch on the air con, even though ah ken it'll freeze the place within five minutes. — Do ye want a drink?

— Red wine. Marianne points tae a bottle on the desk, one of those that ye eywis open because ye subconsciously think thir complimentary, but they never are.

I open it as Marianne collapses in a sprawl on the bed, kicking off her heels. — We doing this, then? she says, looking pointedly at me. In such situations it's best not to speak, and I start removing my clothes. She sits up and does the same. I'm thinking that outside of my ex, Katrin, Marianne is the palest-skinned lassie I've ever set eyes on. Of course, the fabulous architecture ay a woman never fails tae excite, and that arse is as utterly splendid as I have observed-imagined from my youth. One day this magnificent charge will go, like vision, hearing, continence, and I hope it's the very last of them to succumb. Then I realise there's a problem. — I don't have any condoms ...

— I don't have any either, Marianne says, nutter imperious, hand on her lily-white breasts, — because I don't shag around. I haven't fucked anyone in months. You?

— Same here, I concede. I stopped banging young chicks from clubs several years back. They're only really after the DJ, and you're generally a consolation prize. What starts off as succour to the psyche eventually tramples the self-esteem.

— Then let's get it on, she says, like she's challenging me to a square go.

We do, and I try to bring my A-game, in order to show her what she's been missing.

Afterwards, as we lie alongside each other, the distance of an ocean and continent I thought I'd put between Victoria and myself suddenly narrows. Guilt and paranoia rips out ay ays tae the extent that she could be in the next room. Then Marianne says with a harsh laugh, — You were better than I thought you'd be ...

This would have been affirmation had her expectations no been rock-bottom. If I still saw her as the too-cool-for-school chick, it figured that she'd always see me as the socially awkward, ginger-heided loser. We were condemned tae those perceptions ay our fourteen-year-old selves. I can not only feel the 'but' coming; much worse I ken exactly who *he* will be.

— ... But not as good as one person we both know, she says, as her eyes take on a faraway aspect. I feel my spent dick shrivel a little. — He always left me wanting more, and feeling as if *I* could have given *him* more. Teased me, and she looks at me with a bitter smile that ages her. — I always liked good sex, and she spins catlike in the bed. — He gave me the fucking best.

My exhausted cock retracts another half-inch. When I speak, tae break my own ruinous silence, ma voice is at least an octave too high. — Ye let him wreck your life, Marianne. Why? I force my tones down. — You're a smart woman.

— No. She shakes her head, her static blonde locks, like a nylon wig, falling exactly into place, just as they'd done when we'd been going at it full steam ahead. — I'm a fucking child. He's made me that, she states, then looks at ays. And he's here. In Edinburgh, not in London. Up here for Christmas, the cunt.

This was a revelation. Of course he'd be here: his mother, sisters, the big Italian family thing. — Do you know where?

— His sister's, for Christmas, Carlotta, the younger one. But his brother-in-law … She suddenly looks awkward. — I met them in George Street. Simon told me that he was taking his son to the hospitality suite at Easter Road, for the game at New Year.

— Right … maybe see him there.

But I'm a fucking child too. So when Marianne leaves, I find out fae the Hibernian FC website that the game at New Year is against Raith Rovers at home. This is what we now have instead ay the derby. I'm glad I've been spared Hibs, and even fitba, in the last twenty years, becoming an armchair supporter. Ajax went downhill when I started following them. From the European Cup and the last season at De Meer, tae the fabulous Arena, and fucking mediocrity. I cannae even remember my last Hibs game. I think at Ibrox with the old boy.

So I go back tae my dad's down in Leith. He's seventy-five and sprightly. Not Mick Jagger sprightly, but nimble and strong. He still misses my mother every day, and his two dead

sons. And, also, I suspect, his living one. So when I come
into his life beyond the weekly phone call, I take him to
Fishers down the Shore for some seafood. He likes it there.
Over the sublime fish soup, I tell him how it came about
that I'm pally with Franco again.

— I read about him, Dad nods. — Nice to see that he's
doing well. He waves his spoon at me. — Funny, I thought
that art stuff was mair your thing. You were ey a good wee
drawer at school.

— Ah well … I smile, a little infantilised. I love this old
bastard. I look at his white hairs, plastered back in thin strands
like a polar bear's claw on a pink scalp, and I wonder how
many of them are down to me.

— Good that you've put aw that behind youse, he growls.
— It's a short life; far too short tae faw out over money.

— Shut it, ya auld commie. I can't resist the opportunity
to recentre his politics. — Money is the only thing worth
fawin oot ower!

— That's what's wrong wi the world the day!

My work is done! We finish a bottle ay Chardonnay, him
still a bit fucked as he shifted too much whisky – as did I
– on Christmas Day. When he starts tae get a bit woozy in
the chair, I call a cab and drop him off home, then head on
tae the hotel.

As the car trundles through the dark streets, I cannae
believe who ah see begging on the pavement under a street
lamp. Tae my mixed joy and trepidation, it's Spud Murphy,
sitting there, just yards fae my hotel. Ah ask the cabbie tae
stop, and climb oot and pey the boy. Then I walk quietly up
tae Spud, who wears a Kwik-Fit baseball cap and cheapo
bomber jaiket, jeans and incongruously new-looking trainers,
wi a scarf and mittens. He's sat like he's folding in on himself.
Beside him, one of these wee terriers, dunno if it's a Yorkie

or a Westie, but it looks like it needs a wash and fur trim.
— Spud!

He looks up and blinks a couple of times before a smile spreads across his face. — Mark, ah cannae believe it, ah was jist aboot tae pack up. He rises and we share an embrace. A rank odour of stale sweat peels fae him, and ah even have tae fight down a retching impulse. We decide tae get a drink, and repair tae the hotel bar. Spud is a semi-jakeball and has a scabby wee dug in tow, but I've an account at this doss, so despite the barmaid's glance indicating she's singularly unimpressed, they let it slide. This is actually quite big ay them, because, well, ah hate tae be a cunt, but he kind ay fuckin mings, like he hasnae since he was a wee laddie. Well, maybe in the junk days, but ma ain smell probably masked that. We position ourselves in a dark corner, a bit apart from everyone else in the sparsely filled bar. The dug, called Toto, sits silently at his feet. I'm thinking it's strange Spud going canine, as he was eywis a cat obsessive. We inevitably start discussing the Franco phenomenon, and I'm telling him aboot wanting tae square up Sick Boy, Second Prize and the art radge himself. How I need tae find one, how another has vanished, and how the third doesnae want the money he's owed.

— No surprised Franco isnae interested in the dosh, catboy. Spud slurps back a good quarter of the pint of lager, as Toto accepts my pettings under the table. He's a matted-furred minger, but he's cute and sweet-hearted, and his sand-paper tongue slaps ma knuckles.

— What dae ye mean?

— Pure cursed that dosh, likesay. That money you gied ays was the worst thing that ever happened tae ays. A big, big binge ay drugs, the end ay me n Ali. No that ah kin pin ma demise on you, catboy, he helpfully adds.

— I suppose we all make our choices in life, mate.

— Ye really believe that?

So here I am, sitting discussing free will and determinism with a jakey; me on Guinness, him on Stella. And the debate carries on up in my room. — What other option dae ye have but tae believe it? I ask, as I open the door and the afternoon sex smells hit ays, but Spud seems oblivious. — Yes, we've goat strong pulls but we can see what they are and where they take us and we therefore resist and reject them, ah tell him, suddenly realising that ah'm chopping oot the lines ay coke in the bathroom, using ma stainless-steel Citadel Productions business caird.

— Can you no see what you're daein now?

— I'm no in a resist-and-reject mode at the moment, I tell him. — I'm in a getting-through-shit-at-all-costs one. You dinnae need tae join ays. It's up tae you, ah tell him, waving a rolled-up twenty. — Make yir choice: this is mine.

— Aye ... mibbe just tae be social, likesay, Spud says with rising panic, only abating as soon as ah hand the cunt the note that ah ken ah'll never see again. — It's been a long time.

Then we're back oot, at a couple ay bars, which is the only wey I ken I'll get rid ay him, before my eyes start shutting and a pit-bull yawn almost tears my bottom jaw fae my face. I head tae the hotel and try tae fitfully sleep.

The shattering alarm seems tae wake ays ten minutes later. And this is my life, the sheer fucking lunacy of it. I now have to fly back to LA, for one of Conrad's gigs, then return here for Hogmanay, getting in on the morning of New Year's Eve for the big bells party. Then I want to just hole up in Amsterdam for winter and get some work done, but ah need tae go back tae LA again, and put time intae Vicky and me, if I really want things tae take off. And, I reflect, as a ball ay self-loathing sticks in my chest like a tumour, I need tae stop *shagging the fuck aroond*.

So I'm on the red eye tae that fucking blight on humanity that is Heathrow and then up in first class aw the way tae LA. The cunts at security swabbed every inch of my case for traces of ching. But my bank cards show fuck all, and the stainless-steel business caird cleans up a treat.

Hell, it's a long and tedious flight with Conrad, whae connected fae Amsterdam, sitting next tae us. He's bored, sulky and utterly charmless company and I give thanks for the relative isolation ay the individual pods. Conrad is basically mildly autistic, a spoilt fat cunt, but I believe there's a fundamentally decent young gadge in there. I have to believe it. Emily, who is on at Fabric in London, is just young and confused but has a good heart. Then there's Carl. The biggest bairn of them all. What a fucking trio. And now *FUCKING FRANCIS BEGBIE* is back in ma life and I'm seeking out *SICK BOY*.

At LAX, the immigration ratshagger's look is long and searching, gaun fae me, tae passport, tae me, tae passport. This is bad. It means he now has tae say something. — So how long have you lived in Amsterdam?

— On and off, about twenty-five years.

— And you're a manager in the entertainment industry?

— An artist manager, I concede, depressed at the lack of irony in my voice. I watch Conrad, a couple of booths down, breeze through, his doughy digits sweating over the fingerprint glass like sausages on a hotplate.

— Like bands?

— DJs.

He softens a little. — Is that like managing a band?

— Easier. Solo artists. No equipment, I state, then think of the exception to every fucking rule, that fucking Neanderthal

118

Ewart. — Book the plane, transfers and hotels. Organise the press. Fight for publishing royalties, battle promoters for gigs and cash, I rant, managing to stop myself from saying, *and drugs*.

— You come here a lot. Do you plan to move to the USA?

— No. Though I do have an apartment in Santa Monica. It saves on hotels. I'm in LA and Vegas a lot on business. One of my artists, I point at Conrad, now through and heading for the luggage, — he's got a residency at the Wynn. I always travel on an ESTA. I've applied for a green card, and I suddenly think of Vicky, smiling in the sun on the beach, — but even when I get it, I won't be living here all the time.

He looks at me as if he doesn't believe my green card application for resident alien will be accepted.

— David Guetta is one of my sponsors, I offer.

— Uh-huh, he says doomily, then seems all put out. — Why don't you wanna live here permanently?

— Maybe the same reason that you don't want to live in Amsterdam? I like America, but it's a bit too American for ma personal tastes. I suspect you'd find Holland a wee bit too Dutch.

He pulls his lower lip out in dreary evaluation, slumping back into catatonic boredom, as the luminous green light comes on and I print my fingers for the thousandth time, and get my picture snapped yet again. A stamp on the passport and customs form, and I'm back in the land of the free.

The first thing I do – literally – when I land somewhere is hassle the promoter for drugs. Anyone who doesn't have a contact shouldn't be in the fucking game. I tell them it's for the DJs, but most of those boring cunts nowadays never touch anything other than hydroponic grass, my contemporary, N-Sign Carl Ewart, being the exception – yet again. I usually get some gak, just to keep the party going, anything that stops me from reminding myself that I'm the oldest person in the club, unless I'm with N-Sign. I feel sorry for old DJs, they deserve big money, stepping out to that ritual humiliation every night: guys who no longer dance, playing music for people who do. That's why I try to be patient with Carl. I put in my order for the unofficial rider: cannabis, MDMA powder and cocaine. Conrad is slavering so much techy shit about different buds in my ear, I put him straight onto the man.

The deal done, he says, — Where is that cokehead bum N-Sign? Why do you persist with him?

— History, mate, I shrug. I should tell Conrad to mind his own business, but I'm desperate he doesn't go the way of Ivan. And it is his business, as I'm booking Carl gigs on his undercard.

As we wait for our luggage to come onto the belt, a text from the cunt himself: no Carl, but *Begbie*.

When r u next in Embra?

You never know if he's being ironic or dyslexic.

Hogmanay. N-Sign playing.

Would you, Spud, Sick Boy and Second Prize be up for an art project? I want to make casts of your heads.

Can't speak for them, but count me in. Saw Spud, hoping to see Sick Boy Hogmanay.

Sound. Can u do 3 Jan?

Aye.

Conrad gets an Uber to the hotel, on his own, after I explain that I'm meeting my girlfriend. — Dude, he smiles.

When I get back to the apartment to hook up with Vicky, she's so pleased to see me, and me her. I'm thinking about Marianne and *what the fuck was I doing?* Maybe it was something that had to happen. To get it out my system, so I can move on with her now.

After we go out for a meal with her friends Willow and Matt, we head home and are at it like knives. I feel a sort of twang and Vicky feels it too, but we only pause for a second, before finishing. We find that the condom has split. It has rolled down the shaft of my cock, splattered in a mix of spunk and thick menstrual blood; her period has started. I'm relieved but she nonetheless goes for the morning-after pill. — I want to be double-treble sure, I'm just *so not* a mother, Vicky smiles cheerfully.

We fall back into the bed, and for a brief second I hear Marianne's nagging voice: *I don't shag around. I haven't fucked anyone in months.* With her being privy to Sick Boy's movements, I'm just not convinced. But it's drowned out by Vicky's appreciative contentions. — It's great being with you. I've dated boys, nice boys, but boys. It's good to be with a man.

I feel the vice of guilt. I've always enjoyed boyishness, never striven for maturity. Manhood is an ill-fitting cloak on my shoulders, like being dressed by somebody else. But my euphoria breaks its constraints: there is more than one type of man. — You're the best thing that's happened to me in a long, long time, I confess to her. We share a *wow* look; acknowledgement that we're spinning into something and it feels good and right.

Then, of course, I have to leave her. When I get back to Edinburgh, without the smoothing pills, my fatigue is jaggy and acute. Thankfully Carl has not too bad coke, and the home crowd inspires him to play a decent set at Hogmanay. As well as Marina and her boyfriend Troy, I have a twitching Spud and a jovial Gavin Temperley with me in the main guest box. One is skeletal, the other now a fat bastard. In the next box my auld pal Rab Birrell, with his brother Billy, who used to be the boxer. Both look well. It's good to see them.

Afterwards there's a party, but I'm no much company, and I dinnae want tae get too fucked up in front of Marina, so I make my excuses and bow out early. I crash at the hotel and sleep like fuck, right through tae the next night. Then I go doon tae Leith and get a wee dram with the old boy for New Year, and he's made a welcome pot ay stovies.

Then more kip at the hotel and I'm off the next day tae see Hibs. Surprisingly, for a relegated outfit, the club seems a much bigger and more professional operation than ah mind ay it being. The reception area looks like one ay they corporate hotels, and there are now several hospitality suites rather than just the one. — Just gies ays the most expensive package, I tell the woman, who looks at ays like I'm a clown.

— But it's just for you, right?

I realise how pathetically nae-mates this is sounding. — I'm meeting a Mr Williamson here, it's a last-minute thing.

— Right … Is it Simon Williamson? There's a party of six. Would you like tae join them at that table?

— Sound.

I square up on the Visa and head for the stairs. On reaching a reasonably plush dining area, I immediately see Sick Boy, looking much the same, bar the greying locks, sitting wi what appears to be Juice Terry Lawson, still with that corkscrew hair, and four young gadges. I stare at Simon David Williamson, the cavalier shagger ay the Bananay Flats, for a few moments. Yes, the mop has maybe receded a little along with the touches of silver, but he looks well. As I gape, he suddenly rubbernecks. He stares at me in disbelief, then, rising, bellows: — What the fuck are *you* doing here?!

— Wee word, buddy, I say, nodding tae Terry. — Tez. You huvnae changed much! Got tae be fifteen years, easy, I consider, remembering the last time I saw Terry was when we made that dodgy scud film. He had a terrible accident where he ruptured his cock.

— Aye, he smiles, and he kens exactly what I'm thinking, — one hundred and ten per cent recovery!

We exchange pleasantries for a few moments, but I can feel the seethe of Sick Boy, who grabs my wrist and ushers me ower tae the bar. When we get there, I dump the envelope in front ay him. He has zero reticence about immediately snatching it. Snidely looking inside, he discreetly counts it, hudin it close tae his chest, eyes gaun fae the money tae me, tae the people in the vicinity, in an almost Dickensian parody ay furtive greed.

Finally he lets those blazing lamps rest on me. I've forgotten the hurt, questioning, accusation they permanently carry. With an injured pout, he declares, — You ripped me off not once, but twice. The cash I can get past, but you stole the film! I put my heart and soul into that movie! You and that fucking bitch Nikki and that stuck-up hoor Dianne –

— They shafted me as well. I went back tae the Dam with my tail between my legs.

— I came looking for you there!

— I figured ye might, so I moved out of town for a bit. Den Haag. It was a little dull.

— Very fucking wise, I can tell you! he hisses, but he's looking in the package again. He's impressed and cannae even hide it. — Never thought you'd pay me back.

— It's all there. You should've been after Nikki and Dianne for most of it, but I decided tae compensate ye on their behalf.

— That doesn't sound like you! You must be fucking off-the-charts wealthy. All that NA stuff works for rich bastards, who think they can buy their way oot ay the misery they've created!

This cunt has loast nane ay his natural outrage. — Well, there it is. I'm happy to take it back –

— You can get tae fuck!

— Good, cause it's aw yours. Now you can expand Colleagues.

His eyes bulge, his voice goes to a low growl. — What do you know about Colleagues?

I decide it isnae a good idea tae mention Marianne. — Only what your impressive website tells ays. 'Ambitious plans for expansion,' it says.

— Well, yes, naturally. 'We plan to tread water' doesn't really impress, he sneers, looking over at the fellow hospitality diners in contempt.

Ah watch Terry back at the table, taking a keen interest. Sick Boy clocks this n aw, dispensing a quick scowl, then pointedly turning his back to him. As he faces ays, I explain, — The best online calculations for sixty grand in the year 1998 range fae eighty-three thousand seven hundred and seventy quid tae one hundred thousand and nine hundred nicker. Ah split the difference at ninety-one thousand and eighty pounds using a single purchasing power calendar application.

— I could have made a lot more if I'd been allowed to invest *my* money *my* way!

— Impossible tae predict that for sure. Investments can go south as well as north.

He stuffs the envelope in his jacket. — What about the masters ay *Seven Rides for Seven Brothers*?

— Fuck knows. But a fifteen-year-old scud film willnae be worth much.

— Hmmph, he grunts and looks over to his table. — Well, thank you for the money and about fucking time n aw. But this is a social occasion. He points tae the door. — Now go.

— Well, I'll have a little roast beef and watch the game, at least the first half, if it's all the same tae you, I smile. — I did purchase a hospitality package, and it's been a long time since I saw the Hibbies in action. And aren't ye just a wee bitty curious as to why I'm daein this *now*?

Sick Boy rolls his eyes in concession and nods tae the group of Terry and the lads. — Yes. Okay. Just don't expect me tae listen tae any fucking AA/NA tale of woe and step-working, debt-paying bullshit, he says, as we step ower and settle down to join the others.

That pre-emptive speech is useful as that was *exactly* where I had planned tae start. I'm introduced tae Sick Boy's son and nephew, and Terry's two lads. All of them seem nice, normal young guys. But I suppose we did at that age to outsiders. We have a decent meal, a comic tells some gags, then gaffer Alan Stubbs gives his view of the game, before we head into the stand to watch it from nice foam-cushioned seats. My back aches a little, but it's not too bad. I'm sat next tae Sick Boy. — Well, he says, his voice low as he taps his inside pocket, — what's the story? Why this? Why now?

I like the look ay the Hibs midfielder McGinn. Unusual running style, but keeps the baw well. — Begbie, I met him on a flight to LA. Seen him over there a few times since. We're sort of mates again. I had him at our club night in Vegas. He invited me back to his exhibition.

It might have been 'Begbie' but it's more likely 'club night', 'Vegas' and 'exhibition' that ensures I have his full attention. – You're hanging out with that fuckin psycho? After what he tried tae dae … Sick Boy pauses as Hibs attack the Raith goal, orchestrated by McGinn.

— No. That's it. He really has fucking changed.

Sick Boy cracks a high-wattage grin. He points tae a foul on a Hibs player and elbows his son. — The butchers of

Kirkcaldy, he snorts. Then he turns back tae me. — This art shite he got intae? You dinnae think for a second that that headcase has genuinely rehabilitated? He's playing you. Waiting for his moment to strike!

— Not the vibe I get.

— Then I'm delighted for him.

— Ah offered him the money. He refused. The bastard is married tae a Californian beauty. Eh's got two lovely wee daughters, who dote on him, and whom he gets tae watch grow up. I seldom see my boy.

Sick Boy shrugs, but fixes me a look ay understanding. He drops his voice tae a whisper. — Tell me about it. So we both fell a bit short in the paternal stakes, he thieves a quick glance at his son, — what of it?

— So how the fuck did Begbie become the success story?

Sick Boy openly scoffs, in that imperious disdain, which nobody else I've run into in life has ever been able tae emulate. — You must have money! You wouldnae be handing this over if ye wirnae extremely flush. He taps inside his pocket. — Clubs? Vegas? Dinnae come oot wi aw that shite and plead poverty!

So I tell him about my job and DJ Technonerd's breakthrough.

— So you're coining it in fae they fucking shit EDM DJs? These drum machine and stylophone wankers?

— Not really. Only one ay them makes serious dough. One is a charity case, call me sentimental, but I've always liked his shit. The other is a speculative punt, which doesnae look like coming off. That duo cost me practically everything I earn with the big payer and I'm too much ay a sap tae drop them. I'm looking for a fourth and fifth one. I thought, instead ay being a DJ myself, if I managed five at twenty per cent each, it would be just the same. I've got three so far.

Sick Boy is unmoved by my disclosure. He evidently thinks my penury pleas are simply about avoiding any mair hassle n hustle. — I read about that Dutch fucker, Technonerd. That cunt's minted. If you're on twenty per cent ay his earnings ...

— Okay, I've a place in Amsterdam and an apartment in Santa Monica. I'm not starving. I've a few bob in the bank that I haven't spunked on guilt money for you, treatment and care for the boy.

— What's wrong wi the laddie?

— He's autistic.

— Wee Davie ... the spazzy gene? he thinks out loud, in reference tae ma deceased younger brother. His son and nephew turn round briefly.

Anger rises in ays and I fight it doon and look disparagingly at him. — You're already making me regret this, I nod tae the envelope bulging in his pocket.

— Sorry, he says, and it seems semi-gracious, — can't be an easy gig. So why are ye sorting me out now?

— I want tae live. As in *live*, I emphasise, and Vicky's face, laughing, toothsome and blue-eyed, sweeping back stray strands of sun-bleached blonde locks that have escaped their penning, pops into my brain. — Not just exist, I contend as the half-time whistle goes. — Clear away aw the shit fae the past.

— So it *is* all about rehab case atonement.

— In a sense, yes. It gets too much carrying the burden of cuntishness around.

— Advice: Catholicism. Confession, he says. — Better a few quid on a collection plate than ninety grand, and he tips me a wink, tapping his pocket.

We head back inside for our half-time cups of tea and beers and decent meat pies. Sick Boy and I again hit the bar tae blether in conspiracy. — You seem to be doing okay. Better than me, he moans. — Fucking travel everywhere. I never get out ay London unless it's on holiday.

— If you have loads ay girls working for you …

— They make the big bucks, no me. I just hook them up on the app. Dinnae come it, Renton. You're the one with the dosh.

— Stuck on planes, in airports and in hotels, with nowt tae dae but lament how life's passing ays by. I'm wasting that most finite resource: time, chasing the dream that *fucking Begbie* is living! I suddenly erupt. — He's refusing tae take his money, what the fuck is aw that about?

— He's no changed, Sick Boy spits. — He's just fucking with you. Begbie is incapable ay change. He's a warped specimen of humanity.

— I don't even care what he is. I just want tae morally discharge ma obligations.

— You'll never morally discharge your obligation tae me, Renton. He taps his pocket. — This shite doesnae even start tae cover it.

— The film is completely worthless.

— I'm talking about Nikki. You ruined my chances of getting together with a girl I was nuts about!

Nikki was a con artist who took the pish out ay us both. And I dinnae believe for a second that he still gies a toss aboot her. It's aw leverage for future manipulation. — Wake up, mate. She fucked us both over.

Sick Boy seems tae swallow a moothfae ay something that's unpleasant, but perhaps no quite as putrid as he antic-ipated. We go back tae our seats for the second half.

— Listen, I've goat some business fir ye. I need an escort, I tell him, watching his eyes widen. — Not for me, I hasten tae add. I'm trying to be un-sleazy.

— I'm sure that's working for you.

— It's for my young Dutch boy. The DJ.

He looks towards his young nephew. — Can these retards not get a fucking ride for themselves?

— Tell me about it, I'm his manager. I elaborate on the problem. — Guys like Conrad have nae social skills. They smoke weed and masturbate tae pornography. They can't talk tae a girl or have sex with a real person.

— Cyberwanking little creeps. These fuckers are mentally ill, Sick Boy whispers, looking again at his nephew, now playing a video game on his phone, — made so by the world we live in.

What he's saying resonates. The match isnae that bad, and there is something fundamentally wrong about the way the kids are looking at screens instead ay watching what's going on live.

— Even we're tainted enough by our immersion into that world, his elbow digs into my ribs, — although we were schooled up the goods yard!

I cannae even say her name tae myself, but I wince as I think ay ma cherry popping inside her piggy-bank fanny. Unable to look her in the face as ah pushed and shoved through her dryness, tae the low-key encouragement of Sick Boy. Ma eyes watering as they focused on the broken glass and gravel around us. The blue sleeve ay her cagoule we lay on blowing up in my face in the wind. A dug barking in the distance, and a disgruntled growl of *Dirty wee cunts* fae a passing jakey. — Aye ... the goods yard.

— You'd have still been a virgin now but for me taking you under my wing, he laughs, picking up on my discomfort.

I'm now favourably recalling the banging I gave Marianne, as the nephew's head spins round. He meets my eyes, then turns away. I lean in to Sick Boy. — Oh, I'm sure I'd have found a way oot ay that maze, but thank you for inappropriately sexualising me at a tender age.

For some reason, this stings him. — Ye never complained back then!

— But I was sensitive. Sixteen, seventeen, would have been ideal for me. Fourteen was way too young.

— Sensitive ... as in thieving-cunt-who-rips-off-his-mates sensitive? *That* kind of sensitive?

There isnae a great deal I can say tae that. The final whistle blows and Hibs have won 1–0, tae keep the promotion bid on course. Sick Boy shepherds the young lads intae the back ay Terry's taxi. — You chaps go on ahead, the advance party. Tell Carlotta no tae bother expecting me for dinner, I'll grab a bite with ma auld mucker here.

The boys, especially Ben, look disappointed, but not surprised, as Sick Boy slams the cab door shut and hands Terry a tenner. — Fuck off, ya daft cunt, it's oan ma wey, Terry says, then leans out the windae, and oot ay earshot fae the young gadges, whispers, — Anywey, be nice tae check oot your sister again, bud. No seen her in years. Still a looker, ah'm bettin, and now that she's back oan the market ... He tips a wink, leans back and starts up the car.

Sick Boy's eyes protrude. — She's no oan –

Terry pulls away, as his horn blares triumphantly.

— Cunt, says Sick Boy, then laughs, — but good luck tae him. Maybe a Lawson length would help sort her heid out. Her husband's been kicked oot the hoose. He was caught Christmas Day, check this, on video, banging Marianne. Mind ay Maid Marianne, fae back in the day?

I haven't fucked anyone in months. Fucking bullshit. — Aye ... I nod meekly, as we walk across the car park, through the crowds.

— She's always been disturbed, but has now gone full-on psycho. She would fuck a minging dog in the street these days. I'll be telling the brother-in-law tae get checked up, especially if he manages tae get back wi ma sis, he sings, as we cross the Bridge of Doom. — Remember some ay the ambushes here, back in the day? he says, as I feel a phantom itch pepper my genitals. Paranoia rips out of me. *Vicky* ...

He's still slavering away as we go on to Easter Road. Everywhere seems replete with rich memory. We head down Albert Street. I'm thinking of Seeker's flat where we got the skag, the Clan Bar opposite, now shut, and we head to Buchanan Street, where Dizzy Lizzie's pub has been resurrected as a slightly higher-end concern. It actually has drinkable beer now. The barmaid is familiar, and she greets us wi a big smile. — Lisa, my lovely, Sick Boy says, — two pints ay that wonderful Innis & Gunn lager please!

— Coming up, Simon. Hi, Mark, long time no see.

— Hi, I say, suddenly remembering where I ken her fae. We find a corner and I ask him, — Is that what's-her-name?

— The Ghastly Aftermath, yes, that's her, and we share a childish chuckle. She got that name fae a TV advert for washing-up liquid. A posh, hung-over hostess facing a sink full ay dirty dishes exclaims, 'I love parties, but I hate the ghastly aftermath.' The Ghastly Aftermath always hung around at the end ay a party. Ye would find her crashed oan the flair, or on a couch, or sitting watching TV and drinking tea, long after every other cunt had fucked off. It wisnae like she was hanging around tae fuck any survivors, and she wasn't peeving the dregs ay the alcohol or waiting oan new drugs tae arrive. We never quite ascertained what her motivations were.

— Lived at hame wi her ma and wanted tae stay oot as long as possible, Sick Boy decides. — Ever ride her?

— No, I say. I once snogged the Ghastly Aftermath, but that was about it. — You?

He rolls his eyes and tuts in a don't-ask-silly-questions manner. I insist tae him that I'm no sticking around tae peeve

131

it up, as I'm too fucked wi the jet lag. I should feel a retro loser, but it's oddly comforting, being here in Leith with Sick Boy. — Do ye get back up the road much?

— Weddings, funerals, Christmas, so yes, loads.

— Ever hear of what happened to Nikki? Or Dianne?

His eyes widen. — So they really did dae a turn on you as well?

— Aye, I admit. — Sorry about the film. Fuck knows what they did with the masters.

— Threw them on a bonfire, no doubt, he says, then suddenly breaks oot intae gallows laughter. — There we were, two scamming Leith schemies, fuckin rinsed like daft cunts by those cold-hearted bourgeois chickies. We were never as streetwise as we imagined, he muses ruefully. — Listen … does Begbie ever mention me?

— Just in passing, I tell him.

— I've never telt anybody this, but I went tae see the cunt in hospital; after that car tanned him in, when he was chasing you. He clears his throat. — He was unconscious, in some kind of fucking spazzy coma, so I let rip with a few home truths in the veg's pus. You'll never guess what happened next?

— He came out of the coma and grabbed your throat and tore it out?

— Actually, quite fucking close. The bastard opened his eyes and seized me by my wrist. I was shiteing it. Those fucking lamps ay his were a blast ay Hades …

— Fuck sake –

— He sank back into the bed, closed his eyes. The hospital staff said it was just some reflexive action. He woke up proper a couple ay days later.

— If he'd been in a coma he wouldn't be able tae make oot a word you said, I smile. — And if he could and he cared, you'd already be deid.

— I'm not sure, Mark. He's a maniac. Tread carefully. I'm glad I'm no involved with him any mair. I've had considerable personal distress from the spunk-breathed amoeba's poxy obsessions.

— I've another one for ye. He wants to make a cast of our heads. In bronze.

— No fucking way.

I take a long swig of lager and lay the glass slowly on the table. — Don't shoot the messenger.

Sick Boy's head rolls slowly, as his eyes half close. — I'm not going anywhere near that fucking psychopath!

8

LEITH HEADS

As Mott the Hoople's 'Honaloochie Boogie' blasts out from a small radio, none of the three men present can quite believe that they are standing in the same room. An artist friend has given Francis Begbie the use of this attic studio, located in a backstreet zone of warehouses near Broughton Street. Despite the abundant light spilling through the glass ceiling from a sliver of blue sky, two sets of untrained eyes, belonging to Renton and Sick Boy, process the space as a small, dingy factory unit. It has a kiln, and a range of industrial equipment, two large workbenches, acetylene torches and gas canisters. Racks on the wall store materials, some of which are marked poisonous and combustible.

Frank Begbie's protracted yawn signals that, like Renton, he fights jet lag from a long-haul air journey. Sick Boy is evidently vexed, glancing intermittently from the door to the clock on his phone. He decided to come on the basis that being seen with Begbie might give him some leverage with Syme. Already it feels like a mistake. — Where's Spud? Probably just coming fae a fucking bench in Pilrig Park, and of course, he's the one who's late!

Renton notes Sick Boy's nervousness in the presence of Begbie. He hasn't engaged with him, beyond a perfunctory handshake and nod. — Nae word fae Second Prize? Renton asks.

Sick Boy rolls his shoulders in a 'search me' manner.

— I had assumed he'd drunk himself to death, or, even worse, met a nice lassie, settled doon and got lost in Gumleyland, Renton smiles. — He was a bit ay a Holy Joe the last time I saw him.

— That's a shame, Franco says, — I wis gaunny call this piece *Five Boys*. I wanted tae show the journey we've aw been on.

It is the un-Franco-like word *journey* that instantly compels an exchange of doubtful glances between Sick Boy and Renton. Frank Begbie catches this and seems about to say something, but then Spud walks in. Just by regarding his bedraggled, wasted figure, Renton feels his own exhaustion peeling away. Spud's clothing is tatty, but while his face is wizened, his eyes blaze. His movements are at first deliberate, but then break into short, uncontrollable spazzy jerks. — Here we go, Sick Boy announces.

— Sick ... Simon ... long time. Hi, Mark. Franco ...

— Hi, Spud, Renton says.

– Sorry tae be late, boys. Franco, good tae see ye. Last time wis at yir laddie's funeral but, ay? That wis awfay sad, ay?

Renton and Sick Boy look at each other again, this obviously being news to both of them. Franco, however, remains unruffled. — Aye, Spud, good tae see you n aw. Thanks.

Spud continues rambling, with Renton and Sick Boy trying to work out what drugs he's ingested. — Aye, ah'm sorry tae be late, man, ah pure goat involved cause ah ran intae this boy, Davie Innes, you'll ken the boy, Franco, Jambo, but a good lad, likesay –

— Nae worries, mate, Frank Begbie cuts him off. — As ah say, I appreciate you daein this, and he turns to Sick Boy and Renton. — That goes for youse n aw.

It is unnerving for them all to hear Franco express gratitude, and an uncomfortable silence follows. — I'm kind of flattered, Franco ... or, eh, Jim, Renton ventures.

— Franco's fine. Call ays what ye want.

— Mibbe call ye Beggars, Franco, Spud laughs, as Renton and Sick Boy freeze in horror. — Wi nivir called ye that tae yir face but, ay, lads, mind we were ey too feart tae say 'it's the Beggar Boy!' tae Franco's face? Ken?

—Aw ye did, did yis? Frank Begbie says, turning to Renton and Sick Boy who stare at the floor for an excruciating moment. Then he laughs loudly, a blustering guffaw, which shocks them in its hearty joviality. — Aye, ah could be a wee bit uptight back then!

They look at each other and explode into a joint, cathartic laughter.

When it dies down, Renton asks, — But why do ye want tae make casts ay our ugly mugs?

Franco sits back on one of the workbenches and looks wistful. — Us and Second Prize, we aw grew up thegither. Wi Matty, Keezbo and Tommy, who are obviously oot the picture.

Renton feels a lump in his throat at the mention of those names. Sick Boy's and Spud's gleaming eyes tell him that he's not alone.

— My art stuff's in demand right now, Frank Begbie explains, — so I wanted tae dae a kind ay early autobiographical piece. Aye, I was gaunny call it *Five Boys*, but I think *Leith Heads* should dae it.

— Sound, Renton nods. — Mind way, way back in the day, there was a chocolate called Five Boys?

— Ye nivir git that Five Boys chocolate any mair. No seen it for donkey's years, Spud says, his mouth flapping open. He brushes some saliva off his chin with his sleeve.

Sick Boy addresses Franco directly for the first time. — Will this take long?

— About an hour ay yir time, all in, Franco replies. — I know you all have busy lives, and that you and Mark are only here for a short break and probably have family stuff tae dae, so ah'll no keep youse long.

Sick Boy's head bobs in accord, and he checks his phone again.

— It'll no be sair, likesay? Spud asks.

— No. Not at all, Frank Begbie declares, handing them overalls, which they put on, then sitting them down on a set of small swivel stools. He inserts two shortened straws up Spud's nostrils. — Just relax and breathe easily. This will be cold, he explains, as he starts to paint latex onto Spud's face.

— It is. N aw sort ay tickly, Spud laughs.

— Try no tae speak, Danny, ah want this tae set right, Frank urges, before repeating the procedure on Renton and Sick Boy. Then he fits a five-sided Perspex box over the head of each man, the edge of the receptacle sitting about an inch shy of any part of the face, lining up the protruding straws to slip through small holes in the front of the box. Through grooves at the bottom, he slides in two adjustable convex-indented leaves. Those join together, forming a base with a hole that fits snugly around each man's neck. — This is the bit that people get edgy aboot, it's like a guillotine, Franco cackles, to be met with three tight smiles. Checking that each man can breathe freely, he then secures the gaps with putty, and opens the top of the box and starts to pour a preprepared mixture in. — This might feel a bit cauld. There's a bit ay weight in it, so try and sit up and keep your back straight so that it isnae straining on your neck. It'll just be on for fifteen minutes, but if ye experience any difficulty breathing, or any discomfort, just raise yir hand and ah'll open it up.

As the boxes fill up and the compound begins to set, the sounds from outside – the cars in the street, the radio, Franco's own activities – all fade out in the consciousness of Renton,

Sick Boy and Spud. Soon each man can sense only the air entering their lungs through their nostrils, via the straws that poke out from the plaster-filled blocks.

The amalgam solidifies quickly, and Franco removes the Perspex casings and contemplates his old friends: three literal blockheads, sitting next to each other on their stools. Suddenly aware of a tug in his bladder, he heads to the toilets. On the way back, his phone displays MARTIN on caller ID, and he picks up. — Jim, we might have to change venue for the London show. I know you liked that one, but the gallery has suffered some structural problems and the council need them to do work before it's suitable for the public ... Martin's soft American voice is hypnotic after the grating Scots ringing in his ears, and Franco thinks of Melanie. He finds himself loitering in the corridor, looking out through a dirty window at the narrow cobbled streets below, and the random foot traffic cutting between Leith Walk and Broughton Street.

SICK BOY

I put my hand onto my lap to rearrange the erection I feel burgeoning. I don't want Begbie – a closet homo if ever there was one, this art thing shocks me far less than it does the others – getting the wrong idea! In my mind's eye, I'm going back to Marianne, pleading undying love, winning her round, setting her up to be fucked by a gang of strap-on-wearing schoolies from her alma matter, Mary Erskine. Ah, the sweet narratives of pornography. I miss them so. That's creativity, Begbie ...

RENTON

This is so relaxing ... in fact it's the most relaxing time I've spent in fucking years! Just doing nothing, letting your thoughts slowly unravel and meander.

Vicky ... how uncharacteristically quiet she's been the last few days ... no emails or texts returned ... like I've somehow upset her. What the fuck did ah dae? She can't be up the kite after the flunky burst, cause she had her period on, and in any case, she scoffed that morning-after pill straight away.

Does she know about Marianne? Could she tell?

Marianne lied about no shagging anybody, cause she defo rode Sick Boy's brother-in-law. And obviously Sick Boy himself. Who else?

Fuck, they thin wisps ay air coming through that straw ... I cannae hear or see anything ...

BEGBIE!

I'm at his mercy! He could just cut off ma fuckin air supply right now!

What the fuck ... cool it ...

As they say in the movies: if the cunt wanted ays deid I'd already be deid ... stay fucking calm.

Fuckin itchy knob, but I cannae scratch it cause I dinnae fuckin ken whae the fuck's watching ...

SPUD

Funny but this sortay staeted oaf as barry at first but it's gaun aw sortay messed up cause one ay ma nostrils is jist pure seizen up, like, then it pure shuts, like wi aw the ching n snotters ... oh man ... the second yin ... ah pits muh hand up in the air ... ah cannae breathe!

Help ays, Franco!

Ah cannae breeeethe ...

Frank Begbie is still on the phone with Martin, but has shifted the discussion from suitable London exhibition venues onto his own area of interest. — If Axl Rose saw that fuckin catalogue, he'd be right in for that yin ay Slash. Just get it oot tae his people.

— Right, I'll send it to his management, and also the record company.

— Call Liam Gallagher's lot, *and* Noel Gallagher's n aw. And they boys in the Kinks, the Davies brothers. There's a huge market in the music business we huvnae even started to tap intae.

— I'm on it. But, Jim, I'm conscious of your time, and the commissions are rolling in.

— Ah've plenty time.

In the workshop, Danny Murphy, rendered blind, deaf and anosmatic, rises from his stool in terror, tearing at the set block of wet plaster-concrete mix that encases his face. He stumbles over Mark Renton. Alarmed by the weight on him, the sensation of tipping off the stool and tumbling to the floor, Renton reflexively grabs out, striking at something. Feeling a walloping blow to his side, Simon Williamson panic-strickenly raises his hands, trying to pull the heavy object from his face.

Frank Begbie hears the banging, thrashing sounds, and abruptly ends the call. He returns to find the studio in chaos. Spud, arms and legs spreadeagled, lies immobile, on top of a flailing Renton, while Sick Boy has collapsed across a trolley. Franco grabs a huge set of stainless-steel cutters and tears north from the side of Sick Boy's neck, pulling open the block, exposing his grateful face as he fills his lungs. — Fuck … fuck sake … what happened?

— Some cunt was fuckin aboot, Frank says, in a voice that strikes terror into Sick Boy. It is almost signalling the return of someone much feared, whose impending presence is hinted at, but as yet unconfirmed. Sick Boy sees it in the eyes staring at him, inspecting the latex mask, before looking to the imprint in the discarded block, noting it has set as a mould. — Good … Franco Begbie purrs, hauling in a breath, seeming to slip back into the mode of artist Jim Francis.

Franco pulls Spud's almost weightless figure from Mark Renton. He falls to his knees and starts giving Renton the same treatment as Sick Boy.

— Will I take this off him? Sick Boy asks, reaching for the block that covers Spud Murphy's face.

— Leave it! Franco first snaps, then adds, more gently, – Ah'll see tae it ... as he cuts and tears Renton's casing from his head.

A gasping, jerking Renton can suddenly breathe, as he feels the air and sees the light flood in. Then Frank Begbie is lunging at him with a pair of industrial cutters. — NO, FRANK!

— Shut it, I'm taking this oaf for ye!

— Ay, okay ... thanks, Frank ... Renton wheezes in gratitude. — Some cunt fell on ays, he moans, as Frank Begbie springs the mould from him. Then Franco is over to Spud Murphy, now a thin, motionless body sticking out from a block of concrete.

— I was smacked by some bastard, Sick Boy says, pulling the latex mask from his face.

— It wisnae me ... Spud fuckin fell on toap ay me! What was he playing at? Renton rises, staring at the immobile body on the floor. — Fuck ... is he okay?

Frank Begbie ignores them, cutting through the block, then tearing it from Spud's head. He rips off the latex mask. Spud doesn't respond to a hearty slap across the chops, so Begbie pinches his nose and sets to work on him with mouth-to-mouth resuscitation. Sick Boy and Renton look at each other in trepidation.

Frank lurches back as Spud's lungs explode into life, puke shooting across the floor, then trickling out from the side of his mouth as Franco spins him onto his side. — He's awright, he announces, before helping Spud to sit up, propping him against the wall.

Spud gulps in air. — What happened …?

— Sorry, bud, ma fault. Fuckin phone. Franco shakes his head. — Loast track ay the time.

A snigger suddenly ebbs from Renton. First Sick Boy looks at him, then Spud and Franco, compelling him to ask, — What's the worst job you've ever had?

The laughter is loud and tension breaks from them like wild stallions smashing out of a corral. Even Spud, through a fitting cough, is moved to join in. When there's a lull, Sick Boy looks at his phone and turns to Begbie. — Is that us done?

— Aye, thanks for your help. If you have to get off, go ahead, Franco nods, then turns to the others. — Mark, Danny, ah could do wi a wee hand.

— What can we do? Renton wonders out loud.

— Help ays cast my ain heid.

On this news, Sick Boy finds himself inclined to loiter, as they assist Franco in putting on his own latex mask. Then, as he had done to them, they encase his head in the Perspex box, and start to pour the concrete-plaster mix around it. The timer on the clock is set. As the block solidifies, Sick Boy play air-humps at it, to Spud's and Renton's mild amusement. As they know through experience, Franco will hear nothing now, yet they opt to remain silent.

At the allotted time, they tear off the mould. The freed artist calmly inspects the indentation of his own face in the concrete block. — Good work, boys, it's perfect. He immediately starts to cast all the heads from the impressions, filling them in with clay. Once they set, he explains, he will do the eyes by hand, from photographs he takes of them all. Then he'll take the moulds to a specialist forge to be cast in bronze.

Sick Boy is now fascinated, and in no hurry to leave. They chat more easily and when the heads finally come out of the kiln, the others are shocked, not at their own images, but that of Frank Begbie's. There is something about it, gaunt and tense, still with hollows for the eyes that he will add later. It isn't a representation of the man now in their company. The head looks like how he used to appear; full of psychotic anger and murderous intent, and that is before he has filled in those blank voids. It is the mouth; it twists in a familiar cold sneer, which they haven't yet seen in the Jim Francis version. It chills each man to his bones.

The artist picks up on the mood of his subjects and the shifting atmospherics of the room, but can't determine its source. — What's up, boys?

— They look great mate, Renton says uneasily. — Very authentic. I'm just blown away by how real they seem, even withoot the mince pies.

— Nice one, Frank Begbie smiles. — Now as a token of my appreciation, I've booked us a table at the Café Royal. A slap-up nosh on me. He looks at Sick Boy. — You still in a hurry to get off?

— It might be nice to catch up properly, Simon Williamson concedes. — On condition Renton puts his fucking phone away for ten minutes. I thought I was bad, but you have to retain *some* fucking social skills in the digital age.

— Business, Renton says defensively. — It never stops.

— Vicky business, I'm betting, Frank Begbie teases.

Sick Boy's guileful grin slides over Franco and Renton, deft as a pickpocket's fingers. — So he has a proper girlfriend, which he's kept silent about! He *still* reverts to his seventeen-year-old self on such occasions!

— Aye, right, Renton says, his hand wet with sweat on the device in his pocket.

— And on the subject of business, if you gentlemen are ever in London and looking for escort services, and he hands them all an embossed Colleagues business card. — Now, he smiles at Franco, — let us feast!

9

SICK BOY – EXPANDING/ CONTRACTING

Carlotta is constantly on the phone, even though I'm back in London where I can do little to find her missing Thai-hooring husband. She's fucking relentless, so I pick up, as I trek from King's Cross Underground to my office. I can't leave Colleagues for too long. There's only so much you can do online without being at the holeface. The girls form their own bonds with the clients, then conspire to undercut you by making their own deals. There is zero you can do about it. Then they'll rip off, or fall out with the customers, who return like nothing has happened, to use my service again. So you are continually firing and recruiting. And for a pittance. They make the real money.

But Carlotta does not give a fuck about my business affairs, as her sobs heave down the line. — It's killin me, Si-mihn … it's fuckin killin me, as I jink past open-mouthed stunned plebs waiting for the lights to change, hopping over York Way to the Caley Road. This time my sis really is beside herself and making no sense. I'm looking around the tarted-up street, barely able to comprehend what's become of the bookies and the Scottish Stores pub, those once-redoubtable centres of hooring and drug activity that constituted my personal power base. Grim days. Carra can barely speak; thankfully Louisa takes over. — She's in pieces. Still husnae heard *a single word* fae Euan since he went tae Thailand.

The dirty bastard. Lumpy-bawed Presbyterian hoor's erse-ramming cunt ... — Has anybody been able to work out how long he's going to be away?

Louisa is trying to sound outraged, but she can't help a salacious *Schadenfreude* seep into her tones. Nobody could have female siblings like mine and believe in the concept of the sisterhood as anything other than a movable feast. — Only that he bought a round-the-world ticket after sorting out a career break with his employer. Of course his first port of call is Bangkok!

— What the fuck, I hiss, crossing past the old snooker hall, now a shit club venue, copping a lungful of exhaust fumes. A solitary jakey extends a styrofoam and croaks hopefully. His face contorts in a bitter sneer as he sees it's only coppers and a 5p I've deposited. — He must have said when he's planning on returning?

— He told her all this in one email, Lou says breathlessly, — then cancelled his account and shut down his Facebook page. He's even pit off his phone, Simon. She's goat no way ay getting in touch wi him!

The office is located in a backstreet behind Pentonville Road, on the side that has escaped redevelopment. It's a shabby old building above a minicab office and kebab shop, its days numbered with the sweeping post-Eurostar gentrification of the area. I let myself in and feel my feet stick to the carpet as I mount a stair so narrow it could be in Renton's stomping ground of Amsterdam.

In the meantime, Lousia has managed to get Carlotta back on the blower. Of course, her and Ross, to say nothing of Euan's auld mammy back in Wee Free cattle-cowpin land, are worried sick. The audacity of those self-indulgent pansy bourgeois drama queens on their menopausal breakdowns in saying that *I* don't know how to treat women!

A wave of heat hits me as I open the office door. I left the fucking radiator on, and the power bill will be extravagant. Some privatised utility-shareholding one per cent public-school Nazi fuck will be getting wanked blind by a Third World child on a luxury yacht right now. Thank heavens for Renton's money. I tell Carlotta to calm down and assure her I'll be up next week. I ask her if there's anybody else Euan would be in touch with, but she's tried all his workmates and he's just cut them off too. The cunt really has gone native. I never thought he'd have the balls.

Getting her off the phone feels like the psychic version of doing a pish you've long been bursting for. I open the window to let the cold air seep in, then move to my raised standing desk to check my emails and the website. A few lassies have left notices and shots. I'm enjoying their port-folios, and phoning to make appointments, when VICTOR SYME flashes up on caller ID, providing not so much a sinking feeling, as a bitter, rancorous surge of nausea, convincing you that the world is fucking finished.

The snide-couponed sex offender is talking about his urgent desire to meet 'this surgeon felly'. Of course, I have to spill the disturbing news. Inevitably, he's far from chuffed.
— Call me as soon as he's back! Ah dinnae like surprises, he whinges.

That's a cliché all arseholes use: *Ah dinnae like surprises.* Fucking soulless control freaks. And gangsters are just the politicians of the schemes. Now the psychotic fishwife Syme thinks that I'm some kind of PA for this vanishing podiatrist! Fuck me, that cunt's feet must be in bad shape! — He's fled the country, Vic, on a hooring expedition, I'm wagering.

— Well, you'd better git um fuckin well back!

When you're as much of a cunt as Syme, you don't need to be logical, far less reasonable. — Well, Vic, if I knew where the fucker was I'd be right over there, dragging him back myself. But he's gone off the radar.

— As soon as ye hear fae him, ah want tae ken aboot it!

— You'll be the second to know, after my sis, his wife.

— Ah dinnae dae second, Syme says, and I can feel the spiteful malice down the line. Fuck sake, this is one creepy imbecile!

— Did I say second? I meant my sister will be second, I say, examining the profile of Candy from Bexleyheath, 20, student at Middlesex University, tweaking the head of my cherry through black brushed denim and boxers. — You, of course, will be numero uno.

— Count oan it, he snaps. — And dinnae think you're oot ay ma range doon there in London, he says, in that queasy, smug voice that chills me. — Be seein ye.

I cough a goodbye into a dead line.

10

RENTON – BONNYRIGGED

I cannae ignore it any longer; that itching and the watery, milky discharge fae my cock every time I take a single fish. That tenderness around the hee-haws, and now augmented by those sharp abdominal pains. A present from Edinburgh. One that Marianne probably got fae fucking Sick Boy!

The Sexually Transmitted Infections Outpatient Clinic is on the Weesperplein. I inform Muchteld, sitting opposite me, peering over her specs into her laptop, that I have tae nip out for a couple ay hours. There's no reaction from her, as nothing is suspicious about this. She's been with me long enough. When we worked together on my club night, Luxury, I was always sneaking away to pay people off in cash, or even meeting associates tae get fucked up.

We're (appropriately) based in the heart of the red-light district, which retains a strange sleaze during the day. I stroll in the welcome brisk air towards Nieumarket, planning to jump on the Metro 54. I shuffle past two young holiday jakeballs fae the north ay England, preoccupied with ogling a hefty black lass in a window, as their mates urge them tae come doon the street. — This is where Jimmy Savile started out, I tell one. A salty retort comes my way, which I miss as a shivering junky asks ays for cash, and I slip him a two-euro coin. He tears off without recognition, sick wi need. I dinnae take offence, I've been there, and however his condition compels him tae act, he'll be glad ay it. Weaving off tae the sounds ay a hurdy-gurdy,

I head underground. The station is calm and sterile compared tae the chaos above it. As I board the chunky train to ride the two stops I'm thinking of Vicky and there's an ominous tug in my chest.

When I get off, I emerge into bright sunlight. I've always liked this part of town, without realising that the clap clinic was based here. The Nieuwe Achtergracht is one ay ma favourite canals tae walk. It's full ay quirky things to look at, and a real houseboat community; as it's outside ay the four horseshoes in the centre ay toon, tourists rarely meander it. The clinic is housed in an ugly 1970s precast structure oan the corner. It's joined to a block ay purple-bricked eighties-style apartments, which at least try tae nod tae Amsterdam's nautical heritage with a few porthole windaes, aw looking oantae the bustling street. There's a twisted dark canopy ay shame, which ironically looks like a vagina wi open piss flaps, urging 'Come in, big boy!' as ye walk through the doors below. I think ay aw the scabby cocks and putrid fannies of shaggers, innocent and prolific, who have walked underneath it, tae – often temporary – salvation.

The doctor's a young woman, which is embarrassing, but the tests are nowt like the auld Ward 45 ay Edinburgh popular culture, where the wire test-tube brush soaked in Dettol is rammed down the cock hole. Nothing more than blood and pish samples, and a swab of the discharge. But she kens what it is straight away. — It looks likes chlamydia, which the tests will no doubt confirm in a couple of days. Do you wear condoms when you have intercourse?

Fuck sake . . .

I've picked up a fuckin Bonnyrigg Rose, for the second time in my life. At my fucking age, it feels beyond embarrassing, just totally ridiculous. — Generally, yes, I tell her. — Though there has been a recent exception, and I'm thinking ay Marianne.

— The risk, with chlamydia, as with all sexually transmitted diseases, is greatly decreased by use of a condom, but not eliminated. Condoms aren't foolproof, for many reasons, and you can still get sexually transmitted infections despite using one. They sometimes break, she says.

Fuckin tellin me ... I'm now thinking aboot bein wi Vicky and my cock bursting through the tip ay the rubber, and her scrambling in panic for the morning-after pill. For fuck sake.

They sometimes break.

It's all I can hear as she goes on about how the chlamydia infection can spread if you have vaginal, anal or oral sex or share sex toys ... Though the woman is detached and professional, I feel like a chastened adolescent who should know the fuck better.

Afterwards, I sit at the Café Noir on the corner ay Weesperplein and Valckenierstraat. I decide against a beer and have a *koffie verkeerd*, and contemplate the shambles ay a life oscillating between extreme social boldness and cowardice, neither ay them ever deployed at strategically optimum times.

I dinnae even need the test results tae confirm it, as the next day the email comes in:

From: VickyH23@googlemail.com
To: Mark@citadelproductions.nl
(No subject)

Mark,

I've had some bad and very embarrassing news. I'm assuming you know what it is, as it directly affects you too. Under the circumstances I think it's best we don't see each other again, as it clearly isn't going to work out now. I'm so sorry.

Wish you well,
Vicky

Well, there it is. You fucking blew it again. A great woman, who was so into you, and you give her a fucking dose because you cannae keep it in your troosers and have tae bareback ride some slag just because fucking Sick Boy humped her for years and you were jealous. Ya stupid, pathetic, useless and irredeemably weak bag ay shite.

I look at the email again, and feel something inside ays fold in two. My body seems tae go intae shock, and ma eyes water. I slump in front ay the TV in my apartment, letting my emails and calls pile up before deleting them all. If it's important they'll get back to me.

A couple ay days later, Vicky's grim correspondence is confirmed by the test scores. I go back tae the clinic and they put ays on antibiotics for seven days, no sexual contact tae be had within this time. I have tae return in three months tae confirm that I'm all clear. The doctor asks about sexual partners, who I'm likely to have goat it fae, and who I probably gave it tae. I tell her I travel a lot.

I'm sitting back in my flat, smoking dope, feeling sorry for myself. Getting even more depressed through knowing exactly what I'll do tae handle this setback: get wrecked, then sober up and fling masel into my graft. Repeat till death. This is the trap. There isnae a later. There's no fucking place in the sun. There is no cunting future. There is only *now*. And it's shite and getting worse.

The following evening and Muchteld comes tae the door, wi her partner Gert. He's also been wi ays since the early days of Luxury, and they carry big bags ay shopping. Muchteld starts cleaning up the apartment, while Gert skins up and starts cooking a meal. — I have tickets for the Arena tomorrow.

— I don't want to watch football. It just makes me miserable.

Muchteld, throwing takeaway cartons into a black bin liner, looks up and says, — Fuck you, Mark, football will not make you worse. We go to Ajax, then we eat and we talk.

— Okay, I concede, as a capitalised text pops in from Conrad.

WHY ARE YOU NOT ANSWERING MY CALLS AND TEXTS? THERE IS AN ISSUE AT THE STUDIO WITH KENNET. HE IS AN ASSHOLE! I WANT HIM FIRED AND I NEED A PROPER SOUND ENGINEER LIKE GABRIEL!

— You guys, I smile at them, hudin up the phone, — and this spoiled fat cunt, who has never stopped for a second tae think about anyone other than himself, you might have just saved ma life.

— Yet again, *klootzak*! Muchteld laughs. — You must speak to him, Mark, he is bombarding the office with calls. He thinks you do not care about this track he is making.

— Yeah, okay … I say, without enthusiasm.

Gert gets me in a headlock, aggressively rubs my scalp. I can't break free, he's a bear of a man.

— Hey, honey, easy on my boy! Who manages the manager, right, Mark?

I love those cunts.

Part Two
April 2016
A Medical Emergency

11

SPUD – THE BUTCHERS OF BERLIN

People kin be awfay funny, man. Ah mean, ah goat hassle fae Mikey cause ah nivir hud a passport. So the cat made ays git yin, n ah'm thinkin: it pure shouldnae be that wey, needin passports, cause wir aw Europe, likesay. Wis a lot ay hassle n aw, man, hud tae go through tae Glesgey n fill in tons ay forms. N they needed the photaes tae be jist right. Then, whin the passy finally comes through the door, n ah'm ready tae rock, Mikey's naewhaire tae be seen! Took ays ages tae track um doon, but finally found the feral gadge in Diane's Pool Hall, hingin wi some jungle cats. — It's no happenin right now, mate, eh sais.

— Ye mean … yuv cancelled the gig? Ah've pure sortay spent the deposit, man, ah goes, pointin tae ma new trainers.

— Ah widnae say cancelled, Spud, ah'd say mair post-poned. That's how ah wid pit it. Postponed at this stage ay time, is what ah wid say. Then eh goes, raisin ehs voice a bit soas the other gadges kin hear, — Vic Syme n me huv tae sort oot some details, that's aw. Ah ken whaire tae find ye.

So ah goes hame again, n looks at the passport. N it wis like that fir weeks n weeks. Me aw excited, then Mikey sayin: still no go.

Ah cannae stoap gittin the passy oot ay the drawer. It's barry, cause ah've nivir had yin before. It says Great Britain and Northern Ireland and European Community. But wi

Britain mibbe headin oot ay Europe and Scotland mibbe headin oot ay Britain, ah'll probably huv tae get a new yin before long! Mind you, a Scottish passport wid be barry, wi a thistle oan the front mibbe, instead ay that Her Britannic Majesty requests stuff which seems awfay auld-fashioned, and a rip-off offay the Stones, likesay. The Brian Jones cat that's potted heid.

It makes ays feel like ah'm the man though: DANIEL ROBERT MURPHY. A subject ay Her Majesty the Queen. Even though ah'm likesay a pape ay Paddy stock, ah'm just as much ay a subject as any west Edinburgh Jambo or west coast Sticky Bun. Aye, they cats'll no like that but, ay!

The thing is the weeks rolled by n ah nearly forgot aw aboot this big secret-squirrel hush-hush Berlin joab, cause ah gits sorted oot wi part-time casual work, daein forklift drivin in a warehouse. Peys sweeties but it's guid tae graft n git a wage again but, ay. N still gies ays time tae go oan the John Greig doon at the Grassmarket. Spring isnae bad for the mooch cause cats ur aw optimistic n ah kin fantasise that aw they cool office lassies walkin past wid be impressed if they kent ah wis makin a top-secret delivery ay stuff behind the auld Iron Curtain n doon tae the mystic East ay Istanbul. N mibbe it would be pure exotic love in foreign climes, like that Sean Connery cat as Bond. In the aulder Bond fulums, likesay.

Then, one eftirnin, Mikey comes along tae ma pitch. — It's time, eh goes. N man, ah'm pure sortay nervous, cause eh disnae look happy, eh's goat that serious face oan.

— Ah'm ready, bud, ah goes, standin up. But ah wisnae really, cause ah'm sortay happy, ken? Things ur gaun a bit better now. But ah pure took the five hundred up front. — Bring ays yir kidney, Sydney, ah sais oot ay nerves. Mikey isnae chuffed but.

— Shut it. Eh looks around, gesturing ays tae follay him ower tae the pub. — This is fuckin serious. Ah never want tae hear that word comin oot your mooth again. Goat that?

— Aye, sorry, man, ah tell um, n ah git Toto leashed up n wir walkin ower the street.

— Ah pit masel oan the line gittin ye this work, Spud. Dinnae fuck it up. Dae the business n it'll be a regular thing.

So ower in the boozer eh slips ays a wallet wi the plane tickets. A few days later ah'm at the airport, and Toto's wi ays! Ah goat ma sis Roisin tae go oan that Internet thing n check eh wis wee enough tae take oan ma lap. Turns oot ah kin pure take um in this thing called a Sherpa bag, n ah dinnae huv tae pit um in the hold. Ah try tae keep um under eighteen poonds, but ah've let it creep up a bit, so ah'm tryin tae make sure eh disnae drink sae much in case eh disnae make the weight. Ah think aboot the bag, mindin how as a sprog ah used tae watch that *Owen, M.D.* oan telly aboot the Welsh country doaktir boy, n his dug was called Sherpa. But the bag couldnae be named after that canine gadge cause he was a huge dug, n wid never have goat in one ay these boys. Ah pure need the company, man, cause ah've nivir flew before n ah'm excited but dead nervous that mibbe some sneaky terrorist gadge might be oan the plane thinkin aboot another 9/11! Wid jist be ma luck tae be comin up in the world, then git blawn tae fuck by some boy whae wis worried aboot they Molly Malones zappin ehs faimlay. N ah dinnae trust naebody else tae look eftir the dug right.

But oan the plane they gie ye stuff tae eat n a wee peeve, so ah'm sittin back, sayin tae Toto, whae's in the bag at ma feet, — This is the life, pal, but eh's sayin nowt, just wee whines, which the lassie sittin next tae ays picks up oan n tries tae comfort the wee gadge. — He's lovely! What's his name?

— Toto, ah goes. Thinkin barry tae git some convo oan the airy, ken?

— Oh, how sweet, after *The Wizard of Oz*!

— Naw, it wis pure eftir that band Toto whae did that song aboot Africa. Thaire's a barry remix ah heard and ah just thoat: name the dug that. Then ah goat telt by ma gay mate, Poofy Paul, aboot *The Wizard ay Oz* connection, ken?

— Well, I hope you both follow the Yellow Brick Road!

— That wis that Elton John boy though, no Toto, ah goes.

The lassie jist smiles at that. Goat her thaire but, pure bambozzled the dude-ess wi cultural science, man.

— He's ... ah bends ma wrist, — that wey n aw. Nowt against anybody, mind you, live n let live, aw love is beautiful, but ah'm a straight shooter, if ye git ma drift.

Overcooked that chick, man. That's me aw ower. Some gadges ken how tae talk tae a lemon, no me but, ay? She gies a smile that sais 'yir a radge, but hermless enough' which is the worst smile a lassie kin gie ye. — He's certainly a cute one, she goes, pattin the dug's wet beak through the mesh ay the bag again.

So we lands in Turkey n me n the dug gits oot ay the David Narey, n jumps a sherbet tae Istanbul, and it's mental! Man, the place is fair bustling, wi aw they people bouncing aboot. Cause ah'm a fair-skinned gadge wi a dug ah wid sort ay stick oot a bit here, but ah'm in the taxi n wir drivin through the streets. It's like thaire's tons ay guys but hardly any lassies. Rents went ages ago as a student n ah mind um sayin it wis like Leith, but that's aw changed. Ye git tons ay lassies walkin around in Leith now. Ah sort ay thoat thit aw the burds here wid huv veils, n look through thum aw seductively at ye wi big eyes, like in they auld Turkish Delight adverts, full ay Eastern promise, but it isnae like that, likesay. Shame but, ay? How barry wid that be?

But this is good, it's the best wey tae make money, like, bein a middleman. See, ah cannae dae the tea-leafin any mair. Whin ye git aulder, ye git too much ay a moral compass, and it ey points in the 'dinnae rip cats oaf' direction. Can not dae it any mair, man. Just cannae be in some dude's hoose takin thair stuff, n it disnae matter how much thuv goat. It still might be something that means a loat tae them, like a deid relative's trinkets. Could not huv that oan ma conscience, man. Nup. The auld 'feast ay Stephen' jist isnae happinin fir ays any mair.

So ah'm at the station, huvin boat some food, waitin by platform 3 like they sais, n this boy comes up tae me, leathers n a helmet, n looks at the dug. Eh hands ays a cardboard boax wi a plastic handle stickin oot ay it. It's aboot the same size as Toto. The boy sais nowt, just hands ays the boax n a ticket for the train, then eh's away. The boax is heavier thin it looks, cause inside the cardboard thaire's another boax.

The train leaves at nine, but ah lets Toto oot n takes um fir a walk n tae dae his business, so the time goes quick. Ah heads back as it gits dark n huv tae bag the dug up tae git him oan the choo-choo, but ah'm chuffed cause it's a nice wee carriage aw tae ourselves, so ah let him oot. There we are sittin back, bound fir Berlin. Toto's oan the seat opposite, his wee heid bobbin away like a noddin toy dug in the back ay a car windae, as we go past stuff at speed. Ah opens the cardboard boax, n see that the other boax inside is white, n looks like a mini fridge or a microwave cooker. It's goat aw controls n things oan it. Yon kidney'll be inside. Ah dozes off for a bit n wakes up when ah hears the ticket wifie comin. Wir in Bucharest, so ah gits Toto back in the Sherpa bag. It steys thaire for ages. The train disnae seem too busy though.

By the time we gits tae Prague ah'm pure starvin cause ah've eaten aw the stuff ah boat at the station. Ah've let Toto out the bag n ah tells um tae hang loose a bit while ah goes tae the lavy tae take a slash, then investigate the buffet, tae git something fir me n the dug. Ah sees they hot dugs, which sounds like cannibalism for perr Toto, but obviously isnae likes. The lassie pure speaks English, and that's barry, cause nae wey wid ye git a lassie oan the railways in Britain thit spoke German. No unless she wis German. But ah dinnae think any bilingual Deutsch chick wid be wastin her talents trolley-dollyin oan Britain's railways. But cats huv tae dae anything tae make a livin these days, even brainy overqualified yins need tae dae shite joabs. Which makes the likes ay me pretty much useless, man. But no now. Now ah've finally goat a wee tickle; the part-time warehouse gig back hame n the international jet-set boy whae's oan a mission here!

When ah gits back tae the carriage, ah cannae believe it ...

Toto's knocked ower the boax. He's pushed it off the seat oantae the flair. It's opened. Aw that chemical stuff is spilt acroass the flair. *Aw naw, man ... How did it open ...?* N eh's goat the kidney oot n eh's eatin it. *Aw naw ...* — Aw, Toto man ...

He looks up at ays. It's lodged in ehs jaws, wriggling like it wis alive. Ah touches it n it's aw cauld and smelling ay chemicals.

Ma life is ower, man, ah've fucked up big time.

— Droap it, boy! ah goes, n eh does. It's goat ehs teeth marks in it ... That's evidence ... Ah picks it up n it's cauld in ma hand, but no frozen through ... It feels sort ay burnin in ma hand ... Ah tell um tae stey n ah goes outside n lobs it doon the lavy ay the train n flushes it away.

Ah dinnae ken what the fuck tae dae now! The rest ay the trip tae Berlin, man, ah'm jist pure shitein it. Thaire's a rock in ma guts the size ay an asteroid, n ah'm brekin oot in chilly sweats. Ah'm thinkin aboot what Syme'll dae tae ays. Like droonin me. Or burnin ays. Or setting aboot ma nipples wi pliers. Ah'm thinkin: anything but the eyes n baws. N ah cannae even blame perr Toto, no his fault; shouldnae huv left the dug unsupervised. Ah shouldnae huv flung it away: but it hus the dug's teeth marks in it. Whin we gits oaf ah'm still in shock, pure in a trance, n Toto kens thaire's something wrong as eh jist walks alongside ays, lookin up.

So ah'm no really thinkin straight, n ah goes tae a local butcher n buys a kidney tae replace it. Thin ah goes tae the lavy in the station n makes the swap. It looks nowt like the one Toto goat at. It's a different shape n colour, mair ay a broonish thing like a Jambo strip. But ah pits it in the ice boax anyway, n ah ken thi'll find oot, but it just buys ays a bit mair time tae think.

But thaire isnae time tae think cause whin ah gits back tae the platform thaire's a boy waitin thaire, another biker, whae, funnily enough, looks a bit like the last gadge but isnae. This yin talks, seems mair chilled oot. — All is good?

— Aye, sound, ah goes n ah hands it ower tae the guy n eh leaves withoot checkin it or sayin nowt.

Ah suppose they willnae ken till they open it. But if they pill ays up fir it, ah'll need tae hud ma hand up, cause it widnae be fair tae git the biker boy intae bother. As long as they dinnae try n pit this kidney intae a bairn or anything! That wid be the worst … Bit naw, calm doon, thi'll no dae that. Thi'll check it's no right first.

Ah taxi tae the airport tae git the flight back. Ah think aboot steyin here wi Toto, but ah'd nivir survive, ah'm no a cat like Renton or Sick Boy, that kin jist take off like that n everything's hunky-dory. Ah need tae face the music. But ah'm gaun back tae Mikey … and it's no really Mikey, it's the boys behind um, like that cat Syme, and whae kens who else. Ah looks at Toto, whae disnae understand that he's done wrong, it's no the dug's fault, but ah cannae help sayin tae um, — Aw, Toto, what huv ye done tae us, man?

12

RENTON – DJ SHAGGER

That queasy admixture ay sad embarrassment and rip-roaring affirmation kicks in as I feel that *presence ay another* in the kip. And it's somebody that shouldnae be there. And we are, like, where? Amsterdam–Berlin–Ibiza–London ... No fuckin Edinburgh, please no fuckin Edinburgh, and oh fuck ... there she is; so young, and ma lines, jowls, n burst blood vessels are gaunny get the full treatment fae the wrecking sun flooding in through the half-open blinds. She's looking right at ays, her heid propped on her elbow, smiling, eyes hungry and rapaciously mocking, raven locks tumbling, that beauty-spot mole oan her chin. — Mor-ning! You were snoring!

What the fuck tae say? Why Edinburgh? Ewart's birthday bash at Cabaret Voltaire. Conrad, who seems happier about the new track, though he won't let me hear it, tae my amazement, *volunteered* tae come over and play. Of course I realised too late that his purpose was tae play a shit-hot deep-house set and blow everybody away, thus humiliating Carl in front ay his ain people. It worked. The young Dutch maestro took all the plaudits while Carl, coke-fuelled and sour, sloped off with his mate Topsy and their crew, into a dull night and a party in some west Edinburgh rat trap. Rab Birrell stuck around. So did Juice Terry. And Emily was there and did a great set too ... Then I remember her swinging her hips on her cork wedge pumps, saying something vampish like 'I think I'm enticing all the Scottish boys ...' I said something cheesy in retort and her lips were on mine, and then ... for fuck sake.

Ching. Voddy. E: I fucking hate ye. She's tons younger than me. She was pretty dirty, and I lost myself. Fuck sake, I huvnae done some ay they things since ah was thirty!

I got the three-month all-clear a few weeks ago. Huvnae heard fae Vicky since the incident, though I've been tempted tae get back tae her and apologise. She's due that, even if she'll have long moved on by now. But it's no been easy tae pick up the phone: I just cannae let 'sorry about giving you the clap' be my last interaction wi her.

So now I've done what I excel the fuck oot ay: compound a bad situation wi another stupid decision. Emily is my fucking *client*. I slide oot ay the bed, and pull a hotel robe, thankfully close tae hand, round me.

— Where are you going? she asks. — Let's order some breakfast on room service. All that shagging has given me an appetite!

— I'm truly flattered that I'm your son of a preacher man, Emily, but we cannae go any further wi this –

— What the fuck are you talking about?

— Dusty Springfield: 'Son of a Preacher Man'. It was about the only boy who could get this lassie who swang the other way onside.

Emily flicks her dark curls. Her expression is incredulous. — You really believe that's what that song's about?

— Yes. It's about a lesbian having a secret heterosexual affair with 'the only man who could ever teach her ...'

Loud, derisive laughter erupts fae somewhere deep inside her. — Yeah, well, *you* taught *me* zero. Fuck sake, Mark, I have had boyfriends before! Don't flatter yourself that you're some kind of Henry Higgins of cock, she sniggers. — Starr is only the second girl I've gone out with, and her bottom lip quivers a little as her guilt kicks in.

Fuck yes. Ah've jumped ahead ay myself again. Ah still believe – despite all the contrary evidence – that every woman in the world has the capacity tae fall in love wi ays. And that they maybe have to fight quite hard against doing so. That mindset, call it a delusion if ye will, is one ay the greatest gifts I possess. Of course, the downside ay this is that I tend to overreach. — So it's a phase?

— Oh fuck off, Mark. How old are you? Sixteen? It's called life. It's called 2016. I don't see the choice of sexual partners as binary. If I find somebody attractive, then I'll sleep with them. You're an interesting man, Mark, don't devalue yourself, you've done a lot. Luxury was one of the best clubs in Europe. You always booked female DJs. You brought big-time success to Ivan.

— Yes, but he fucked off as soon as he broke huge, I remind her.

— You need to start talking more about music again, Mark. You were really passionate about it. Now you just listen to any mixes some arsehole with half a following sends you. You're looking for the next big thing, rather than letting the music lead you.

She's so on the money it's fucking scary. — I know that. But I'm an old cunt and I look silly lurking in the shadows of a nightclub full of kids.

— You think of me as a kid?

— No, of course not. But I'm still ages with your dad and I'm your manager, and you're in a relationship, I say, suddenly thinking of not Starr, but Vicky, then trying not to.

— Oh, don't give me that buyer's regret shit.

— What do you expect me to say? I'm glad our slivers of existence intersected in a Venn diagram between the crushing slabs of oblivion on either side of them, but –

Emily's finger shoots over my lips, silencing me. — Please, Mark, not the old guy's mortality speech; always that sad and tiresome conversion of sex into death.

— How many older guys have you slept with? I instantly regret asking that.

— However many, it's a damn sight fewer than the young club girls I've seen you slope off with.

— Not for a while now. And never with a client: that's just wrong, I contend, unwisely adding, — And Mickey would kill me.

— What the fuck has my dad got to do with it? I'm twenty-two, for fuck sake! You're as weird as he is!

Jesus fuck, that is much mair than half my age. — Quite a lot if he finds out, I should imagine, and I go into the bathroom and pick up my electric shaver.

— Don't tell him then, she shouts through, — and I won't tell your dad. You do have a dad – I mean, is he still alive? He must be like, ancient!

I drag ma shaver ower ma coupon. I stare back at masel in the mirror: a hollow fool who has learned fuck all. — Yes. My dad's a bit older and frailer than he used tae be; he has a dodgy pin, but he's hanging on in there.

— What would he say if he knew you were sleeping with somebody young enough to be your daughter?

— *Did* sleep wi, once, in a drunken accident, I stress. — He wouldnae think very highly of it, but he's way past bothering about anything I do.

— And my dad should be too. It's creepy.

— He only wants the best for ye because he cares, I tell her. I cannae believe the pathetic words stumbling weakly from my mouth, or that I'm defending Mickey, who seems tae heartily dislike me. I've just banged the lassie aw weys, now I'm almost telling her she should study hard or she's grounded.

I emerge from the bathroom as thankfully my phone is going again and I have tae take this call as it's Donovan Royce, a promoter for Electric Daisy Carnival in Vegas, who *never* returns calls. — Mark! The fuck, bro!

— Hey, Don. So what's the story on a slot for my boy? In the hallway mirror, I watch Emily bristle. But I have tae work for my guys too.

— I'll be straight, EDC, the Ultra EDM crowd thing … they just ain't for N-Sign. They're too young, too musically uneducated for his sophistication.

— Don, come on. He's putting a lot intae this comeback.

— Mark, it's N-Sign Fucking Ewart! I grew up fucking chicks at high school under his poster! The man is a house-music legend to me! It's not me *you* have to sell N-Sign to. It's *me* who has to sell him to kids who have goldfish attention spans. Who don't even wanna dance, just want to punch the air and go 'yay' and grind up against each other as another small segment of a pop hit comes on. They don't wanna go on a journey with an old maestro. It's apples and oranges.

— Let's educate them then, Don. You used to be a true believer. I glance ower at Emily who has stretched forward in the bed, her long, thin frame almost in a yoga pose.

Loud laughter erupts down the phone. — You gotta be desperate to pull that old number. It's business, bro, as in 'regrettably in this instance we cannot get it on and do any'.

The conversation is depressing as fuck. But it's the basic truth: Carl will never get on the bill for an EDC or Ultra unless he has another pop hit. Ironically, the cunt is capable ay daein just that. But first I have to get him back into a place he now hates: the studio. I look back at Emily. — What about my girl, Emily, DJ Night Vision?

— I like her shit, but she isn't that sexy.

— I disagree, I say, genuinely stung. *My ravaged baws say otherwise.*

— Okay, seeing as it's you; the Upside-down House, an afternoon slot. Tell her to show some skin. Maybe a bit of cleavage. She has a pair of titties, right?

For fuck sake. Who is this cunt? The Upside-down House too; it's the smallest stage. — Early evening. Wasteland. It's right up her street.

— Wasteland is booked solid with reserves in place. I can do her a Quantum Valley slot, provided she can do trance.

— She fucking *is* trance, mate, I wink at Emily, who is nodding fifty to the dozen.

— Four till five.

— An evening slot, mate, help a brother out.

A loud sigh down the phone, then, — I can do 7.15 p.m. till 8.30.

— Done. You are a fucking man-ride and you are getting rammed till your eyes pop out your head on stalks and swing so far doon your body they are like all-seeing testicles, I tell him. *The fucker is getting objectified and sexualised right back.*

— Wow ... thanks, I think, he says.

As I click off, Emily shoots tae alertness. — What the fuck was that?

— Got you a slot at EDC, I say, keeping it low-key, pulling on my clathes. I find wi DJs, well, mine anyway, if ye fist-pump the air aboot a gig, bristling wi enthusiasm, the cunts will moan about it no being good enough. But play it low-key, and they squeal with excitement.

— EDC! That's a big deal!

— It's only Quantum Valley, early evening, and you'll have to load it with a trance vibe, I say in fake dreariness.

— But that's fucking great! Quantum Valley is the best space at EDC! You rock, Mark Renton!

170

It's aw about expectation management. — Thanks, I smile, as the phone goes again.

— Switch that thing off and come back to bed!

— I cannae, babe, this isnae a good idea for either of us. If I shag one ay my DJs I have to shag them all. It's called democracy. And I was always useless at swinging the other way. Let's leave it at that and discuss later, I offer, as the phone rings off.

— You won't say that I fucked you to get this gig?

— Don't be silly: I'm your manager. It's *my* job to get metaphorically fucked in order to get you gigs. And if you want to sleep your way to the top, fuck promoters, not somebody who's already into twenty per cent of you.

Emily flops back, thinking about this, then springs up abruptly. — I've a theory about you, Mark Renton, she says, arching a teasing brow. Here we go: every woman in her early twenties must buy handbags with a Penguin Freud stitched intae the lining. — That you were a young guy who was self-conscious about your ginger hair and pubes, and hung out with a mate who was a bit better looking, maybe had a bigger cock, who was more confident with girls ... How am I doing?

— Way way waaay off the mark, as in distinctly not Renton, babe, I tell her, pulling on my shoes, as Sick Boy's name flashes up on my phone. — Si ... right. On my way.

— Where are you going? says Emily.

— Working for you lot twenty-four/seven, sweetheart, I tell her, tapping the phone and heading for the door. I invited Sick Boy along tae our show. He appeared and is now helping ays oot wi a management problem. The recurring one: getting Conrad laid. Since I've squared Simon David Williamson up, we've become online buddies. Sharing links ay old band videos, new songs, humorous news items about sexual disasters and mutilations, the usual psychotic shit people bandy about nowadays.

In the hotel lobby Sick Boy is waiting wi an escort girl who scrutinises something on her mobile. She's a pretty enough brunette, though with a flinty-eyed professional hardness. Sick Boy's talking on one phone, while trying tae text on another. — Yes, I know what I said, Vic, but I didn't expect the cunt tae abscond tae fucking Thailand ... No indication when he's due back, he won't answer any emails or texts, has gone offline ... Yes, he's a surgeon, Vic ... Yes, I'm still in Edinburgh. I can't stay up here, I have a business tae run in London! Yes, okay! Right. He ends the call, evidently distressed. — Fuckin mongols! Surrounded by them! The lassie looks pointedly at him, and he composes himself. — Not you, my darling, you are the one shining light in an otherwise permanently murky scenario. Mark, meet Jasmine.

— Hi, Jasmine. I hand her the key to Conrad's room. — Be gentle with him!

She silently takes the key and vanishes into the lift.

— Don't be such a smarmy sleazebag, Sick Boy reprimands. — That woman is providing a service, so treat her with respect. I plan to recruit her for a possible Edinburgh operation. Most of our girls are MBAs.

If that lassie was awarded an HND in secretarial studies at Stevenson College, then Spud is professor of global finance at Harvard Business School. — Being given a lesson by you on sexism. Next week, Fred West on patio building. Or Franco on art.

— Don't, Sick Boy says, pushing index fingers into a throbbing temple. — Just don't.

— You seem stressed.

— So do you, he snaps back in defensive truculence.

— Well, apart fae being still jet-lagged tae fuck, oan an Amsterdam–LA–Vegas–Ibiza circuit for the last five months, having this birthday gig for Ewart, then flying tae Berlin for

172

the big show at the Flughafen tomorrow, with a DJ I can't find, him now lost in Jamboland somewhere, and I'm tempted to add *plus ditched by my girlfriend because of you, ya cunt,* — I'm perfectly fine. And you?

— First World problems, he says pompously. — My brother-in-law, who is being hassled by a psycho to do work for him, has fucked off tae Thailand, left Carlotta and the kid. Guess who's been stalked by the nutter, and the sister, for months? He slaps his head in the manner of old. — When did I become the radge designated tae sort oot other cunts' problems?

— Sortin oot other people's crap is the shittiest, most thankless deal you'll ever get, I empathise.

— And while we're running around like daft fuckers, Begbie is lying in the Californian sun, Sick Boy spits bitterly. — But you know what? I think you could be right about him. From deadly psychopath to arty wee pussy!

13

BEGBIE – WILD ABOUT
HARRY

The cunt got a fuckin shock when he came intae his hoose
n pit oan the light. There wis me sitting in the chair behind
ehs desk, pointing ehs ain fucking shooter right at him. Had
it in his top right-hand drawer, the fuckin spazwit! Polis? That
cunt? Seen fuckers in *Edinburgh* that would pit that wanker
tae shame.

— What the fuck ... How did you get in here?

— Do you really want the boring details? ah ask him. Ah
wave the gun a wee bit. The cunt properly registers it for the
first time. Disnae like it. — Now give me one good fucking
reason, after you harassing my wife, why I shouldn't shoot
you now.

— You're a murdering scumbag and she should know that!
N eh points the finger at ays.

This cunt isnae wise. — That's another good reason *why
I should* shoot you. I was asking for one why I shouldn't.

The prick faws silent at that yin: did not fuckin like that
at aw.

— Thought we'd just have a wee chat. About you bugging
my missus.

With his slitty black eyes, he looks angry rather than
scared. Fair fucks tae him.

— Hear you like a peeve. Ah point tae the bottle ay whisky
that ah've placed between us on the desk. — Take a wee drink.

He looks at me, then the bottle. He wants it awright. Hesitates for a few seconds, then pours a gless. Knocks it back slowly but steadily.

— Go on, have another! Sit doon. Ah gesture tae the chair. — I'd join ye but I've stopped. Never leads tae good places.

That scoobies the cunt. He stares at the empty gless. He's fucked his life up, his shite cop life, wi the auld Christopher Reeve. That boy isnae bothered whether yir polis or a villain: he just wants tae send ye tae hell. Ah've done aw that shite. This Harry cunt seems tae make a calculation that there's nae wey oot for him, so he pours anyway, n takes a seat, oan ma second promptin, wi the pointin ay the shooter. He looks at ays, eyes narrowing that accusing wey. — You killed those drifters, and the cunt tries tae stare ays oot.

I glower back at the cunt, my lips sealed. Gaze intae that cop soul. They're aw the same, despite the TV shows that portray them as the big heroes. Ah jist see the gossiping, sweetie-wife, fussy essence ay a wanker programmed tae serve others.

Harry blinks first. Clears his throat. — They were pieces of shit, but you murdered them in cold blood. The two that threatened Mel and the kids, he contends, tryin the fuckin stare again.

Cheeky cunt. Breathe. One … two … three …

These wee black beady eyes. Like a fuckin hamster looking at ye fae its cage. Like the yin we hud at school. The raffle tae see whae got tae take it hame for the holidays. Aw the oohs and aahs and the trepidation oan the teacher's face when they saw whae fuckin won. *Poor Hammy, he's going to Begbie's for the summer! Last we'll see of him!* N it wisnae misplaced. The poor wee golden bastard never came back. It wis natural causes – the fuckers just last a year – though nae cunt ootside our hoose believed that. They aw thought some cunt had stuck him between two slices ay breid.

— You couldn't let it go, could you? Couldn't leave us ... the police ... to deal with it, this Hammy, sorry, *Harry* cunt goes. — Because that's who you are ... that's what you do. You've done ... you've ... you ... The cunt's speech slows tae a mumble as ehs eyes get aw heavy.

— GHB, mate. Sodium gamma-Hydroxybutyrate, a designer drug with anaesthetic properties. The sex offender's game. Dinnae worry, ah stifle a wee chuckle, — you're no getting rattled. Or even hurt. I'm just removing you from the game.

— What ...? His eyes are closing, his neck heavy as his heid faws forward. He grips the rests oan the chair.

And the cunt looks at the hosepipe, which ah pick up by the nozzle and fling ower the ceiling beam. I'm making a noose at the end ay it. His weary eyes trace back tae where it comes in fae the gairdin, via the windae. Dib dib dab, ya polis bastard. Boy's spangled now, just aboot able tae show a slab ay fear through the confusion in his glazed eyes.

— Disgraced alco cop suicide, ah explain tae the cunt. — I never liked the fuckin polis, mate. I thought it was just back hame, in Scotland, and that American cops would be different. But naw. I hate all polis. Everywhere.

Eh tries tae stand, but faws oot the chair, tumbling oantae the rug. Ah bend ower him and slap his chops. Nowt. The cunt is out for the count. Ah wipe the gun clean n pit it back in the drawer. I get the noose aroond his neck and pull him back up on the chair; thankfully, he's no that heavy, aboot five-eight, 150 pounds, a welterweight, would be ma guess. The makeshift rope, gaun over the beam and oot through the windae, is attached tae the hose reel, which is bolted oantae the garage wall. I'd staked it out earlier. It should make a strong enough wrench.

I open the windae and step ootside. Ah go tae the reel n start winding it in. Looking inside ah kin see the cunt starting tae revive, his mooth flapping n his eyes doolally under heavy lids he struggles tae keep open. I'm yanking the fucker tae his feet, as his tired airms reach up, groping at the rope, trying tae loosen it. The daft cunt falls nicely intae ma trap by getting oan the chair, tae try and get some slack on the rope that's throttling him, but that's exactly where I want um! Fucker jist gets one shot tae try and pull the noose off before I furiously wrench it up, baith hands on the handle, tae take the slack and tighten it again, forcing the dopey polis bastard oantae his toes.

— Ye dinnae fuck aboot wi me n what's mine, mate, ah say as ah climb back in and blooter the chair oot fae under his taes. The cunt's swinging there, eyes popping oot, tongue hingin oot his heid, n ah'm gled ay the croakin sounds as ah've heard mair than enough words fae a snide copper mooth. Then a tearing, screeching noise, but comin fae *ootside*, n ah look tae the hose wheel, starting tae fuckin buckle under the weight.

I step back ower tae the windae and slam the cunt tight, tae take the strain offay the reel. Then ah'm back tae this Hammy the fuckin hamster cunt; watching his spazzy eyes bulge as he gropes and splutters, swinging and kicking away, but fair play tae the cunt, he's still pittin up a fight.

Hurry up and die, ya fuckin polis bastard!

Ootside ah sees the hose wheel's bending, so ah tries tae push the windae frame's edge even tighter against the rope tae jam it in, n tae relieve the pressure oan it. But then, as ah'm concentrating oan shuttin the windae, there's a creaking and snapping noise fae behind ays. Ah turns tae a huge fuckin crash fae above and the whole fuckin ceiling caves in! The fuckin beam's broken in two, and this cop cunt's oan his hands n knees covered in dust and plaster, scrambling across the flair tae his desk, trying tae pill the noose oaffay his neck. Aw fours, jist like that fuckin hamster! There's no wey I'm gaunny get there before him so ah grab the hose and pull it wi baith hands, tryin tae reel this cunt in like a fish, but thaire's too much slack oan the fuckin rope. He's goat tae his feet n eh's reaching across the desk, fastening one hand oantae the edge ay it, n the other's gaun tae the drawer where I put the gun back ... Ah've goat tension oan the hose now n ah'm tryin tae pull him back ... but ya cunt, eh's goat the fuckin drawer open ...

Ah lits go ay the hose, so the cunt faws forward acroass the desk, but his hand's in the drawer! Ah'm no gaunny git there quick enough, n thaire's nae time tae open the windae so ah dives right through the fucker, shatterin the gless, landin oantae the gress, and I'm oan my feet and fuckin offski, cursing this gammy leg Renton gied ays, as I bombs ower the fuckin yard.

Ah hears a rasping cry and a shot ring oot and ricochet, hitting against the fuckin garage or one ay the other outbuildings. Ah gits roond the corner and thaire's a second shot; thankfully the fucker sounds further away, no that ah'm stallin tae find oot. This place is isolated up here in the woodland hills, which means it's good for what ah planned tae dae, but nae use when it aw goes fuckin tits-up and you're the cunt hunted by a bam wi a fuckin shooter!

The motor's parked on a dirt track windin up the bank, by an overhanging bush. It seems like there's nae pursuit, but ah jump in and get the fuck away, no easin oaf the gas till ah git doon the slip road n oantae the freeway. At first ah worry that this fucker is gaunny grass me right up, but if he does, Mel's tape comes oot, and anywey, it's that cunt's word against mine.

Ah'm cruisin along the freeway, breathin nice and easy, but cursin my bad luck. Fuckin woodworm! Ye think yuv planned for everything, stakin the place oot since fuckin

Christmas! Now aw ah've done is made a dangerous enemy even mair motivated tae take ays doon.

But lookin oan the bright side, ah've just gied masel even mair encouragement tae fuck that cunt right up. It's him or me now. N it's no fuckin well gaunny be me, tell ye that for nowt.

Ah haul in ma breath. Nice n slow. Breathe ...

That's the fuckin game. Suddenly ah feel masel shakin wi laughter. Thinkin aboot that cunt's pus when eh wis gittin throttled by that noose: it wis a fuckin treat! Goat tae enjoy what ye dae: ye dinnae enjoy it, dinnae fuckin dae it.

In the rear-view mirror, the sun's in the background, fawin ower that range ay hills. It's no been such bad day, at least weatherwise. Ye cannae really feel shite for long in this climate.

14

SICK BOY – ALL THAI'D UP

I emerge from the building site at Tottenham Court Road, and a skyward glance shows darkening clouds bunching together. There's a sharp chill in the air, as I dig oot my phones from the inside pocket of my Hugo Boss leather jacket. All messages to be disregarded, except the one from Ben:

Just got here, will get them in.

I've been steadfastly avoiding Edinburgh, but *it* hasn't been avoiding me! I'm ruing that festive day I put the MDMA powder in that self-indulgent, weakling sex case's drink. I couldn't have envisaged that my playful alchemy would have meant fucking months of fielding correspondence from a heartbroken Carlotta and the weasely brothel-keeper Syme.

There is fuck all I can do to bring their boy back from Thailand. Pompous Presbo shit with his fucking round-the-world plane ticket and his career break. *It's something I have to do*, said the prick in his last ludicrous email, before going completely offline. Leaving his missus and son distraught, punishing them for his nefarious misdeeds! What a cunt! I fight through the blocked-off roads into Soho. The IRA or ISIS never created anything like as much chaos and demoralisation in London as the neoliberal planet-rapists with their corporate vanity construction projects. Sure enough, a steady rain is beginning to fall in cold splatters.

My son has asked me to meet him for a drink in a public house of zero repute, a bland haunt of office workers and tourists. It dawns on me that I've spent practically no time with him recently. I'm feeling guilty, as I enter a busy bar. He's already gotten a seat in a corner, where two pints of Stella fizz on a wooden table. We are close to an imitation fire with a low grate. A pleasing smell of polish fills the air.

We exchange greetings and Ben, who looks troubled, suddenly fixes me in a gaze. — Dad, there's something I need to say to you …

— I know, I know, I've been a self-absorbed wanker. I've just had so many things on, this mess back in Scotters, with your uncle freaking out and your aunt being in pieces, it means I've had to –

— This isn't about *you*! Or them! he snaps, like he's at the end of his tether. His neck is red and his eyes glisten.

This startles me. Ben has always been a cool, taciturn lad, more placid Englishman, or even stoical Scot, than tempestuous Italian.

— I told you I was seeing somebody.

— Aye, this wee bird you're knocking off, you sly –

— It's not a *bird* … he pauses, — it's a bloke. I'm gay. I have a boyfriend, and he spits the word out, indicating how he resolves a certain issue I now presume he has to contend regularly with. He's looking at me with a belligerent counter-aggressive set to his chin, as if he expects me tae freak out and gie him the shit he probably got from those cunts in Surrey.

But all I feel is a warm, relieved glow. While I never saw this coming I'm absolutely delighted, as I've always secretly hoped for a gay son. I would have hated to have that hetero-shagger competitive thing that my dad had with me. — Excellent! I sing. — This is great! I've got a gay son! Good on you, bud! I punch his arm.

He looks at me in shock, his brows rising. — You ... you're not upset?

I jab a finger at him. — We're talking gay, totally gay, not bi, right?

— Yeah, I'm only into guys. Not girls at all.

— Brilliant! This is the fucking best news ever! Cheers! I raise my glass in a toast.

He looks flabbergasted, but clinks it with his own. — I thought you'd, well ...

I take a gulp of Stella back, smacking my lips together. — I would probably have been a bit jealous if you were bi, as you'd have more shagging options than me, I explain. — You see, I always wanted tae be bisexual. Could never get it on with men, though. But I do like a lassie to put on a strap-on and give it tae me up the –

Ben starts flapping and cuts me off. — Dad, Dad, I'm delighted you're taking this well, but I don't want to hear all this stuff!

— Fair enough. But it's no skin off my nose; we're Hull v Wasps, different codes, union v. league. You're not likely to bring in some hot wee torpedo-titted vixen, to make me jealous, like I did with my father. What about the Surrey people?

— Mum is pretty upset, while Gran is just inconsolable. She can barely bring herself to look at me, he says, genuinely saddened.

I shake my head slowly in disgust, as old bile, dredged up, ferments in my gut. *Fuckin old boiler. Wisnae shy aboot taking a Jocko-Eyetie portion, back on that Tuscan holiday, yet would deny her first grandchild the same pleasure.* — Fuck those bigots: it's the twenty-first century. I don't care who you shag, as long as you shag with a vengeance!

His face lights up at that one. — Oh we do. In every conceivable way. I'm moving into his flat in Tufnell Park, and already the neighbours have been complaining about the noise!

— That's my boy, and I punch his arm affectionately again. — Right, you fucking raving arse bandit, up to that bar and make mine a double Macallan's!

He complies and we both end up in a bit of a state. My son is gay! What a fucking blessing!

As I'm on my way home in a cab, I look at my phone and there's a text from Victor Syme:

Get your arse up here. I've found your boy.

What the fuck? Either Syme wants me urgently, or Euan really has returned to Edinburgh. A year of absence my hairy hole, he's only been away a few months! I type a response:

Euan McCorkindale is in Edinburgh?!

Aye. Get your arse up here.

Jumping on a shuttle first thing in the morning. See you.

A reply from that maggot would have been too gracious.

15

SHAGGING HOORS WILL NOT BRING YOU PEACE

He realises that he hasn't dodged the lines between the paving stones since he was a child. Now he's avoiding them in an even stride, enjoying the rhythm of his feet on the cold slab. The brogues: always a good stout shoe for this sort of weather. Trainers – those incubators of foot disease – not so much. He's lost count of the number of times he's told Ross not to constantly wear them. The strange dislocation he feels, that sense of being completely in touch with *the other*, one of the multitude of alternative characters we repress in order to complete our chosen daily life; it makes him sick and giddy with fear and exhilaration. To walk this familiar city as a man without a home is just like walking new streets in a new world.

On his return to Edinburgh, he got a new phone and email address. He wanted to call Carlotta, but couldn't face the further humiliation of having only been able to stick less than four months in Thailand, after his declaration that he would be away for a year. At first he felt fabulous out there. He was free. The break, the new place, and Naiyana, the girl he'd taken up with. But the novelty quickly wore off, supplanted by an emotional downer. He missed Carlotta and Ross, craved the order of his old life. Now he is home.

Euan McCorkindale doesn't know at this stage whether or not he will return to his podiatrist duties at the Royal

Infirmary following his career break. Everything is still up for grabs. After checking into the cheapish-but-clean budget chain hotel on the Grassmarket, his next move was to reset the Tinder app on his new phone.

And then he's off onto the streets and into a cafe, sitting opposite Holly, thirty-four, recently divorced, two kids. She says she doesn't want anything 'too serious' at this point in time. Euan finds he's augmenting himself in such encounters, not necessarily lying – women generally find his career as a podiatrist quirkily interesting enough – but adding to himself, pushing his parameters further. He once took Spanish classes with Carlotta in preparation for a holiday. After the event, he was keen to continue, but she didn't see the point. That tuition will be resumed and from now on he will be self-describing as a *Spanish speaker*. And although he's only played a few times with a colleague from work, he is designating himself a *squash player*. Life is about perceptions, of the self as well as others. You can either sell yourself short or claim something, own it, and grow into it.

Holly is a strong prospect, but Euan leaves her an hour and twenty minutes later, with nothing more than a peck on the cheek. *Never give it up right away, if they're worth fucking more than once, keep them waiting for it. Then slam the very fucking soul out of them, leave them wanting more.* To his complete dismay, Simon Williamson's oddly restrained words resonate in his ear. *This psychotic pig is still guiding me! Marianne was right!*

Euan's spirits sink further, despite re-emerging onto brighter, warming streets. Summer is digging in, Scotland's most anticipated guest, who generally arrives late and is usually the first to leave. Euan was uncertain of where he was going but he instantly knows when he gets there. It's where he was yesterday, a building down a side street with an orange sign that says TOUCHY FEELY SAUNA AND MASSAGE.

Thankfully Jasmine, whom he visited the previous evening, is working her shift again. This time she takes him to what she describes as the 'special suite for preferred customers'. It certainly seems impressive enough. There is no bed, just piles of giant red cushions of all shapes and sizes strewn over a floor with indented lights. There's a big TV set on one wall and, most theatrically, a red velvet curtain on the other. The cushions, though decorated with gold lace trimmings, are designed to facilitate various sexual positions; some are wedged, others rectangular, and Jasmine is skilled at the configurations they offer. Euan is excited, yet senses that something is off in her performance. He finds Jasmine tense and wary, her distracted eyes tinged with trepidation, a contrast to the highly engaged, cheerful and performative woman who serviced him yesterday in the less salubrious chamber. He wonders if it is bad protocol to visit the same girl two days in a row; if it marks him in her eyes as desperate, damaged or sleazy. Then he's aware of another presence in the room. He turns to see a man in a suit, his face hard and weaselly, all sharp angles, standing over them. Sweating, the man rubs at his neck with a hanky, although it isn't hot. Euan realises that he's been behind the red curtain, which is open, indicating a small, recessed stage. — What's … what is this …? and he ceases his activity. He looks from Jasmine to the menacing interloper.

— Sorry to interrupt, but we have enough for a special VIP tape. The man points to a security camera above the door, its red eye blinking. He hadn't even seen it.

— What's going on? Euan looks at Jasmine, who can't meet his eyes. As he dismounts her, she rolls away and promptly shrinks out of the room.

186

— Doctor Who? Welcome tae the Tardis. The man flashes a direful, violating smile. — I'm the owner of these premises. The name's Syme. Victor Syme.

— What do you want? Is this how you run a business –

— I want you tae go and see your brother-in-law. Up at the City Cafe in Blair Street. In half an hour. He'll tell you all you need tae know.

The podiatrist is chopped to the quick by the sneering certainty of this man. Deathly still, it's his piercing green eyes that do the real talking. In an attempt to grab some control of the situation, Euan finds his professional voice. — But why are you taping me? What's it got to do with Simon?

— I don't like repeating myself, Doc. If you make me do it again, you'd best use your inside knowledge and tell me now exactly which A&E unit you would prefer to be taken to, Syme says, so cold and inanimate. — One more time: the City Cafe in Blair Street. Now go.

Held fast in a vice of his own silence, the naked podiatrist pulls on his clothes. All the time, he feels the pimp's eyes on him, and is relieved to get outside.

On his way up to the City Cafe, Euan's brain is a riot of confusion. The violent knot in his gut tells him that this latest disaster has made an already-terrible situation interminably more perilous. His certainty is that this is a blackmail scenario. The concept of forgiveness from Carlotta is like an elusive radio frequency which his mind tunes in to and out of. One minute totally dead, the next blaring beautiful, infinite possibilities at him. The confusion of international travel followed by the ambivalence of the last few days, on Tinder and in the saunas, that incessant veering between elation and despair; it now merely seems training for this new horror, which has yet to fully unravel.

I should have stayed on the year's career break, travelled round the world, whoring my heart out. Why did I come back?

187

But indulging his baser instincts only seemed to make matters worse. *Or maybe go back to work*, he considers, *rent a flat, be a dutiful weekend dad to Ross, and live as a single shagger*, the life that he obviously felt, beneath the threshold of consciousness, was groundlessly denied him. Even with Syme's intervention and this horrific tape, the latter still seems the most rational course of action.

But there is Carlotta, his beautiful Carra … though he's burnt his boats there, surely. Erred fatally. Neither his wife nor his son could un-see those horrible, perverse images. They sickened even him, the loose skin on his arms, the sack of flesh across his lower gut, his beady, budgerigar eyes. Then he vanished for months off the face of the earth. And now they might be seeing even more, the model husband and father with a prostitute!

And fucking Simon!

He steps into the City Cafe, enraged as he sees, sitting at a table in the corner, the man who has occasioned all this torment and twisted liberation. Simon David Williamson looks up at him with a sad smile. He has an Americano coffee, turning the large cup in his hands, never taking his eyes off Euan.

— What the fuck is going on, Simon? Why are you here?

— Carlotta asked me to find you, Simon Williamson says.

— I've been coming back up here every fucking weekend, he exaggerates, — when I should be running my fucking business. Colleagues London and, potentially, Colleagues Manchester. Not Colleagues Edinburgh. You know why? Because I haven't fucking set up a Colleagues Edinburgh … He cuts himself short as he seems to really see Euan for the first time. — You look gey shelpit, he says, surprising himself with his couthie Scots affectation.

— I've been travelling, he says, unable to stifle a sad groan in his voice. — How are Carlotta and Ross?

— You fuck off to Thailand, and don't call them. Disappear off the fucking face of the globe. How the fuck do you think they are?

Euan hangs his head in miserable shame.

— Fucking hooring over there and doing the very same back here, I'll wager.

Euan glances up at Simon. In his brother-in-law's eyes he sees himself as old and depleted, pathetic and wretched. — And now your friend Syme has fucking filmed me with a prostitute!

Simon Williamson looks around, casting a sour eye on the premises and its patrons. The City Cafe hasn't changed, but it now seems long past its cool heyday and the clientele has aged with it. He waves his phone. — First, he's *not* my friend, he emphatically states. — But yes, he took great delight in telling me. I had asked him to look out for you, but I didn't think you'd be so daft. Or that he'd stoop so low. I overestimated you both. You should have stayed the fuck in Thailand.

— What do you mean?

— I mean you fucked up badly. A gentleman is always discreet. And this life, Euan, it isn't you …

— Well, it obviously is, as it's the one I'm leading.

Williamson's eyebrows rise. — Yes, so I've heard from Syme, the proverbial horse's mouth on these matters. To paraphrase James McAvoy as Charles Xavier in *X-Men: First Class*, 'Shagging hoors will not bring you peace, my friend.'

Euan meets his brother-in-law's stare with a cold, implacable one of his own. — To paraphrase Michael Fassbender as Magneto's reply, 'Not shagging hoors was never an option.'

Sick Boy cackles loudly and rocks back in the chair. — Fuck me, I've created a Frankenstein's monster here, he says, then leans forward, putting his elbows on the table, resting his head on his fists and letting his tone assume gravity. — I

189

never thought I'd utter these words in a million years, but for God's sake, think of your wife and kid.

— That's what I've been doing. It's why I couldn't stay in Thailand. I need to see them ...

— But?

— But I'm coming to terms with the sort of man I really am and I'm thinking that they are far better off without me. I've had those desires for years. The difference is that I'm now acting on them.

— That's a big difference. That's the *crucial* difference. So stop all the proddy bullshit.

— I don't think I can stop seeing other women now. Euan shakes his head sadly. — Something has been unleashed.

Williamson looks around the premises again. A DJ whom he recalls playing lots of cool shit back in the day now sits slaughtered at the bar, a semi-jakey, slavering about the pomp of Pure, Sativa, the Citrus Club and the Calton Studios to a bored, younger barman. — Do what we Catholics do.

— What's that?

— Lie. Be a fucking hypocrite, Williamson shrugs. — I never rattled as many women in my life as I did when I was married to Ben's mother. Rode the mother-in-law, the wee sister, banjoed the fucking maid of honour on the night before the wedding; the whole shebang, for fuck sakes! I'd have rammed the old boy if he'd had a fanny. If I had my way I would have drugged that cunt, given him a gender reassignment operation, had him ganting on it, then made him my bitch and treated him atrociously, he declares, visibly warming to the thought.

Euan finds himself sharing guilty laughter, surely a measure of how far he's fallen, before he reflects in sad resignation, — My life is a mess ...

— Listen, mate, you have to go back and try to make amends.

— It's not possible. You saw the video. You witnessed her reaction. Her fury was beyond incandescent. She was totally broken and completely disillusioned, Euan whines, refusing to drop his voice, even though two couples have sat down at the table next to them. Foam spills from the ripped leather seats between them.

— She was in shock, ya radge, Simon declares. — People are adaptable. I'm not saying you're her pin-up boy and she's coming round a hundred per cent, but she needs to see you. It's been months. She's had time to process it all.

This observation provides Euan with a smidgen of comfort.
— Yes, he concedes, — I can see that.

— Well?

— Well, what?

— Do you want to return to normal family life?

— Well, yes.

— But still shag around on the side?

Euan reaches into his heart. Trembling, he looks at Simon. Nods grimly. — But thanks to your friend Syme, the first is no longer an option.

— We certainly can't let Carlotta see that video, Simon says. — Or it's over, and he passes his phone to Euan, who is stunned to see an image of himself, having sex with Jasmine in the sauna, only thirty minutes ago.

— How did you –

— Technology will kill us all. Williamson screws his face up, as if in edgy recall. — I can get Syme to erase those videos. But you need to work with me. That means doing him a wee favour. If not, he puts this shit online and not just Carlotta and Ross, and her friends and his classmates, but all your colleagues and patients will see this. They will form an opinion as to the type of man you are. A one-off mistake is one thing; a serial philanderer and pervert, exhibitionist hoor-monger is something else.

Euan wallows in his despair. The images with Marianne were devastating for the family. But this stuff the world would see. The credibility he's built up over the years would be trashed and he would be humiliated in his profession, a laughing stock and a pariah ... He struggles to make sense of the nightmare. — How? Why? Why me? What does Syme want with *me*?

His brother-in-law swivels his eyes around the bar, and sighs. — It was my fault. I was looking for you, at Carlotta's request, and I took that Christmas picture around the saunas. Syme heard about this, came after me, and was curious about what I wanted with you. He obviously thought I was the polis at first, then perhaps some kind of grass. I told him the situation and let slip that you had medical skills, at which point he suddenly took an interest. Then you vanish off the map for months, and I have to deal with the hassle from this murderous buffoon, who fucking well thinks we're both at it. Then you come back and he rumbles you rifling one of his Roger Moores in the sauna. Bang to rights.

— He ... this Syme character, he wants me to *look at his feet*?

— He has a job for you. Simon Williamson notes a swaggering posse of lads enter the bar. He puts on a Wild West frontier accent. — Some kinda doctorin work, I'm supposin. With Euan evidently unmoved, he adds abruptly, — That is as much as I know.

— But I fail to see how – how can *you* do this to me?! This is blackmail! We're family!

Simon Williamson's features seem to turn to cold stone. He speaks in a clipped, staccato rhythm. — Let me make one thing clear: you are *not* being blackmailed by me. For both our sakes, I wish that were the case. We are *both* being fucked over by a very dangerous cunt indeed. You should not have gone to the saunas, Euan. I would have set you up with a tasty wee bit of –

— It's your set-ups that have ruined my fucking life already!

— Look, we both fucked up. Simon suddenly slaps his own forehead. — We can point fingers at each other till the cows come home, or we can try and sort it. I'm suggesting the latter course of action. If you disagree, feel the fuck free to have this argument with yourself. I'm off.

Euan is silent in the face of Simon Williamson's cold logic.

— It's broken, but it can be fixed.

— What do you want me to do?

— *I* don't want you to do anything. But this cunt, and I use the term advisedly, he apparently needs your medical skills. What for, I can't even imagine.

Euan contemplates his brother-in-law. — What sort of world are you mixed up in? What kind of a person are you?

Simon Williamson looks at him in injured disdain. — I'm as desperate as you, and I've been pulled into this world by you shagging about!

— You gave me that fucking drink spiked with MDMA! Your drugs started –

— Fuck you and your First World problems! If every cunt that had taken their first ecky committed adultery by jacksie-rifling the first psycho fucker who smiled at them, not one worthwhile relationship in Britain would still exist! Either you man the fuck up and we sort this shite out, or everything, your family, your job, your reputation, are all down the fucking swanny!

Euan sits trembling in the seat. His hand fastens around the glass of vodka and tonic. He downs it in a oner. Asks Williamson, — What do I have to do?

16

OUT OF THE SHADOWS

For some time anonymous shapes and shadows, their identities almost but not quite discernable, have haunted Danny Murphy. They swagger out of Leith Walk's pubs for cigarettes, sprawl in duos or groups to the next howf, or stare out as menacing smudges from behind dirty bus windows. His heart jumps beats in anticipation as echoing footsteps in the stair outside intensify, only to die out on the floor below, or slap past his door bound for the top-floor flats. But as the days roll by, he finds himself reacting less. The unlikely scenarios of comfort he's formulated and magnified start to achieve dominion in his mind. Perhaps the biker crashed and the box somehow opened, and it was presumed that had ruined the kidney. Maybe he was in the clear.

One evening, all this changes. Indoors with the dog, watching TV, he hears the familiar steps on the stair. This time there is something about them, perhaps their weight or rhythm, that indicates a dread purpose. This sense is shared by Toto, who looks poignantly up at his master and lets out a sad, barely audible whine. Danny Murphy sheds a skin, and he almost breathes a sigh of relief at the bang on the door, which he opens up to the inevitability of Mikey Forrester. — Mikey, he says.

Forrester's face has been pulled an inch south. His hands are clasped together in front of him. — You fucked this one up big time. You've cost my partner, Victor Syme, a great deal of money and –

As if on cue, a man pushes past Mikey, who, in timid deference, gives way for him. Whereas Mikey is all performance, Victor Syme carries an overwhelming air of reptilian menace, speaking with the certainty of a man already privy to the conversation he is about to have. — You, he points at Spud, — you tried tae take the fuckin pish!

— Ah'm sorry, man, Spud desperately blurts out, taking a backward step, as Forrester slides in and shuts the door behind them, — it wis an accident, likes. The dug knocked ower the ice boax and ate the kidney! Ah jist pure panicked, ay, but ah'll make it up tae ye –

— For fuckin sure, Victor Syme says, before turning to Forrester. — So this is the boy you vouched for. He struts down the hallway, scanning its squalor in disgust. — A fuckin jakey.

— Tae be honest, ah didnae ken he'd fallen on such hard times, Vic, I thought –

— Shut the fuck up, Mikey. Syme dismisses Forrester with a raised hand, closing his eyes, as if not trusting himself to even look at his supposed business partner.

Mikey's plummet into screaming silence sets off a sickening confirmation deep inside Spud that this isn't going to end well. Victor Syme moves towards him, seeming to glide as if on castors, and ushers him over to the window. — Nice view. He gazes outside to street activity barely visible through the grime on the panes.

— Eh, aye … Spud says, his head bobbing and jerking. Blood pours from the side of his mouth. He sees Syme register it. — It's aw the speed, ah need it tae distract ays fae the peeve.

— Aye, no such a nice view in here, the brothel-keeper smiles, looking at an implausible stack of old Pot Noodle containers.

— Ah ken that Pot Noodles urnae good for ye and ah shouldnae be eatin thum –

— Nonsense, you've got everything ye need in them. Chinese folk live for ages. He turns to Mikey. — Think ay the Master in *Kung Fu*.

— Ah suppose thaire is that, Spud smiles wanly.

— What dae ye see oot there, mate? Syme asks, attempting to envision what it would be like occupying the mind of a man like Daniel Murphy, trying to comprehend how it would feel to see the world through his hollowed, veering squirrel eyes. This exercise fills him with corrosive distaste and a sense that obliterating such weakness would constitute a service to humankind. He puts one arm around Spud's thin, trembling shoulder as he smoothly slips a cosh out of his pocket with his free hand.

— Ah dunno … likesay buildins and shoaps n that …

In one violent predatory movement, Victor Syme jumps back and batters Danny Murphy over the head. Mikey Forrester, forced to bear witness, cringes in guilt and revulsion as the assailant hisses through clenched teeth, — What do ye see now?!

Spud howls out in a primal shriek, overwhelmed by a surge of nausea and the most terrible pain, as if his skull is cracking open, like a nail is being driven into the centre of his brain. This thankfully only lasts for a couple of seconds, and he feels his own vomit spill from him, as the floor ascends to meet him.

Toto starts to yelp, and then licks at Spud's head. Mikey's face takes on a rubicund flush, his bottom lip trembling. Spud's rolling eyes have receded into his skull, his breath emitting in soft but audible pants. Syme picks up the dog, who whines in misery. — Never was much ay a dug man, he says to Mikey, whose countenance is now a funereal grey.

*

A red velvet curtain dominates the largest suite in the basement premises that Victor Syme uses for his trade. The rest of the windowless room, uplit by a series of floor-mounted spotlights, is festooned with scarlet cushions, bordered with gold lace. These litter a sandblasted floor of varnished timbers. One other feature of the room: a large flat-screen television, fixed on a wall.

A handset held by Victor Syme snaps the images on the screen dead. The proprietor has just played Euan McCorkindale the video of him engaged in sexual congress with Jasmine, forcing him to view it in silent purgatory. — Why make me watch that? the podiatrist groans.

— Tae bring home tae ye, dear Doctor, Syme's slimy fake Morningside tea-room accent making Euan shudder, — that you are in fucking shit street. Well, Doc, you can get out of it, if you play your cards right.

Euan can't arrest his returning drift to a deep, beaten silence.

Sick Boy, sitting in the corner, his perusing of the video punctuated by the odd disdainful sigh that added insult to Euan's injuries, suddenly rises. — Great. Well, I'll just head off and allow you fine fellows to negotiate your own deal, as my services are now superfluous.

A shaky plea tears from Euan's throat, — You can't leave –

— Aw naw, you wait here, Syme snaps in accord. — Ah've heard aw aboot you, mate. You take ownership ay this problem, he demands of Sick Boy. — Ah found yir brother-in-law here.

— Aye, but now you're blackmailing him. So I'd say we're even.

— Disnae work that wey. Syme almost presents himself as a reluctant enforcer of oppressive rules devised by another party. — Youse need tae square this wi your sis, he looks at Sick Boy, — and your wife. Euan is treated to a creeping, diseased wink. — And yis urnae gaunny dae that wi this vid in circulation.

— Please ... how much do you want for it? Euan pleads.

— Shhh, Victor Syme urges. — Your bro-in-law understands this world, Doc. You're a fuckin tourist here.

— Fuck off, Sick Boy says defiantly, — I don't work for you.

— Oh yes you do, Syme sings, Christmas-panto style, drawing open the velvet curtain behind them. It reveals, hung upside down, a bound and gagged Spud Murphy.

Sick Boy gasps and takes a step back.

– Now it's up to you two. Syme's tongue darts across thin, bloodless lips. — Youse can walk oot ay here. But if yis do it's endy story for this boy.

Euan's head jerks back. — I haven't got a clue who that is.

Then Victor Syme waves the embossed Colleagues business card, the one he removed from Spud's pocket, forcing Simon Williamson to admit, in a pappy voice, — I do.

— But you'll get to know him, Doc, Victor Syme's lofty tone pledges to Euan, as his pasty, noxious smirk freezes the souls of both brothers-in-law. – Oh aye, you will get tae know him most intimately. Because right now you have work tae dae.

17

SPUD – UNSUPERVISED MEAT

Ah'm walkin through this graveyard but it's aw covered in mist. Ah kin see heidstanes, but no make oot anything oan them. Toto's lying doon by a grave, his wee paws ower his eyes, like he's greetin. Ah go acroass n try tae talk tae him but he doesnae move they paws. Ah read the inscription on the stane. DANIEL MURPHY ...

Aw man ...

Then Toto's paws go doon n ah see it isnae him, it's a demon wi a reptile heid n it's lookin right at ays ...

Ah turns tae run n these radges wi big bulbous faces grab ays n one slams a chib intae ma gut ...

NAWWWWW!!!!!

When ah comes to, it's pure like the bad dream's still gaun oan, cause it's naewhaire ah've been before, yit still sortay ken, but ah kin hardly breathe. A sharp smell ay pish tickles ma nostrils. Ah huv tae fight through this pain, and a seek feelin in ma gut, tae make ma napper obey basic commands. *Keep they blurry eyes open. Git that chokin tongue offay the roof ay the mooth ...*

Aw man ... ah'm in a bed n shiverin like a kitten. Ma eyes are bleary like thir fill ay gunge n ah keep blinkin n the vision finally pills intae focus. Thaire's a plasma bag on a metal stand, wi a tube coming fae it ...

What the fuck, man ...

I can hardly believe that this tube's gaunny lead intae ma boady, even if ma brain's sayin it's a cast-iron cert! Ah lift up the thin covers n trace the tube under thum, tae track it gaun intae a bandage in the side ay ma stomach. Ah jump up in shock. Ah'm seek and sair and ah raise ma heid, tryin tae gain mair focus. Thaire's stale lime-green waws, painted over auld patterned wallpaper that shows through. A stained maroon carpet. The room is pure seventies, a time warp ay aw the bedsits and shabby flats that have been the stages for aw the dramas ay the boy Murphy's life ...

That sickening feeling in ma tremblin boady: aw man, that's awfay familiar. The air aw rank n fusty.

Ah hears a coughin n ah suddenly realises that thaire's other cats in the room! Mikey Forrester's there, so is that Victor Syme boy. Ah think he banjoed ays. That evil pus, man, it pure fills the room. — You ruined ma property. Destroyed it. Made it fuckin worthless.

— It wis an accident ... ah find my voice, still croaking aw sair like ah've gargled broken gless. — What have you done ...?

Syme looks at Mikey, then at two other gadges whae step forward ootay the shadows. One's Sick Boy! The other yin's the boy ah saw when ah wis hingin upside doon, aw trussed up. — Si! What happened? ah'm raspin. — What happened, Si?!

Sick Boy comes forward wi a gless ay water. — Here, Danny, drink this, pal. He helps ays sit up n huds it tae ma mooth. The tepid water seems tae roll ower the caked slime and scum in ma gob n throat. His beak twitches, n ah ken it's cause ay ma breath. — Slowly, he says.

— I'll leave you tae fill him in wi the details, Syme sais tae Sick Boy, and heads fir the door. Eh turns the handle and pulls it open, but stoaps n looks at Forry. — And get the rest ay this sorted oot! It's on you, Mikey. Dinnae disappoint me again.

Mikey goes tae say something, but the cat's words seem tae stick in his craw, just like mine, as Syme swaggers out ay the room.

Ah'm fuckin shitein masel, n ah pushes the beaker away. This isnae right. No at aw. *N whaire's the dug?* — Si ... Mikey ... what happened? ah goes.

Sick Boy n Mikey look at each other. Sick Boy stands back n Mikey shrugs n goes, — Syme wanted payback for the kidney you'd ruined, so he felt he was entitled tae take one ay yours.

Ah touch the bandaged wound. Look at the tube. — Naw ...

— It was either that, or, Sick Boy runs his hand ower his throat, — Finito. It took aw ay our joint powers ay persuasion, believe me. He looks tae Mikey. — He'll tell ye!

— Aye, Mikey nods. — Ye were very lucky that Syme thoat he had a recipient that matched ye. It's goat tae match, see?

— Whaaaat ... Ah dinnae believe this! Ah try tae sit up proper, but ma whole boady is in pain n ah've nae strength in ma airms ...

— Shhh, dinnae distress yourself, mate, Sick Boy sort ay coos, easing ays back doon intae the bed, makin ays sip mair water. — It was removed by Euan here, eh nods at the other gadge, — who is my brother-in-law, Carlotta's man, and a qualified doctor. You were in the best possible hands, buddy boy!

Ah'm just glarin at this boy, but eh cannae look ays in the eye. Eh's just shuffling aboot, eyes shiftin fae flair tae waws. Ah raises ma hand and points at um. — You, you took ma kidney? In here? Ah looks around at the pure squalor. — You're a butcher!

— I've been dragged down a sewer, the boy sais, shakin his heid, but it's no like he's talkin tae anybody. — I only went out for a fucking drink at Christmas, on my *birthday* ...

201

— IT'S YOUR FAULT! ah screams, pointin at Mikey, and then Sick Boy. — Youse two! Supposed tae be mates! Supposed tae be ma-hay-haytes … n ah feel the tears streamin doon ma face …

This is like, fucked …

Mikey turns away in shame, but no Sick Boy. Aw naw, no him. — That's right, blame me! That cunt Syme was gaunny kill us all! I only got roped intae this because he wanted revenge and payback after *you* cost him thirty grand with that kidney! IT'S FUCK ALL TAE DAE WI ME! He pummels his ain chist in outrage, as his eyes protrude and his Adam's aypil bobs. — NANE AY IT!

— Ah didnae ken … ah goes, — … it wis the dug, ah mean it wisnae his fault, jist an animal … didnae understand …

— What were you thinking, taking the fucking dug with you?! Leaving meat, unsupervised, wi a *dug*?

— Wisnae meant tae go doon like this, Spud, n Forrester backs Sick Boy up. — You sais nowt aboot bringing yir daft wee dug oan the trip.

— Ah couldnae git anybody tae look eftir him, my voice screeches oot. Then ah gits a surge ay pure fear n ah'm lookin aroond, in panic. — Where is he? Whaire's Toto?!

— He's fine, Sick Boy goes.

— WHAIRE?!

— Syme has him at one ay the saunas. The lassies are dug-sittin. They'll be spoiling him, taking him oot for walks.

— Ye cannae leave a perr wee dug wi that cruel bastard! He'd better no hurt Toto!

— Toto's insurance, Mikey goes.

— For what? For what?! What ye sayin, Mikey?!

Mikey says nowt but looks at Sick Boy, whae raises his palms. — It was me, well, me and Mikey here, that convinced

202

him to spare us wi this eye for an eye thing. It took some daein, that cunt is a fucking animal. His heid weaves fae side tae side, then he breks intae a smile. — But, throughout this fucking mess, there's at least some good news!

Ah cannae believe this. — What? What's good aboot this?!

— The kidney Shictor Schlime took, Sick Boy goes in that annoyin Bond voice, like it's aw a joke, — for a client … it turns out that it was incompatible with his recipient after all.

— What … ye mean it didnae need tae come oot?! Ah hear ma ain voice, whimperin. — Yis took it oot fir nowt!

— Aye, but it can go back in again.

— Where … where is it?

— Back in Berlin. Sick Boy reaches intae his jaykit and pills oot some plane tickets, hudin them in ma face. — So we need to fly there, post-haste, and get you refitted. You'll be as good as new, apart fae the Mars bar.

— As good as new, ah'm mutterin aw tae masel in misery, as Sick Boy shares a raised eyebrow with Mikey Forrester and this doaktir boy Euan turns away, sayin something under his breath ah dinnae catch.

— What's he sayin? Ah points at him. — What's yir doaktir boy sayin?!

The Euan felly turns n goes, — It's crucial to move quickly.

Ah just groan, aw feverish n seek. Ah'm burnin in hell here, man. Ah feel that ill, ah ken ah'm no gaunny make it oantae that plane tae Berlin.

18

SICK BOY – ALL ABOARD THE RENFREW FERRY

I accompany a furrowed-browed Euan back to his hotel, issuing the caution, — Nae hooring tonight, bud, plenty feather and flip, a big day the morn.

He departs, ghoulish and jerky, to the lift and his lonely room in silence. I head back to the McCorkindales' sprawling well-appointed Colinton villa, *sans* the man of the house. Crackers Carra is giving me a hard time, her saucer eyes protruding as if the lids have been ripped off, her jaw grinding fiercely, her pus reminding me of the time I ran into her and her mates at Rezerection. Fuck me, how long ago was that? — But how do you ken he's back? Have ye seen him?

— No, I fib, deciding that telling her would only compromise an already-desperate enterprise. — But he's definitely been sighted, by reliable sources.

— Who? Tell me who's seen him!

— A few people. He was in my mate Terry's cab. I spin another *harmless wee* white lie. — Coming out the Filmhouse. Look, that's why I'm here, to find him.

A matt finish to her popping lamps shows me that Carlotta is doped up on something or other. Her black hair is greasy and shows grey roots, something she'd never tolerate before. — This is tearin us apart … she pleads, in a voice like a coffin creaking open.

— Look, you're stressed, go and lie doon.

Her lip curls south and she bursts intae tears. I take her in my arms and she collapses like a puppet with the strings cut. I have to practically carry her up the stairs and put her to bed, kissing her sweated brow. — I'm on it, sis, I tell her. Although drug-stunned, Carlotta still has a face on her like a well-skelped bahooky and glances at me from under the duvet like a small, cornered animal, as if ramping up for some aggro. I'm happy to make my escape. Why the drama? Fuck me, she's still a fine-looking woman who will get paired up easily. She'll get the hoose, and child support for the boy, till he leaves home with a good degree to secure exciting work in the retail sector. Then she can downsize and get a comfy pad and a young lover, with perhaps the annual lumb-sweeping sex-tourist holiday in Jamaica flung in, just tae keep the buck on his toes.

As I get downstairs Ross immediately ambushes me, his imploring eyes igniting through a forest of spots. Every time I see him, the wee bastard asks me when he's getting his hole. If the laws of natural selection were properly applied, he'd remain a virgin for life. Like Renton should have done. *This is what I get for fucking with nature.* — You sais the next time you were up!

Saved by the bell! The phone goes, and I wave him into silence, taking my call out in the garden. Talk about timely! Syme's at least had the decency to offer to help me with this issue. — Your wee problem is soon going to be sorted, he declares as I go behind the shed, away from the prying eyes of the hapless wee runt staring out through the windae at me.

— Thank you, Vic, I tell the pus bag, as I shiver in the cold, — but let me get back to you. I might be able to complete the job in-house. I'm a little out of the Edinburgh scene, but I still have an address book I can work, I declare, as the meaty-titted hoor from next door flings open a back-bedroom windae, allowing Tiffany's 'I Think We're Alone Now' to spill out into the air. Is this a come-on?

I sniff the creosote on the hut as Syme growls something indecipherable. It could have been scorn or tribute; I know not and care less.

So I succumb to my debt of honour. I've got Ross in a cab – not Terry's, the man has zero discretion where other people's sexual affairs are concerned – and we're heading for the same hotel Rents used, where I book a room online and call Jill to meet us there.

We wait for a bit before she appears in a wrap-around pencil skirt, black-and-white-striped top and bobbed haircut with purplish-black lippy. I intro them, and Ross's eyes have a hard-on, but she's underwhelmed to the point of disgust.

— No fucking way, she says, pulling me aside and hissing in my ear, — he's not a businessman!

Ross does look like a pizza-faced prepubescent Aled Jones on meeting his new adoptive parents, Fred and Rose West. — He's a prodigy, a youthful high-flyer: a sort of junior William Hague at the Tory Party Conference type of character.

— I'm no a paedophille, she snaps, as Ross's lips tremble.

— Lassies can't be nonces, I tell her. — It's no like there's a beastesses' wing at Cornton Vale. You'd just be popping the boy's Renfrew Ferry. A social service, really.

— Fuck off …

— C'mon, babe … unprofessional behaviour, I tell her, as poor wee Pitch and Toss's eyes flick from me to her.

— Aye, on your part. I thought Colleagues was a high-end escort agency, no about daft wee bairns wanting laid, and she turns on those high heels and heads off.

— Fair enough, I tell her retreating figure, — we can work something out, but she's no listening. She is so fucking out ay there.

So I'm compelled to dive back into the swamp, and take Syme up on his offer. It's the only way to shut wee squeaky baws up. Ironically, he sends Jasmine along to the hotel, the very bird that did Ross's old man. I suppose there's a certain symmetrical poetry to it all!

Jasmine looks Ross over. He's like a refugee being shown to his dormitory in Auschwitz.

— Gonna leave you guys alone for a bit, I grin.

Ross goes to say something, but Jasmine takes his hand.
— It's okay, honey. Tell me about yourself.

This lassie has got the goods. I split and hit the bar downstairs.

Well, thirty-five minutes later, as I'm just about halfway through my third Stella and the *Guardian*, Jasmine comes down alone. — He's sorted, she says. — He's just getting dressed.

— Great, I tell her, slipping her another twenty over and above the agreed tariff. She looks at me in mild disappointment before she departs. If I'd gied her a hundred, I'd have gotten the exact same look. I didn't have the heart to tell her it was the son of the guy she made the sex tape with, whom her boss is now blackmailing.

Pitch and Toss arrives downstairs a few minutes later, very dazed and confused. I swear it's as if his face has been steeped overnight in a vat of Clearasil. The pus seems to have been sucked out his spots like the spunk from his baws.

— Job done?

He nods blankly, stuffing his hands into the pocket of his hoodie.

I get him outside, down George IV Bridge, and we take a stroll across the Meadows. It's a beautiful spring day. — So how did it go, pal?

— It was okay ... no like I thought but. I was nervous at first, but then she started kissing me and then ... his eyes light up as his voice drops and he glances over to a football game, — ... she sooked my cock. She said it was really big!

I'll bet she did.

— When I sort of ... got it ... more up than in, really, she said that she couldnae believe it was ma first time, that I was a natural!

I'll bet she did.

The sun is hotting things up, burning off the meagre cloud cover. It's now more like summer. I pull some Ray-Bans out my pocket and stick them on. Ross havers in unbridled enthusiasm. — That she couldnae believe how good it felt for her, and that ah made her come, he squeals, turning to me, wide-eyed, looking for confirmation, as a woman passes us pushing a pram. — That ah really knew how tae make love tae a lassie and ah would give any girl the time ay her life!

Jesus fuck, whatever Syme is paying this yin isnae enough!

— Did she get ye licking her oot?

Ross's jaw seems to spasm a little, as if in muscle memory. – Aye, he blushes, — she showed me that bit that's sort ay at the top ay the fanny. Ye never hear aboot that in the online sites.

— You're going on the wrong ones, I tell him. — Fuck that dude stuff. Try lesbian sites instead. Here's a tip: there are three keys tae being a good lover: fanny-licking, fanny-licking and fanny-licking. Tip two: surround yourself with women, women and more fucking women. Work with them. Become a hairdresser, a bingo caller, a cleaner, do those sorts of jobs. Shagging is a disease of association. Tip three: don't speak; just listen to them. If you do speak, ask politely about *them*, what *they* think of this or that. As he goes to comment, I wave a silencing finger. — Just listen. Tip four: don't go near other guys; they are the fucking useless stupid enemy. They are *not* your brothers. They are *not* your mates. They

208

are obstacles at best. They will teach you less than nothing, and get in your way with their fucking stupid pish.

I watch him trying to take this in.

Fuck me, that Jasmine is getting so poached for Edinburgh Colleagues.

We stop off at a store and to his delight I buy him some decent trainers. — The cover story for your mamma, when she asks you where we were. And also a reward for being a top shagger. I give him a playful nudge.

— Thanks, Uncle Simon, squeaks the dazed Colinton gigolo.

When we return to the ranch, Carlotta is up and we tell her about the trainer shopping. But she's still going on about Euan, lost in her own despair. This problem will hopefully be sorted out soon. I check my phone. Sure enough, there's an email from Syme with an e-ticket in the attachment for myself and Euan. Economy class. I get onto the airline and upgrade mine to business, using the Colleagues account. Of course Carlotta is clucking, hovering over me, trying to see what I'm doing. — I have a lead, which I'm following up first thing tomorrow morning, I tell her.

— What kind ay a lead?

— Just some people I've been talking to. I don't want to get your hopes up, Carra, but I'm giving this everything I've got.

— You cannae keep me in the dark like this!

I pat her softly on the cheek. — As I say, something or nothing, and I head up the stairs, opting to retire early.

After a decent kip, I rise the next brisk morning, and taxi to the airport. Yes, I'm meeting Euan, among others, to make the direct flight to Berlin. I text Renton:

When did you say you were going to Berlin?

An almost instant reply:

Here now. Big gig at Tempelhofer Feld tonight.

Life's ironies: when I was hunting for Renton, I couldn't find the bastard anywhere. Now our stars are so aligned that I can't get rid of the cunt.

Espied timeously in the departure area: Mikey Forrester, clad in semi-decent Hugo Boss brown corduroy jacket, carrying an Apple Mac in a leather shoulder bag. He's with Spud, who looks like he's been rejected as an extra from *The Walking Dead* for being too decrepit. Murphy sports a crappy old green dress jacket and a Ramones *Leave Home* T-shirt, through which seeps a stain of blood and something else, even though he's well bandaged. Then I catch Euan, the obtuse cunt, standing apart from us, looking anxiously at his watch. As we clear security, Mikey picks up his cue and moans something about time.

— Relax, boys, I tell them, even though I'm anything but, in fact absolutely shiteing it about what we're about to try and pull off. Fear, though, is an emotion best not expressed. Once acknowledged, it spreads like a virus. It's ruined our politics: the controllers have been dripping it into us for decades, making us compliant, turning us against each other, while they rape the world. You let em in, you let em win. I cast an eye over at my motley cohorts. — Looks like the gang's all here!

Mikey drops his passport and I pick it up. As I hand it to him I see his full name: Michael Jacob Forrester. — Michael Jakey Forrester! You kept that quiet!

— It's Jacob, he protests belligerently.

— Whatever you say, I grin, throwing my bag on the belt and heading through security.

19

RENTON – DECKED

Never work wi a Jambo cunt fae the west side ay Edinburgh. Being steeped in a broth of Gumley mediocrity, schemes too drab tae be offensive, snobby-but-shite bungalows and that dark tumour on the city that is Gorgie-Dalry tenementland, serves to leave an indelible stain of moral weakness. Carl vanished after his birthday bash and finding him was a nightmare. I eventually tracked him down at the BMC club yesterday, where he helpfully introduced me as a 'Hibs cunt, but awright' tae the ching-snorting, crap-beer-guzzling occupants ay this seedy blood-relative-battering shithole. It gets even worse as I have Conrad and Emily ootside in the limo on Gorgie Road. When I manage tae get Carl, who apart from his two fucking heavy record flight cases has nothing but the clathes on his back and whae smells like a cross between a blocked lavy and the local brewery, intae the vehicle, the Dutch maestro roars, — You smell bad! I must sit up front!

So fat boy moves up beside the driver, leaving me sitting bitch between minging Ewart and Emily, who keeps groping my thigh. Carl can smell nothing outside the rancid chemicals clogging his ravaged nostrils and sinuses, but he witnesses her actions through a drunken, sleepy haze and gies ays a creepy, licentious smirk. Then he bursts intae 'Happy Birthday to Me' which segues intae 'Hearts, Hearts, Glorious Hearts', before he passes out.

— Fuckin B-side cunt, I laugh. The limo driver is Hibs and gets the joke.

When we arrive in Berlin, Carl, comatose on the flight, is suddenly animated again. I pick him out a couple ay T-shirts fae the Hugo Boss shop at the airport. — Cool, he sais aboot one, and, — My ma wouldnae dress me in that shite, Renton, regarding the other. He cheers up when we meet Klaus, the promoter, at the hotel bar. A dance-music veteran, he makes a big fuss ay Carl, immediately sorting us both out with ching. — N-Sign is back! I was at that party outside Munich, many years ago. The crazy one. Your friend ... he climbed onto the roof!

— Aye, says Carl.

— How is that guy?

— Deid. He jumped off a bridge back in Edinburgh, shortly after that.

— Oh ... I am sorry to hear this ... Was it the drugs?

— Everything is the drugs, mate, Carl says, signalling for another lager. The first never touched the sides, and you can *see* it flooding back into the toxic reservoir inside him, recharging it. This could be a shit gig.

Conrad starts moaning about his room being too small. The cunt is acting out because my old homie is getting the star treatment from Klaus. Then Emily's all nippy, because my little boys' club is sooo much more important than her. I'm fucking exhausted and we've only just got here. This *will* be a shit gig.

The Tempelhofer Feld is on the site of the old Berlin Flughafen, which shut down several years back. They plan to make it into a refugee camp. Now the youthful, colourful ravers are cultural émigrés from the old, clapped-out, straight society of capitalism that can't pay them a living wage and exists solely to suck the wealth of their parents into its coffers through debt.

The Nazi-era terminal, said to be the biggest listed building in the world, is stark, imposing, gloomy and beautiful. Its giant hangars curve out implausibly under a column-free cantilevered roof. In its flightless era it's mostly leased out, and one of the biggest tenants are the *Polizei*. Two cops with machine guns look stonily at us as we head into the building, our pockets stuffed with wraps of cocaine. We find the offices, in a glass-fronted control centre overlooking the big arena and its stages. Besides the cops, Berlin's traffic-control authority and the central lost-property office are based here. There's also a kindergarten, a dancing school and one of the city's oldest revue theatres. We watch the out-of-town ravers, milling about, gaping in awe at this strange utopia the locals casually accept. — This is some gaff, I concede to Klaus, who practically ignores me. Now that the festival is under way, he seems tae have ditched sociable and turned intae a narky fascist cunt, snapping orders at stressed underlings. I go off to check things out as the arena fills up, shimmying through the revellers. A skinny young guy I've never heard ay plays an interesting set. I'm getting into it. I head for the DJ box, wondering if I can get a word when he's done, when I see that there are no decks there. *Ewart. The place does not have record decks. Fuck. I realise that I forgot to arrange for turntables to be there.*

I hurry back to the control centre, flustered. I've stated repeatedly tae Carl that he needs to move with the fucking times. All I get in response is a shrug and him muttering about how 'we'll sort something out', usually as he chops oot another line ay coke. Emily and Conrad probably wouldnae remember their SD cards and headphones if I wisnae constantly chasing them up, but they are of a different era. The culpabilty is mine, though: I ought to have mentioned this on the rider.

I've haven't had dealings with Klaus before, and tell him about our decks problem. He laughs in my face. — We have not had record turntables in here for over a decade!

— Is there nothing around, on any of the other stages?

He looks at me as if I'm tapped, shakes his head slowly.

— Fuck. What can we do? Exasperation has made me publicly air my concern. Big mistake. Ye never show your doubts or fears in this game. Suck it all up.

The promoter shrugs. — If you cannot play, we cannot pay. Somebody else will do the slot.

Carl, loitering at the long Formica-topped bar, has caught this exchange and comes over. The bastard is already ablaze with ching. At least that makes my next question to Klaus superfluous. — Mark, you're a manager, aye?

I ken exactly where this is gaun, but my lot in life is tae play this tedious game out. — Aye.

— So fucking manage. Find a set ay turntables. Should not be mission impossible here in Berlin. Still plenty time before the gig. Now I'm going tae wander the festival site, have a few drinks, and try and get ma cock sucked. I've always liked German birds.

I'm sucking down my wrath, at him, yes, but also at myself. There's little tae be gained in protesting impotently and I've been here before. As galling as it is to admit, the cunt is right. It *is* my job tae solve problems and right now we have a big yin. But I cannot believe this fuckin doss cunt. — DJs huvnae used vinyl since John Robertson was a Hibby. If you'd spun since fuckin 9/11 you'd fuckin well realise that. That's why you have airms like a fucking ape, cartin they boaxes aboot. A fuckin USB, that's aw you need. You dump your set into the Pioneer, press play and pump your fists in the air like a daft cunt. *That* is DJing now. Get teckied up, no eckied up!

Conrad and Emily seem friendlier; they've been working together in the studio, which is good news. I'm concerned with his secrecy about this track, though. I hope the fat fuck isn't cutting a deal with somebody else. He comes over, drawn to our conflict, and wobbles his head, sniggering in derision. — So unprofessional.

Carl responds in haughty disdain. — Others might get doon wi aw that shite, bro, he says to me, not even looking at my Dutch star, — that's no fucking DJing but, no tae me, he sings in defence. But he's covering up the fact that he's embarrassed. Carl is more like a fish out ay water every day and I ken exactly how the poor bastard feels.

So I'm off, oot ay the site, intae the street, trying tae get a fucking signal on the mobby tae find music-equipment stores, which is almost impossible with the crowds milling around, all on their phones. Eventually, the bars pop up and I'm scrolling around, looking for some kind ay shopping district, but there seems to be nothing around for miles. The sky is blackening and it's starting to drizzle. I wander despondently for a bit, heading through a big flea market.

I can't believe it.

I'm normally as blind as a Scottish referee over long distances, but desperation has given me X-ray vision. Literally fifteen minutes outside the site, in this market, is an electrical goods stall. I still have to walk closer to confirm that jumping the fuck out at ays among knock-off fridges, freezers, amps and stereos, there really are two old-school Technics decks! My heart is pounding, and even more uncannily: THEY HAVE NEEDLES AND CARTIDGES! *Thank you, God! Thank you, God of Edinburgh dance music* ...

I approach a young Middle Eastern-looking kid in an Everton FC football top. — The decks, do they work?

— Yes, of course, he says. — As if they are new.

— How much?

— Eight hundred euros. His expression is gravely serious.

— These are ancient, I scoff. — Two hundred.

— They are vintage, he says coolly, brows arching, lips riding back to display a set of dazzling white choppers. — Seven hundred and fifty.

— No way. They probably don't even work. Three hundred.

The kid's face does not change one reflexive muscle. — They work as new. I can only go to seven hundred. You look anxious, as if you need them urgently. You must think of this as a favour I am doing you, mister.

— Fuck … I delve intae ma pockets and count out the poppy. Thankfully, a manager eywis needs a wad. There's eywis some cunt – drug dealer, hotel doorman, taxi fucker, hanger-on, security, polisman – who wants paying off or needs a bung. The wee cunt is now smiling, serenading me with a chorus ay — As new, my friend, as new …

— You're a manipulative, unscrupulous, little fucker. I hand the boy the cash and issue him ma embossed card. — Ever contemplated a career in the music business?

20

SICK BOY – BUSINESS CLASS

Sitting up in business class is an unmitigated delight. It's not so much the benefits of the actual service; more knowing you've got your status over the plebs officially confirmed for the next three hours. From my seat, I pull an obligatory face of impatient disdain as they pass by me, on their walk of shame to steerage. That aside, it gives me the luxury of territory and time to think things through.

Across the aisle, there's a gay bastard; blond hair, tight trews, blue round-collar T-shirt, and he's being outrageously loud. I kind of wish Ben was like that. What's the point of having a buftie-boy son who isn't outrageously effete? Who just wants to live a boring hetero life? Oppression breeds struggle, which engenders culture, and it would be shite if swashbuckling camp was to vanish from the globe just because some uptight cunts have finally discovered that the world is round. This boy, mid-thirties, is a bit of a star. Even the stewards – outrageous ferrets to a man – are all cast as Ernie Wise in face of his swaggering affectation. In the name of sport, I decide to compete with him to see who can be the most mincing, self-indulgent, attention-seeking cunt on the plane. — Try-ing to get a drink on this death trip. I shake my hand enough to indicate nerves, but also to suggest that the wrist is a bit rubbery.

This ploy backfires spectacularly when the raving arse bandit takes a massive shine to me, seeing my narcissistic

Olympiad as a form of buftie seduction. — I dee-tect Celt in that brogue! the queen squeals in excitement.

— Oh you do, I storm back, — courtesy of me being back this side of Hadrian's Wall for the first time in a long time. And there was *me* thinking that my inner Mel Gibson was a dormant force!

— Oh no, I assure you he's alive and kicking, but *sans* the fetching plaid!

Suddenly a stewardess is upon us, bearing glasses of champagne. — An angel of mercy. I down one instantly as my hand reaches to another. — May I?

She smiles indulgently.

— You'll have to forgive me, I hold the spare glass of champers to my chest, — I am *such* a nervous flyer!

— Oh stop, says the queen, taking his glass, — I am so anxious as I have my dogs in the hold, two labradoodles, and they aren't used to travelling.

As I quaff the extra champers, and we taxi, then take off, I tell the frantic buftie a horror story about two pit bulls in a plane hold, one of whom ripped off the other's bottom jaw. — They turned on each other after the luggage shifted and crushed against them. I lean over and drop my voice. — They don't look after animals on these flights. You do have insurance, yes?

— Yes I do, but –

— But that doesn't bring those gadges back. I get it.

He gasps in fear as the plane levels out and the seat belt sign goes *boing*, and I rise to investigate the lower orders, leaving him to chew on the nightmare his trip has now become.

The economy portion of the plane is essentially a scheme in the sky. Spud is crammed into the window seat. Fuck me, that South Leith scruffbag literally does look like death

218

warmed up. Mikey sits tensely next to him, while Euan is somnolent across the aisle in his grim and depressive thoughts. Amazing this world that we live in, where poking your cock in a hoor's erse for ten minutes can wreck your life.

— How are the men? The *real* men, I roll my eyes, still in camply-cruising-at-thirty-thousand-feet mode, — the foot soliders, toughing it out back here in economy class?

— Dinnae you talk tae me! Spud shouts.

Da fellah Morphy won't be after bein told, sure now he won't. — I saved your bacon, ya daft muppet! Once again: it was *you* whae fucked up a simple task for that psychopath, Syme. And you, I snap at Forrester.

— Ah'm his –

— I know, his partner.

— That's right, Forrester says defiantly.

— And how is it you git tae sit up in business class? Spud moans. — Ah'm the yin that's sick!

Mikey, and even Euan, breaking out of Tranceville across the aisle, look at me in accusation.

— Eh, because I paid for an upgrade? Under normal circumstances I'd be *delighted* to spring a biz-class ticket for you boys, but the cost was prohibitive. I couldn't put it through the company account, as you are not employees of Colleagues. I pause. — The taxman's hackles would have been raised and I don't want an audit from those fucking cocksuckers at HMRC right now, thank you. Besides, I look to Mikey, — as Vic Slime's distinguished partner I would have thought you'd be joining me with the Kate Winslets, Miguel.

Forrester has to eat that one in silence.

I go back to biz class and the queen formerly known as flamboyant still frets in stricken silence. As this broken pansy is now of little interest to me, I opt to chat to the hostess, the one who brought the drinks. Thought I detected that

219

spunky edge of shagger's glint in her eye. I get a little flirty with Jenny, eventually asking her if she thinks there's any call for a male escort agency like Colleagues, for travelling women like her. She says it certainly has possibilities, and we swap contact details. Time passes nicely, even if Jenny is forced to bunk off occasionally, to attend to the morose business bores I have to share this compartment with. Then we get an announcement that we're landing in fifteen minutes. So I quickly head back down to steerage where I reckon it's time to tell Spud the good news.

Mr Murphy is zoned out. His head, leaking from rheumy eyes, snottery nose and slavering gob, rests on the shoulder of an uncomfortable-looking Forrester. I gently shake him awake, and he jumps with a start. — Daniel, mein burden, I'm afraid to say that we haven't been quite straight with you.

Spud blinks awake and gapes at me in confusion. — What … what dae ye mean …?

I look to Euan, he and Forrester both tensing in grim concern, as I hunker down in the aisle. Then I turn back to Spud. — Call it poetic licence, deployed in order to keep the patient in a strong frame of mind, and gain his coopera-tion in expediting our task.

— What … he touches his wound, — what did you dae?

— We didn't take your kidney. We aren't butchers.

Spud rubbernecks to Euan, who confirms, — You still have two kidneys.

— But … but what am ah daein here? What are wi gaun tae Berlin fir? What's that wound meant tae be fir?!

His high, yelping voice incites a few heads on the plane to turn to us. I glance at Mikey and then Euan, leaning forward, whispering, — You see it wisnae what we took oot ay ye, it was what we had tae put *in*.

— What?

220

— Skag: several kilos of uncut pharmaceutical heroin. I swivel round. A fat cow who was all ears *seems* to have returned to her knitting. — Apparently there is a bit of a drought in Berlin right now. Something tae dae wi a big bust.

— You put *skag in me*? Spud gasps in disbelief, and then looks to Euan. He lurches to me but Mikey pulls him firmly back into the seat.

My brother-in-law can't look at him.

— See when we land, ah'm gaun straight hame –

— Suit yourself, bud, but I wouldn't recommend that course of action, I stress, scanning the locale and edging closer again. — Your body fluids will soon break down the latex bags and discharge the auld Salisbury Crag right intae your system. What a way tae go though! There was once a time we'd have thought ay that as a result! And … Toto is still in Syme's hands, mind?

Spud sits back, bug-eyed and open-mouthed, taking in the horror and impotence of his situation. I feel sorry for him. He was foolish to take this job, daft to bring along the dog and crazy to leave it unsupervised and underfed with the goods. The punishment, however, as it always is for those who suffer from the disease of poverty, is very excessive. — How could you dae that? he squeals at Euan. — You're a fuckin doaktir! He lunges across the aisle and swings at my bro-in-law, swiping air.

Mikey grabs him and pulls him back into the seat. — Chill, Spud, you'll burst the fuckin stitches!

The knitting munter glances from us to her shite jumper, in order to ensure that this comment doesn't apply to her. The completed garment will go to a poor nephew or niece, securing them ritual playground beatings for retardedness.

— This isn't my fault! Euan pleads.

I beg with Spud to see sense. — Do you think we wanted this mess? Syme literally had a gun to our heads, Danny.

221

You've witnessed how he operates at first hand. He was going to kill us all, our fucking family members, and every cunt we ever sat beside on the 22 bus! Get real!

Mikey turns away. — Business partner, he mutters, in a self-denying plea.

— But this is ... it's aw wrong, and fuck me if ma auld mate poor Danny Murphy fae Leith disnae start tae fucking greet, here on the plane. — It's jist aw-aw wrong!

I have my arm round those pieces of bone they call shoulders. — It is, bro, it is, but we can sort it ...

— Aye, it is, but whae dragged us intae this mess by fucking up a simple delivery? Mikey suddenly barks, turning tae his broken travelling companion. — Me n Sick Boy ur jist tryin tae fix the mess!

— Speak for yourself, I tell him, — I'm being blackmailed. Threatened. Forced into this fucking nightmare, by your business partner.

Mikey slumps down in a wee sulk.

— And you try to rectify this ... by blackmailing *me*, Euan hisses.

The stewardess, not the lovely Jenny I was chatting tae, but a low-rent, pleb-serving, varicose-veined battleaxe, bike-rode into decrepitude over decades by the few hetero pilots, without even a hint of a sparkler thrown into the mix, is right over, her crabbit pus rammed into my coupon. — Please, take your seat! We are about to begin our descent!

I comply, thinking that *my* descent started a long time ago, when I was stupid enough to come back tae fucking Edinburgh for Christmas. That crazy Marianne bitch! I resolve tae pay her back with fucking interest!

Tis a relief to be on the ground, and more so for the squawking queen who is haranguing airport officials about his dogs, as we head out to the taxi rank. In the cab I try to make light of things by telling the tale of the buftie and his labradoodles, but this backfires, only reminding Spud of Toto. — If he hurts that dug, ah'll kill him, ah'll no care! Spud bleats. I do believe Murphy would actually *try* to do this.

The ride through a zone of shabby warehouses and dilapidated slums – I suspect the old East Berlin – hints that the clinic will be highly insalubrious. But even this scuzzy approach has failed to give myself and obviously Euan, mouth agape with incredulity, an impression of the teeming squalor that greets us.

We've alighted into the car park of a three-storey disused building, its ground-floor windows smashed and boarded. Mikey, his leather manbag swinging, nods at a battered aluminium entryphone box. I press practically all its buttons before it yields a tepid buzz allowing me to shoulder open the heavy door and gain admittance. Inside, it's almost pitch black. I bang my shins on something, and my eyes adjust to reveal a commode with the top of a packing case over the shitter. I look to Mikey who flashes sheepish confirmation that this forms the 'wheelchair' he contended would be available at this 'hospital'. At his request Spud sits in it, and Mikey pushes him slowly down the empty, ghostly corridor. As we traverse it, our shoes crunch on broken glass. I wish I had a torch; the barricaded windows permit only meagre light to shoot through the spaces between the edges of the wall and the wooden panels. The building is institutional, probably an old school or insane asylum. Under his breath, Euan spraffs some gibbering nonsense. The impact is like Dick Dastardly's sidekick, Mutley, trying tae recite Muriel Spark's *The Prime of Miss Jean Brodie*.

We get into a goods lift smelling of stagnant urine, the sort formed by cheap, acidic alcohol. Even a minger like Spud is sensing this is not kosher. — This isnae a hoaspital … he plaintively whimpers as the elevator creaks upwards before coming to a sudden, jaw-rattling halt on the second floor. We walk down another long, dark, unlit corridor. The windows at this level remain largely unbroken, but are so filthy that the only light shoots through in beams from the odd breached pane. Mikey delves into his bag, producing a large T-shaped key, opening up a battered, reinforced steel door that reminds me ay Seeker's old skag base in that top-floor tenement in Albert Street. We step intae a dirty and dingy room with a floor of cracked tiles that looks like an old industrial kitchen, except that it contains two metal-framed hospital beds. In one of them lies a fat Middle Eastern-looking man in a filthy vest, sitting bolt upright as we enter. He seems both vaguely annoyed and guilty, and I suspect we've interrupted a masturbation session. Then he breaks into a big smile. — I have company ... he chuckles, waving his big hands at us. — I am Youssef! From Turkey.

Mikey and I introduce ourselves to the Ottoman, obviously, by his dark, circled eyes, another patient of sorts, as Euan's neck twists and his lamps swivel around in horror. — This is outrageous. The place is insanitary ... it's ... it's more like a medieval torture chamber than an operating theatre, he gasps, — I can't work under these conditions!

— Have tae, Doc, or the patient is history, I say, saluting the Youssef gadgie.

— Just git that shite oot ay me, a bug-eyed Spud flaps, climbing out of the commode, lying out on the second bed as he removes his clothes down to his underpants. — Now!

— See, I challenge Euan. — Danny Murphy. Balls the fucking size of Leith. Now you, step the fuck up!

— I ... I can't ... Euan pleads, looking fae me tae Mikey.

— You ... you call yirsel a medical man, likes? What sort ay doaktir are you? Spud barks, then winces in pain.

— I'm a podiatric surgeon.

224

— A what? Spud sits up.

— A foot doctor, if you will, Euan says meekly.

— What?! Spud looks at me. — You've goat a fit doaktir operating oan me? Oan a bag ay skag in ma gut?

— Aye, Spud, but dinnae worry, I pick the skin around my nails, — Euan put it in, so he can get it back oot, I try to reassure him. *I need snout badly.* — Right, Euan, get Danny boy under the anaesthetic.

— I'm not an anaesthetist, Euan snaps indignantly. — It's a highly skilled and specialist profession! They said there would be one here!

— I am the anaesthetist, Youssef smiles, and rises, heading tae the sink, washing his hands, then splashing some water on his face, and putting on a gown and mask, a selection of which hang fae a rack. — Shall we begin?

Euan turns to me. — We can't … I can't …

My brother-in-law is getting on my fucking nerves. — Options. Gies yin. Dinnae just say 'we can't' like a fuckin fanny. I turn to the rest of them. — One thing that gets on my tits in life is cunts that just go tae fucking pieces under pressure. Yes, we're in the shit. I suggest we work together to get the fuck out of it!

Euan eats that one up. Glancing at Spud, he goes to the surgical gowns. As he, Mikey and I robe and mask up, Youssef starts tae administer Spud the anaesthetic. — It will be all good, my friend, his big, dark eyes laugh over the top ay the mask.

He's the only cunt here giving me confidence. — This is a fucking man, I shout, looking at Euan and Mikey. — Act like men!

Mikey starts to light up a fag.

— Are you crazy? Euan gasps.

Mikey looks at him in seething rage for a second, then ceases his activity, as Spud turns tae me in panic and grabs my gown, drawing me close. — Promise me one thing ... if ah dinnae make it, you'll look eftir Toto.

That'll be right. — That fuckin mutt got us intae this mess in the first place. Mair than you. Mair than any cunt!

— Promise, Spud urges in fear as he slumps intae the pillow and his eyes roll intae the back ay his heid before shutting. As he slips under, I say in soothing tones, — Aye ... then add a crisp, — *right*. The torment is still etched on his face, as he drifts off into deep sleep.

Now that he's unconscious, Mikey gets the fags out.

— But – Euan starts.

— Crash the ash, Mikey.

— Only one left. He flashes the packet with the solitary cancer stick.

— Fuck. I suck it down, contemplating the others. — The biggest problem is that we haven't told him exactly what Syme is making us do ...

— This is absolutely crazy! Euan suddenly bellows at the ceiling.

That fucker is losing it. And now is *not* the time. — Your fanny-curious Wee Free proddy bell-end set this mess up, ya Calvinist cunt. I shake my brother-in-law by the shoulders. – Don't fucking wimp out on us now!

Euan breaks my grip and pushes me away. — I'm not a fucking kidney surgeon! Can't you get that through your head?

This cunt needs tae calm the fuck down. — The principles of surgery are generic. I lower my voice to a hush, pulling the laptop from Mikey's bag. — We have a good YouTube video on the subject. I watch Euan's face crumple further in disbelief. — Backup, likes.

— A YouTube video?! Are you kidding?

— Do not worry, my friend, Youssef smiles, — I am not really an anaesthetist either!

As desperate as it is, I feel a snigger rupture uncontrollably from me at that one.

— What …? Euan gasps.

— Well, I anaesthetised animals, in Baskent slaughterhouse back in Ankara. A place of the very highest standards. It is the same principle, just a different dosage. Enough to put them to sleep a little, but not enough for good! I have done those operations before many times and never lost anybody yet!

I haven't a clue whether this cunt is joking or not, but he seems tae ken what the fuck he's daein. Well, Spud looks like he's kipping, rather than being broon breid. Mikey has the laptop fired up, and the video is on, and we're quickly going through it on fast-forward. — I'm hoping this is ringing some fucking medical student bells, I snap at Euan.

— But I need to see it all the way through, I need time –

— We don't fucking have time. The video will be playing as you're operating, and I place the laptop on Spud's milkbottle white, pancake-flat chest, delighted to cover those incongruously red nipples that look like lesions. — You'll have an ongoing tutorial.

Euan shakes his head in resignation, as Mikey and I lay out the equipment and instruments to his specifications: the knives, clamps and swabs.

I nod to the shiteing podiatrist, and he starts peeling off the minging bandages to expose an angry, weeping wound. I'm seriously crapping it now too, the tension rising through me, as sharp as those scalpels. I almost want to cry 'stop' but there's no going back at this stage. Taking him tae a hospital isn't an option. They wouldn't let us keep Syme's skag and they'd throw us in jail. And then there's the other matter, of our real purpose here …

As Euan opens up the stitches, I suddenly realise that the fucking laptop is running out of juice. It blinks on the emergency power indicator. — Fuck … Mikey, gies ays the fuckin mains cable, I snap. — We're nearly oot ay Robert the Bruce.

Mikey nods, goes into his leather bag. Then looks back up at me.

Surely fucking not. — What …? I hear the word wheeze out. — Dinnae fuckin tell me!

— You sais bring the laptop! Ye said nowt aboot a fuckin charger or a lead!

— Jesus fuck!

— I can't do this! Euan pleads in that girly voice that is getting on my tits.

— We will make a great team! Youssef cheers in enthusiasm.

— Let me call Renton, I shout. — He's here! The festival site is only twenty minutes away. He's always got his Apple Mac with him!

21

RENTON – THE CHARGER

I'm fucking stressed enough through getting the decks here, and I'm supervising a thankfully very German technician efficiently connecting them up to the mixer and amp, but now Carl has gone fucking AWOL. I turn round and Klaus is right in my fuckin coupon. — Where is your DJ?

— He'll be here, I tell him, checking my phone. I don't believe this cunt. I try to call him, then text:

Get the fuck here now please, mate.

Klaus sweeps his long fringe out of his eyes to show me him rolling them in exasperation, and steps away. Conrad is across, a big smile on his face, Jensen, who arrived on a later flight, by his side. — He will have gone to pieces. Taken cocaine, alcohol and run away. Thinking of his wife who is now being fucked by another man, he says with malice, as Jensen chuckles malevolently. — He is finished. It is all over for him.

I can do without this bullshit from that fat cunt, and AAAGGGHHH …

… I can do withoot Sick Boy phoning ays up! I should ignore it, but for some reason, I take the fucking call. The reason being that the cunt won't stop until I pick up or block him.

– Mark, it's a long story, but I'm here in Berlin. With Spud and Mikey Forrester.

— Spud? Forrester? In Berlin? What the fuck? I hear myself exhaling sharply. — Well, the answer is aye. Youse can get on the GL. Ah'll leave passes for the three of yis at Will Call, I say, ma tones terse and clipped. I do not need this right now.

— That's not what I'm after, but if it all goes okay it'll be welcome. Right now I need you tae bring the lead fae your laptop, the power lead, fae your Apple Mac, right?

— What?

— Is it a Mac?

— Aye it's a Mac, but –

— I need you tae bring it tae the address I'm going to text you. I need you tae bring it, *right now*, Mark, he stresses, adding, — Spud's life literally depends on it.

— What? Spud? What the fuck is up wi –

— Mate, listen. I need you to do this and I need you to do it *now*. I'm no fucking aboot.

By his tone ah ken that he isnae. What the fuck are they involved in? The text drops in with the address. By my rudimentary knowledge of Berlin, it's pretty close. — Okay, I'm on my way.

I grab my Apple Mac and tell Klaus that I need a driver, as I know where Carl is. He reluctantly nods tae a big, muscular bouncer-type guy who intros himself as Dieter, and we're off the site and intae the car park, then in a people carrier and heading tae the address. We cross the river and drive through a warren of backstreets adjacent to a huge expanse of railway tracks and sidings, heading in the direction of the Tierpark.

After about twenty-five minutes Dieter pulls up outside an old, dark, three-floored industrial building, in a desolate quarter ay disused and squatted spaces. A weak sun sneaks timidly behind the back of it, almost synchronised with us stepping out the car. There's an eerie silence. The vibe isnae right but it gets even worse when ah buzz a battered intercom, then, leaving the driver, go inside and head down a darkened, fusty-smelling and broken-glass-strewn corridor. At the end of it I see what looks like a ghost, and a freeze spreads up my back, but it's Sick Boy, dressed in sterile hospital gown and mask. I'm now even mair curious as tae what the fuck is going on here. — Quick, he says, gesturing me into a creaky old goods lift.

— What the fuck?

He's explaining, but it's in a rant and it's aw gaun ower my heid. I'm struggling tae keep up with him as he bombs doon the corridor and opens a steel door. I follow him inside. A guy I dinnae ken, wi a Scottish accent, thrusts a gown and mask at ays. — Put these on.

As I comply, I'm looking over his shoodir and cannae quite believe what I'm seeing. An unconscious man is lying oan a bed, in robes, a laptop oan his chest. *There's a wound in his stomach, held open by surgical clamps.* He's hooked up tae a drip in what seems tae be a makeshift operating theatre …

Fuck me, it's Spud Murphy …

Mikey Forrester is also robed up, as is this outrageously fat gadge, and that Scottish guy I've never seen before.

— Rents, Mikey nods.

— Gies that lead … the fucking laptop is aboot tae die, Sick Boy barks.

I hand him the lead and eh plugs it in and scrolls back this online video. I can't believe it. *Sick Boy* and *Mikey Forrester* are *operating* on Spud Murphy!

— WHAT THE FUCK! I shout. — What is this? What the fuck are youse playing at?

— Have tae dae this, this cunt's hands were fucking shaking, Sick Boy growls, nodding tae the guy wi the Scottish accent. — A Nicola Sturgeon, my fuckin hole. Stey or go, Mark, but shut the fuck up, because ah need tae concentrate. Right!

231

— Right. I hear the word creep oot fae some dark corner ay ma soul.

— I'm a podiatrist, the boy sings in a long, piteous bleat, holding the clamp, and Sick Boy's right, the cunt's hands are shaking on it.

— You get the clamp fae him, I'll make the cut, Sick Boy says tae Mikey, who is *smoking a fag*. Mikey looks at him and hands him the snout. The fat guy is monitoring the mask over Spud's face. This is like walking intae a nightmare and for about five solid heartbeats ah think I'm still at the fucking gig, spiked on something hallucinogenic, or kipped in ma hotel room dreaming. Sick Boy nods at Mikey, removes the cigarette from his mouth, and takes a drag on it. — Let's rock the fucking discotheque!

— Watch it, the podiatrist guy says tae him, — you're dropping cigarette ash into his wound!

— FUCK, Sick Boy snaps. — Mikey, go n fuckin clean that bastard, swab the fucker oot! He drops the tab and crushes it under his heel. — Gently ... he says, supervising Forrester, who is poking around inside Spud, — it's only ash. Marlboro, low tar, he adds. — Right, have you got that clamp on there, Euan? Can you see where it is? Same place in the vid?

— I ... I think so ... the Euan guy stammers.

— You should fuckin *know* so! You trained in medicine as a physician! You studied fuckin surgery! Sick Boy's eyes ignite ower the mask. — Is it on the same bit as the video!

— Yes!

— Right. I'm going to cut it ... now ... right?

— I dunno, I ...

— Ah sais *right*! Either we sit here aw day or I fuckin cut! Is this the right place? It looks likes it on the video! Is it the *fucking right place*, Euan?

232

— Okay! Yes! Euan shrieks.

— Here goes!

I look away, my arsehole clenching, then turn back, and Sick Boy snips it and he's hudin the clamp on the bastard. And as there's no blood spurting like a fountain, I have tae assume that it's fucking working.

— *Yes! Ya fuckin beauty!* Sick Boy roars. — Now let's lift that bastard out! Mikey, git that fuckin boax ower …

Forrester wheels a trolley across to the operating bed. There is something that looks like a miniature fridge sittin on it. With these long surgical tongs, Sick Boy lifts this slithery thing out of Spud's body … fuck me, this is like a scene fae a fucking sci-fi alien intrusion movie, cause this bloody thing wriggles, as he drops it into this high-tech box. I feel boak rise inside me and fight it back down into my acrid guts. Ma legs are weak and shaky, and I grip the back ay a chair for support.

Mikey seals the box up, as he catches ays looking at it. — State-ay-the-art technology, Mark. This is a Lifeport organ-recovery system. Ah thoat it wid jist be an ice boax like ye huv tae keep bevvy cauld, but naw, it's aw sophisticated. Ye dinnae want tae ken the favours ah hud tae pill tae git this beauty!

— What is this … this fuckin dystopian science-fiction shit?! What did ye take oot ay him? WHAT THE FUCK IS GAUN OAN?!

Sick Boy punches the air as the Euan guy starts tending to Spud. — I'VE SAVED THE FUCKIN DAY AS USUAL, he roars, then points to Euan. — Suture! Stitch the cunt up! Quick!

— I am! Euan hisses. Then he turns tae me, his eyes filled with trauma above the mask. — I only got into this mess through going out for a Christmas drink. He spiked my drink with Ecstasy –

— Ecstasy? What the fu—

— That's right! Why not blame Simon? Sick Boy snaps, but he's euphoric, as if he's scored the winning goal in a Cup final. — Something of a cottage industry in these parts! I'm the only cunt whae hud the fucking baws tae sort oot this fucking mess! And did I no sort it? Surgeon Si! He bursts into song, pointing at himself, — Like a surgeon ... cut for the very first time ...

My heid is spinning. I'm getting phone calls and texts from Klaus, Conrad ... and now Carl, but I dinnae gie a fuck. We're sitting there, watching Spud unconscious, beyond white, already looking like a corpse, the big gash in his stomach being sewn up by this Euan gadge.

— What's in that box? What did you take out ay him?

— A kidney, Sick Boy says. — It had a Graham Parker and the Rumour on it.

— Cause that's what youse cunts specialise in, life-saving surgery, ah mean, what the fuck is wrong wi hoaspitals? Fuck it, ah throw my hands up, — ah dinnae want tae ken!

— It's for the best, me old chum, Sick Boy says.

— This is what's best for Spud, is it?

Sick Boy seems tae come doon instantly, and looks sheepishly at me. — Believe it or not, yes. Which shows the extent ay the fucking mess we've got into. But, he taps the white box-like device, — we finally have a ticket out of it.

Forrester and the Turkish-looking guy have been rummaging in a stainless-steel fridge, I thought for some medical supplies, but they return with some bottles ay German beer. Mikey opens them and passes them aroond. My hands are shaking as I take one.

— Any ching? Sick Boy asks ays.

— Well, aye ...

— Rack them the fuck oot then.

234

Right now I cannae think ay a reason no tae get ripped and stey ripped forever. — Whae's in?

Forrester nods in agreement. So does the Turkish boy, introduced finally as Youssef. The Euan gadge looks away, so I rack up four on a stainless-steel table.

— I could have been a surgeon, if I had the training, likes, Sick Boy advances. — But they say surgeons are cold and mercenary. I'm probably too Italian, too warm-bloodied.

They tell ays what's been happening, and I cannae believe it. How the fuck did Sick Boy and this Euan guy, whom he tells me is his sister Carlotta's doctor husband, get involved wi some gangster called Syme? — And what the fuck are you going to dae with Spud's kidney? I ask the last one out loud.

— He owes it tae Syme, Mikey says.

— He's donating a kidney ... for money? Tae this Syme boy?

— Sort ay. He wrecked one ay Syme's. No actually one ay Syme's, but one Syme peyed for, Mikey explains.

— Jesus fuck, you guys really are off yir fuckin heids!

Sick Boy looks gloomy at me. — Unfortunately we've no telt Spud yet ...

Then I hear the croaky voice from the rattling bed behind us. — Telt ays what?

22

POST-OP BLUES

The people carrier twists, stalls and tears through the choked streets of rush-hour Berlin. Mark Renton sits up front alongside Dieter the driver, talking softly into his phone. Spud Murphy, whom they'd had to carry to the vehicle, sits in the back, barely sentient. Flanked by his medical team of Youssef and Euan, he feverishly struggles to make sense of the latest twist in the grim saga of those last few days. Extrapolates this shit-show to his life in general. He tries to think of the turning point, the moment when it went bad. He looks at Renton, the ginger-brown fuzz on his scalp greying, thinks of that money his friend gave him, all those years ago. It set him right back on a drug path he's rarely deviated from since.
— Tell ays again … he begs Simon Williamson, Michael Forrester, Euan McCorkindale and the Turkish man he knows only as Youssef.

— Yes, you now only have one kidney, Sick Boy glumly confirms. — It was the only way we could square things with Syme.

— But how …? Spud touches the bandaged wound. It is sore. Despite the painkillers he's been given, his body burns in agony.

Mikey, who sits in the middle seats with Sick Boy, explains, — Syme had tae have it fresh, and getting ye oot here was the best way tae dae it. The skag deal wis an opportunity. Two birds wi one stane.

— So ye didnae really pit ... skag ... in ays ...

— Aye. Mikey holds up a red-stained plastic bag of white powder. — Two birds wi one stane but, ay, he repeats emphatically. — Thaire wis a drought oan ower here, n Syme kent a boy, so ...

Spud can't speak. He shakes his head slowly and sinks back into the seat. To Euan, he looks like a jumble of rags. The foot doctor feels moved to make a plea of innocence to his patient. — I only got involved because I'd never been with another woman properly ...

— You, Spud points at him, — you're married tae his sister ... His eyes burn into Simon Williamson.

— Yes, Carlotta, Euan sadly nods.

Spud's eyes grow wistful. — She was beautiful ... as a young lassie ...

— Still is, Euan says, adopting Spud's baleful tone.

— Ye love her?

— Yes, Euan says, with tears in his eyes.

— What aboot me? Spud starts whimpering. — Ah'll never be wi a lassie again! Ah've no hud ma hole in years! It's aw ower for me n it never even started!

Sick Boy turns to Spud. — If that's aw you're worried about, I'll sort ye oot for fuck sake, then he scowls at Euan. — I'm used to sorting out retards who cannae get laid!

— Yes, you are, Euan shoots scathingly back at him. — A fucking pimp. What a noble trade!

Simon Williamson heatedly retorts, — Aye, well, you and your dippit wee laddie wirnae exactly complaining when youse were sticking your dicks intae hoors!

The crash inside Williamson on this reflexive disclosure is mirrored in his brother-in-law's expression. Euan looks like he's just run into a brick wall. He gasps in stunned silence. Then he hauls in a breath, the veins in his neck bulging.

— Ross … WHAT DID YOU DO WITH ROSS? his voice roars out, crackling in his throat.

— I helped him oot! Something you should have done!

— You fucking sleazebag! Did you set your own son up with a prostitute when he was below the age of consent?!

— He never asked ays tae, as he didnae need it, Simon Williamson declares, suddenly, mordantly, thinking of his son sucking another man's cock. — He was brought up the right way!

— Not by you obviously! Do you know that what you did to my son is illegal? It's fucking child abuse! Fucking paedophilia!

— Fuck off! The wee radge begged ays tae set him up wi a woman. Now he's as happy as a fly in shite! Where were you when he craved the cherry-popping advice? Thailand, banging fucking hoors! You've no seen him since Christmas, ya fucking hypocritical cunt!

Euan lets his head fall into his hands. — It's true … we're lost … the human race is lost … we have no discipline and we just look to loud-mouthed, lying tyrants to punish and reward us for it … we're gone …

— Nae cunt got snout? Mikey asks.

Youssef pulls out a packet, issues one to Mikey, who sparks up, and Sick Boy.

— There is no smoking in here, Dieter the driver barks.

— What? Mikey snaps in anger.

— If you want to smoke, you can walk.

Mikey and Sick Boy suck it up, the former looking at the GPS on his phone. On Mikey's instructions they pull up on a slip road, by some shops, just before a busy crossroads. Then Mikey, handing the Lifeport to Sick Boy, who sets it on his lap, gets outside, immediately sparking up, prior to dialling on his phone. Renton is trying to talk but Sick Boy urges silence as he attempts to eavesdrop on Mikey's conversation with Syme. — All good, Vic. Aye, Vic. Conditions were sanitary, Vic.

Then they hear the approaching rumble of a motorbike, which soon pulls up alongside them.

— He's here, Vic. Ah need tae go, but it's mission accomplished.

Sick Boy sits, both relieved and still racked with tension, the Lifeport box on his lap. Spud shouts at him, — Gies ays that boax! It's mine! It's ma kidney!

Sick Boy ignores him, passing the box out the window to Mikey and the biker. — It's Syme's, Spud, he says, looking back. — He needs tae get it or we're aw fucked!

— No until ah git Toto back! Spud squeals in horror, as Mikey Forrester and the biker put the box into a storage unit on the back of the motorbike. The driver remounts and speeds off, receding within seconds into Berlin's traffic and the mottled evening light.

Mikey climbs back in and Renton nods to the nervous-looking steroid bouncer, who starts up the car and heads for the festival site. Spud, sprawled on a seat in the back, is ranting as if still groggy from the anaesthetic, or perhaps it's a fever, Renton worries. — It's mine … gies it back … Ma dug … Ah need it tae git ma dug … Mikey … what did Syme say aboot Toto?

— Sais eh wis fine, Spud, bein well looked eftir …

Spud tries to assimilate this, decides that he wants to believe it. *Has* to believe it.

— I gied you something worth more than a kidney, Danny, Sick Boy says soberly. — I gied ye your life.

Renton glances back at Sick Boy, shakes his head, as the vehicle navigates the Berlin streets. — I do not know what this is, but I know that not one of these guys is DJ N-Sign Ewart, Dieter says to Renton, looking pointedly at him.

Renton feels his hand going to his wallet and extracting more euros from the wad. — Aye, I got a message that he found his own way back. For your trouble, and he hands over the notes. Dieter stares at him doubtfully for a beat, before pocketing the money.

— What aboot … what aboot *ma* kidney? Spud babbles.

— It's gaun tae a wee lassie in Bavaria, Mikey rubbernecks. — The kidney, likes. Will save her life, mate. The bairn's been on dialysis for donks. Must make ye feel barry but, ay!

But now Spud can't even speak. He sits with his eyes closed, his head back on the seat rest, sucking air through his teeth, in hard, sharp bursts.

They drop him off at Renton's hotel, with Euan and Youssef. As Renton, Sick Boy and Mikey make to leave, Spud panics, — Where are youse gaun?

— I have a gig, mate, Renton says. He looks to Sick Boy.

— Worry not, Danny boy, Sick Boy coos, — Euan and Youssef here, he nods at the semi-pro Turk anaesthetist, — will keep an eye on ye. You really are in the best possible hands. Euan's cleaned oot aw the muck and he'll gie you something for the pain. You'll soon be kipping like a bairn. Nae sense in us hingin aboot. Sick Boy looks to Mikey Forrester, who nods in agreement.

— But youse'll come back …

— Of course we will, mate, Renton says. — But try and get some solid snooze in. You've been through a big trauma.

— Yes, Sick Boy trumpets, — rest is the best medicine.

By the time the trio reach the festival site, Renton feels as shattered as Sick Boy and Mikey Forrester both look, but without being anything like as buzzed. He watches them high-five as Sick Boy roars, — The Nicky Sturgeons did the fucking business, mate. Best left tae the low-grade care team now. Our specialist skills are no longer required, and tonight we celebrate!

As Renton tries to find his game face, Sick Boy and Mikey make their way to the guest bar at the back of the main stage. Sick Boy holds out his hand. — The number ay lassies this boy has fingered, and they try and tell *me* aboot the steady hand and the deftness ay touch required tae be a surgeon! Fucking amateurs!

— Goat tae admit but, ah wis shitein it, likes, Mikey nods, grabbing two bottles of beer.

— But we held our fucking riverboat gamblers' nerves while the posh trained cunt went tae fuckin pieces! Sick Boy beams in triumph, as they clink the bottles. Three girls, standing close, look him over, clocking the euphoric power he radiates.

A few seconds ago, Renton didn't care about anything, but now he's clicked back into managerial mode. He notes with relief that Carl is present, sitting drinking on a sofa underneath a giant Depeche Mode poster. But something is not right. The DJ looks downcast, and Klaus, standing by the bar close to Sick Boy and Mikey, is visibly angry.

Renton flops down next to his DJ. He goes to speak, but Carl gets in first. — I can't do it, mate.

— What ...? Renton says, surprising himself at how much he still cares. — What, the gig? Why? It's your big shot tae get back in the frame! Out of the corner of his eye, he sees Conrad and Jensen, who have been hovering by the fridge and table, eating the rider pizza, inching towards him.

— I've lost it, Mark, Carl says sadly. — I really appreciate everything that you've done for me, he points to his chest, — but N-Sign is finished, mate.

Conrad, listening in, springs over, pointing at the stricken DJ. — I told you he was the drunk and the drug addict and the bag of nerves who is now of zero use, he laughs at Renton.

Carl turns away and snivels, as if he's going to burst into tears. It cuts through Renton, and makes him flash a reprimanding stare at his cash cow.

Conrad laughs again, then folds over a wedge of pizza, better to cram it into his mouth. Red grease dribbles onto his top. A publicist runs forward and dabs at it with a wet cloth.

— Well, that's it then, Renton says, in grim resignation, talking to Carl, but taking in everybody assembled. — I've spent a fortune on this cunt of a gig and we won't get paid now, and probably will get sued.

Klaus looks on, his stern face and tight posture confirming this.

As Sick Boy represses a mirthful shrug, Carl suddenly bursts out in loud laughter. He points at Renton. — Got ye, ya fuckin Hibs wank! Then he springs forward and addresses Conrad. — As for you, ya fucking useless fat tub ay lard, come and watch a real DJ blow this fuckin place apart! He turns to Klaus. — Hope you've got insurance for death by astonishment, mate, because that's what half those cunts out there, he gestures to the crowd, — are gaunny fuckin well die of!

— Ja, this is good!

Conrad looks open-mouthed, dropping paper plate and pizza on the floor, then turning to Renton. — He cannot talk to me like that!

— He's a cunt, Renton gasps in relief. — A total cunt.

Carl struts out into the box, nodding to the departing DJ. He thinks about Helena, how blessed he was to be with her. But now there are no tears at having fucked up. He thinks of his mum and dad, what they gave him, and sacrificed. Now there's no sadness, only a burning flame igniting within him, a desire to do them proud. He thinks of Drew Busby, John Robertson, Stephane Adam and Rudi Skacel, as he bellows into the mike, — BERLIN! ARE YOUSE FUCKIN READY TAE HAVE IT??!!

The crowd greets him with a wild, cacophonous roar, as he drops 'Gimme Love', his breakthrough hit, setting out his intentions, following up with a mesmerising set. The livewire audience are eating out of his hand, and at the end they are begging for more. As he walks off to choruses of 'N-SIGN ...', he ignores a wide-eyed Conrad, going to Mark Renton with five fingers raised in the air on one hand, and one on the other. For once, Renton couldn't be more delighted at this irritating gesture. — Stenhoose sex bomb, he whispers in his ear.

— Believe, Carl retorts.

Conrad, edgy and demoralised, follows him onto the stage, as the floor instantly thins out. He gets it partially back by throwing in his two big hits earlier than planned, but doesn't look happy and the audience scents his desperation. It's Renton who quietly saves the day, encouraging his star from the wings with the thumbs up, as the nervous DJ glances at him.

Suddenly Sick Boy is on Renton's shoulder, clutching a beer, waving a small baggie of coke and nodding to the toilets. — That cunt is shiteing it, he says. — I'd like to see him remove a kidney!

— He'd probably eat it, Renton laughs, following him. — It'll dae him nae harm tae play second fiddle for once. This is an older crowd of seasoned house heads. People who appreciate good music. And they remember.

They get to the toilet. Sick Boy racks up, looking at Renton, feeling a strange love and hate he can't explain. Both seem compromising, but also uplifting and essential. As Renton snorts up the line, Sick Boy says, — You know, I've been thinking of how you can pay Begbie his money back.

— It's nae use. The cunt has me where he fucking wants me. He'll no take it. He knows I'm in his debt forever and that it's fucking killing ays.

Sick Boy takes the rolled note, arching an eyebrow. — You know how he's having the exhibition over in Edinburgh, right?

— Aye, we're playing at it. Renton opens the toilet door slightly, to look out over to Conrad, and then spies Carl, now cavorting with Klaus and several women, including Chanel Hemmingworth, the dance-music writer.

As he shuts the door, Sick Boy hoovers back a line, standing up stiffly. — And a couple of days before that, he's auctioning the *Leith Heads*.

Renton shrugs, gets on the other poodle's leg. — So?

— So buy the heads. Bid them up, then win the auction, pay over the odds for them.

A smile explodes across Renton's face. — If I bid for these heads and buy them for mair than they're worth …

— You've *forced him* to take the cash. Then you've discharged your obligation, paid the cunt back what you owe him.

— I like it, Renton smiles, checking his phone. — Speak ay the devil, he says, showing him a text that has just come in from 'Franco'.

Have hospitality tickets for Cup final at Hampden for you, me, Sick Boy and Spud.

Eyes bulging, Sick Boy says, — Now that cunt *Begbie* has done an unsolicited act of goodness, for the *very first time* in his entire life. What a fucking day!

— Oh, but that's him now, Mr Goody Two-Shoes, Renton says.

23

BEGBIE – CHUCK PONCE

Ah minded ay meeting the boy, back in the jail. Ah wis pretty surprised that a big Hollywood star would come and see us, in the fuckin nick. But funny, he wanted me tae help him prepare for this hard-man part he'd goat. He needed tae dae the accent cause it was based on a book by some crime writer, that this European art-house director wanted tae film. Fair play, the cunt that wrote it selt a ton, but I never liked these books. Written for straight cunts: always makin the polis oot tae be the big fuckin heroes.

The polis urnae the big fuckin heroes.

First thing I did when ah saw this handsome but diminutive leather-jacketed young man wi the slicked-back dark hair was tell the cunt the score. I said I wisnae being wide, cause I assumed it wisnae like in America, but Chuck Ponce was a funny name in the UK. Telt him he was makin a right cunt ay ehsel ower here, wi a handle like that. Of course he kent aw that shite; telt me his real name was Charles Ponsora, and yes, he was now aware that it meant something different in the UK, but he was stuck with it. The cunt's agent had told his name was 'too Latin' and would go against him for Waspish lead-man roles. Just like Nicolas Coppola became Nicolas Cage, so Charles Ponsora became Chuck Ponce.

So we worked together in the jail, him listening tae me and some ay the boys crackin oan. We made tapes wi his dialect coach, a bools-in-the-mooth fucker that slavered pish aboot the accents ay Scotland. Cunt was fuckin useless. I telt Chuck stuff, about the jail, about enforcing for the likes ay Tyrone. Did him fuck all use but; his accent in that film was still ridic, like if ye goat that groundskeeper cunt fae *The Simpsons* n hud the fucker oan skag in the Kirkgate for five years. But the boy had a way about him, looked at ye like he was really listening, like ye were special. He made aw those big declarations that we'd be brothers forever. He'd see me in Hollywood!

His words.

Never heard fae the cunt again for six years, even after being back oot. Even after getting my agent tae send him an invite tae the exhibitions, tae my wedding, and my bairn Grace's christening. Ah learned fae this that actors were fuckin liars, and the best liars believed their own bullshit when they spouted it. Then, a few months ago, he comes along tae one ay ma shows. Just wanders in with this wee entourage. Telt me that he wanted a heid made ay Charmaine Garrity, his ex-wife, but wi specific mutilations.

I telt him that I liked to keep they commissions confidential. Could we meet for a wee coffee? So Chuck called and I drove tae San Pedro, and now we're walking along the clifftops together. Although it overlooks the port, this is a private place tae talk, particularly this deserted ocean side, a sheer drop tae the grey rocks below and the incoming tide that laps them. I'm telling him how ah love the sounds ay the waves crashing, the gulls squawking. — We used to go down to Coldingham when I was a kid. It's in Scotland. Cliffs, with rocks below, like here, I tell him. — My ma always told me to keep away from the edge, I smile. — Of course, I never listened.

Chuck shimmies forward, wi that big grin on his pus. — No, I'll bet you didn't, dude! I was the same! I always had to dance to the brink of that goddamn cliff, and he ambles tae the verge. Shuts his eyes. Stretches out his arms. The wind whips his hair into the sky. Then he opens those peepers again and looks doon tae the rocks. — I had to do all that shit too! That's the way we're made, bro, we dance to the edge and then weeeeeeeeeeeeaaaaahhhhh—

My hearty shove oan Chuck's back sends him intae that void, squeezing his voice intae a decelerating, dissolving scream. Then nowt. I turn away fae the brink, roond tae feel the sun on my face, raising my hand tae cover my blinking eyes. I haul in a deep breath, and turn back tae glance down at the body lying broken on the rocks. It puts ays in mind ay how he was at the end ay *They Call Him Assassin*, as the incoming tide froths around him. — I was bullshitting ye, mate. I did listen tae my ma. You should have listened tae yours n aw.

Part Three
May 2016
Sport and Art

24

RENTON – THE 114-YEAR-OLD PARTY

Despite us leaving Edinburgh early, the 'stretchy' is crawling along the M8. It's surely the most woeful major road between two European cities. Franco got the Cup final tickets fae a collector of his work. He claims he's no really bothered; it's just a freebie. Sick Boy seems the most enthusiastic, he hired the tacky limo tae take us through tae that desolate graveyard ay dreams in the south side ay Glesgey. I'm so-so about it, though concerned due to Spud's medicated but valetudinarian form. — Widnae miss it but, he constantly says.

Franco is the only one who doesnae ken how Spud got into this state, and he's curious. — What the fuck's the story, then?

— Aw, eh, a wee kidney infection, Franco, Spud says.
— Hud tae huv it removed. Still, ye just need one but, ay?

— Too much fuckin drugs inside ye ower the years, mate.

On that matter, Sick Boy and I are indulging in some champagne and toot, Spud and Begbie baith passing for reasons ay health and lifestyle choice respectively. The driver's a sound enough cunt and he's getting well bunged tae stay cool. There was something I meant tae say tae Franco, and ah suddenly remember. — That was weird about Chuck Ponce, ay, mind he was at your exhibition?

— Aye, a shock right enough, Franco agrees.

— Ah liked that film *They Did Their Duty*, Spud croaks.

— Shite, Sick Boy contends, hoovering up a line. — *Prizefight: Los Angeles*, that was good.

Spud ponders this. — That's when eh pretended tae be an android prizefighter, but eh wis really a mutant wi superpowers ...

— Aye.

— A guy that had everything tae live for, ah shrug, — aye, it's a funny auld life.

— Always seemed tae have issues tae me, Franco sais. — Ah mean actors, stardom, aw that stuff. They say if ye become famous, ye naturally freeze at that age. And he wis a child star. So eh steyed a bit ay a bairn really.

I'm fighting down saying: *like being in the jail long-term*, but he looks at me wi a wee smile as if he kens what I'm thinking.

— What the fuck was the imbecile doing with a name like Ponce? Sick Boy snaps. — Did nobody tell him he was making a royal cunt of himself?

— It doesnae mean anything in the USA, Franco shakes his heid, — and it wis some kind ay shortening ay his real name. Then, when he broke big, everybody drew it tae his attention. But by that time he'd established himself as a ponce, so tae speak.

— It happens, I go, telling them the story ay how a mate ay mine in the dance-music industry met Puff Daddy. — He said to him, 'Do you realise that in England your name means homosexual paedophile?'

— Right enough, sais Sick Boy. — Who advises those cunts?

When we get into the stadium, I'm suddenly a suffering bag ay nerves. I realise that Hibs are like heroin. I once shot up after being off it for years, and I felt aw the horrible,

252

nauseous withdrawal fae every hit I'd ever taken. Now I can feel every terrace and stand disappointment coming back tae haunt ays, no just previous games but fae the non-attendance ay the ones over the last two decades. And it's the fucking Huns, ma auld man's team.

But I cannae believe it's possible tae attend a big fitba game wi Begbie and feel so relaxed about the potential ay violence. Instead ay scanning the crowd, as was his auld modus operandi, his eyes are totally locked on the pitch. As the whistle blows, it's Sick Boy who's uptight, his patter setting my fucking nerves oan edge. He refuses to sit down, standing in the aisle in spite of grumblings behind us and looks from the stewards. — They are never going to let us walk oot ay here with that Cup. You know that, right? It just won't happen. The ref will be under strict Masonic instructions tae ensure that – YA FUCKER!! STOKESY!!!

We're aw jumping aroond absolutely fuckin demented! Ah realise through a rid smoke flare behind the goal at the Rangers end that Stokes has scored. Their half ay the stadium is completely stationary. Our half is a bouncing sea ay green, apart fae poor Spud, whae cannae move, just sittin thaire crossing ehsel.

— Git oan yir feet, ya daft cunt! a boy behind shouts, ruffling his hair.

We are looking good. Hibs are playing nice stuff. I watch Franco, Sick Boy and Spud. We are kicking every ball with them. It's going so well. It's going too fuckin well: it has tae happen. Things get very fucking dark. Miller equalises and I sit in numb despair till the ref blows for half-time. I'm lamenting a life full of what-might-have-beens, thinking of Vicky and how I fucked that one up big time, as Sick Boy and I head tae the toilet. It's rammed but we manage tae get a cubicle for the ching. — If Hibs win this, Mark, he says as he chops out two fat lines, — I'll never be a cunt tae any woman again. Even to Marianne. She's the one that caused aw this bother, with Euan, and through him, Syme. Funny thing is, I've been trying to call her. Normally she cannae wait for me to phone; her keks are aroond her ankles quicker than it took Stokesy to hit the net. Now she's obviously had enough of my games. And the strange thing is, his dark eyes glisten sadly, — I miss her.

I dinnae want to dwell on Marianne. Sick Boy treated her like shite over the years, but there's always a strange proprietal reverence in his voice when he talks aboot her. — I know what you mean, I declare. — If Hibs win the Cup, I'll try and square things with this woman I was seeing back in LA. I had real feelings for her, but I fucked it up, as you do, I lament. — And I'll look after Alex.

We shake on it. It seems utterly pathetic, and it is: two coked-up wankers in a toilet, planning their future actions in life oan the outcome ay a fitba game. But the world is so fucked right now that it seems as rational a course ay action as any. Then we go back down, and the coke buzz is still searing when Halliday's strike fae naewhaire puts them in front. For the umpteenth time a guy behind us urges Sick Boy to sit down. Begbie starts breathing in a controlled manner. This time Sick Boy complies, sitting wi his heid in his hands. Spud groans, a deep pain, as injurious as any that has been physically inflicted on him lately. Only Begbie seems unconcerned, now oozing a strange, relaxed confidence. — Hibs have got this, he sais tae me wi a wink.

A text from ma auld boy, who is watching on the telly:
EASY! WATP;-)
Auld Weedgie cunt.

— We were wrong to believe, Sick Boy groans. — I told you, it's the lot ay Hibs tae never win that fucking thing. And they've still to get their obligatory late penalty. 3–1 Rangers: racing fucking cert.

— Shut the fuck up, Begbie says. — It's our Cup.

I have tae admit tae being in the Sick Boy camp. It's the way ay the world. We really are destined never tae lift it. I'm growing despondent as I'm flying tae Ibiza at 6 a.m. from Newcastle airport, tae meet Carl, who is doing a gig at Amnesia. At least ah'll git some kip now as it'll be an early night. He'll be ripping the fucking pish oot ay us, wi mair 1902, 5–1 shite. And there it is, already on my phone:

HA HA MUPPETS! SAME OLD STORY! HHGH 5–1, 1902.

I suddenly feel very depressed. Hibs huvnae given up though. McGinn makes a couple ay tackles, playing like a man who wants tae physically drag the team back intae a contest that's slipping away fae them. The fans aroond us are still defiant, but a little downcast. Then another chance for Stokes, but it's saved …

— Fucking nearly men again. How many times, Sick Boy, back on his feet, despite more protests, snarls doon towards the Hibs bench, as Henderson lines up a corner. — I'm delighted that I've shagged loads ay women and taken tons ay drugs because if I'd relied on a poxy fucking football team to give me ma jollies in life – STOKESY!!! YA CAAAAHHHHNNNNNT!!!!!!

Again! Anthony Stokes wi a header fae Hendo's cross! Game back on! — Right, I announce, — I'm dropping an E!

Begbie looks at ays as if I'm crazy.

— I'm doing this because I'm fucking shiteing myself, I explain. — I've walked oot ay this stadium a miserable cunt

255

so many times in ma life: even if we lose I'm fucked if I'm daein that again. Anybody else in?

— Aye, says Sick Boy, and he turns round to the guys behind us. — And don't ask me to fucking sit again because it isn't going to happen! He pounds his chest in aggression.

— Sound wi the ecktos, echoes Spud. — Ah wish ah could stand ...

— Fuck off wi that shite, says Franco. — And you, he turns tae Spud, — you must be crazy.

— Ah'm too like nervous tae git through it, Franco. Ah dinnae care if ah die ... jist look eftir Toto for ays.

Three out of four ain't bad. They go down the hatch. I'm on my feet, standing next to Sick Boy.

I don't think I've ever been so tense at a game ay fitba. I'm waiting for Sick Boy's declaration tae become manifest: the obligatory soft Rangers penalty. Although the ref has been great so far, he'll be saving it for the dramatic last minute. These cunts are aw the fucking same ...

Oooh ... ya beauty ...

I'm suddenly feeling a nice melting in ma guts and there's a surge ay euphoria as ah look at Sick Boy, and in profile, his face contorts, as a weird, joyous ache ay a roar goes up and time freezes and JESUS FUCK ALMIGHTY, THE BAW IS IN THE RANGERS NET!! Hendo got another corner, whipped it ower, some cunt heidered it in, and the players are all over David Gray, and the crowd are going absolutely fucking mental!

Sick Boy's eyes are tumescent. — DA-VIE-FUGH-KIN-GRAYYYY!

SHOOOOMMM!!!

A boy jumps on my back, a stranger, and another gadge kisses ma foreheid. Tears are streaming doon his face.

Ah grab Sick Boy, but he brushes me off in combative petulance. — How long?! he screams. — HOW LONG BEFORE THESE MUPPETS STEAL OUR FUCKING CUP?!

— It's our Cup, Franco says again. — Settle doon, ya fuckin bams!

— Ah'm pure nervous n ah think they stitches might have burst … Spud wails, biting his nails.

The whistle goes, and astonishingly, the game is over. I hug Spud, whae is in tears, then Begbie, whae is jumping aroond in euphoria, eyes bulging, punching his ain chest, before forcing himself tae take deep breaths. We move towards Sick Boy, who again brushes off my lunging arm and jumps up and down and turns to us, the sinew straining in his neck, and goes, — FUCK EVERY CUNT!! I WON THIS FUCKING CUP! ME!! I *AM* HIBS!! He looks over tae the downcast opposition supporters, just a few rows away from us in the other half ay the North Stand. — I PUT A FUCKING HEX ON THOSE HUN BASTARDS!! And he surges doon the gangway towards the barrier, joining the multitude who trickle, then deluge, onto the pitch through the flimsy net of security personnel.

— Daft cunt, says Begbie.

— If ah die now, Mark, ah'm no really bothered cause ah've seen this n ah didnae think ah wid ever see the day, Spud sobs. Draped over his bony shoulders: a Hibs scarf dropped in the revelry.

— You're no gaunny die, mate. But see if ye do, right, yir no wrong, it widnae matter a fuck!

Ah didnae quite mean it tae come oot like that, and poor Spud looks up at me in horror. — Ah want tae see the victory parade though, Mark … doon the Walk …

There are bodies everywhere on the Hibs half ay the field. A small number cross over intae the other half tae wind up

Rangers fans, and a few of them come on tae meet the challenge. After some minor scuffles, the polis gets in between the small groups of would-be swedgers. On the Hibs half ay the pitch, the fans are joyously celebrating the end ay a 114-year-auld drought. The cops are trying to get the field cleared before the Cup presentation can be made. Nobody on the pitch is going anywhere fast, as goalposts and turf are torn down and ripped up as souvenirs. It takes ages, but it's brilliant: the medley of euphoric Hibs songs, the hugging of total strangers and the bumping intae complete newcomers and auld friends. It's hard tae distinguish between the two, every cunt is in a strange trance. Sick Boy returns with a big piece ay turf in his hand. — If I'd had this shit the other day, I'd have planted some inside you, mate, he says tae Spud, pointing at his gut.

It seems like an age, but eventually the team comes back out and David Gray lifts the Cup! We all erupt in song, and it's 'Sunshine on Leith'. I realise, that through all our years ay estrangement, this is the first time that Franco, Sick Boy, Spud and myself have actually sung this song together. Individually, it's been staple fare for aw ay us at weddings and funerals for years. But here we are, aw belting it oot, and I feel fucking amazing!

As we stream outside the stadium, euphoric in the Glasgow sunshine, it's obvious that Spud is totally fucked. We put him in the limo bound for Leith, Hibs scarf round his neck. As a departing shot, Sick Boy sais, — If ye gie yir other kidney, we might win the SPL!

I see Begbie register this, but he says nowt. We shuffle into a mobbed-out pub in Govanhill and manage tae get served. Everybody is in a dreamlike fugue. It's like they've just had the best shag of their lives and are still spangled. Then we walk intae toon, hitting a few pubs in Glasgow city centre. It's party time, aw the wey back through tae Edinburgh oan the train. Central Edinburgh is crazy, but when we get down tae Leith Walk, it's just fucking unbelievable.

I have a car picking ays up at 3.30 a.m. fae my old boy's place, tae take ays tae Newcastle for the 6.05 easyJet to Ibiza. I'm no fussed aboot leaving the party, as I have every confidence that it'll still be on when I get back. I've got loads ay texts fae Carl. They chart his descent fae denial intae hostility, acceptance and finally grace, confirming the momentous nature ay the occasion.

WTF?

SPAWNY BASTARDS!

ABOUT FUCKIN TIME, YOU LEITH CUNTS!

LUCKY CUNTS, HALF OUR FUCKIN SONGBOOK DESTROYED!

FUCK IT, FAIR PLAY TO YOUSE.

I get down tae my dad's tae gloat, but the auld Weedgie Hun bastard is in his bed pretending tae be asleep, and just in case he isnae kidding, I dinnae want tae wake him. I write 'GGTTH' on a bit ay paper and pin it oan the kitchen board for him tae see. I cannae sit here though; I'm back oot in Leith, and hooking up wi the boys again, starting at the Vine.

Sick Boy and I are hammering the ching, with loads ay others. As the night tumbles on uproariously, a sea ay faces slides by as if on a carousel; some long forgotten, others half remembered, more eagerly rejoiced with in an endless stream of bonhomie. Ah decide tae get Begbie while he's in a good mood and gie it one last shot, before ah pit Sick Boy's plan intae action. — That money, Frank, just let ays gie it tae ye. Ah need tae.

— We've discussed this, he sais, and his eyes are fucking glacial, cutting through my intoxication. I'd thought he'd forgotten how tae dae that stare. And I certainly neglected to recall how it freezes ma soul. — The answer is always gaunny be the same. I dinnae want tae hear about it again. Ever. Right?

— Fair enough, I say, thinking: *well, I gave the cunt his chance*. Now I'm gaunny have tae look at him, Sick Boy and Spud, as well as myself, every fucking day, because those *Leith Heads* will be mine. — The next words you'll hear from me are, and I stand up and burst into song: — WE'VE GOT McGINN, SUPER JOHN McGINN, I DINNAE FUCKIN THINK YOU UNDERSTAND …

Franco smiles indulgently, but doesnae join in. He seldom did fitba songs. But Sick Boy duets with gusto, and we share an emotional embrace, as the ditty is taken up for the millionth time around the bar. — Everything you've ever done that's fucked me over, I forgive you, he contends, wired tae fuck. — I wouldnae have missed these moments for anything. We are lucky, he turns tae Franco, — lucky tae be fae Leith, the greatest fucking place in the world!

Franco responds tae a speech he would have been euphoric tae hear fae Sick Boy's lips years ago (but which would never have been made) wi only a minimal shrug. Life is so fucking bizarre. The ways we stay the same, the ways we change. Fuck me: it's been a roller coaster couple of weeks. Seeing Spud in a makeshift operating theatre with his insides hingin oot, having one ay his kidneys removed by Sick Boy and Mikey Forrester, was crazy, but naewhere near as mind-blowing and unexpected as watching Hibs win the Scottish Cup at Hampden. We head to Junction Street, and the Fit ay the Walk, moving back up towards toon. We must have hit every bar in Leith. Begbie, without either punching a soul or necking a drink, lasts until nearly 2 a.m. before he jumps a cab tae his sister's place.

We carry on, then I call the car tae pick ays up at the Fit ay the Walk, which is mair mobbed than ah've ever seen it, and the atmosphere is incredible. It's way past just a Cup win; it feels like some magical catharsis for a whole community that's been carrying an invisible injury. I cannae believe the enormous psychological burden that's been lifted offay me, as I didnae think I'd gied much ay a fuck aboot Hibs or fitba for years. Ah suppose it's aboot who you are and where ye come fae, and once you've made that emotional investment, it might lie dormant, but it never goes and it impacts on the rest of your life. I feel beyond fucking brilliant and spiritually connected to every Hibby, including this car-hire driver whom I've never set eyes on in ma puff before the day. But I really need tae kip cause the drugs are running doon and exhaustion is banging at the door ay this incredible high, and he's droning on about the game, euphorically slapping the roof ay the cab and tooting his horn intae the empty night, as we storm doon the deserted A1.

Ah'm comatose as I get on the plane, and despite the revelry ay the package-holiday mobs around ays, a deep torpor descends on me. Three hours later I'm rolling off, crusty-eyed, beak both runny and blocked, Carl meeting ays at the magic island's airport, having jumped off the Gatwick flight an hour earlier.

— Where's the car? I groggily ask.

— Fuck the car: I've drinks set up for us in the bar.

— I've been up aw night, mate, ah need tae git some fuckin kip. Ah went intae this coma oan the flight and –

— Fuck your kip. Ye just won the Cup, ya daft cunt. One hundred and fourteen years! Carl is caught between an abject despair and a phantom elation that he cannae quite figure oot. But he tries. — I hate you bastards and it's the strangest day ay ma life, but even ah want tae mark it. The stick ah've gied you, wi the 5–1, ye deserve it.

Ah think aboot the 7–0 stuff ah gied ma brother Billy, and Keezbo, ma poor auld buddy fae the Fort. Ah realise that it probably never means as much tae them as it does tae you. It just worries me tae think that they thought ah wis just some kind ay dull, retarded simpleton, like ah thought ay Carl. Still, the auld man is fucking getting it tight later!

We head tae the bar. It takes ays two beers and a couple ay lines ay ching, but ah dinnae feel fatigued any mair.

— Thanks for this, mate, ah tell him. — It was what I needed, and it'll keep me awake long enough tae get through your gig – you're going to kill it, just like you did in Berlin.

— Aw down tae you, Mark, he says with glassy-eyed emotion, squeezing ma shoodir, — you believed in me when I had stopped believing in myself.

— Conrad might need some therapy though!

— A slap across the chops will be good for the arrogant wanker. Now here, one for the car, he says, ordering up two half-pint glesses ay neat vodka.

— Ah cannae drink this … ah protest, knowin that's exactly what ah will dae.

— Fuck off, ya Hobo lightweight. One hundred and fourteen years!

We stagger oot tae the motor, the sun blinding. The boy isn't too happy about being kept waiting, telling us he's another job on, obviously setting us up for the bung I'll gie him. Carl is peeving the neat voddy effortlessly. This is suicide drinking, there's fuck all whatsoever social about it. — Mate, the gig's in a bit. Maybe you want to ease up.

— It's been *eight fucking years* since I was last in Ibiza. I used tae be here every summer. *And* I'm drowning my sorrows. The Hobos won the cup. This changes ma fucking life as much as it does yours. He shakes his head in despair. — When ah wis young, even though ah wis surrounded by Jambos, aw my mates were Hibbies; the Birrells, Juice Terry … now my manager. What the fuck is going on here?

— I'll turn you yet, mate. Leave the dark side, Luke.

— Fuck off, not a chance …

It's blinding in the sun and I'm stuck with that albino Jambo vampire cunt, each shaft ay light seeming tae go through him as if he's translucent. I can practically see all the veins and arteries in his face and neck. It's a forty-minute trip and I'm wired for every fuckin second ay it. By the time we get tae the hotel, I want tae crash. – I need tae sleep.

Carl produces the bag ay coke. — You just need another wee livener is aw.

So we go up tae the hotel's rooftop bar. It's a predictably beautiful day. Cloudless and hot, but fresh. No sooner is the gak fighting through a plug of mucous tae get up ma Vespa, when the phone rings and Emily pops onto caller ID. In my gut: an ominous bolt of something wrong as I pick up. — Sweetheart!

— I'll give ya fucking sweetheart, a male cockney voice grates back at ays. *Mickey. Her dad.* — My little gel was left waiting at the airport. You call that fucking management? Cos I don't call that fucking management!

Shit.

— Mickey … you're in Ibiza?

— I jumped on a flight from the Canaries to surprise her. Just as farking well I did, innit?

— Yes, mate, I'll sort it out. Can you put her on?

Some grumbling and then the voice changes. — Well then?

— Em … alright, babe?

— Don't fucking babe me, Mark! There was no pickup!

Fuck … — So sorry. That car firm, I'm no using these wankers again. I'll get right onto them now. Fucking outrageous. Doesnae help you, ah know, but let's get you billeted then we'll get some lunch, I coo, managing to pacify her and end the call. Fuck, forgot to email Muchteld in the office. Again. Like in Berlin wi Carl's decks. The coke is blasting more holes in a brain already like a Swiss cheese. But Hibs won the Cup, for fuck sake, so fuck everything!

Carl looks at me in quizzical evaluation. — You rode her? Young Emily? The Night Rider, he laughs.

— Of course not, she's a client. It would be unprofessional, I say pompously. — And she's too young for me. I feel the roar ay the coke, thinking ay Edinburgh. A terrible error ay judgement fae us both. Especially me. But fuck it; it was great n aw. And it was just sex. And there were condoms. Nobody was hurt in *that* particular shag. — I'm no like you, Ewart.

— What's that meant tae mean?

— Ye cannae bang every young lassie that looks like Helena, thinking that's gaunny bring back that romance, I say, tipping some ching into my pina colada.

— What the fuck –

— Accept that we fuck up in relationships. It's what human beings do. Then we hopefully learn that our selfish, narcissistic behaviour bugs the fuck oot ay the other party. So we stop it. I stir the drink with the plastic straw and sip.

He looks at me, a fucking milk bottle with eyes. — So this is you stopping it then, gadge?

— Well, I'm trying to … trying to provide … I burst oot laughing and he does n aw, — a professional management service tae ma exciting client base … we're sniggering and then laughing so much that we can hardly breathe, — … but you fuck it up and enable ma bad behaviour, ya Jambo cunt …

— Some fucking management …

— I've made you three hundred fucking grand this year! After you bombing out your film scores and no DJing for eight years, just sittin oan a fuckin couch smoking dope! Three hundred grand, for *playing fucking records* in nightclubs.

— It's no enough, Carl says, and he's deadly serious.

— What? What the fuck *is* enough?

— I'll tell you when you bring it to me, he smiles, and he isnae joking. — Fancy daein some DMT?

— What?

— You've never done DMT?

I'm embarrassed, as it's the only drug I huvnae done. It never appealed. Hallucinogenics are a young cunt's drug. — Naw ... Is it a good high ...?

— DMT isnae a social drug, Mark, he contends. — It's an education.

— I'm a bit long in the tooth for drug experiments, Carl. So are you, mate.

Thirty-eight minutes later, we're in his hotel room and a punctured plastic litre bottle is filling wi smoke fae the drug he's burning on aluminium foil on the nozzle, displacing the water that leaks fae the boatil intae a basin. When it's done, Carl takes the burning foil off its neck, and ma mouth is round it. The acrid shit razes my lungs worse than crack. — As Terence McKenna says, you have tae take the third toke, he urges, but I feel fucking overwhelmed already. There's an almighty rush in my heid and the sense that I'm physically leaving the room, even though I'm still here. What keeps me persisting, though, is the utter lack ay danger and loss ay control you normally feel when ye dae a new drug, especially one that takes hud ay ye tae this extent. I keep forcing it back intae ma lungs.

I slide back in the chair, resting my heid, wi my eyes shut. Brightly coloured geometric shapes appear, and dance in front ay me.

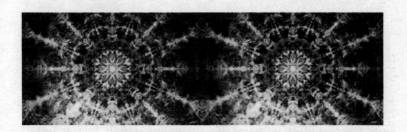

I open my eyes and Carl looks at me in an intense awe. Everything in the world, from him to the mundane objects in the room, is heightened. — You have the 4-D vision, he says to me. — Don't worry, it'll adjust to normal after about fifteen to twenty minutes.

— Can I no just keep it? I've never had such fucking depth perception, I grin at him, then start to haver. — I was happy just tae be, man. That strange contentment, the bizarre sense that it was familiar, that I'd seen it before. It stopped ays fae freaking oot at the weird things I saw.

— It is mental. Did you see the wee Lego dwarfs? Like sort of acid-house garden techno gnomes?

— Aye, they wee people; they seemed tae alternate between a physical presence, clear and real, almost digital, and a spectral form. They were genuinely happy tae see ays, without being all frivolous and fussy about it.

— Were you happy tae see them?

— Aye, those wee cunts are brand new. And you ken the strangest thing? Nae comedown. I feel in my body and mind like I've never taken anything. I could go for a run or to the gym right now. How long was I under for? It must have been at least twenty minutes, maybe forty?

— Less than two, Carl smiles.

So we sit for hours, engaging in discussion. Most of all, the conclusion is that visiting *that place* answers everything about the great dilemmas we ask ourselves, about human society, the individual and the collective. It tells ye that it's *both* that are sovereign, and that our politics of trying to resolve the two are utterly futile. That we are aw connected to a greater force, yet retain our unique singularity. Ye can be as much or as little ay one or the other as ye like. They are so integrated that even the question, which has haunted philosophy, politics and religion for all time ceases tae exist. Yet at the same time, I never cease being aware that I am Mark Renton, a breathing, human organism, sitting oan a couch in a hotel suite in Ibiza town, and my friend Carl is in the room, and I just need tae open ma eyes to join him.

I want every cunt in the world tae be right in on this. Then Carl hands me a wrap of cocaine. — I'm not wanting fucking ching, Carl. No after this.

— It isnae ching, it's K. I have tae play later and I don't want tae start hitting this, so you take it.

— Fuck sake, you no got any willpower?

— Nup, he says.

I pocket the wrap.

25

SICK BOY – BRINGING IT ALL BACK HOME

I don't want this staggering trip to end. It has changed life as we know it. — It's time to put everything you think you were sure about in this whole wide world to one side, sis, I tell Carlotta, as the Hibernian team bus approaches so slowly, inching through the hysterical, dancing and shell-shocked but *appreciative* crowds that bellow out 'Super John McGinn' and 'Stokesy's On Fire'. — You need to be with him, I implore, looking over at Euan, who stands a few feet away on the corner of the side street, by the cherry-popped Ross and his spazzy wee mate whom he is doubtlessly now lording it over.

The favour I've done that whingy little cunt cannot be overstated. Early on in life, I sussed out that this gig was all about impressing women. The hard man, the joker, the intellectual, the culture vulture, the moneymaker; all of them trying so hard, but ultimately just aspiring to be the shagger. So much easier tae simply be that guy from the off, and cut out all the other wearisome pish. I passed that knowledge on to a gormless little spunker, *gratis*. Now Ross and his dippit comrade are standing there with their fresh glory-hunter Hibs scarves on, chin spots rashing, eyes scanning the lassies in the crowd.

But poor Crackpot Carlotta, *la mia sorellina*, has tears in her eyes. — He did me wrong, she sobs, sounding straight outta Nashville, but she's now at last permitting the wound, rather than talking from inside a fuddled suit of antidepressant armour.

— I spiked him with MDMA powder, sis, and I tuck some of her inky hair behind her ear, letting soul seep into my eyes. — All Euan talked about was you, and then he was cynically seduced by that maniac, who was just trying to get back at me. I place my hands on her shoulders.

— Cheer up, hen, shouts a nearby half-pished unhelpful fat cunt in a Hibs strip that clings to him like a body stocking in a chubster's sex club, — we won the thing!

I half acknowledge the blob with a weary smile. I hate to see an overweight Hibs fan: fuck off to Tynecastle if you've no self-control or self-respect. — You mind of Marianne? I urge her to recall. — She came to the door with her old man, back in the day, up the duff, throwing accusations around. Of course, she got rid ay it.

Carlotta looks at me in scorn, but isn't pushing me away. — I think so. Another one you treated like shite.

I'm not loosening my grip, just letting it dissolve into an easy kneading of her tense shoulders. — Heyyy … I wasn't blameless, far from it, but it cut both ways. So anyway, let her take it out on me, I implore, — not a reliable pillar of the Edinburgh medical community. I drop my hands, ending my massage, lifting up her fallen head. — That's her level of spite though. She knows family is the only thing I care about.

Carra hauls in a deep breath, glances over to where Euan stands, then faces me with her wild eyes. — But he was *fucking her up the arse on a video recording*, Simon, she shouts, as a few Hibby heads turn round. Somebody shouts something about Stokesy and Tavernier, which I have to stifle a giggle at. I crack an appreciative smile at the nearby group, but they are quickly distracted as the chants intensify with the bus edging nearer. With the crowds trying to get closer, a crush is developing, so I steer Carlotta back down the side street, more proximate to where Euan stands. — It's just genital interaction

270

and drugs. There's no love on display. All I saw there was – I'm about to say 'the tentative technique of the amateur' but manage, — somebody having a glorified wank. Go to him, Carra, I beg, nodding to Euan. — He's hurting as much as you. He's had his life wrecked too. Heal. Heal together!

Carlotta purses her lips, her eyes stockpiling tears. Then she turns and heads over to him, and as David Gray holds up the cup to ecstatic acclaim, before passing it to Hendo, she takes her beleaguered hubby's hand. He contemplates her, also displaying impressive waterworks, as I signal to Pitch and Toss and his daft sidekick to stand over by me. Ross looks at his sobbing parents in awe. — It's a funny old life, buddy, I ruffle his hair.

This wee cunt shouldnae be riding hoors! He's barely mature enough to have stopped climbing trees! Maybe Renton was right, and I made a mistake inducting him into the world of minge, projecting my own teen vices onto an obvious novice. I was differently made: at his age I had testicles as vicious and hairy as the heads of two ferrets.

This Sunday Cup parade is the best! The crowd is an endearing mix of families and the many casualties who have carried on through the night, and for whom probably the only respite from alcohol in the last thirty-six hours was that beautiful ninety-four minutes of football!

There are loads of old faces around. The Exercise Bike (every cunt has pumped it and it doesnae move) approaches me. Her face is set in the tentative slouchiness of Leith Academy days. A cigarette dangles from her 22 bus and the bag slung over her shoulder has a frayed strap, which, in combo with her vacant eyes, suggests that they might be strangers by the end of the day. Not that one can conceive of this day *ever* ending. — Funny tae see ye back up here in Leith, Sihmin, she says. I can't for the life of me recall the Exercise Bike's first name, but do recollect that I was the only one in that goods yard train of scurrilous villains who treated her with r-e-s-p-e-c-t.

— Hi, gorgeous, I say, in lieu of her moniker, pecking her on the cheek.

— Crazy here, ay? she declares, in a high, shrill sound. I swear the aroma of rancid spunk from every diseased cock she's ever sucked wafts into me like a cosmic force, setting up home in some decrepit *credenza* of my psyche. But even though I've absolutely zero intention of slipping her a length, I'm excited to see her – this Cup win heightens every experience – and text Renton:

How is Ibiza? Exercise Bike on the prowl in the Walk! Blast from the past! Not with yours, matey!!

I'm looking at her company, seeing if any of them register on the fanny Rolodex, but that familiar toxic need is dripping out of her like radiation from stricken Chernobyl victims, and I have to get the fuck away. As she becomes distracted by the trivial intervention of a cohort, I take the opportunity to slip my marker and get talking to a lassie with a pretty, oval-shaped face who seems on the fringe of the group. Despite being obviously up the duff, she's quite steaming drunk, wearing a ludicrously tight, sexy minidress. Showing like that, this woman is a nutty raver. — Your dress is perfect. It leaves little to the imagination, yet demands a great deal of attention. That's a winning combo.

— It's a special day, she says, holding my gaze and dispensing a big, toothy smile.

It sets off a twinge in the baws. — Did you go?

— Naw, never had a ticket.

— Too bad. Great day out.

— I'll bet, she smiles again, eviscerating my libido's guard with her dazzling white teeth and keen, dark saucer eyes.
— I watched it on telly.

— You know, that's what I'd love to dae now, just chill with a couple of tins of beer and watch it again on the box.

I'm pretty much done with crowds, I state, looking around at the chaos, avoiding the hungry eyes of the Exercise Bike.

She half glances to her lump. — Aye. Me as well.

— I'd invite you back to mine, but I live in London. Been up for the game and visiting family.

— Come tae mine if you like, ah'm just in Halmyres Street. She points down the Walk. — Ah've got some beer and the whole game is up on YouTube. Ah can play it through my telly.

I nod to her lump. — Won't your felly be a bit miffed?

— Who says I've got a felly?

— Didnae get there by itself, I grin.

— Might as well have done, she says with a shrug. — One-night stand in Magaluf.

So we slip away from the Exercise Bike's mob and slither through the crowd back tae hers. She's not letting me ride her at first, though if Jimmy Dyson could emulate her suction power in his next model, the cunt would make a second fucking fortune. We watch Stokesy's first goal, then fast-forward to that last ten minutes of euphoria. I'm patting her belly, but stop when I recall my words at my old man's similar fascination with the lump of Amanda, my ex, when she was carrying Ben. I told the cunt tae at least have the decency to wait till the bairn was born before he started fucking noncing it.

However, we're snogging in celebration and eventually she relents, and we hit the bedroom. I've got her splayed forward on the bed and I'm rifling her from behind. Haven't rode such a heavily pregnant bird since the ex-missus, and I have to confess that I'm enjoying the novelty. There's some-thing grotesquely beautiful about the form. We crash out afterwards and I'm glad of the kip, but I snap into conscious-ness that way you do when a whole swathe of peeve has left you in a oner, and you're suddenly wide awake. She's lying on her side, and I slip out the kip and leave a note, slightly concerned that I never got her name. I mean, she did tell me, but it's been an emotional time.

You're wonderful x

Defo worth another bang after she pops. Also, potential Edinburgh Colleagues personnel if she can dump the bairn with her mother.

Unfortunately, she springs awake. Sits up in the bed. — Hiya ... you going?

— That was great, it was really lovely meeting you, I say, lowering my weight onto the bed, taking her hand in mine and stroking it gently as I look into her eyes.

— Will I see you again?

— No. You'll never see me again, I tell her, sad and honest. — But it's for the best.

She starts to cry, then she apologises. — Sorry ... it's just that you were so nice ... my life's going tae total shit. I've had to stop working. I dunno what I'm going to do. She looks at her lump.

I lift up her chin and kiss her softly on the lips. My hand rests on her swollen belly. I gaze into her wet eyes, letting my own mist up, through recounting childhood injustices visited upon me. — First World problems. You're a beautiful woman and you'll get through this bad patch and off this scary path that you're on. Somebody will love you, cause you're the sort of person who gives out love. You'll soon forget me, or I'll only be a nice but fuzzy memory.

She shakes in my arms, and the tears are streaming down her face. — Aye ... well, maybe, she bubbles.

— Tears are the beautiful, sparkling jewellery of the feminine soul, I tell her. — Men should cry more, I never, ever cry, I lie. — But it's good to cry together, and I feel my own tears come on

274

cue; gritty and thick, along with ching snotters. I stand up, wiping them away. — This never happens to me ... I have to go, I tell her.

— But ... this is ... I thought we made some kind of ...

— Shh ... it's all good, I coo, slipping on my jacket, and stepping out the room, as she erupts in loud sobs.

I leave the flat with a jaunty step, bouncing down the stairs, pleased with my work. A memorable entrance is fair enough, but the best thing to do is provide the *emotional exit* that breaks the other party in two with a crippling sense of loss. *That's* what leaves them wanting more.

Through the chaos I have to walk towards Meadowbank before I find a cab and get back to Carlotta and Euan's. I hit the hay again about 6 a.m. Monday morning, but, unable to sleep, I watch the entire game twice. I do one on BBC, and one on Sky, with the latter by far the best. The British imperialist state broadcaster is full of wet-eyed Unionists, with no pretence of impartiality, bleating because their chosen outfit got severely rogered. I phone up two women in Edinburgh, one of them Jill, and three in London, to tell them that I'm madly in love with them and we need to talk about our feelings for each other. I scour Tinder's constant stream of headshots while watching Stokesy's brace and skipper Sir David Gray's winner again and again. The best thing about it all is the Huns taking the strop and not coming out for their losers' medals, nor doing any interviews. It means that the coverage is just solid Hibs, our sheer joy uninterrupted by the unwanted, though probably hilarious, intrusion of sourpusses. The pundits and commentators just don't get it: every time I hear a bitter, snidey, sweetie-wife tone deploying the term 'tarnished' to reference the pitch invasion, I just feel the entire occasion being massively further enhanced. This is a victory for class, for Leith, for the Banana Flats, for the Italian-Scots. I say this because I regard Hibs as essentially an Italian rather than Irish outfit. Hibernia may mean Ireland, but it means it in *Latin*. So the club's real origins pre-date both Scotland *and* Ireland.

Renton calls and I pick up. — Unless you have decent drugs, end this conversation now, I tell him, as I've arranged to meet Jill for a ride. Spunk is already trickling back intae the baws from some factory in that little annexe of heaven deep within my life force. I also need to start phoning round for some more ching. Could handle a belt up the Vespa scooter.

— I don't want to end the conversation, Renton says. — Prepare to be astonished.

— Hibs just won the Cup after one hundred and fourteen years. What the fuck is going to astonish me now?

The answer comes a couple of days later when Renton is back in town. He has summoned myself, Begbie and Spud up to his spacious, well-designed hotel suite with its soft lights and luxury furnishings (and this is a cunt who says he isn't rich). He has the paraphernalia spread out across a low-slung Arabian coffee table, and I cannae believe what the fuck he's up tae. Does the cunt want us to hit a fucking crack pipe?

— What does DMT stand fir? Spud asks, still looking like shit.

— Danny Murphy's a Twat, I tell him. — I should have pummelled that gash in your gut when you were under. Would have at least then have gotten a fuckin ride out of you, and I dry-hump his wound, perhaps a little robustly.

— Get off, it's sair. Spud pushes me away as I catch a stare from Begbie. It goes from me to Spud and back to me again. Not quite as psychotic as of old, but still with enough reprimand in it to calm me down. Ching. It can compromise one!

— Frank, are you up for this? Renton asks.

— I've telt ye, ah stoaped aw that shite, Franco says. — Ching n bevvy were the only drugs ah did, n ah'm done wi aw that now.

276

— Honest, Frank, this isn't a drug. It's not a social thing. It's an experiment, Renton stresses.

— You're an artist, Frank, I volunteer, trying to subtly get at the cunt, — see it as a new frontier to explore. I've heard it's an incredibly visual experience.

— The Leith heids, Renton smiles.

All eyes are on Begbie. He cracks a low, reptilian grin. — Awright. But only for art's sake.

— Top man. Renton starts preparing the DMT, as tutored apparently by that fucking Jambo drug apparition Ewart. — This will blow your mind, but at the same time, you'll be totally relaxed. My theory is that it takes us back tae a time before we were born, or after our death, and in the process exposes human mortality as just a sliver in between, and, I think –

— Shut the fuck up, Renton, I tell him, — I've done every drug except this one. Listening to you is like working through the box set ay *Breaking Bad*, getting tae the final season, then having some cunt tell us what happens in the last episode.

— Aye, Mark, lit's huv this convo eftir the collies, catboy, Spud agrees.

I'm first on that fucking bottle. It's not that hard on a *smoker's* lungs …

ONE …

TWO …

THREE …

FUCK THIS SHIT! AVANTI!!

I'm sitting back and dissolving into somewhere else …

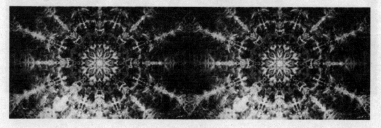

277

278

I sense the drug is leaving me and it's over. When I exit the trip, I'm still on the couch. Renton, Spud and Begbie are all in the 4-D vision Mark was havering on about; it's sharper with dramatically greater depth perception. In fact, they seem like translucent computer windows, stacked in front of each other. Renton looks at me like a scientist does a chimp he's just given a new drug to.

I look over at Spud, whose eyes are blinking, trying to find focus.

— Whoa, man ... Spud gasps, — how mad was that!

— That was pretty fucking phenomenal, I concede. Most times in your life you have to be cool, even blasé. Call it dignity. But there are others, where you just need to surrender to the power of the situation. These are very few. But, like the appearance of your first – *wee Dawn no* – child, and Hibs winning the Cup, this is certainly one of them.

What the fuck just happened to me?

— Too fucking right, Renton says, and we start to swap experiences, focusing on the similarities: the geometric shapes and colours, the little people, the positivity and lack of threat, the sense of being welcome and guided by a higher intelligence. Then we move on to the differences; me sliding face first through snow down the side of mountain, then rocketing upwards, and Spud elaborating about a very warm, womb-like chamber, conscious that he was heading down steps, that notion of descent being his overriding sense of things . . .

. . . I can't help smugly think that it's typical of fannybaws Murphy to be consigned to a fucking dungeon, while Super Si explodes up mountainsides and surfs the blue skies. Begbie remains silent, starting into space. Renton, his sly rattishness enhanced by my special eyesight, says, — See, oan ma trip wi Carl, the walls fell away like boards, opening up intae a clear blue sky. I soared intae this flame, which blasted ays intae the stratosphere. He blows out air he's compressed in his cheeks.

We look at Begbie, who has opened his eyes, and is rubbing at them. He obviously has the layered vision, like I still do, though it's less pronounced and settling down now. — What did you get out of it, Franco? I ask him.

— Fuck all, he says. — Just some vivid colours n flashin lights. Only lasted a couple ay minutes. Load ay shite.

Renton and I look at each other. I can tell he's thinking exactly what I am: *This cunt? An artist? My fuckin baws.*

— Did you take the third hit right back? Renton asks.

— Aye, of course I did. You fuckin gied ays it.

— Spud?

—Ah feel bad, man, thinkin aboot aw the chorin ah did, he says in agitation, — n that's how ah'm aw ill now, Mark, but ah nivir –

— It's okay, man, take it easy, Renton tries to calm his rambling.

I turn to Begbie. — Well, I experienced a lot more than some flashing lights, Franco. That was fucking phenomenal. I had a sense that I had fused with every member of the human race and I was moving as one with them, yet still somehow an individual.

— Did you see the wee Lego dwarfs? Renton enquires.

— Yes, but mine were more like spherical. Not exactly like acid-house smiley guys, but definitely from the same stable. It defies easy explanation. It was so vivid, but now it seems hard to put together in words exactly what I did see.

— I took off, Renton says. — I stepped into these flames and shot right intae the sky. I could feel the wind oan ma face, smell the ozone in the air. Did anybody experience being present at a feast, like the Last Supper? That's quite common.

— No, I tell him, and look to Spud.

— Naw, man, ah just went doon aw these stairs intae that cellar, but no scary, like aw comfortin and warm, like gaun back tae the womb.

— Franco, nae Last Supper images? Rents presses.

— Naw, says Franco, looking annoyed, — like ah sais, jist some flashing lights.

Then Spud goes, — Ah'm really no feelin sae well ...

— Yir heid? Renton asks.

— Naw ... aye ... but ah feel aw seek n dizzy, and then he lifts his T-shirt. The wound is damp with leakage, some sort of discharge. Spud groans, and his eyes roll into his head and he flops back into the couch and passes out.

Fuck ...

26

SPUD – HOSPITAL EYES

I'm pure seek, man, really seek but, here in the hozzy, n Franco's come tae see ays, which is an awfay surprise cause eh's no that sort, n that isnae meant as any diss oan the cat. It's jist that ye think eh likesay disnae care aboot folk. Ah mean, eh's goat ehs new burd fi California and his bairns, the new yins, no the auld yins, n eh seems tae care aboot thaim. So ah suppose that hus tae count for something. Aye, ye huv tae be fair n say that cat has made the transition fae sinking fangs intae prey in the jungle, tae sittin in a comfy basket in front ay the fire n huvin a long purrrr tae ehsel. He tells ays that ah've been oot for twenty-four hours. — Aye, ah goes. They cleaned and dressed ma wound and ah'm oan an antibiotic drip, n ah shakes ma airm n looks at the bag hooked up. — Ah mind ay nowt, ah tell um. — Thoat it wis yon DMT.

— Listen, mate, Franco goes, — ah ken thaire wis something dodgy that went on wi this kidney stuff. Ah'm no gaunny press ye though. But if something did happen, ye kin talk tae ays aboot it. It's no like ah'm gaunny go oan the warpath n set aboot any cunt. Those days are long gone, that's just no my world any more.

— Aye … ah ken that, Franco, changed man n aw that. That wis mad the other night thaire but, ay?

— Aye, Franco says, then eh admits, — Played aw that DMT stuff doon. It wis fuckin wild but ah didnae want Renton tae ken. Him and Sick Boy thegither: it eywis annoyed the fuck oot ay ays when they went on aboot drugs, fuckin drugs, fuckin drugs aw the time. Ah mean, take the cunts or dinnae; but dinnae fuckin talk aboot them twenty-four/seven!

— What did ye see but, Franco?

— Enough, mate, Franco says, like it's a wee warnin.

But ye kin git away wi mair now wi Franco, n ah've goat the licence ay invalid status, so ah pure press it a bit. — What dae ye mean, but?

— Ah mean ah dinnae want tae talk aboot it, eh goes. — It's personal. It's in ma heid. If ye cannae keep what's in yir heid private, wir aw fucked, ay.

Ah'm gaunny say, but *we* telt *you*, but ah jist goes, — Fair dos, catboy. When ye gaun back tae the US of A?

— Soon, mate. We've got the big auction comin up this week, follayed by the exhibition next weekend. Melanie's come ower, n we're enjoying huving time thegither withoot the bairns aboot, much as we love they wee angels. We're steyin at ma sister Elspeth's. It's aw workin oot nicely.

— How's Elspeth?

— Fine … he goes, — well, no that great, but ah think it's aw jist wimmin's stuff, ay?

— Aye, it's good whin yuv goat people. Ah've jist goat Toto but he's at ma sister's now. Andy, ma laddie, he's daein well, but he's doon in Manchester. Lawyer but likesay, ah hear the pride crack ma voice. Still cannae believe it but. Takes eftir Alison in the brains department. — Comes up tae see his ma … You mind ay Ali, aye?

— Aye. Is she well?

— Barry. Teacher now, ay? Got another felly eftir me, hud another bairn, a laddie again. Ah feel masel choking up. Ah did huv chances tae huv a better life. Ah loast love. That hurts, man. That hurts ye in places other things cannae. — Aye, it's jist me n Toto now. Ah worry cause ma sister'll no

look eftir him if anything happens tae me. The doc said ma
hert stoaped n that ah wis deid for four minutes.

— This is connected tae the kidney thing?

— Sortay naw, but aye. It weakened ays gaun through aw
that n pit a strain oan the hert.

— This kidney thing, he looks at ays again, — ye want
tae tell me what happened? Ah swear it stays between us.

Ah hus a wee idea n looks at him. — Awright, but you've
goat tae tell ays aboot your DMT trip first.

Franco hauls in a breath. — Awright, but likewise for your
ears only, right?

— For sure, catboy.

Franco's eyes sortay widen. Ah mind ay whaire ah seen
um like that before. Whin we were bairns n thaire wis a deid
dug oan Ferry Road: a gold Labrador. Perr animal hud been
hit by a car or a lorry gaun tae the docks. Back then people
didnae eywis look eftir dugs right. They wid git a dug, then
jist lit it roam durin the day. Sometimes dem poor puppies
wid mob up in Pilrig Park, n even go feral, till cooncil dug
catchers goat them and pit them doon. We wir aw sad, at
the deid dug, likesay, lyin thaire, stomach ripped open, head
smashed in, gore n blood streakin ower the road. But ah mind
ay Franco's eyes, they were sort ay aw innocent and wide.

Like now. He clears ehs throat. — I'm sitting roond a
table and there's a bunch ay us, aw eating nice grub fae these
big plates. Ah'm at the top at the table. The settin is fuckin
opulent, like some sort ay olde worlde stately home.

— Like Jesus at the Last Supper? What Rents wis on aboot?

— Aye, ah suppose so. But aw that Last Supper stuff pre-
dates the Bible and Christianity. It comes fae the DMT, which
humans have eaten before Christ was even thought ay.

The cats at St Mary's Star ay the Sea or South Leith Parish
Church widnae like that. — Wow … so it's like Christians

are just nosy straightpegs that, like, watch other people get messed up oan drugs and record aw their stories ...

— Ah suppose it is, mate, Franco sais. — Anyway, the thing that struck ays was that aw the other people roond the table wir deid. He stares at ays. It's a funny look.

— Like zombies?

— Naw, like people who are no longer wi us. Donnelly wis thaire. Big Seeker n aw. N Chizzie the beast ...

It's like ah ken what eh's sayin. *Eh killed them aw*. Ah kent aboot Donnelly n Seeker, n ah wis wi Chizzie just before eh goat his throat cut but they nivir caught the boy that did it ... but surely thaire wisnae mair ... — How many wis thaire? ah ask.

— A few ay them, Franco carries oan. — So ah wisnae chuffed being there wi they bams, but everybody was sound. Ken what ah took fae that?

Ah'm lookin at him, feelin aw hopeful aboot the world. — That people are okay n we should aw git oan?

— Naw. Tae me it said nae cunt's gaunny be bothered, even if ye fuck them right up. The next life is too big tae get aw het up aboot what ye dae here in this yin.

N ah think aboot this in terms ay ma ain life. Aye, ah've messed things up, but mibbe it disnae matter. Ah suppose it works fir Franco, n eh could be right. — It's mibbe a good wey ay thinkin, man, ah tells the cat.

27

THE AUCTION

As the tourist crowds infest the city, Edinburgh does its habitual spring tease, providing a few glorious days. Then it's time for the usual about-face; the deliverance of the traditional smoky clouds and sudden downpours of heavy rain. Citizens and incomers wander around pinch-faced, looking cheated, many a little lost, and perhaps in need of a friend. Nobody more so than Mikey Forrester, who is happy to take Simon Williamson's call and meet up at an impersonal bar near Edinburgh's Waverley Station. Mikey is aggrieved; he thinks he's avoided the rain as he walks down Cockburn Street and Fleshmarket Close, but it suddenly teems down and he's soaked to the skin by the time he slips into the pub.

Williamson is already standing at the bar, looking down at his fellow occupants of the boozer in arch disdain. Mikey nods to him and heads over. Sick Boy elicits strange emotions in him. He envies his effect on women; that seemingly effortless ability he has to charm them into bed had never deserted him over the years. Mikey is burdened by a belief that if he watches people closely enough, he can identify and appropriate their abilities for his own. As a life strategy this has afforded him limited success, but having internalised it, he can't quite shake it off.

Sick Boy has set up a Diet Coke for himself and, without asking him, orders up a vodka and tonic for Mikey. — How goes, Miguel?

— No bad. How's Spud?

— He was a wee bit dodgy, Sick Boy says, in mild understatement, accepting the proffered drink from the barman in exchange for notes, — but the hozzy say he's going to be fine. Watch ... and he steers Mikey down the bar, where he stands close to him. Mikey can smell fresh garlic on his breath. Sick Boy always ate well. Probably Valvona & Crolla, he guesses, or perhaps his mother's or sister's home cooking. — I have a wee proposition for you. Could be lucrative.

— Ah'm daein awright, Mikey Forrester says defensively.

— Ye can drop the patter, Mikey, Sick Boy responds, quickly adding, — I'm no here tae judge anybody. Let's face it, we all shat it offay Syme, yes wi good reason, but tae our eternal shame.

Mikey is about to intervene in protest, but no words are coming.

Sick Boy continues. — Thing is, he's off our backs now. I know how tae keep him away fae your wee goings-on, and also ensure that he retains his gratitude tae ye.

— We're partners! Mikey bellows, bunching his fists, massively overplaying his hand.

— Easy, bud, Sick Boy whispers, urging him to drop his voice. Sick Boy thinks perhaps it wasn't such a good idea to meet in this spot. After all, there were few better places for low-life grasses to congregate than in boozers close to railway stations, and a fat semi-jakeball in a tracksuit and skinhead cut seems to be taking an interest in the conversation. Mikey acknowledges his folly with a terse nod, and stands closer to Sick Boy.

Simon David Williamson knows never to kick away a man's crutch unless you offer him a superior replacement. — Have it your way, but my proposition could be very advantageous to you. Obviously, this is all in confidence. Do I have your ear, or should I go?

Eyes darting across the bar in a quick scan, Mikey Forrester takes a sip of his vodka and nods in the affirmative.

— Let me ask you: who does Syme fear? Sick Boy raises his eyebrows. He knows how to hook Mikey, namely by placing him at the centre of a compelling drama. With that very sentence, by urging his strategic counsel, he's hinted at Mikey having an elevated status in the city's underworld. The expansion of Michael Forrester's pupils and the swivel in his neck tells Sick Boy he's pressed the correct button.

Mikey's voice stays low. — Naebody. No now that Fat Tyrone's away. Nelly'll no go up against him. Nor will the Doyles. They've just divided Tyrone's wee empire up between them. The young team arenae ready, no since Anton Miller got done.

Sick Boy maintains only a rudimentary knowledge of the Edinburgh criminal scene, and has also extricated himself from the London one. Fundamentally, he dislikes gangsters. He is solely interested in women, and finds it difficult to engage at even a cursory level with most other men for any length of time. And ones who are more interested in the shifting hierarchy of power, rather than the sweet music of romance, bore him senseless, though he is too politic to show this disdain. — I was thinking of a certain Leith psychopath we both know well.

— Begbie? Forrester laughs, before lowering his voice again. — He's in America, a fuckin artist now, oot ay that life. Besides, he looks around, noting that the chubby skinhead has drunk up and gone, — him and Syme are probably tight, the way they boys ey are.

— Syme's West Side, Begbie was always Leith and the toon, mobbed up wi Tyrone, Nelly, Donny Laing, aw that crowd. Different circles. Syme was intae scrubbers, never really Tyrone's thing. He was always loans, debt collection, extortion, Sick Boy explains, thinking: *This is obviously pish; nutters always know each other, and generally side together against the civilians they prey on.*

But it proves a convincing enough narrative for Mikey to embrace, and he nods along in conspiracy.

— Begbie's back in Edinburgh for this auction and an exhibition ay his art, Sick Boy offers, then advances, — You and Renton, youse were never really bosom buddies, were yis?

Historically, Mikey Forrester hadn't got on with Mark Renton. The reason was trivial enough. Mikey had long fancied a woman, who had been stringing him along for free drugs, and whom Renton subsequently enjoyed a meaningless copulation with. This bugged the shit out of Mikey, and he had made his hostility apparent down the years. Age, however, had given him perspective and he now bore Mark Renton no ill will for this incident. Indeed, he felt a tinge of shame that he'd made so much of this now-petty grievance. — He helped us in Berlin.

— Doesnae make ye bezzy mates.

Forrester looks forlornly at Sick Boy. You can't unsay the things you've said over the years. This only makes you look even weaker than the original running off at the mouth. — He's a fuckin grass who steals fae his ain.

Sick Boy shouts up more drinks, this time joining Mikey in the vodka and tonic. — How about if I told you I know a way to piss off Renton and get in Begbie's good books? he purrs. — To the extent that it would buy you more respect from Syme, and get you right back in easy street. Intae a place where you'll be a genuine equal partner. What do you say?

Mikey is all ears. Of course, he would never be an equal partner with Syme, but Sick Boy knows that his vanity will always stubbornly allow the possibility. — What ur ye proposing?

Sick Boy tries not to register his distaste at Mikey's sour breath. It's like he's been gargling menstrual blood. He idly wonders if Mikey is a pussy eater, whether he goes south on rag week, and if he brushes his teeth after. — Renton might find that Begbie's art will cost him more than he's bargained for, especially if some cunt is bidding against him. And he really wants it, so there is no way he'll let anybody else win.

— So ...

— So you go there and bid the cunt up. Clean the fucker right oot. Begbie gets big bucks oot ay it all and Renton is totally skint, having peyed way over the odds. All thanks to one Michael Jacob Forrester. He points at Mikey. — Once Slimeball sees that you are *the fucking man*, right in with the viciously repped Franco Begbie, he starts to treat you with a bit more r-e-s-p-e-c-t. Get my drift?

Mikey nods slowly. — But ah've nae money tae bid for art pieces.

— You lose the auction to Renton.

— Aye, but what if he pills oot n ah win?

— I cover it, he says thinking of the money Renton gave him. — But if you stop the bidding at the figure we agree, that won't happen.

Mikey raises his glass, takes a sip. It makes sense. Or perhaps it doesn't. But what it does do, and what Sick Boy judges correctly is utterly irresistible to him, is place Michael Jacob Forrester right at the centre of an impending commotion that the city's underworld will talk about for years to come.

The auction takes place inside a four-pillared pseudo-Athenian temple, cast in the grey stone and with the arched windows often favoured in Edinburgh's New Town. Regarded as one the most beautiful salesrooms in Britain, the building is tucked in a maze of backstreets between the East New Town and the top end of Leith Walk.

Inside, it is a cross between an old church and a theatre. The stage, which holds the auctioned items to the rear as well as the auctioneer's lectern to the fore, is the centrepiece in an inverted U-bend that runs around the hall. It looks onto a wooden floor partially covered by a giant, ruby-coloured, patterned rug, with around fifty people sitting on neatly lined-up gold-and-red chairs. Above the wings are balconies, supported by black cast-iron pillars, under which sit officials, who record the proceedings.

The room is a hub of chatter and bustle. Some serious collectors are present, evidenced as recipients of hushed comments and reverential stares. The air is stuffy and slightly rank, as if some of the ageing pieces and collectors past have deposited a lingering scent. Close by those who dress and smell of ostentatious wealth, sit a few shaven-headed wideos of varying degrees of status in the local thug hierarchy. Jim Francis, the artist formerly known as Frank Begbie, stands at the back of the room with his agent Martin Crosby, looking over at them in an affectionate disdain. — The boys. Come tae have a wee neb at how much money auld Franco's makin oot ay this art game!

Martin nods, though he's only able to make out the bones of what Jim is saying. Back on home turf, his client's accent has thickened up considerably. Martin flew in from LA yesterday, and prior to today claimed never to suffer from jet lag.

Then Frank Begbie can't believe his eyes as he spies Mark Renton sitting at the front. He moves down and slips into a seat beside him. — What are you daein here? I thought you had nae interest in art.

Renton turns to face him. — I thought I'd put in a cheeky wee bid for the *Leith Heid*s.

Frank Begbie says nothing. He rises and returns to Martin, who is talking to Kenneth Paxton, the head of the London gallery he has got Jim Francis attached to. Franco barges in without any concern for protocol. — Who's the main man here?

Martin Crosby flashes the gallery head a look of apology that says *artists* ... but defers to Paxton. — That guy, Paul Stroud, the gallery owner calmly announces, pointing at a bald-headed, abundantly bearded fat man sweating in a linen suit, fanning himself with a hat. — I mean, he's not the collector, but he's the representative and buyer for Sebastian Villiers, who is big news.

— Seb's a major collector of Jim's work, Martin says to Paxton, *and* the artist, as if to remind him. — If he wants *Leith Heads*, then they're his.

Frank Begbie's surprise is compounded when he sees Mikey Forrester standing nearby. His eyes go from Renton to Mikey, both looking decidedly uncomfortable, Mikey obviously aware of Renton's presence, but not the other way round. *What the fuck is gaun oan here?*

The auctioneer, a thin man with glasses and a tapered beard, points to four heads mounted on a display sideboard. — Our first item for auction today is *Leith Heads*, by acclaimed Edinburgh artist, Jim Francis.

In the front row, Mark Renton stifles a guffaw that originates from somewhere in his bowels. He glances at the group of wideos, some of whom send vague bells of recognition ringing, and finds he isn't alone in his mirth. Renton looks at the Sick Boy head. It captures him a little, but the eyes are too serene. He arches round to see if his old friend has shown up, despite his assurances he wouldn't, doubting Sick Boy could resist succumbing to the vanity of his own image on display.

— One is a self-portrait, the auctioneer continues, — the other three representations of his boyhood friends. All are cast in bronze. They come as one lot, rather than separate items, and I'm instructed to start the bidding at twenty thousand pounds.

A paddle is raised in the air. It belongs to Paul Stroud, the agent of the collector Sebastian Villiers.

— Twenty thousand. Do I hear twenty-five?

Mark Renton slowly and tentatively lifts up his paddle, as if this action might draw a sniper's bullet. The auctioneer points at him. — Twenty-five. Do I hear thirty?

Renton puts up his paddle again, occasioning some strange looks and a few laughs.

The auctioneer pulls his spectacles down over his nose and looks at Renton. — Sir, you cannot bid against yourself.

— Sorry ... I'm a novice at this game. Got a wee bit excited.

This sets up a series of guffaws from the punters, which die out as Paul Stroud raises his paddle.

— I hear thirty thousand.

— Thirty-five. Renton raises his hand.

— A HUNDRED THOUSAND! comes a shout from the back of the room. It is Mikey Forrester.

— Now we are getting serious, the auctioneer declares, as Frank Begbie remains composed, and Martin Crosby shimmies to the edge of his seat.

You have got tae be fuckin jokin, Renton thinks. Then he sucks in some air. *Fuck him. He won't beat me this time.* — ONE HUNDRED AND FIFTY THOUSAND!

— What the fuck is going on here? Frank Begbie asks Martin Crosby.

— Who cares!

Stroud pitches in, paddle flapping. — One hundred and sixty thousand!

Renton is back. — One hundred and sixty-five thousand!

Forrester shouts, — One hundred and seventy thousand! Then he dies a death as Renton hesitates, blinking like a small mammal in car headlights ...

— One hundred and seventy-five thousand, Renton croaks.

— I'm hearing one hundred and seventy-five thousand, says the auctioneer, looking at the sweating Stroud, heading to the exit, frantically trying to get a signal on his phone. — One hundred and seventy-five thousand ... going ... going ... sold! To the gentleman down the front, and he points at Mark Renton.

Euphoria and despondency battle in Renton. It is around five times what he wants to pay, but he has won! The *Leith Heads* are his. But now he is beyond broke. Had he not been on such an uncompromising mission, and known how much pain he saved a long-standing rival by his final bid, Renton might have shut up. As it is, Mikey Forrester breathes a massive sign of relief. He goes up to Renton. — Well done, Mark, the best man won, mate!

— Mikey, what the fuck, who are ye bidding for?

— Sorry, bud, got tae nash, Mikey smiles, making way for the advancing Frank Begbie, and dialling Sick Boy as he sharply exits.

Renton goes to follow but is intercepted by other attendees, offering him congratulations. He looks at the heads, and for a second, he thinks the Sick Boy one is smiling. Renton maintains his push to the exit, but is stopped by Franco, who shakes his hand. — Congratulations.

— Thanks ... What the fuck was Forry daein bidding?

— I'm as scoobied as you are.

— Whae was the other bidder?

— His name's Stroud. He works for this boy Villiers, a big collector. Must have breached his agreed limit, and he was trying to call the boy to get him to up it. But you were victorious.

— Aye, well, who was Forrester working on behalf of?

— Somebody who loves me and wishes me a fortune. No many ay them in Edinburgh! Franco laughs, looking at Renton, then considering. — Or …

— … some cunt that hates me and wants tae see ays broke. That's a slightly longer list … Renton lets out a long, tight breath, glancing again to the four heads, and fixating on one in particular. — Sick Boy was the only cunt that kent how badly I wanted to buy the heads. It was the only wey I could pay you back.

Frank Begbie shrugs. — Well, you got what ye wanted. The *Leith Heids*. Delighted for you, he says, lips pushing together tightly. — Now if there's nothing else …

— Maybe a thank-you?

To Renton's shock, the animation drains out of Begbie's face, as a dark thought seems to crystallise behind his eyes. — I've changed my mind. I want my fuckin money back. That fifteen grand.

— But … I … Renton stammers in disbelief, — I'm broke! I've peyed massively ower the odds for they heids! That was my wey ay peying ye back!

— You bought some pieces of art, Franco's voice, so slow and deliberate, — your choice. Now I want my money back. The money for that drug deal, back in the day.

— I've no fuckin got it! No now! No after breaking the bank tae buy … He looks at the heads and stops himself from saying *that load ay fuckin shite*. — No after buying the heids!

— Well, that's too fuckin bad, for you but, ay?

Renton can't believe what he is hearing. — But we're mates again, Franco, out in LA … the Cup final … we had a bonding experience ... the four ay us ... the DMT ... he hears himself havering, as he looks into insect eyes, containing nothing but cold treachery.

— Still a fuckin druggie, ay, mate? the unmoved Franco Begbie half sneers in Renton's bemused face. — It stipulated in the sale that the heads would be available tae the buyer after the exhibition next week. So let Martin know where ye want tae have them shipped tae, he nods over to his agent, — and he'll arrange it. Right now we've got a wee table booked for lunch at the Café Royal. I'd invite ye tae join us, but let's keep things on a business footing till ye pey me back the money ye owe ays. Till then, he smiles, turning to his advancing agent and high-fiving him.

Renton is in a daze as he exits and heads down the Walk. He registers a red disabled mobility scooter coming towards him. A small dog sits in the basket on the front. It's being driven by Spud Murphy.

— What the fuck ...

— Nifty, ay, catboy? Pride Colt Deluxe. Up tae eight miles an ooir. Ah got a hire ay it fae the social. Was headin up the toon tae the hotel tae see ye. He hands Renton a tan Hugo Boss bomber jacket. — You left that up the hoaspital when you brought ays in.

— Thanks ... Renton takes the garment, looks across at an Italian cafe. — A wee cup ay char, bud?

28

BEGBIE – A HISTORY OF ART

The cunt stands in front ay the big, grey, marble fireplace. He raises an eyebrow, then his gless, and looks at me. Melanie, sitting next tae ays, wears a light brown backless dress, and a nice lavender-scented perfume. — A highly successful auction, Iain Wilkie, the well-known Glasgow painter, now 'exiled' in the New Town, as the cunt puts it, sais tae us. His wife, Natasha, curves trying tae burst oot ay a short black party dress, gies ays a wee smile. The ride pours some mair San Pellegrino intae ma gless. They're Mel's mates, here in the art world, n you've got tae make a wee effort. Ah'd rather be at the boxing club wi the boys … well, maybe no. It's a big myth that ye move intae a new world when ye leave the auld yin. What ye usually move intae is fuckin limbo.

What ah miss is being in the studio, daein ma stuff. Aw this exhibitions n auctions shite n dinner parties, they dae ma heid in. Ah jist want tae work oan ma paintins n sculpture, n hing oot wi Mel n the bairns. Gaun for walks doon the beach, wee picnics, aw that sort ay stuff. That wee Eve is a scream. Cracks ays up the things she comes oot with. Grace n aw, but she's mair like her mother. When aw that good stuff, my work and my girls, when that gets taken away fae ays, then that's when ah git tempted by the auld diversions. I feel the fuckin urge tae hurt some cunt.

This Wilkie gadge is rabbitin shite aboot how he needs tae drink, has tae get fucked up tae express his creativity. It's a veiled dig at me being the only sober cunt here: anybody can see that. Natasha fills up ma gless wi more sparkling mineral water. If it had been peeve in that gless her man would be up the Royal by now, gittin a fuckin tanned jaw reset.

— I like life better without it, I smile at him, — it only takes me places I don't want to go.

Natasha grins again. I ken I could ride her nae bother. These people are like that. It's the wey they are. That's how she sees me; savage, untamed Frank Begbie, the real fucking deal, no like the poofy 'bad boy' of Scottish art, the title they gied tae that poseur. Or used tae. Before ah came along. Now he's aw keen tae be best mates.

— We're running a little dry here, Wilkie goes, draining the last ay the wine.

— I'll nip out for a couple of bottles, I tell them. — I'll get decent stuff, I'm quite *au fait* with vino now, Mel always sends me oot, ah wink at her.

So ah slip oot doon tae the offie. It's a posh fuckin shoap in a basement. Ah picks oot some Napa Valley Cabernet that seems dear enough, n it's what Mel and her mates drink back in California. While ah'm inside, settling up, ah hears a bit ay a commotion gaun oan fae the street. Ah peys up n gits ootside swiftish, right up the steps, intae the dark road, tae see two young gadges, early twenties, shoutin at each other. One boy roars: — Ah'll fuckin take ye any time! Think ah'm fuckin feart ay you?

The other gadgie seems cooler, mair in control, n a bit less pished. — Moan then, doon thaire, n eh points tae the wee lane. They head off, and I'm thinking: *Yes, ya fuckin beauty ... two juicy flies gaun right intae the spider's fuckin parlour ...*

Ah follays them doon and sure enough, thir tradin blows n then the less pished gadge has got the loudmouth oan the deck. He's oan him n batterin the fuck oot ay him, pounding um in the coupon. The loudmouth's goat his hands raised n screamin, — FUCKIN LIT AYS UP, AH'LL KILL YE, YA CUNT!

Ah pits the bag ay wine doon against the waw, n ah'm right up behind them. — Nae sense in him littin ye up, if yir gaunny kill um, ya daft cunt.

The mair sober boy turns roond, looks up at ays n goes, — What's it tae dae wi you? Fuck off or you'll git some n aw!

Ah gies him a grin, n ah sees the cunt's expression change, as ah steps past him n boots his grounded mate right in the chops. The boy screams oot. The other boy jumps right off him, springing tae his feet n squarin up tae me. — What ye fuckin daein? This isnae your bus—

Ah kick him in the baws a beauty and the cunt yelps oot. He's bent ower n trying tae crawl oot ay the dark lane, back oantae the lit-up street. — Uh-uh-uh, you're gaun naewhaire … n ah grabs him by the hair and drags him ower tae the decked cunt oan the cobblestanes. — Apologise tae yir mate.

— But you … you kicked him in the face!

Ah bangs the cunt's heid oaf the waw, twice, n his heid bursts open on the second bang. — Apologise.

The cunt looks fuckin spangled, n ah'm twistin his hair away tae keep the blood offay ma clathes. — Darren … ah'm sorry, mate … eh groans oot.

The Darren boy's tryin tae stand, pillin ehsel up the waw. — What's the fuckin story …?

— Take a fuckin shot at this cunt's pus, ah tell him, ma grip still oan the other gadge's hair.

— Nup …

Ah batters the other boy's heid oaf the waw again. The cunt's shitein it. He's beggin the boy he was just batterin a minute ago. — Aw … dae it, Darren … just dae it!

The Darren boy's jist standin thaire. He takes a look back doon the alley. — Dinnae think aboot fuckin runnin, ah warn the radge. — Hit the cunt!

— Dae it! Jist dae it n wi'll git doon the road! the other boy begs.

The Darren felly punches ehs mate. It's no much ay a dig. Ah steps forward n hooks the Darren boy in the pus. It's a beauty n eh topples doon oan his erse. — Git up! Git up n hit um right, ya fuckin mongol!

Darren gits tae ehs feet. Eh's greetin, n ehs jaw's aw swollen. The other boy, ah kin feel um shakin like a fuckin leaf, ma grip's still tight oan his hair.

Ah looks at the Darren boy. — C'mon, ya cunt, wiv no goat aw fuckin night! The Darren boy looks at his mate aw sad and guilty. — Git oan wi it, ah'm fuckin well runnin oot ay patience here!

Ah loosens ma grip as the Darren felly panels his mate, goodstyle, fuckin droaps the other boy wi a solid smack tae the chops. Ah jumps forward, rams the fuckin nut oan this Darren cunt, whae faws in a heap beside his mate. Ah'm bootin baith cunts. — Back each other up, ya fuckin poofs! Ah immediately think ah shouldnae have said that, cause it might be construed as homophobic. Nae time for aw that nonsense these days. Tons ay gay friends in California. Ye get back intae bad habits ower here though, right enough.

Thir lying thaire, groaning, burst mooths, and ah sees the other boy look oot through a bloody, crusted eye tae the Darren yin.

— Shake, ah goes. — Ah hate tae see mates faw oot. Shake each other's hands.

— Okay … please … sorry … the less drunk cunt goes. His hand reaches oot n grabs Darren's. — Sorry, Darren … he goes.

301

The Darren boy, baith his eyes slits in purple bulbs now, dinnae ken if that wis me or his mate; he's moanin, — S'awright, Lewis, s'awright, mate … let's just go hame …

— DMT, boys, if yis huvnae tried it, gie it a go. This disnae matter, this is jist transitional, ah tell the cunts.

When ah leave the alley, thir groanin away thegither, tryin tae help each other tae thair feet. Aw mates again! That's ma fuckin good deed for the day!

As ah make to leave the alley, ah pick up the bag wi the boatils ay wine, breathin nice and even. Thaire was rain earlier, n the bushes are wet, so ah rub the bloodied hand on them, removing as much ay it as ah kin. By the time ah'm oot the alley ah'm no Frank Begbie any more. I'm the celebrated artist Jim Francis, and I get back to the palatial New Town home of my friends Iain and Natasha, and my wife, Melanie.

— There you are, we were wondering what was keeping you, Mel sais, as I come through the door.

— You know, I just couldn't make up my mind, I'm afraid, and I put the bottles on the kitchen worktop and look at Iain and Natasha. — That's an amazing selection ay wines they've got, considering it's a local shop.

— Yes, the guy who opened it, Murdo, he's got another branch in Stockbridge. Him and his wife Liz, they go on wine-tasting holidays every year, and they only stock from a vineyard they've personally sampled, Iain goes.

— Is that right?

— Aye, and it makes a big difference, that attention to detail.

— Well, I'll take your word for it. I'm pretty boring these days, having shed all my vices.

— Poor Jim, this Natasha hoor goes, aw pished. If I didnae love my wife and daughters, I'd probably bang it. But I dinnae hud wi that sort ay behaviour, no when you're mairried. Some people, it means fuck all tae thaim. But it disnae mean fuck all tae me. Ah puts my airm roond Melanie, as if tae tell this Natasha yin tae git tae fuck.

Then ah heads through for a pish, n gies ma hands a proper wash, in case anybody notices. Knuckles a bit scraped, but nowt else is a problem. Ah goes back through n curls up oan the couch, aw contented eftir ma wee fix. But the only thing that'll pit this right is getting intae the fuckin studio and back tae work. Cause ye cannae go around battering the fuck oot ay cunts. It isnae very nice, and ye can git yersel intae bother.

29

WANKERS AT AN EXHIBITION

Edinburgh's art cognoscenti are uncharacteristically nervous and self-conscious, filing into the prestigious Citizen Galleries in the Old Town. Within a gutted Victorian exterior with decorative facade, this functionally modern, three-storey space, with its high ceilings, white walls and pine floors, central lift and steel fire-escape stairways, is more than comfortable. But it's their fellow clientele, rather than the premises, which is the source of the artsy crowd's discomfort. They are in the novel situation of rubbing shoulders with the shaven-headed, tattoo-covered, Stone Island-bedecked hordes they perhaps distastefully spy from their estate cars, swaggering their way to Easter Road and Tynecastle stadiums, or to Meadowbank or the Usher Hall for a big boxing event.

These two Edinburghs rarely dally in the same zone too long for any serious cross-cultural pollination to occur, but here they are, moving through the gallery to the middle floor, united, to witness the exhibition of the work of one of Leith's most infamous sons, Jim Francis, better known locally as Franco Begbie. Surprisingly, it's the toffs, on their home turf, who make the early running for the complimentary drinks, the baseball caps standing back, perhaps a little unsure of the protocol. Then Dessie Kinghorn, a CCS veteran, ambles up to the bar, looks at the nervous server, and asks, — This free, mate?

The student, gamely paying off loans with a quarter-dozen jobs, is not going to argue details, and nods in accord. Kinghorn grabs a full wine bottle and a fistful of beers, turning to a group of hovering, emboldened faces and shouting: — Free fuckin ba-ar, ya cunts!

A stampede follows, the bourgeois mob melting to the side of the room in a manner some CCS vets haven't seen since the nineties. As if on cue, the man of the moment, the artist Jim Francis, enters with his wife, Melanie. The artsy crowd pounce on them, offering congratulations, as the thug element look at Begbie's mounted heads and paintings in doubtful bemusement, checking out the price tags and the positions of the security cameras and guards.

Mark Renton arrived earlier with Carl Ewart and Conrad Appledoorn, who is now following the silver-tray-carrying servers. Despite nodding to a few old faces, Renton feels safer behind the makeshift DJ booth, set up for the after-show party. The bank was broken to own the *Leith Heads*, displayed to the rear of the gallery, now it's to be disastrously trampled by Franco for a further fifteen grand that isn't there. The useless bronze heads stare back at him from their plinths. The expression on each, even his own, screams: *mug*.

— Do I really look as snidey as that heid?

— Got ye tae a tee, buddy, Carl Ewart says, observing the milling crowds. — Stacks ay fanny at these art dos but, Rents, he says, taking the words out of his manager's mouth. Both men have lived too much of their lives in clubs, surrounded for too long by women too young, sexy and beautiful for their rougher male cohorts to ever believe in any form of social justice. Yet Renton has discerned, within the ranks of Edinburgh's female artsy bourgeoisie, a serenely arrogant poise and entitlement, which might have been expected at a bigger urban centre, like New York or London.

— When you get this amount of stuck-up, quality birds on a Tuesday night, it can only mean that independence is in the offing.

— It isnae the Busy Bee or the Cenny, for sure, Carl acknowledges. — I'm surprised Sick Boy isnae networking ... he begins, stopping instantly as he sets eyes on Simon David Williamson, raffishly at the centre of a posh-frocked squad of beauties. — Scratch that thought. And look ...

Renton cannot bear to set eyes on Sick Boy, who has made no attempt to engage with him since the successful but catastrophic auction. *All that money. All that travel. Hotel rooms. Clubs. Tinnitus. All for fucking Frank Begbie! All because of fucking Williamson, the cunt.*

Carl has spotted Juice Terry, chatting up one of the female catering staff. — Terry isnae aspirational socially, just sexually, Carl ruminates. — He walks into a room, and he just sees fanny, full stop. He fastens on to one and if she tells him tae fuck off, he moves on to the next ...

— ... Whereas Sick Boy, Renton interjects, warming to Carl's theme, — sees a woman's minge as essentially a device, a conduit to the greater prize: the control ay her mind and, ultimately, her purse. Fanny, mind, purse, that's always been his trajectory. Getting them into bed is the end ay the line for Terry, but only stage one for sly Si. He is a cunt. Renton focuses back on his old friend.

I gave that prick ninety-one thousand quid and he set ays up tae be shafted for Begbie's bronze heids for another one hundred and seventy-five. And that fucker Begbie wants another fifteen four hundred and twenty on top ay that!

Renton feels giddy, almost physically sick. His nausea rises further as he overhears a sincere Sick Boy contending, — Classic Motown, classic Motown and classic Motown, in response to a question regarding his musical preferences.

— Note the words *classic* and *Motown*, he adds, just in case there is any ambiguity.

— The boy's a fuckin bastard, Renton begins, before he feels Carl's elbow banging his ribs. His client is pointing to an apparition standing in the doorway, looking inside in spooked awe.

— God sake, says Renton, — that fucker should be in his kip.

Spud Murphy staggers towards them, taking a glass from a waiter's tray, looking at the young man as if expecting it to be snatched away at the last second. — Mark ... Carl ... ah feel shite, man. This kidney, it's pure no workin right. It's like it's hard tae pish ...

— Ye shouldnae drink, Spud, you've only got one tae take the burden now. Time tae ease up, mate. Renton looks at his old friend in concern. — You seem out ay it. Ye taken anything?

— Ah'll come clean, mate, that jaykit ye left at the hozzy, thaire wis a bit ay how's-yir-faither in thaire n ah sortay taxed it ... Ah just snorted some lines the now ... rough as fuck but, man ...

— Fuck ... that's no ching, Spud, it's K, Renton turns to Carl, — the stuff you gied ays, mind?

— You're welcome to it, Spud, Carl says.

— Right ... ah'd better git back hame then, left the pavey scooter ootside ... Spud turns to Renton. — Sub ays, mate ...

Renton despondently pulls out a twenty from his wallet.

Spud gratefully snatches it. — Ta, mate. Will replace it and the collies whin ... well ... later ... His head jerks round. — No gaunny go withoot sayin goodbye tae Franco but ... legs awfay heavy though, man, like ah'm pure wadin through treacle, he says, then lurches away from them.

Renton makes to follow, but Carl says, — Naw, leave um. Let Franco sort him oot. You have a needy client. Tell me about this Barça deal again.

Mark Renton cracks a smile and watches, with a malicious glee, as Spud Murphy lumbers, zombie-like, across the floor, towards Francis Begbie. The artsy entourage fussing over the star scatter like pins in a bowling alley, as Spud finds his target.

Franco greets him through clenched teeth. — Hi, Spud. Nice to see ye here. You sure ye feel good enough tae be oot though?

— Ah'm gaun hame now ... ah just wanted tae see ... this exhibition. This is likesay weird, Franco, Spud says, stroke-victim mouth flapping open, — like Hibs winnin the Cup or me losin ma kidney. It's mental ...

— The world throws up shocks, bud, Franco agrees. — The plates are shifting. It's aw up for grabs, mate.

— Ah'm pleased fir ye though, Franco, dinnae git ays wrong ...

— Ta, bud. Appreciate it.

— ... Cause you've really changed, man ... and you've likesay goat everything n ye pure deserve it.

— Thanks, Spud, nice ay ye tae say so, mate. The artist hauls in a deep breath, battling a fundamental resentment at being cast as Franco Begbie, fighting to keep grace in his voice. He was the artist *Jim Francis*, from California, here with his wife and his *agent, for fuck sake*. Why couldn't they just let him be that? What the fuck was it to them?

— Aye, you've changed awright, Spud insists.

— Thanks, Franco repeats. He scans around the milling, chattering crowds, all their eyes on *his* paintings and pieces of sculpture. Except the doolally set in front of him. He looks for a potential upgrade on the company, and a sucker to entrust Spud to.

— Aye, you've no goat the same eyes, mind they killer's eyes ye used tae huv? Spud demonstrates by trying to force

308

his bug-eyes into slits. — Thaire's just pure love in they eyes now.

— Again, thanks, Franco says through a locking jaw, waving to Melanie.

— Ah see it when ah see ye look at yir wife ... n she's tidy, Franco, if ye dinnae mind ays sayin likes. Spud feels a roll under his feet like the wooden floor is uneven, but he steadies himself. — She looks like she's a kind person n aw, Franco ... Great thing whin ye git a good-lookin lassie ... that's a kind person n aw. Did she make you a kinder person, Franco? Is that the answer? Love?

— I suppose it is, Spud. Frank Begbie feels his fist tighten on the glass of sparkling water in his hand.

— Ah hud love wi Alison. N it wis good ... it wis the best ever. But ah couldnae keep it, likesay. How's it you dae that, Franco ... how's it ye keep it?

— Dunno, mate. Luck, ah suppose.

— Naw it's mair thin luck, Franco, Spud says, his voice cracking with sudden emotion, — it's goat tae be poppy n aw. N success. Like you stumbled oan this hidden art talent. Ken? That's ma problem, he laments, — nae talent tae speak ay.

Frank Begbie hauls in another breath. Sees the opportunity to introduce the levity he badly needs. — You were a decent housebreaker and no a bad shoplifter.

Spud shuts his eyes, opening them after a couple of beats, and takes in the strangeness of the room. — Aye, n ye ken whaire they talents took me, he says. — But you've done well, Mark's done well, though we ey kent that, he went tae university, the lot, n Sick Boy ... as long as there's chicks tae exploit, he's ey gaunny git by. But how did it happen tae you, Frank? How did Frank Begbie ... how did Frank Begbie ... come oot ay aw this as the cat that goat the cream?

— Look, mate, ah told ye, Franco says impatiently, — it just happens. Meet the right person at the right time, get a bit encouragement, find something ye like daein ...

He is relieved when Martin approaches them. His agent is a very composed man, but his eyes are glazed and his pupils enlarged in excitement. He points to a big canvas on one of the walls. It depicts a man tied to railway tracks. — *Blood on the Tracks*, it's been bought by Marcus Van Helden for one million, Jim! One painting!

— Quid or USD?

— Well, USD. But it's more than *twice* the highest amount you've sold a single piece for!

— Gallery gets half, so that's half a mil. You get a hundred grand, that's four hundred thou. Taxman gets a hundred and fifty, that's a quarter ay a million bucks, or aboot one hundred and eighty thousand quid.

Martin's brow furrows. He struggles to understand his client's mentality. What others were in receipt of seems to be of far more concern to him than his own substantial remuneration. — Well, that's life, Jim ...

— Aye, it is.

— It's a single piece and it sets the bar high for your other work. It establishes you as a premium artist in the eyes of collectors.

— Suppose so, Jim Francis says without enthusiasm, as they move across to the picture, Spud staggering along behind them. The piece depicts a bloodstained figure bound to a railway line. — That pure looks like Mark, Spud sings excitedly.

— It does a bit, Franco grudgingly concedes, looking over at Renton by the decks. — I wisnae thinking ay him, though. Must have been subconscious.

— This art gallery, man ... it's awfay posh n gies ays the heebie-geebies just gaun in. So ah've goat this ketamine, n that's the only wey ah kin git through it, Spud announces to Begbie and Martin, then suddenly lurches to the steel stairs.

Franco looks at Martin in semi-apology. — An old pal, fallen on somewhat hard times.

Instead of going down the stairs to the exit, Spud, his mind now succumbed totally to a blank limbo, lurches up to the vacant top floor. The room is the same as the one below, but it's empty.

Where is everybody ...?

He is scarcely aware that he is taking a fire hose from the wall. Starts to unravel it. Looks down at it. Throws it away. Turns it on at the tap, then wanders off, oblivious to it jumping over the floor like a demented snake, shooting out a high-pressure jet of water. He stumbles back to the fire escape, then feels himself falling downwards, but not safe like the DMT trip, and a javelin of panic skewers through the drug anaesthetic as he reflexively reaches out to arrest his decline, grabbing out at an exposed pipe, using it to steady himself. He is aware of gently sliding again, as it wrenches from the wall. Then it snaps. Spud tumbles down a few steps, and a river of cold water skooshes from the burst duct into the stairwell.

Assisted by the banister railing, Spud manages to pull himself to his feet. He descends the stairs, almost blind, following the music, nearly knocking over a server with a tray. People gasp and move aside as Renton runs from the decks to intercept. — Fuck sake, Spud. He grabs his friend's scrawny shoulders, placing a glass of champagne in his hand.

— The system, Mark ... it's beat us aw, Mark.

— No, mate. We're the undefeated. Fuck the system.

Spud lets out a high hyena-like laugh, as Renton helps him sit down in a chair by the decks. Carl N-Sign Ewart plays smooth, soulful house as the various associates of Franco

– boxers, ex-football thugs, jailbirds, construction workers and taxi drivers – start to mingle with the genuinely libertine among the artsy crowd, while the poseurs make for the cloak-room, like *Titanic* passengers for the life rafts.

Renton is trying to coax a bored Conrad to play for a bit. He has the big headlining SSEC gig later. — It's still early. Do a wee turn.

— They do not pay.

— A wee favour for your manager?

Conrad looks at Renton as if he's crazy, but gets up to play anyway, Carl happily giving way for him. The overweight young Netherlander drops the first track to cheers, promoting his manager to slap his back. — Go on, the Dutch master!

Then Conrad shouts at Renton, — There is a girl who is hot. He points to a young woman, sipping water by the side of the dance-floor area. She has killer cheekbones and hypnotic ringed green eyes.

— Play. I'll get you an intro. Are you going to showcase the new track?

— Invite her to come with me to the SSEC gig. If she comes, you do not need to go, he says with a grin, then cuts back to a petulant, reprimanding scowl. —You, and the world, will hear the new track when I am ready!

— Sound. Renton focuses on the positive; a get-out-of-jail-free card is in the post. As Conrad gets back to work, Renton and Carl go over to Juice Terry. He greets them with hugs. — The Milky Bar Kid is back in town! And the Rent Boy tae!

— I love you, Terence Lawson, Carl says.

— Lean Lawson! Did you go tae the final? Renton asks.

— Hud a fuckin ticket, ay, but ah ended up baw-deep in this tart.

— Nice one, Tez, Carl says.

312

— Aye, ah wis watchin the game oan the telly while pumpin it aw weys. Hud her ower the couch, then oan the bed tied tae the metal frame wi her ain Hibs scerfs. Best ay baith worlds. When those cunts went 2–1 up, ah kept up the pressure till Stokesy equalised. Still at her whin Gray goat the winner. Final whistle, ah jist punched the air n blew ma fuckin muck right up her! Best fuckin ride ah ever hud!

Renton laughs, then nods towards the object of Conrad's desire. — Who's that lassie?

— Used tae be a gangster's pump, but ah got her ootay that and intae the scud, Terry says. He starts to tell Renton about some fairly recent gang war. A young team boss had perished, as did Tyrone and Larry, two old associates of Franco.

Renton, Carl and Juice Terry are joined by Sick Boy and the Birrell brothers – Billy 'Business' Birrell, the ex-boxer, and Renton's old pal Rab, who wrote the script for the porno flick they made. Spud is still in the chair, head twisted, eyes rolling, drooling out the side of his mouth. Franco is close by with Melanie, chatting to some guests. — Can't wait tae get home, Renton hears his old pal sing in an accent more Californian that Caledonian. But, he reasons, his own one is blanded out through living in Holland. Sick Boy has also picked up a dreary, poncey metropolitan ubiquity, though Leith was seeping back into his tones. Only Spud, he looks at the mess, crumpled into the seat beside the decks, is keeping it real.

Nobody notices that the ceiling has been bellying out. Sick Boy is avoiding the substantial cleavage that is being thrust in his face, looking over her shoulder at Marianne, who is wearing a blue dress. She arrived with a younger man and woman. Terry peels off the company and is straight over to her. *He's firing a volley of questions at her, the usual Lawson technique* ... — Excuse me, Sick Boy says to the busty woman, moving across the room to where Terry and Marianne are in conversation.

Renton watches him detach Marianne from an irate Terry, and lead her to the fire escape. Just as they disappear, the ceiling collapses and water cascades down.

— Save the work, screams Martin, pulling a painting from the wall.

Everybody freezes in amazement, then they rush to avoid the water and falling ceiling debris, or try to move the artwork. Frank Begbie remains impassive. — If there was a fire in a flat at Wester Hailes, wi a family trapped in a blaze, and the chance tae save them, the services would be called here tae save the art first. Ah dinnae git that.

— Jambo scheme, Renton says, — I get it.

While Franco laughs, Renton takes his opportunity. — One question, Frank, he coughs out exigently, — this money ... the fifteen grand, why now? Why do ye want it back now?

Frank Begbie pulls Renton out of earshot from Melanie, who is helping Martin and an attendant remove *Blood on the Tracks*. — Well, after a bit ay mature reflection, I think you're right. It'll help us all move on. Get rid ay aw this shite aboot the past, ay?

— But ... surely ... ah boat they heids. For way ower the odds. That's us mair than square.

— Naw, mate, you bought some art. It says so on the bill of sale. That's goat fuck all tae dae with our debt.

— You're no gaunny hit me with that ... please, Frank, I'm struggling, mate, ah've got –

— I'm no hittin ye wi anything. I don't do that any more. You stole fae us all; you eventually offered to pey it back. You

314

peyed back Spud. You peyed back Sick Boy, only tae rip him off again.

— But I peyed him back again! Renton cringes at his own voice, a high, infantile shriek.

— Anyway, I decided that I didnae want tae touch that money. Then you tried tae manipulate me by buying the heids, which ye hud nae real interest in.

— I was trying tae get ye tae take what wis due tae ye!

— That wisnae the motive, Franco says, as sirens wail from outside. — You wanted tae feel better aboot yirsel. Tae square the account. The usual AA or NA shite.

— Does there need to be a dichotomy ... a separation ... Renton stammers, — a difference between the two, do they need to be apart?

— Ah ken what a fuckin dichotomy is, Franco snaps. — I told ye, I got past the dyslexia in the jail, and huvnae stopped reading since. Did ye think ah wis bullshitting ye?

Renton swallows his own patronising silence. — Naw ... he manages.

— Prove that was your motive then. Prove that I entered intae yir calculations. Franco cocks his head to the side. — Make it right. Pey me my money back!

And Frank Begbie walks away, leaving Renton's mind unspooling through time and across continents, as he stands in the chaos that Spud has created. The gallery owner looks on in a helpless loathing as Martin runs around with staff, removing the last of the pieces. Conrad is upset about the water in the DJing equipment, and is shouting loudly. Carl can't get why, all that's his are the headphones and the USB card. Firemen and plumbers arrive in almost indecent haste, as maintenance men go about their business and guests gasp, moan and chatter. Outside, a screeching drama queen of a fire alarm continues its beseeching appeal long after everything seems in hand. Renton is rooted to the spot, with one thought burning in his mind: *Begbie knows I'm skint. He's beaten me again. I can't let that happen.*

And then there is Sick Boy, who has cost him everything, egressing with Marianne. Begbie would have been happy with twenty grand for those heads, but Sick Boy, through Forrester, had set him up to clean him out. That was not acceptable.

30

SICK BOY – MARITAL AID

Begbie's ridiculous exhibition was a must. I so craved seeing Renton's upset pus, knowing that I had primed Mikey to fuck his finances by bidding up Franco's useless work. Of course, the bronze head looks nothing like me. Yes, the defined cheekbones, solid chin and noble nose are present, but it fails to capture those swashbuckling pirate eyes. But Franco provided the bonus ball of the icing on the cake: the temperamental artiste decided that he wanted the drug money back after all! Salt in the Rent Boy wounds, and a deft touch I'd never have associated with Frank Begbie. Mikey informed me that Renton's treacherous ginger pus was a treat! Pity I missed that.

At the gallery Renton keeps his distance, fronting nonchalance, but not trusting himself around me. He slopes about the decks with Ewart and his fat Dutch kid. But all this is just a welcome prelude to the main reason for turning up, the presence of Marianne, who floats into the exhibition like a willowy ghost in a blue dress. Mazzer is in the company of a young guy and woman; two good-looking but shallow and disposable cunts to be found behind the velvet rope in any overpriced George Street hole. Whether the young boy is a lover or the girl's beau, he is effortlessly elbowed aside when Juice Terry hones in on her.

Time, therefore, suddenly becomes of the essence. I leave my unsavoury associates, and saunter over to them. — Terry

… if you'll excuse us a wee second. Marianne, we really need to talk.

— Oh, do we? She shoots me that look of cold derision, the one that always gets me right behind the baws. — You can fuck off.

— Aye, this can wait, ya cunt. Terry gies me the evil eye.

But Marianne isn't taking hers off me. She's heard my deceitfully seductive lines so often before. How many times can I do this? How many times can I make her believe? I'm feeling that power of pathos mashing me up inside, as I envision both of us being stricken down by a terminal disease, each with just months to live. A farrago of Bobby Goldsboro's 'Honey' and Terry Jacks's 'Seasons in the Sun' plays in my head as my voice goes low and deeply resonant. — Please, I say in a deathly plea, — this really is important.

— It had better be, she snaps, but I'm in the fucking game!

— Too right it better, Terry says in rage, as I take a reluctant Marianne by the hand and we depart for the fire escape. *Lawson! Cock-blocked by Williamson! The rampant Stenhouse forward was through in on goal and seemed certain to score, but the Italian central defender, the Leith Pirlo, came from nowhere with that well-timed tackle!*

On the fire-escape stairwell, she's looking pointedly at me. — Well? What the fuck do you want?

— I can't stop thinking about you. When you threw that drink in my face at Christmas –

— You fucking deserved it. And more! Treating me like shite!

I suck in more air and let myself shiver with cocaine withdrawal. — You know why I do that, don't you? Why I'm drawn to you and then push you away?

318

She remains silent, but her eyes are popping like she's been jacksie-rammed. Not by Euan's paltry Presbyterian penis, but by a proper monster, the size of the Holy Papa's staff. By an Italian stallion!

— Because I'm crazy about you, I say soberly. — Always have been, always will be.

— Well, you've got a funny way ay showin it!

Sloppy defending – presents a scoring opportunity! I raise my hand to her face, pushing aside the static hair to stroke her cheek, as I stare deeply into her eyes with my own moistening ones. — Because I'm fucking *scared*, Marianne! Scared of commitment, scared of love, and I let my hand fall to her shoulder and start to kneed. — You know that 10cc song 'I'm Not in Love'? Where the guy sings that song, because he's desperately in love, but vigorously trying to deny it? That's my song for you, and I watch her face involuntarily ignite. — I'm that guy! Scared ay the intensity of the feelings I have for you.

— Oh fuck off, Simon –

— Look, you don't want to hear it and I don't fucking well blame you. I know what you're saying to yourself: how has he suddenly got the balls to man up, and act on his fucking feelings? I look at her. — Well, the answer is *you*. *You've* stayed the course. *You've* believed in me. *You've* shown me love over the years, when I was too scared to give you it back. Well, no any more. Now I'm done with running and hiding, and I fall to my knees at her feet and whip out the ring. — Marianne Carr … I know you've changed your name, I add, forgetting her current moniker, — but you'll always be that to me, will you marry me?

She looks down at me in total shock. — Is this for real?

— Yes, I tell her, and I break into a sob. — I love you … I'm sorry for all the hurt I've caused you. I want to spend the rest of my life making it up to you. This is as real as real ever gets, I say, imagining her repeating that line to a mate in some George Street wine bar. *He sais that this is as real as real ever gits.* — Please say yes.

Marianne gazes into me. Our souls melt together like pastels in a hot mouth – her hot mouth – and I'm thinking of the first time we fucked, when she was fifteen and I was seventeen (at that age classed as stoat rather than noncing), and all the decades I've seduced her – and been seduced by her – since then.

— God … the fucking mug I am but I believe you … Yes! Yes! she sighs, as a torrent of water comes tumbling down the stairs, soaking my legs and her feet.

— What the fuck? I stand up and there's Renton. I glance down at the wetness on my trousers and then outstretch my arms. — Mark! Guess what! I just –

His head flies into my face –

31

RENTON – THE PAY-OFF

My forehead connects wi a sweet, satisfying crack oantae the bridge ay the cunt's nose. He slams a hand on the railing, which rings like a gong doon the stairwell, but cannae prevent his fall. Watching the wanker tumble doonstairs, like one ay those auld toy slinkies, almost in instalments, is a beautiful sight. He comes tae rest in a crumpled heap oan the cold metal ay the fire-escape stair bend, soaked by the water cascading doon the steps. For a few seconds ay fear grips ays: I'm scared he's been badly hurt in the fall. Marianne is doon tending tae him, hudin his heid up, as blood gushes fae his bent, cartoon-like nose, oantae his blue shirt n beige jacket. — Fuck sake, Mark, she screams up at ays, her eyes crazy wi rage.

I take a step forward. I'm bordering on penitence, till I hear him protest, — A cowardly attack ... so undignified ...

— That's what a hundred and seventy-five grand feels like, ya cunt!

Marianne, teeth barred, nose tip red, roars at ays, — How could you do that?! I've no fucking feelings for *you*, Mark! That was a one-off! And after what you gave me?!

— I don't ... I –

Sick Boy staggers tae his feet. His nose looks crooked and misshapen. I feel uneasy again, as if I've found and then ruined a hidden treasure; in its newly-mangled state, it's easy tae discern that formerly noble proboscis as a major source ay his charisma. Now the mess spills thick droplets ay claret down his garments and oantae the dimpled metal floor. His glassy eyes brim with focused rage, switching from me tae Marianne. — WHAT THE FUCK IS AW THIS ABOOT?

A bunch ay art worshippers tiptoe past us, tense and sheepish.

Does Marianne mean that I gave her ... Vicky ... fuck sake, I've probably gied Sick Boy a Bonnyrigg! It's time tae make masel scarce. — I'll leave you lovebirds tae work it all oot, I tell them, heading back intae the chaos. The door flies open, almost smacking ays in the face, as another school ay punters pass me, their feet splashing in the water.

Back in the exhibition space, everybody appears concerned but Begbie, who seems no tae gie a fuck about the possibility ay his artwork being damaged. Water still cascades doon the walls, but he's standing back wi that *satisfied* smile he used to deploy eftir he'd just caused carnage in a pub or on the street. He's gone fae being the uptight cunt who goes radge at nothing, tae the fucker who doesnae gie a toss aboot anything. I look for Conrad, only to have it confirmed that the obese young Dutch master did indeed vanish into the limo with the scud model, and down the M8 to his gig. Then I'm oot ay there, heading acroass tae the other exit, in order tae avoid Sick Boy and Marianne. I get oot through the departing crowds, into the still night, and walk back tae the hotel. I pass Spud, parked on the pavement, slumped over the handles and basket of his mobility scooter. He's in a deep sleep. If I woke him now, I would put him in greater jeopardy as he'd try and drive the thing hame. Best to leave him, and I weave up and down the city's medieval steepness tae my hotel room.

After a profound, satisfying slumber, I rise the next morning tae see Conrad sitting wi the green-eyed honey at the hotel breakfast. Anybody who thinks that wealth and fame are not aphrodisiacs should look at this wee beauty wi that blobby mess. I gie them a nod and smile, and sit alone, a couple ay tables apart from them. I loathe hotel buffet breakfasts, and order some porridge and berries off the menu. I get on the phone tae ma bank in Holland, checking on ma finances in increasingly exasperated Dutch and English, getting transferred between various specialist staff. I'm watching Conrad, as he leaves his girl *three times* during my convo to refuel; scrambled eggs, bacon, sausage, black pudding, tattie scones (my fault, I oversold them tae him), beans, tomato, toast and bakery goods – pain au chocolat, croissant – and, almost perversely, a portion ay fresh fruit and yogurt. Then, as the model lassie slavers on aboot addiction, he's horsed the lot and I'm still oan the line, trying tae work oot how they can pey me ma cash. Well, not just mine any more. I'm three grand short and have tae arrange an overdraft, but they gie ays the clearance on the money I'm owing Franco.

Now I need tae head ower tae the Scottish bank, where the wire transfer has been placed, quickly telling Conrad I have an emergency and will meet him back here in an hour tae get the Amsterdam flight. The bank is a trek down tae the New Town, and there's nae cabs till the Mound, when I'm practically already there. They issue the poppy, the fifteen grand four hundred and twenty that Franco changed his mind aboot. This on top ay the other money I shelled oot for those fucking heids, soon tae be en route tae Amsterdam. It's this smaller amount that's cleaned ays oot. And for this yin, Franco refused tae gie bank details, demanding a cash payment. So I'm totally skint, and ma only assets are the Amsterdam and Santa Monica pads, one ay which I'll probably now have tae sell. But Frank Begbie, or Jim Francis, or whatever the cunt calls himself, has issued the fucking challenge, and I'm rising tae it.

At my request I meet him at a cafe on George IV Bridge. He's already there when I arrive, wearing shades and a blue Harrington, nursing a half-finished black coffee. I sit down wi my tea and slide the envelope across the table tae him. — It's all there: fifteen grand, four hundred and twenty quid.

For a second ah think he might just laugh it off, n tell ays he wis takin the pish. But naw. — Nice one, he sais, pocketing the cash and rising. — I think this concludes our business, he goes, like a twat in a bad soap opera, and the cunt just walks oot the door withoot looking back.

Whatever's in my chest cavity crystallises intae rock and sinks doon intae my gut. I feel mair than just betrayed. I realise that this was how Franco felt all these years ago, and he wanted me tae experience it: that total and complete sense ay rejection. Spurned. Disposable. Worthless. I really thought we were mair than that. But he did too, back then, in his ain fucked-up wey. So the cunt has beaten me, and he's emerged victorious by confronting me with the shallow twat that I once was, or maybe still am. I don't even know any mair. Ah ken fuck all.

Except the realisation that there's nae wey I could ever have won. As well as my fear, it was my guilt: it bugged the fuck oot ay me ower the years. Franco's willnae even exist tae gie him any sleepless nights. That cunt doesn't care about other people. He's still a psycho, just of a different type. No physically violent, but emotionally cold. That's poor Melanie's cross tae bear. At least I'm done with him. I've totally fucked masel in the process, but I'm finished with the cunt for good.

I sit back, aw hollowed oot but finally free, and check the emails on my phone. There's one from Victoria's friend, Willow ...

willowtradcliffe@gmail.com
Mark@citadelproductions.nl
Subject: Vicky

Hi Mark,

It's Willow here, Vicky's friend. If you recall, we met on a couple of occasions in LA. Just to say that Vicky is going through a bad time at the moment. I don't know if you heard, but her sister died last week in a road accident in Dubai. Vicky is back in England now, and the funeral is the day after tomorrow in Salisbury. I know you guys had some sort of falling-out – what over, I don't know – but she really does miss you and I know she'd appreciate you getting in touch at this very difficult time for her.

I hope you don't think it too presumptuous or inappropriate of me contacting you like this.

Hope you are well. Matt says hi, he's taken your advice and signed up for the screenwriting program.
Best wishes,
Willow

Jesus fuck almighty …

I call Conrad, citing a personal emergency. He's surly about it, but that's just too fucking bad, he'll have tae travel alone back tae Amsterdam. I book a flight tae Bristol and a rail ticket tae Salisbury.

32

TAKING THE SHOT

It's job done and the enriched and satisfied Jim Francis allows himself to relax, enjoying his debut first-class flight. They certainly spoil you. It will be hard now to go back to economy. But he refuses the complimentary drinks proffered by the smiling air hostess. He thinks about how free bevvy could turn any occasion into a potential bloodbath. The bloated, tomato-faced businessman sitting in front of him, obnoxious and entitled, so demanding of the stewardess. A face that would burst open under just one punch. And those capped, whitened teeth, so easily loosened by a well-executed hook to the jaw. Maybe a chiv, like a conductor's baton, rammed into that liver-spotted neck, drinking the shock in his bulging eyes as that rich blood jetted across the cabin from his carotid artery. The screams and shrieks of raw panic, that orchestra Jim Francis, no, Francis Begbie, would extol to such efforts by his deeds.

Sometimes he misses a peeve.

It's still a long flight, though. Protracted and exhausting as always. A first-class seat makes it more bearable, but it doesn't change what it is. He feels its reductive power. Drying him out. The jail was healthier. How do people live like this? *Renton: never off fucking planes.*

Melanie, sitting next to him, is uncharacteristically edgy. This concerns Jim Francis, as he both admires and draws strength from his wife's natural calm and serenity. While he watches his movie, he feels her eyes going from her Kindle to his profile. — What are you thinking about, Jim?

— The kids, Jim turns to her. — Looking forward to seeing them. I don't like being away from them, even for a few days. I feel that I want to drink in every second of them growing up.

— I'm scared shitless about bringing the girls back home from Mom's, knowing that he's still stalking us.

— He'll have calmed down, Jim says evenly, as a vision of the purple-faced Harry, swinging from the hose-noose, tongue protruding obscenely, flashes through his brain. — Besides, we still have the tape. He'll behave himself, see the error of his ways, get some treatment. I thought he said he was doing AA.

— I'm not so sure.

— Hey! You're the liberal, meant to see the best in people, he laughs. — Don't let one pathetic, weak radge undermine your belief system!

But Melanie isn't in the mood to be teased. — No, Jim, he's obsessed! He's mentally ill. Her eyes widen. — We could move down to LA. New York even. Miami. There's a great art scene there ...

— Naw, he's no gaunny make us run, Jim Francis says coldly, in a voice that concerns them both, as it's one from a past that they both know so well. He quickly switches to bland transatlantic, contending, — We've done nothing wrong, *I've* done nothing wrong. Santa Barbara is your home. It's my home.

It certainly has been an eventful trip back to Scotland. *Renton, trying to be fucking wide by purchasing* the Leith Heads. *Well, he got them alright, at a price! Be careful of what you wish for, Rent Boy!* Jim permits his triumphant relaxation to meld into drowsiness through his in-flight entertainment

327

choice, Chuck Ponce's Gulf War movie, *They Did Their Duty*, the one Spud recommended.

Ponce plays a Navy Seal who bursts out of an Iraqi prison, coming across an encampment in the desert where a team of aid workers are held hostage by the enemy. He infiltrates the stockade, only to find out that the elusive weapons of mass destruction are stored there. He falls for one of the aid workers, played by Charmaine Garrity. There follows a strong action sequence with the actor depicted hanging from the wing of a plane, proving Chuck had a head for heights. But in real life it was essential to have those green screens, safety harnesses and stunt doubles. Jim dozes off just after Chuck's most memorable line, where he drawls to an Iraqi general, — You can tell your boss, Mr Saddam Hussein, that this American does not like sand in his turkey and has kinda got his heart set on getting these good people home for Thanksgiving!

At the airport, they retrieve the station wagon from the long-stay park, and Jim takes the wheel on the two-hour stretch out to Santa Barbara. Picking up their daughters and Sauzee, the French bulldog, from Melanie's mother's place, they gratefully continue on. Melanie drives this leg, with Jim in the front passenger seat. Grace is delighted to be with them, as is the younger Eve, but she fixes Jim in a reprimanding stare. — I don't like it when you go away, Daddy. It makes me angry.

Jim Francis looks round at his daughter. — Hey, Snottery Sleeve! When things make you angry, you know what you do?

Eve shakes her head.

— Pull in a very deep breath and count to ten. Can you do that?

The child nods, closing her eyes and aggressively filling her lungs with air. Melanie and Jim exchange a smile as the station wagon leaves Highway 101.

That night, after they put the kids to bed, and fatigue begins to creep up on them, Melanie, sitting with her husband on the couch, squeezes his hand and declares, — I'm so proud of you. You've come so far. It's not the money, even though it opens doors for us. We really can go anywhere now.

— I like it here, Jim stresses. — Santa Barbara's a great town. The kids love it. They love to see your folks. Grace is getting on great at the school, Eve will be there soon. Don't worry about Harry, he'll come to his senses. And we've got the tape.

Harry was good at stakeouts. He'd felt anxious and excited in equal measure when he learned that the Francis family had returned. He hadn't dared to go back to the house, but had waited outside the older girl's school till it was finally Melanie, not the kid's grandmother, who picked her up. Harry drove back to circle the neighbourhood, where he found that Jim was also present. He risked a glimpse in the rear-view mirror as he passed, and saw him, deathly still, as he supervised a shitting puppy on the front lawn. Turning onto the slip road that snaked above the block of houses where the Francis home was situated, Harry then pulled up. Vaulting over the barrier, into the forested verge that sloped towards the backyard of the target dwelling in that cul-de-sac, he scrambled down the bank, the leather bag containing the assault rifle slung across his back. From above, he could still hear the rumble of the traffic on the freeway. Keeping his distance behind a small oak, shielded in some thick foliage, he found an ideal station.

Taking out his rifle and assembling it, Harry attached the sights. His heartbeat pumped up when he saw to his amazement that his quarry was now in the backyard! Harry scoped Jim Francis, as he bent down to pick up one of the kids, the younger, more demanding child. To his shock and cold revulsion, he found himself moving the sights down past Francis, onto the chubby head of his young daughter. *That* was the shot that would hurt Francis, and her, Melanie, the most. The urge to just squeeze made him giddy and he felt the rifle shaking as, with a concentrated effort of willpower, he unhooked his finger from the trigger.

No no no ...

Not the children. And not Francis either, at least not until Melanie was forced to confront what he was. Until he confessed to her about those men he'd slain on the beach. Killing was easy. But it was a poor compromise. True vengeance, total justice and complete redemption, those were the building blocks of grace, and Harry had to strive for them.

He again focused on Francis, as the kid ran into the house. His prey was looking off into the distance. Even from this range, and with Harry having the power of death trained on him, there was still something about this motherfucker that gave him the creeps. He felt the phantom constriction round his throat, and the rising of his heartbeat was real enough.

Maybe just take that shot ...

The sun was almost overhead. Soon the lens of the scope would glint through the bushes, and Francis would pick it up on his blazing, swivel-eyed radar. Harry lowered the weapon, bagged it up and threw it across his shoulder. Clambering up the slope, he pulled himself back over the barrier to the slip road. Got in the car and drove onto the freeway.

The behaviour of his nemesis had convinced Harry that there was now only one way to resolve this. When he struck, it would be decisive, and Jim Francis would be no more. But that alone wasn't enough. She would know, oh yes, Melanie would know, exactly what she had married, what a tawdry and pathetic lie her life was.

Part Four
June 2016
Brexit

33

RENTON – VICTORIA'S SECRET

The train rolls into Salisbury Station. I'm exiting, saying my farewell tae two young squaddies I chatted wi on the short journey fae Bristol. We were swapping stories and I told them about my brother, blown up in Northern Ireland three decades ago. I felt instantly bad about that disclosure, as it left them oan a bit ay a downer. The older ye get the harder ye have tae fight against being socially inappropriate, becoming mair prone tae narcissistic emotional outbursts. They were nice lads and the fact that they're in soldier uniform is constant proof that a nation state isnae a kind construct if you urnae rich.

I'm nervous as I'd got no reply after texting Victoria to tell her I wis en route tae Salisbury, and what train I was coming off. I said ah'd see her later at the crematorium. I'm thinking that Willow maybe read this all wrong and the guy who gave her a dose ay the John Knox is the last person she wants tae see at her sister's funeral. But tae ma surprise, she's waiting there, on the station platform. She now looks smaller, older and frightened. Circumstance has stripped the vivaciousness fae her. The Californian sun-bleached blonde hair is already fading tae a murky Blighty brunette. She seems both surprised and relieved when ah take her in ma airms and hold her. It was either that or touch her hand and say something too cold. — Oh, Vic, I'm so sorry, I gasp intae her ear, and her tense body relaxes in my embrace, telling me it was the right move. And tae think I had rehearsed clichéd shit like 'how are you bearing up?' So irrelevant, as the tears streaming doon her cheeks and her choking sobs provide aw the requisite information. It's like hugging a pneumatic drill workmen use tae dig roads. But aw I can do is hud oan till they subside a little, then whisper in her ear aboot getting tea.

She looks up, her eyes wet. She wisely hasnae worn mascara. Her lips curl doon in an oddly childlike parody ay misery, which ah've never seen fae her before. I take her airm, and as we exit the red-bricked Victorian station, the first thing ah see is the beautiful spired cathedral, which dominates the toon. She takes me tae a touristy tea room on a winding shopping street. It's a fussy wee low-ceilinged joint, where two women, one an older, determinedly *manageress* type, the other a younger trainee, are chatting and busying themselves behind the counter. I order some tea and scones, and we sit doon away fae the windae, at Vicky's urging. Of course: she'll no want tae display herself tae her home toon in this frame ay mind. — You didn't need to come down here for me, Mark, she says plaintively, her voice breaking.

— Maybe we're just going to have to agree to disagree on that one, I tell her. Fuck me, I would take on aw the pain in the world right now, just tae alleviate one moment ay her throttling sadness. I can't believe I left it so long to see her.

— I'm so sorry, she says, fighting back tears, as her hand reaches across the table and fastens onto mine. — This is so stupid and horrible, and yeah, so fucking embarrassing. She forces a big breath into her lungs. Her voice still seems so small, like it's coming fae somewhere much deeper inside her than is normal. — I was kind of seeing somebody for a while, this guy Dominic … She halts as the younger lassie nervously approaches wi the tea and scones I ordered, setting them doon oan the table. I smile at her, catching the disapproving eye ay the manageress, who looks at ays as if ah intend tae pimp the girl oot.

As she leaves, Vicky continues. — Dominic and I weren't exclusive, but you know that ... and he didn't look after himself ...

Fuck ... I don't believe it ... Not Vicky, no my English Rose ... my English Bonnyrigg Rose ...

— ... You were away, and we hadn't really talked, like defined where we were going with all this, she looks downcast, — ... I felt a vibe, but I worried that I was being presumptuous ...

Fucking hell, man, what the fuck ... The tea room is so *frightfully English*, with its drapes, cluttered faux-country artefacts, and delicate bone-china cups and saucers. I feel like we're two sticks ay Semtex in a decorative cake tin. — We really don't need tae do this now, honey, I tell her, but I know she couldnae stop if she wanted tae.

Vicky shakes her head and smiles tightly, no really hearing ma intervention. — Anyway, he gave me something, brought me a present back from Thailand ... She looks up at me.

This is so hard for her tae say. It's horrible seeing her like this, but if she only knew how much ay a relief it also is for ays tae hear this, thinking it was *me* who had given the present tae *her*.

— This really was before you and I got properly ... well, whatever we got, she chews on her lower lip. — I didn't know, Mark. I gave it to you, right? I did. I'm so sorry.

I slide my chair round next tae Victoria's, pulling her to me, my arm around her shoodirs. — It's just one ay those things, babe. A quick visit tae the doc's, a week on the anti-biotics and it was gone. It's no important.

— It's the first time in my life I've ever picked up an STD. Honestly, she says, gaping lamps, the palm ay her hand literally on her heart.

335

— Unfortunately I can't say the same, I confess, — though it has been a while. But as I say, these things happen. And I cannae point any fingers at you, for going with somebody else. My instinct is tae run when feelings start tae get intense in that way.

— You said you were with that woman, Katrin, for quite a while. You're maybe not as much a commitmentphobe as you think, she says generously.

— That was an emotionally barren relationship, and it probably suited ays at the time, I tell her, glancing at the manageress looking at me like I'm a Rottweiler who has just shat on the lawn ay her country garden. — Then Alex came along, and he had certain needs, so I stuck around way too long, trying tae make it work.

— I wish you weren't so nice about this … I mean, you give a guy a dose of the clap and he says it's not important … but I know it was. I know that's why you didn't get in touch.

— No … I saw somebody else too, I admit. — From my own past. It was nothing, and as you say, terms were never defined, but I thought that *I'd* given it tae *you*.

— Oh God, what a pair we are, she gasps in something like relief. I'm wondering if she believes what I've said or thinks I'm just making it up tae help her feel better. — How did you … did Willow … does she know about the STD?

— Yes, she did, and no, she doesnae ken aboot the Maria von Trapp. As I said, these things happen. It was just a daft wee accident. Your sis, honey … that's the real deal. I'm so sorry. I squeeze Victoria tighter. Then a juddering bolt surges right through ays as Marianne and Emily gatecrash intae ma thoughts and ma fingers painfully intertwine with hers.

— You're really are a nice guy, Mark, Vicky says, tearing me away fae my ain pulsing angst. This is a fucking roller

336

coaster. I cannae even speak. I thought getting older would make things easier. Does it fuck.

Her big haunted blue eyes. I want tae swim in them. I'm barely reacting tae the worst compliment you can gie tae somebody like me: *a nice guy*. Tae my Leith lugs, it's always a euphemism for a sap, even if she doesnae mean it that way. Sometimes ye have tae step past yourself. Past aw those voices you've always heard in your heid. All the shite that you've let define ye: that ignorance, certainty and reticence. Because it's fuckin crap, all of it. You're nothing but a work-in-progress until that day you fall out of this world into the land ay dead men's trousers. — I love you.

Vicky lifts her head, and looks at me, joy and pain bursting out through her tears. A snottery bubble explodes from one nostril. I pass her a napkin. — Oh, Mark, thank you for saying it first! I missed seeing you so much. Christ, I love the shit out of you, and I thought I'd blown it!

I'm fuckin useless at receiving praise and this is as high as it gets. I respond wi humour, tae reduce the unbearable tension and the strangulating rapture inside ay me. — If you're referring to your nose, then yes, you just did. If you mean you and me, I'm afraid you're no getting away that easily.

Vicky puts her beautiful, reddish, blubbering face onto mine and her lips send soul-scorching kisses through me. I can taste the salty discharge fae her beak, trickling over our lips, and I love it. We sit there for ages, oblivious even tae the undoubted scrutiny ay the manageress, and talk about her sister. Hannah died in a car crash in Dubai, where she was on a break fae her duties working for an overseas aid organisation in Africa. A driver in a car in the opposite lane went into cardiac arrest, lost control and smashed intae her head-on, killing her instantly. Ironically, he survived, and was resuscitated with minor injuries. Vicky looks at her watch, and ye sense that she's been putting it off. — We should make our way to the crematorium, she says.

I pay the young lassie, leaving a decent tip. She smiles appreciatively, as the manageress tracks our departure, her face set in Thatcherite cheerlessness. Ootside, we walk through the Queen's Gardens, along the grassy banks ay the River Avon. — It's pretty cool here. Wish thaire wis time tae see Auld Sarum and Stonehenge.

— Honey, we are going to have to continue this romance in LA, because your accent has gotten so thick, I can barely understand you, and she *laughs* and my soul ignites.

— It has, hasn't it? Been back a lot lately, seeing some old pals.

— I'm dreading seeing mine, cause they were Hannah's friends too.

Fuck me, ah wish ah could take her pain, but that's the narcissistic element ay love talking. It's no yours tae take. All you can dae is be there.

It's maybe a crass thing tae say, but wi its big chessboard walls oan the main building and the tower, Salisbury has the coolest crematorium ah've ever seen. As the mourners acknowledge each other, I leave Vicky tae her grim meet-and-greet duties. An attendant, noting me taking in the architecture, explains that Scandinavians designed the facility. Tae me it feels uplifting rather than morose, reminding me ay the DMT trips, like a launchpad tae the next life. Nonetheless, the funeral is shite, as the untimely death ay a young person always is. I obviously didnae ken Hannah, but the outpouring ay grief and torment is real enough tae evidence a pretty amazing and deeply loved woman. They talk about Hannah's VSO work, culminating in NGO stuff in Ethiopia and Sudan, then working for a human rights charity based in London. The sort ay person a total wanker, that never did a thing for anybody in their lives, least

338

of all themselves, would dismiss as a do-gooder. — I wish I'd known her. I kind of miss not knowing her, I tell Vicky.

Instead I get tae meet Victoria's remaining family and her friends. Her mum and dad, the dimmed life-essence in their eyes set in ashen pallor, have had everything ripped out ay them, and are clearly broken. I've lost two brothers and my ma but I still feel it doesn't give me a notion of the kind ay road they have tae go down in order tae get back tae any sort ay normality. Vicky helps, and they cling tae her like limpets. They can see the bond between us and don't seem tae be unhappy about it. They probably wish I was a bit younger. Fair enough, I feel the same way.

As funerals do, it made ays think ay the people I know. How I have tae make mair time for them. It takes practically two minutes to put this resolution tae the test as I switch my phone back on after the service at the chapel of rest. I'm rereading that old email from Victoria. She wisnae ditching me, she was assuming *I was ditching her* because she gied me a dose. I then see three missed calls from an Edinburgh landline number. My first thought is: *my dad*. He's healthy, but he's no young any more. Things can change so quickly. When the same number goes again, I pick up as I watch Vicky and her parents shake hands wi the departing mourners.

— Mark, it's Alison. Alison Lozinska.

— I know who you are, Ali. I recognise the voice. How are ye?

— Good. But it's Danny.

— Spud? How is he?

— He's gone, Mark. He died this morning.

Fuck.

No Spud.

No my snottery-nosed old comrade in misadventure ... Berlin ... What the fuck ...

339

I'm feeling bits ay masel breaking off inside. No believing a word ay it. Not fucking having it. — But ... he was getting better ...

— It was his heart. They said it was weakened after the poisoning, following that kidney donation.

— But ... oh fuck ... how is your son, the name pops into my head, — how is Andy taking it?

— He feels terrible, Mark, he thinks he should have tried to help his dad more.

— He couldnae be Spud's parent, Ali, it's not on him.

Ali is silent for such a long while, I'm wondering if she's hung up. As I go to speak, her voice starts again. — I'm just glad Danny did something so good wi his life, donating that kidney tae save that bairn.

This is obviously the narrative that's been spun, so I'm fucked if I'm ruining it. – Aye, it was a great thing he did. How did he — what happened?

— He had a big heart attack a few days back. That almost did him, and the doctors telt him that a second yin was in the post. Listen, Mark, Danny left something for ye. A package.

— I'll be back up tomorrow, I say as I see Vicky coming towards me. — Strangely enough, I'm at a funeral right now, down in England. I have tae go. Ah'll call you later and see ye the morn.

I'm instantly at one wi the funeral party. No longer a tourist in their grief, but stewing in my ain bubble ay numbness. We head back into town, tae the King's Head Inn for the reception, which, in my distraction, I can't fucking well stop calling the after-party. I've been in club-land too long. Following a bit of small talk, Vicky says tae ays, — I need some air. Come and walk down Fisherton Street with me.

— Anywhere you want tae go, I tell her, taking her hand.

When we get outside, I start talking about Spud. I instantly apologise, telling her that I realise this isnae his or my time, but I just heard it and it's hit ays hard. She takes it well, pulling me intae the doorway ay a wool shop, and wrapping her airms roond ays and squeezing. I whisper, — I'm not going to say I know how you feel, because I don't. My brother Billy and I had a very different relationship fae the one you had with Hannah. But we were young when I lost him. I'd like to think we'd have been closer now, had he lived, I tell her. I can't believe my own ears. I don't understand why I'm mourning Billy now, after all these fucking years, as much as Spud. I'm snivelling thinking about them, and old mates like Tommy, Matty and Keezbo too.

— Hannah and I fought loads, she laughs. — We were only a year apart and had the same taste in boys. Can you imagine?

As we press on down the street, I'm thinking that Billy and me never really had the same taste in girls, although ah did fuck his pregnant fiancée in the toilet after his funeral. I rub my eyes as if trying tae erase the memory. Aye, I definitely would class that as iffy behaviour. Then Vicky suddenly shudders, as if reading my thoughts, but she's reacting tae something else. It's two girls, giggling, playful, walking down the shopping street of narrow white buildings. Probably going to a bar or somewhere else on that trail she and Hannah regularly traversed as teens, or when they returned home to catch up. Every gurgling fountain of their girlish laughter must be a devastating blow to her right now.

I stay the night at Victoria's parents, sleeping with her in a single bed. It isn't actually her old one, she explains; that was thrown out when they got the room done up, about a decade ago now. I tell her that Dad still has my room pretty much the same as when I left it, even though I never considered it home after the Fort. We whisper and kiss and make love tenderly, both having tested clear from chlamydia after the three months. It's hard tae leave her the next day, I want us tae be together until we both go back tae California, but her parents need her time more than ah do right now. I can't face even a short flight, so ah take the long train ride up tae Edinburgh, reasoning that it will gie me mair time tae think.

When I get intae the city early evening, I head tae my dad's, letting myself in wi the spare key. He isnae in, it's the night he goes tae the Dockers Club with some auld mates. His routine is etched into my consciousness from a million phone calls. Fuck knows how he would have reacted had he seen the contents ay the Sellotaped brown-paper package Alison brings round.

Alison looks quite different. She has put on weight, but carries it with an almost luxuriant swagger. Underneath her upset about Spud, she has an underlay of contentment. She was always a vivacious soul, though one permanently on the run from a dark cloud that hovered above her. That seems to have gone.

I contemplate the brown package on my lap. — Shall I open it now?

— No, Ali says urgently. — He said it was for your eyes only.

I put it under the bed and we head out tae the big Wetherspoons at the Fit ay the Walk for a drink. Ali's done alright; went tae university as a single parent to study English, then Moray House, and now teaches at Firhill High School. Yet she doesnae see this as a triumph. — I'm massively in debt and will be forever, in an incredibly stressed job that's killing me. And everybody tells me how successful I am, she chuckles.

— The only successful people are the one per cent. The rest ay us are just fighting over the crumbs those bastards spill fae the table. And their media are constantly telling us it's all good, or it's our ain fault anyway. Probably right about the second: ye get the pish ye put up wi.

— For fuck sake, Mark, this convo is depressing the fuck out ay me, ah hear it in the staffroom every day!

I take the point. Nae sense in dwelling on the world's shit, even though it's pilling up mair every day. — Hibs won the Cup! Impossible not tae believe in the revolutionary, transformative potential ay the human citizenry in such circumstances!

— My brother was on the pitch. He's worried cause he's already on a life ban from Easter Road. I'm glad Andy never had much interest in football. It's like everything else in working-class culture now, a route tae jail for doing practically nothing.

— Now who's the depressing yin? I laugh. She joins in, and it rolls years off her face.

It's great to see Ali again, and we have a decent drink, both a little tipsy when we leave. We exchange emails and swap hugs and kisses. — See ye at the funeral, I say.

She nods and I head down Great Junction Street. This stretch of Leith has struggled since as long as I recall; my auld girl and Auntie Alice taking ays up to the Clocktower Cafe in Leith Provy Co-op for juice; the auld State Cinema, long closed, where I watched the matinees on Saturday with Spud and Franco; Leith Hospital, where I got my first stitches, above my eye, after some cunt smashed the swing seat in my pus at the playground. All ghost buildings. Crossing over the bridge at the river, a place of phantoms.

Dad's still out, the boozy auld fucker, so I open the package. On top, a card. It just says:

Mark

Sorry, mate. Did not think at the time that it would mean so much to your folks.

Love

Danny (aka 'Spud') x

The card sits on a pair of jeans. Levi's. 501s. Washed and folded. My first thought is: *what the fuck*, and then I see it all. The Nick Kamen advert. Billy getting dressed in them, pulling them on, the cool stud who fancied himself, going out tae fuck Sharon or some other wee bird. While me, the reluctant virgin, lay on my bed, reading the *NME*, thinking aboot the lassies fae the school, and ma burning desire to pop ma cherry up the goods yard. Where no goods trains had run through for years. Willing the posing cunt tae leave so that I could pull the end oaf it tae the images of Siouxsie Sioux and Debbie Harry, kindly provided by IPC magazines.

Then my mum, storming in fae the drying green, teary mascara eyes like Alice Cooper, screaming, speaking her first words I remember since Billy's death, about how they've taken everything, *they've even taken ma bairn's jeans* ...

Spud had kept them all this time. Couldnae even flog them or gie them away. Too shamed tae hand them back, the sentimental snowdropping gyppo cunt. I could see him in my mind's eye, sitting shivering with junk withdrawal in a back pew at St Mary's Star ay the Sea, watching ma old girl light another candle for Billy, maybe overhearing her say, *Why did they have tae take his clathes, his jeans ...?*

Billy was always a thirty-four, me a thirty-two. I'm thinking that they bastards'll fit me now. — Who knows the mystery

344

ay the Murphy mind, I muse. Ah cannae tell Ali aboot this, at least no now. It's her son's dad.

Then, the packet underneath the jeans. I open it up. It's a thick manuscript, typed, with some handmade corrections. Astonishingly, it's written in the same style of my old junk diaries, the ones I always thought I might do something with one day. In that sort of Scottish slang that takes a wee while tae get on the page. But after a few pages of struggle I realise that it's good. Fuck me, it's very good. I lie back on my pillow, thinking about Spud. I hear my auld man come in, so I put the chunky document under the bed, go through and greet him.

We put the kettle on and talk about Spud, but I can't tell him about Billy's jeans. When he turns in, I find sleep impossible, and I need to converse more, to share all this grim news. I can't talk to Sick Boy. It's pathetic, but I just can't. For some reason the only person I can think ay telling the now is Franco, no that he'll gie a fuck. But ah send him a text for old times' sake:

No good way of saying this, but Spud died this morning. His heart gave out.

The fucker bats it right back at me:

Too bad.

And that's the extent tae which he cares. What a first-class cunt. I'm enraged, and I text Ali to tell her.

A charitable response comes back immediately:

It's just his way. Go to bed. Goodnight. x

34

THE FORT VERSUS THE BANANA FLATS

The sun beams obstinately in the cloudless sky, as if offering any potential troublemakers planning to drift in from the North Sea or the Atlantic a pre-emptive square go. Summer has bubbled its usual promise, but now there are signs of real traction. The old port of Leith seems to sprawl in heat's lazy vulgarity around the churchyard of St Mary's Star of the Sea, from the run-down 1970s Kirkgate shopping centre and flats on one side, to the dark lung of dock-bound Constitution Street on the other.

Despite the grimmest of circumstances, Mark Renton and his girlfriend Victoria Hopkirk are powerless to resist a nervy onset of levity occasioned by her first meeting with Davie Renton. Mark's father has never set foot inside the Catholic church. As a Glasgow Protestant, he initially resented it on ecclesiastical grounds, but when his stubborn sectarianism finally started to wane, he grew to see it as a rival for his wife's affections. It was his Cathy's place of refuge, indicative of a life he couldn't share, a competitor. Guilt wracks him, as it all seems so trivial now. To calm his nerves Davie has taken one nip too many. On seeing his son, in the churchyard with his English, American-based girlfriend, he undertakes a rakish Bond impression, kissing Vicky's hand and stating, — My son never showed good taste in women, then adding the waspish punchline, — until now.

It is so ludicrous they both laugh out loud, forcing Davie to join in. However, this reaction excites a chastising look from Siobhan, one of Spud's sisters, and they rein in their mirth. They greet the other mourners sombrely, filing into the church. In the icon-laden camp palace of unreformed Christianity, Victoria is struck by the contrast to her sister's cremation. In the coffin, the body of Daniel Murphy lies out on display in an open casket, in preparation for the full requiem Mass.

Renton can't avoid running into Sick Boy, who is present with Marianne. After a terse nod of acknowledgement, they are silent. Each wants to speak, but neither can bypass the powerful saboteur of pride. They studiously avoid meeting each other's eyes. Renton registers that Vicky and Marianne have exchanged glances, and is keen to keep them at a distance.

They file past the coffin. Renton notes uneasily that Daniel Murphy looks positively wholesome, better than he's done in about thirty years – the undertakers deserve a medal for their craft – the Hibs scarf he found at Hampden folded on his chest. Renton thinks of the DMT trip, and wonders where Spud is. It brings home how life-changing that experience was, as he'd previously simply have thought of him as completely extinguished; like Tommy, Matty, Seeker and Swanney before him. Now he genuinely doesn't know.

The priest gets up and gives a standard speech, Spud's extended family shivering under the meagre psychic comfort blanket he provides. The proceedings are uneventful, until Spud's son, Andy, gets up into the polished pulpit to make a testimony to his father.

To Renton, Andrew Murphy looks so like a young Spud, it's uncanny. The voice coming from him instantly undermines this impression though, a more educated, blander Edinburgh, with a hint of north of England. — My dad worked in furniture removals. He liked that manual labour, loved the optimism people felt when they were moving into a new home. As a young man, he was made redundant. A whole generation were, when they shed all the manual jobs. Dad wasn't an ambitious man, but in his own way he was a good one, loyal and kind to his friends.

At these words, Renton feels an unbearable tug in his chest. His eyes glass over. He wants to look at Sick Boy, who is sitting behind him, but he can't.

Andrew Murphy continues. — My dad wanted to work. But he had no skills or qualifications. It was important to him that I got an education. I did. Now I'm a lawyer.

Mark Renton looks to Alison. Through her tears, she glows with pride at her son's performance. Who, he thinks, will provide a testimony to him? Thinking of Alex, something catches in his throat. When he's gone, his son will be alone. He feels Vicky's hand squeezing his.

Andrew Murphy changes the mood. — And in a few years, maybe five, maybe ten, I'll be as redundant as he ever was. The lawyer will be gone, like the labourer before him. Made obsolete by big data and artificial intelligence. What will I do? Well, then I'll find out just how much like him I am. And what will I say to my child, he points at his girlfriend, her belly swollen, — in twenty years' time, when there are no labourers' or lawyers' jobs? Do we have a game plan for all this, other than wrecking our planet in order to give away all its wealth to the super-rich? My father's life was wasted, and yes, a lot of it was his own fault. Still more of it was the fault of the system we've created, Andrew Murphy contends. Renton can see the priest tense up to the point where the pressure in his arsehole could crush a solar system. — What is the measure of a life? Is it how much they've loved and been loved? The good deeds they've done? The great art they've produced? Or is it the money they've made or stolen or accumulated? The power they've exerted over others? The lives they've negatively impacted upon, cut short or even taken? We need to do better, or my father will soon seem a really old man, because we'll all start dying again before we reach fifty.

Renton thinks about Spud's manuscript. How Spud's life wasn't all wasted. How he sent it off to that publisher in London, with some minor modifications. He imagines he can feel Sick Boy's gaze, rapacious, on the back of his neck. However, his old friend and nemesis has averted his eyes to the floor. Sick Boy fights down a poignant, undermining reasoning that significance in life is only found in relationships with others, and we've been cruelly hoaxed into believing that it's all about us. A pain is intensifying behind his eyeballs, a sour sickness curdling in his guts. It shouldn't be like this; Spud dead, Begbie absent, him and Renton estranged. He's trying to convince himself that he tried to save Spud but his friend was let down by two people: his brother-in-law Euan McCorkindale, and brothel-keeper Victor Syme. — They fucking killed Spud, he raises his head and whispers to Marianne, — that two who urnae here.

— Begbie?

— No, not Begbie. Sick Boy scans the mourners. — Euan. He shat out of doing his duty as a doctor, couldnae even stop Spud getting infected. And I reunited that cunt with my sister!

'Sunshine on Leith' strikes up as the mourners rise and file past the coffin, paying their last respects. Spud, strangely, scarily, doesn't even look deceased. There isn't that lifeless, soulless, toneless quality dead bodies generally have. He looks like he could spring up and demand an ecky, Sick Boy thinks.

He crosses himself as he looks at his friend's face for the last time, and heads outside the church, lighting up a cigarette.

He overhears a conversation between Mark and Davie Renton, and Renton's girlfriend, whom he annoyingly finds exceptionally fit. He's surprised that she's English, rather than American. When he hears his old rival mutter something about his flight to LA, he cringes, and steers Marianne away. Renton will make the money back, he bitterly considers, scum rises to the top. Of course, Syme wouldn't show his face, but Sick Boy is disappointed at Mikey Forrester's absence.

Marianne asks him about attending the reception at the hotel on Leith Links, where the mourners are all heading.
— No, I'll spare myself the bleatings of victim plebs. Embittered anger and self-pitying grief love a spurious mission, and pissing it up with losers now has zero appeal. You move forward in life or you don't move at all, he scoffs as they head into the Kirkgate. — Even the church was almost unbearable, despite the palatial holy surroundings. The Murphy family, though, they always did embrace the wrong elements of Catholicism. To me the only part that makes sense is confession, emptying the sin bin when it gets full, to make room for new, incoming ones.

— His son gave a really nice speech, Marianne observes.

— Aye, a bit too close to communism for the old priest, decidedly *not* a liberation theologist.

She looks thoughtfully at him. — Do you ever think about dying, Simon?

— No, of course not. Though as long as there's a priest by my side I couldn't give a toss how or when.

— Really?

— The deathbed repentance, the Davie Gray winner in the game of life deep in stoppage time, as I think ay it. No prods need apply.

— Hey! Marianne pushes into him. — I was christened Church of Scotland!

— Nothing sexier than a Scottish proddy bird with an arse like yours. Wait till I get you in the sixteen-ninety position.

— Aw aye, what's that then?

— It's the sixty-nine but with a really skinny fucker and a fat cunt standing on either side of youse, just watching as you go at it, maybe frigging themselves off.

The lovers double-back down Henderson Street, opting for a fish restaurant on the Shore. In a favoured surrounding, overlooking the river, Sick Boy continues to grow more effusive, after his moment of reflection. — Alas poor, skint Renton, he pours the Albariño, — now penniless despite his cowardly attack on me. I'm betting he actually thinks that it bothers me: it was a pleasure to finally out him as the Fort yob he really is, strip him of his pathetic, cultured affectations. Leith south of Junction Street bred only thuggery; north of that great cultural divide was all port sophistication.

— You both came from minging schemes, Marianne laughs.

— Aye, but Fort House was never a Cables Wynd House. One is demolished, the other designated a listed building and deemed essential to our city's architectural heritage, Sick Boy snootily retorts. — Case rested.

Then Simon Williamson rises to head to the bathroom. Looks at himself in the mirror. His nose has set better the second time around. The A&E at the Royal was a painful nightmare, the beak still twisted after it was done. Apart from the unacceptable aesthetics, breathing through one nostril was proving difficult. And you could forget the ching. So Williamson was compelled to go private and have it reset under general anaesthetic at the Royal Free in Hampstead.

But Marianne at least has been fussing over him. He now has her at an advantage. — I know you slept with that treacherous ginger bastard, my lady. Of course, I'll keep this knowledge to myself and let you spoil me in your guilt. As for fucking Renton ...

Mark Renton is across Leith in the small hotel, conversing with Spud's family, his father, Vicky Hopkirk, and Gavin and Amy, the Temperley siblings. To satisfy a growing niggle in his bladder, he heads to the bathroom. En route, a cadaver-like man intercepts him. Seeming hollowed out by some virulent wasting disease, he bares his upper teeth in a death's-head grin. — Ah hear you've got some money for me.

Renton feels the breath being knocked out him, as he contemplates Rab 'Second Prize' McLaughlin.

35

BEGBIE – BREXIT

Wish ah could have made it ower for Spud's funeral the other week. Too bad. But ye cannae just keep jumping on eleven-hour flights. Shame though. Harmless cunt. Aye, it's a long way tae come and that jet lag is a killer, but Elspeth has had a tough time and she is ma sister. Didnae like the idea ay leaving Mel, no wi that fuckin Hammy the Hamster creep hanging aroond. But she took the kids to her ma's, and it's only for a few days.

Nae messing aboot; I take the tram fae the airport right tae Murrayfield. It's cauld for June, no like last month at the Cup final, and the exhibition. What a week that wis. Hibs win the Cup, and I make a fortune flogging ma stuff! That's a fuckin result! Hoping for another yin this time roond.

When I get tae the hoose, Greg's just leaving with the boys. They're shocked to see me, showing up like this. — Uncle Frank, Thomas, the younger, goes.

Greg looks up. — Frank ... When did you ... What are you ...?

— Came over tae see Elspeth. How is she?

— She had the op yesterday, and came through it well. I went in to see her last night ... We're just going there now.

— Room for another in the motor?

— Actually we're walking, he goes, n sees me lookin doubtful. The Royal is miles away and even the Western's a fuckin trek. — She's in the Murrayfield Hospital. We had it done privately, through BUPA, on the dependants company policy at my work.

— Nice one. Lead on, I say.

— When did you get in? Greg asks.

— Just now. Came straight fae the airport. Ah look at the two boys, George and Thomas. Fuck me, they're getting big. — How's the Young Murrayfield Team? ah joke. They look coyly at ays. Good laddies.

Greg smiles at them, then turns back tae me. The thin sunlight is being blocked oot by that big fir tree. — Are you sure you don't want to come inside and rest for a bit, maybe have a cup of tea? It must have been a tiring flight!

— No, ah'm best keeping gaun till I crash.

— Well, she'll be delighted tae see you, Greg says, as we make oor wey oantae the main road. — Hear that, boys? Your Uncle Frank flew in all the way from California, just to see your mum!

— Didn't Auntie Melanie come with you? says Thomas.

— Naw, she's got the girls to look after, pal. They all send you guys their love, by the way, I go, enjoying watching the poor wee cunts get a beamer.

It's only a ten-minute walk. It doesnae look like a proper hoaspital tae me, mair like a bank that smells ay bleach, a place where they just take yir poppy. Suppose that's mainly what it is. Elspeth is sat up in bed watching the telly, but she isnae looking well. She gapes at ays in disbelief. — Frank!

I gie her a hug, smelling the hoaspital and auld sweat on her. — How are you?

— Awright, she says, then goes aw hesitant, her brow furrowed, — well, aye and naw. I feel bloody weird, Frank, she says, as she greets Greg and boys. — But here are my big, strong men!

— Bound tae, ah nod, — a hysterectomy's a big thing for a woman, ah'm gaun. Though ah ken fuck all aboot that. But when you're a bairn in Leith, ye hear wifies gaun 'she's pit oan an awfay lot ay weight since her hysterectomy.' Ah dinnae ken whether that's through depression wi 'the change in life', as they caw getting yir fucking womb ripped oot, leading tae overeating, or if the metabolism just slows doon. Either way, Elspeth hus tae watch cause she's packin oan the coral as it is.

— That's what I've been saying, Frank, Greg cuts in, — there's bound to be an emotional reaction.

Ye kin see that this bugs the fuck oot ay Elspeth, but she's biting her tongue. She goes tae me, — So what brings you over then? Another show? Some business?

— Nah, just flew over to see you. I was worried.

Elspeth doesnae believe a word ay it. But at least she isnae takin the strop. — Pull the other yin, she laughs, — it's goat bells on it.

Ah look at Greg. He's a trusting cunt, but even he's doubtful.

I turn back tae her. — Naw, really, I came to see ye. Nae ulterior motive. I was worried, I had air miles wi aw the travelling ah've been daein, so I just went tae the airport n jumped oan a standby flight.

Elspeth bursts intae tears, and extends her airms. I step intae her grip. — Aw, muh big brother, muh Frankie boy, I've been awfay hard on you. You've changed, you really have changed, my darlin Frankie . . . she's slaverin pish now, but I let her carry on. She came late tae the perty, but she got there.

I tell her, Greg and the laddies a few wee tales, about collectors ay my stuff, n the people that commission ays, like poor auld Chuck. A young doctor cunt comes in wi a big smile on his face, looking at me. — It is you, he goes. — I love your work.

— Ta.

Elspeth's eyes are popping oot her heid, she probably fancies this doctor cunt n she's aw flushed. — This is Dr Moss! Ma brother Frank!

The boy starts asking me about exhibitions and what ah'm workin on. It makes ays think that ah should be in ma studio now, grafting, no hinging aboot ower here, but faimlay is important. For the first time since I brought her back chips fae Methuen's, eftir comin fae the pub when she was a kid, I've got my sister feeling good about ays. That hus tae count for something.

When it's time tae go, ah think ah'm gaunny have tae shout for an orderly tae get Elspeth tae release her grip. Eventually we're outside under the squally grey sky. Greg wants ays tae stey at thair place, but I telt them I'm spending the night with an auld pal.

— She was quite emotional, I says tae Greg, whae's a wee bit glassy-eyed himself.

— Yes, a hormonal thing. Look, Frank, I can't thank you enough for making that awful trip, it hardly seems –

— No hassle. Sitting on the plane wi my sketchbook, working on new ideas, it's bliss tae be honest. And nice tae see you guys again. Maybe California for the school hollybags, boys?

The laddies look excited at the prospect. Nae wonder. Couldnae get tae fuckin Burntisland when ah was their age!

It's rainy but quite warm when I get off the tram back in toon. I meet Terry, in his cab as arranged, parked in that wee shagger's lane ay his in the East New Town off Scotland Street. The lassie's sittin in the back. I nod to her and she heads off, and I take the bag ay tools. — Thanks for sortin this oot, Terry, I appreciate it, ah say, pillin on a set ay water-proof trousers.

— Ma pleasure. You mind the code tae text?

— Aye, as if I could forget, ah nod. Then I head doon the street, following the lassie fae a distance back, watching her head doon the steps ay the basement building acroass the road. This section ay toon is cameraed up tae fuck, there's yin ower the way, but the punters comin tae a knockin shop generally dinnae want tae be seen, so a black beanie cap n dark blue waterproof cagoule n trews disnae exactly stand oot as ah walk doon the steps. A quick glance ower tae the wee knot ay folk huddled intae the bus shelter, tae escape the rain that's comin doon heavier. Breathe … nice n easy.

The door's no locked, so ah let myself in. The gaff smells ay bleach and old spunk, and it's caulder inside than oot. Ah can hear noises, first the lassie's voice, then, as it stoaps, a sly cunt's takes ower. It sounds agitated. As ah get closer, ah see through the crack in the door the bird gieing that Syme boy a gam. I place the bag oan the flair, open it up and pill oot the sword. Feels fuckin barry.

Ah raise the sword ower ma heid n spring through the door, interruptin the blow job. The lassie jumps back at the right time like ah said, n jist as well for her, or her fuckin neb would have come right off n aw. Ah wisnae hingin back, swinging it doon the opening space between her coupon n his groin. The Syme cunt is shriekin oot, — WHAT THE FU— and he's lucky his erection fuckin crumbled quick n eh turned tae the side slightly, or the best part ay his knob would be oan that fuckin tiled flair. As it is ah've just sortay filleted the base ay the cunt's cock wi ma blade, and as it travelled doon, sliced open a baw. Ye git an exquisite split-second glance ay the blood sluicing in the gash, before it flows. It's like slo-mo choreography with this cunt sliding tae his knees n the bird rising fae hers at the same time. It's a thing ay beauty, as eh cups his weddin tackle n the blood explodes through the fingers ay his hands. He's lookin fae his sliced baws tae me, n soas the lassie, n eh goes tae speak, — What the fuuuck …

Aye, the cunt was lucky. But that luck isnae gaunny fuckin last. — Shhh, ah goes, n turns tae the lassie. — If ma lovely assistant here could help me …

She's on her feet, dragging the bag in and getting a throwin knife oot. She hands it tae me.

— WHAT IS THIS?! WHO ARE –

— TELT YOU TAE FUCKIN SHUT IT, ah goes, hurlin the knife at the cunt.

It thuds right intae the fucker's tit as eh lets oot another scream. — WHAAAAT … WHAT THE FUCK …

Terry did fuckin good getting they throwin knives. Ah hand yin tae the lassie. — Take a shot. Goan!

She looks at ays and huds the knife.

The Syme cunt's eyes are bulging, that barry mix ay fear and rage. Ye kin see that fuckin self-loathing at his ain stupidity, at bein too arrogant tae ever see this day comin. Eh takes one bloodied hand away, leaving the other yin tae hud his cock n baws thegither. He raises the blood-soaked free hand slowly as he looks at the lassie. — What?! You'd better fuckin no—

She screams in his pus, — You think I am fucking scared of you now?

— C'moan, darlin … he pleads, as she lets fly at his face. It skites off the side ay his coupon opening up a wound oan his cheek. — FUCKIN HOOR!.

— Nice yin, hen, ah goes, — but mibbe best you dinnae witness the rest. Go on, and meet ays later as we arranged.

She nods and slips oot the door.

Ah'm lookin at the state ay this cunt. Squeezin his ain baws, the blood fae them trickling through his hands. — Funny auld trade, hoormaisterin. Aw aboot selling lassies tae the highest bidder n keepin them controlled by bein the biggest, baddest wolf in the pack, ah grins at the cunt. Ah've reached intae the bag n ah'm feelin the weight ay another throwin knife in ma hand. — Then one day, a higher bidder and bigger wolf comes along and, well, you ken the rest. This is that day, mate.

— Who are you … What dae ye want … What's aw this aboot …? He's lookin up at ays. The pressure in his eyes, like something's gripped the fucker fae inside and is squeezing the life oot ay him.

— You've been pittin it aboot that you did Tyrone. Dinnae like people that claim the credit for other folks' work, ay.

The cunt's slitty wee lamps expand. — You're Begbie … Frank Begbie … they said you were away! Please, mate, ah dinnae even ken you … Ah did nowt tae you! What huv ah done?!

— It's no just aboot the work, ah confess tae the cunt. — Ye see, ye bullied an auld mate ay mine. See this as you gittin bullied back. This counts as bullyin, aye?

— Danny Murphy … Ah heard the boy passed … Ah didnae ken eh wis your mate! Well, ah've learned my lesson, no tae mess wi Frank Begbie! Is that what ye need tae hear fae me? he sais, aw hopeful. Ah'm just lookin doon at him, kneelin oan that flair, bleedin fae the baws, his face cut, a knife stickin oot ay his chest. — What is it ye want, mate? Ah've goat money –

— It's no aboot money, ah cut the cunt off, shakin ma heid. — It gits oan ma tits the wey people think everything's aboot money. Boy wis mair than a mate, eh wis faimlay. Okay, sometimes he got on ma nerves, but he was faimlay.

You never liked him. Probably reminded ye too much ay yirsel, ay, mate?

Syme looks up at ays n gasps oot, — What d'ye mean …?

— They tell ays they called you the Poof at school. They battered you. But you fought back, mate.

The Poof, as ah now think ay Syme, looks at me and nods. Like ah understand him. — Aye … they did.

— That wee laddie, he's eywis inside ye, waiting tae git oot.

The Poof looks at his baws n cock, bleedin through his fingers. Then up at me. — Please …

— Ah dinnae want tae see him. That fuckin wee poof. Ah want tae see you. Tell ays tae fuck off! Tell ays that you're Victor Syme! TELL AYS!

— AH'M SYME, he roars. — VICTOR FUCKIN SYME … His eyes go doon tae his baws again. — VIC … VICTIHR … Victor Syme … He starts tae bubble.

— That's no what ah'm seein. Aw ah'm seein is the Poof.

— Please … ah'll make it up tae ye … for Murphy. For Danny. His family. Ah'll see them awright!

Ah raise ma hand. — But pittin him aside, there's another reason ah'm daein this, ah smile. — Which is: ah just like hurtin people. No killin them, that bit ah'm no keen oan, jist cause it spoils it aw. If they're deid, ye cannae hurt them any mair, ay?

— Well, you've hurt me awright, ah'm sorry aboot Danny … Didnae ken he wis connected … Ah kin make it up tae ye, he whines, lookin doon tae his baws, — now ah need tae git tae the hoasp—

—Ah dinnae *like* killin people, but it makes things messy leavin them lyin around in bits, ah cut the cunt oaf, — so sadly ah'm compelled tae go aw the wey. But mind thit ah dae this purely for the love ay it, rather than the money. So call ays an artist, or a psychopath, makes nae odds tae me, ah goes, hurlin another knife intae the cunt.

It sticks in that soft bit between the shoodir n the chist, n Syme faws oantae his back, littin oot a long groan. — Ah didnae keh-heh-hen …

Ah'm right oan him, smashin the next blade intae his gut, tearin at the flesh. — Ignorance … ay the law … is nae excuse. You've goat something ah need … It belongs … tae ma mate!

Takes ays fuckin ages tae git them oot, n ah'm surprised that the cunt holds oan that long. Fuckin guts, they spread oot like fuck. Dinnae expect a big pile ay giant pinky-grey spaghetti tae spill oot ay the cunt n slide acroass the flair. Fuckin state ay that, but. Then, eftir draggin Syme's boady intae the cleaning supplies cupboard the lassie n Terry telt ays aboot, n lockin the door, pocketin the key that's awready in thaire, ah has tae wash doon the cagoule, the waterproof trousers and the shoes, n gie the place a good mop n clean. Feel sorry for the cunts that work here, cause it'll be fuckin mingin soon, wi it bein summer.

When it's aw done, ah text Terry:

Still cannae get ower that game, amazing how it aw went tae plan.

Right back:

GGTTH. That Davie Gray winner …

Me:

Even better on the replay. Left the opposition destroyed. GGTTH!

It's about ten minutes later when ah git the text:

We've got McGinn, super John McGinn.

Which tells ays that Terry's parked back doon his shag lane at Scotland Street. So ah head oot the door, collar up, beanie doon over the brows, skerf roond the mooth, just another guilty punter who played away fae hame. Coast's clear: bus must have come. Ah get tae the cab and we speed off tae the airport. When we arrive, Terry hands me two commemorative Hibs Scottish Cup mugs. — Wee pressy.

— They snide?

— Of course they are.

— No sure ah'm wantin them. Dinnae like the idea ay being mixed up in anything illegal, ah sais. We get a barry giggle at that. As ah say goodbye tae Terry, ah feel that sense ay loss and regret that ah ey dae on such occasions, realisin that ah'll never see they throwin knives or that fuckin sword again. They have tae be destroyed or planted on some noncey paedo sex case that Tez has awready earmarked. But ah'm upset, as that sword n these knives, they just fuckin handled that well. Unusual tae git a weapon ye huvnae had any time tae practise wi, that just feels so right, never mind *two*. Fuckin craftsmanship. In a perfect world ah'd be able tae keep them, but thir jist jailbait. Gutted though – yir only as good as yir tools.

The lassie is waiting at the airport and I pay her off, slipping the folder intae her bag. — What's your plans?

— I'm going home.

— Where's that?

— Bucharest.

— That's what ah should dae, book a rest, ah tells the lassie. She looks at me like ah'm a radge. — I'm gaun home too. Got an early flight the morn. The night ah'm treatin masel tae that Hilton Hotel here, cause ah couldnae git a first class at short notice withoot the cunts takin the pish.

— So where is *your* home?

— California.

She heads away and I buy a newspaper, that *Independent*, and walk ower tae the Hilton. Ah pey in cash, checking in as Victor Syme, using his driver's licence as ID. Ah look fuck all like the cunt but the photae is shite n the lassie barely glances at it.

They've goat Sky in the room, and thaire's golf oan. Ah dinnae mind watchin golf oan telly cause it's barry when some cunt fucks up an easy put. I call Melanie, tell her Elspeth's okay, and I'm looking forward tae getting hame. The papers are aw full ay that vote the morn aboot leaving the EU. One thing ye can guarantee is, whatever happens, things'll be shite for maist cunts. The wey ah look at it is that it's a short life, look at poor Spud, so ye might as well just dae what makes ye happy!

Gutted tae have missed his funeral, but this is a better wey tae pey ma respects.

Each tae their ain.

363

36

RENTON – DOING THE RIGHT THING

Sometimes it's mair complex than just daein the right thing. It's working out what the right thing is when every cunt's dangling wrong yins in front of ye. I've made the call that the right thing for me is tae keep the Santa Monica gaff and stay clean. So instead of bringing out Conrad's new track, I left it to Muchteld, while I engineered three generations ay Renton to be together.

Taking Alex fae Amsterdam, out ay social services and the care home, tae my dad's place at Leith, was quite an ordeal. But I decided possession was nine-tenths ay the law. Instead ay one ay our regular outings tae the Vondelpark for ice cream and coffee (that was a fucker ay a battle, autistic kids are programmed tae routine), I took him tae the passport office. Then, after dropping Alex back at the amusement park, as I call the home, I went tae the seaside tae visit Katrin and tell her ay my plans.

— It is good you are taking this interest, she said in her usual offhand way. She obviously didnae gie a fuck, and indeed, was happy tae have him out ay the way. I couldn't believe I'd spent so many years sleeping in the same bed as this stranger. But I suppose that's the nature of love: we are either creatures ay the present and have tae live with the trauma and misery if it goes tits up, or doomed tae loneliness. I might no have taken much interest ower the fifteen years ay his life, but it's still a fucking sight mair than she ever did. When it was obvious that there were issues with Alex, she had said wearily, — It is useless. There is no communication.

Her coldness and detachment always intrigued me when it was just the two ay us. Then there was somebody else, who was totally dependent on us, and it didnae play so well. She basically fucked off and lumbered me with the kid, taking an acting job wi a touring theatre company. That was us done. I found Alex a place in a care home, so I could keep working.

As I left her, probably for the last time, she loitered in the big doorway ay this Zandvoort mansion she shares with her architect boyfriend and their two flawless blonde Nazi children, and, in gesture and descending tone I could no longer interpret, said, — I wish you well.

Conrad keeps phoning but not leaving messages. I need to get back to him, but I can't bear to hear him tell me he's signed up with some big agency. Even though not picking up makes this all the more likely. Muchteld put out his single, 'Be My Little Baby Nerd', quirky, dancey, pop, and it's tearing it up.

Of course, I had to take the auld man as well. Ordinarily there was no way the stubborn auld Hun would get on a plane to America, but Alex being in the package changed everything. On the flight tae LA I realise that ma faither is the chronic autism whisperer. He could always calm or distract my wee brother Davie, and he does the same with Alex. My son sits in silence, without any customary loud outbursts or agitation. I hear him repeat, under his breath, — I asked for one, not two.

— One what, pal? Dad asks him.

— It's just something he says.

But every single time he repeats it, my father asks the question ay him.

Vicky meets us at the airport. She smiles and greets Alex, who looks blankly at her, mumbling stuff under his breath. Driving us up to Santa Monica, Vicky leaves us to get settled, as she puts it. Dad and Alex have the apartment's bedrooms, while I'm on the couch. It's too small for the three ay us, and will wreck my back. I really need tae sort something out.

37

SICK BOY – GIVE ME YOUR ANSWER DO

Marianne moved down to London with me, to my new Highgate flat, courtesy of Renton's cash. It's a short walk from Hampstead Heath, and satisfyingly bucks my downwardly mobile trend. Ever since Offord Road in Islington, back in the eighties, neoliberal economics have been chasing me out of the city. Time, gentlemen, please, it insists, as it cock-sucks shadowy fifth-home oligarchs from Russia and the Middle East, who deign to show up two weeks in the year to get cunted in this particular one of their gated gaffs dotted throughout the globe. We treated ourselves to a hooker and some ching last night and are exhausted from our efforts. So she lies in, but I'm up early next morning, on the tube down to King's Cross, to interview some more girls for Colleagues.

I stand behind my raised desk in the small office that serves as the nerve centre of the Colleagues empire, a bunch of phones spread in front of me like playing cards. The buzzer goes and I press it, and several moments later can hear a woman walking up the stairs, her breath, like her expectations, falling away steadily as she comes into the office. If the landlord would get a fuckin windae cleaner in so we could see ootside, let in some light, it might make the place less dreary. I really do need to get a more salubrious suite. Maybe Clerkenwell, or perhaps even Soho. The woman looks at me, and her anxiety at the sleaze can't wipe out the shagger's glint in her eye and filthy set to her mouth. She's the first of eight I have to see today.

I'm zonked when I get home, but I still have enough juice in the tank to pummel Marianne under the beef cosh, while igniting her with the creeping love bombs of obscene speech. Keep them well shod and well shagged: the only decent advice my father ever gave me in the affairs of the heart department. The only decent advice the cunt gave me in *anything*.

My mouth is dry and my head spins satisfyingly as we lie in bed. Then we shower and get dressed, heading out to dinner with Ben and his boyfriend, who have moved in together, close by in Tufnell Park. I've told them to forget about decent restaurants in that area. — I booked up this place, I inform Ben on the phone. — I hope Dan likes seafood.

I've only met Dan once, and I like him. He seems good for Ben, who, as tough as it is to admit, is a bit fucking straight. Sadly Surrey and soul just don't go. We rendezvous at FishWorks in Marylebone High Street. Is there anywhere else more acceptable for seafood in London? I sincerely doubt it. Despite arriving before us, the boys thoughtfully take the two chairs, leaving us the grey padded bench seating opposite.

I order a bottle of Albariño. — I find most whites a little acidic for me these days but this works, I say. — So, how are the Surrey people reacting to my upcoming nuptials?

Ben, wearing a black jacket and a green crew-neck top, says, — Well, Mum's been a little quiet. He breaks into a smile. — Sometimes I think she still holds a candle for you.

Of course she does. Batters it into her fanny every night, while thinking of the best cock she ever had or ever will have. I almost say this out loud, but check myself. After all, it's the boy's mother and he dotes on her. — Understandable. Once you've perused the goods in the Simon David Williamson

368

emporium, I look at Marianne and drop my voice to a playful growl, — it's very hard to shop elsewhere.

— Copy that, Marianne grins, winking at the boys. Then she looks at my nose. — I just hope that bruising goes for the wedding photographs!

Must this spectre be continually raised? — A cowardly attack, I explain to the lads. — I cost an old pal a bob or two as payback for some considerable emotional chaos he caused, and he can't take it like a man.

— Ooh er missus, Dan laughs.

Yes, I do like this guy. — That's the spirit, Dan. I look at Ben. — I'm glad you didn't take up with one of those boring homosexuals, son.

— Dad ...

— No, fuck that, I say, as the menus arrive with the white wine. — It's just the same as a boring heterosexual. If you're gay, just be a *proper fucking poof*, would be my advice. The waiter opens the bottle and pours the wine for me to taste. I take a sip, and nod in approval. While he fills the glasses, I warm to my theme. — Be a lisping, gossiping, flamboyant, outrageous, scandalous queen! Don't be a suburban Charlie with a boyfriend called Tom, with whom you go kayaking at the weekends. Ram strangers in toilets! OD on Oscar Wilde! Get your cock sucked by rent boys in the park ...

A couple at the next table look round.

— Simon, Marianne warns as the waiter departs.

Marianne and Ben are looking edgy, but Dan's loving it, so I speak a little louder. — Seduce a straight fucker and wreck his life, then, after he's divorced, become BFF with his ex-wife, make each other wild cocktails and gossip about what a lousy lay he is. Discover a passionate love of musical theatre. Go to underground techno nights in Berlin dressed in lederhosen.

369

— We'll bear that in mind, Dan laughs, turning to Ben.
— So Germany it is for the holidays then!

Ben blushes. He's a couple of years younger than Dan, and it shows. I wonder if he's getting rammed, or doing the ramming, the saucy wee devil. I suppose the benefits of poofery is that you get to mix it up. Lucky bastards.
— Good! I don't want you guys squandering your gift of homosexuality on dating apps, mortgage brokers, estate agents, architects, adoption papers, meeting with surrogate single hoors who will take you to the cleaners, and arguments about fucking fabrics!

— There are no arguments about fabrics with us. It's my way or the highway, Marianne says, as she rises to go to the toilet.

— I like her, Ben says. — I'm happy for you, Dad.

I move in close and lower my voice. — She's either a predator or a victim. Like Churchill said about the Germans, at your feet or at your throat. It's great living with her, it keeps me on my toes. She tries to undermine me as much as I do her. Every day is a fucking joust, I punch the table in euphoria,
— I have never felt so alive in my life!

— That doesn't really seem like a recipe for –

I cut him off right away. — Three words: make-up sex. Or is that two?

The boys look at me, and giggle a little. Not in a faggy way, more a what-the-fuck-is-that-embarrassing-old-cunt-saying-now manner. It's taboo talking sex to youth: they don't want to envision middle-aged sleazebags banging away. I was the same at that age. Still am now.

— Enough said, I tap my nose, and fuck me, it's sore. *Renton. That cunt.*

Ben's voice rises to an acceptably fey pitch with the wine, and his camp mannerisms become more pronounced.

— That's it, lads, you can dispense with all the Hollywood closet-case stuff and let it all hang out. I'm straight, but I'm still as camp as a row of tents.

— He is, Marianne agrees, returning from the toilet to slide back into her seat beside me.

— That's because I was rifling you aw weys, I laugh, enjoying the wine, as she digs me in the ribs. I look at them. — Well, why should you raving buftie boys have all the fun? No offence meant, my *bellissimi bambinis*!

When they get off the tube at Tufnell Park, Marianne and I have a drunken argument. — You don't have to try and outperform them, they're just young lads, she says.

I know that look, and it calls for an olive branch. — You, my darling, are exactly right as usual. I was remiss, please forgive me. I guess I'm just nervous. My boy moving in with a new partner. But he's a nice lad.

— They're a great couple, she says, assuaged.

The next day we are off to Edinburgh on the train. The journey is very pleasant; it beats flying hands down. I love the way it gets progressively more beautiful the further north you go.

— Do you think this is a good idea? Marianne asks.

— Not particularly. Richard Branson is a wanker and I hate giving money to him. But flying is such –

— No, I mean this dinner!

— Yes, I insist, thinking about that cunt Euan. A sapling whose weakness led to Danny boy's sad demise. — I spoke to my mamma on the phone. She's all excited, I could *hear* her crossing herself. 'My-a boy finally settling doon and getting married ...'

— But she doesn't know it's tae *me*, Simon. We have history. And your sister ...

— Carlotta and Euan are fine now. They'll just have to accept you, or we won't be seeing any of them. Simple as, I tell her. — They have to learn that it can't all be about them, that fucker Euan leaving a trail of devastation with his dick, then going back to playing bourgeois happy families when it suits him ... I look her in the eye. — Not on my watch.

— I just wish I hudnae ... you know ... Her gaze is penitent, as well it might be. A terrible slut, but I really would not have her any other way. — I was so angry with you at the time. She squeezes my hand.

— I don't care about that ... well, only in so far as it sparked off a twisted chain of events, but it was Euan's folly that messed it up.

Marianne sweeps her hand through her hair. It falls back into place instantly. — But won't they be freaked out that it doesn't matter to you, likes, about myself and Euan?

It only matters to me that you shagged fucking Renton. — I'm not a man prone to jealousy. It's only a ride. I drop my voice as the trolley dolly creaks past. I consider shouting up a Stella, but decide against it. — You're a hot vixen slag and that sort of wanton, reckless behaviour just makes me desire you more.

She fixes me that 'I'm game' look and we repair to the toilet. I sit on the lavy seat, her straddling me, and we're banging away. Suddenly the door slides open and a chunky cunt in a Sunderland strip stands looking at us, mouth open. Marianne turns round. — Fuck ... Simon ... I slap the shut knob and it slides back, and this time I remember to press the locking button. The bloater's intervention has upped the horn stakes and we shit-talk each other into a joint shrieker of an orgasm.

Staggering back to our seats, we regard the rest of the carriage in languid, superior, sex-case snide. The train rolls into Waverley, a little delayed, but I've texted Mamma, and we shouldn't be too late. We jump in a cab up to the Outsider restaurant in George IV Bridge. It's a favourite haunt of mine when I'm back in town. Great locally produced food, and a friendly but unfussy service.

— I'm nervous, babe, Marianne says.

— Fight through that shit, oh cherishable force. I'm proud of you, doll, and nobody is snubbing or disdaining you on my watch, I tell her. — Bring it on! Tony Stokes!

It's kid sis who looks up first, as her darling brother walks in arm-in-arm with his lovely fiancée. I'd decided that this would be the best entrance we could make. Carlotta's eyes bulge in disbelief and she sits in a choking silence. Louisa notices and looks shocked, but almost pleasantly, and her man, Gerry, turns to her, trying to work out what's going on. Then Euan, doubtlessly sensing the disturbance in the air, glances up from the menu to see us standing above them, about to sit down.

— Cards on the table time, I announce to the aghast company, getting in my seat, Marianne following stiffly, — there's a wee bit ay history for us all to get past, it might make your hearts go oh, oh, oh, oh ... but we're all grown-ups and we don't care what the –

—AH DINNAE BELIEVE IT! YOU BRING HER HERE! Carlotta wails, as diners' heads swivel round to us. — YOU ... YOU'RE GAUNNY MAIRRAY ... She turns to Marianne. — AND YOU ... YOU'RE GAUNNY MAIRRAY HIM?!

— Carlotta, please, Mamma appeals, as the shocked diners tut and the maître d' hovers nervously.

— Sounding gey Bananay Flats thaire, sis, I smile for levity.

Of course, it falls on unreceptive lugs. — C'MON! Carlotta grabs Euan's hand, hauling him to his feet and pulling him through the scandalised diners towards the door. He looks briefly back, spazzing in confusion, like a lamb in an abattoir, bleating consoling inanities at his wife.

— Typical, I shrug, — make it all about her! I turn to my mother. — Mamma, this is Marianne, the love of my life.

Marianne glances to the door Carlotta and Euan are crashing out of, then smiles at Mamma. — It's a pleasure, Mrs Williamson.

— I think I remember you …

— Yes, Simon and I went out many years ago.

— Aye, I mind, Louisa smirks, as Marianne tenses up.

— It's been a rocky road but the path of true love never ran smooth, I declare, summoning the waiter. — Sorry about the fuss, brother, emotional time … I address the table: — Who's for champers? A wee swally ay Bolly?

— What happened to your nose? Mamma asks.

— A cowardly attack, I tell her, — but it's all good!

— Well, this is a turn-up for the books, Louisa grins like a demented Cheshire cat with its furry balls caught in a vice.

The waiter reappears with that thickset glass fucker in an ice bucket. He pops and pours to my unbridled delight. — Cheer up! I raise my glass. — There is absolutely nothing bad happening anywhere in this big wide world at this precise moment in time!

374

38

RENTON – DON'T BEG THE BEGGAR BOY

On the road, the afternoon light thickens in a gaudy, retina-scorching burst. I take my shades from my shirt pocket, stick them on and floor it, as Vic Godard sings about Johnny Thunders on the stereo. I motor smoothly up the Pacific Coast Highway, the vibrant blue sky clashing with the scrub-covered brown hills. As I head to Santa Barbara, I'm aware that I'm risking it all. Happiness with Vicky, with my dad, trying to build a home over here for Alex.

I was skint anyway but Second Prize has cleaned me out completely. I've zilch and my main source of income, Conrad, is as good as away to a big agency. The worthless *Leith Heads*: fucking Sick Boy and, most of all, that cunt Begbie. I'm not going to beg the Beggar Boy. All I can do is ask. And if he says no, then I'll offer the cunt a square go. I feel an avalanche of rage gather in my chest. Constricting my throat. Tightening my muscles. My back throbbing in its old spot. We'll see if the artsy poof Jim Francis is all that's left ay Frank Begbie. At this moment, I feel the very same way he probably did when I betrayed him: like everything has been taken from me. Well, Williamson fuckin got it, and now Begbie will. And there he is, standing as a man wi a wife and two young daughters, a proper man, in the way he never was back then; one who looks after his family. Like I'm striving tae. But how much empathy does the cunt have? None. Spud's in the fuckin groond and he couldnae even bother showing up. Never sent a wreath, a caird or fuck all.

The ride gets good when I hit Ventura as the road hugs the coastline, the breaking waves lapping up along the shore. My shades are on, the window is rolled down and I've keyed Begbie's address into the GPS. This hire drives nicely, responsive tae my touch on the wheel, as I weave smoothly in and out of traffic.

I need that money. I need it tae be able to build a life here, and I need it right now. No in six months' time when Conrad's royalties come in, cause that will be my last payday there. He's building up tae say something; he'll be off tae a bigger manager, like Ivan did.

So this is how it has to happen. Franco's beaten me at what I value most – art – and now I have tae have this dash wi the cunt; face him on *his* home turf of violence. If I stand over him, the battered artist, I've won the duel. If he beats ays tae a pulp, I've also won: I've shown the cunt up for what he is, and what he'll always be. And me? What am I? Spud, God rest his soul, is more creative than me. He produced something more detailed, clever and meaningful about our life on skag than anything that was in my diaries. I'm glad I sent it off to that publisher.

I play my messages back over the car speaker. Conrad first:

What is going on? I need you to phone me! I am in Los Angeles! There are things we need to talk about! Where are you?!

Muchteld:

Mark. This is not good. You have been been absent with the track coming out. Conrad is pissed off. You need to deal with this and everything else at Citadel. Call me.

Fuck them all. I've bigger fish to fry. I'm fighting for my future, and also my son's and my dad's.

When I get on the turn-off for Santa Barbara, I pass fresh roadkill by the side of the highway. It looks like a domestic pet; a cat or a small dog. I think ay Begbie, and how one ay us is fucking getting it.

39

BEGBIE – HOSTAGE

It's just got dark. There's the cool breeze coming oafay the ocean, and that scent ay eucalyptus fae the trees in the garden. Mel is in the hoose, putting the kids tae bed, and I've just stepped out tae take the trash tae the dumpster in the alley at the back ay the yard. Have tae gie the cunt his due, he's fuckin quiet enough. Hear nowt till I feel the gun barrel. Naebody's stuck one ay them in the back ay ma neck before, but ah ken what it is right away. — Just walk back in here, he sais, pushing it harder against ays.

So we cross the yard and enter the kitchen through the back door. Probably this is where I should pivot and ram the nut on the cunt. But he might pull the trigger. Aw I'm thinking of is Melanie and the girls, through in their beds. So when ah realise we're gaun intae my workshop, which is attached tae the house, ah'm no resisting, as it's the furthest point fae the bairns' bedroom. Ye sometimes get a chance, one chance, in a situ like this. Ah made a mistake ay no striking right away, but ah didnae git a sketch ay the cunt tae tipple how gone he was. — You … he turns me round, — put your arms behind you.

The cop cunt. Harry the fuckin Hammy Hamster.

Ah comply, as I've nae doubt he'll pull the trigger. His voice is tellin ays he's fucking away wi it. That he's gone tae a place in his heid where he's set out the path ay action and willnae deviate fae it. Clipped, precise and certain. What d'ye dae at times like these? Obey and hope something turns up, n if it does, grab the fucking opportunity.

He gets me tae sit in one ay the metal chairs ah keep for visitors. They replaced a couch, as I didnae want people getting too comfy in ma place ay work and distracting me. He moves behind ays. — Put your hands through the back of the chair.

As I comply I feel the metal harshly clasping ma wrists. A long time since I've known that sensation. Nowt like it for making yir guts sink. Ah kin hear the bats squeakin ootside in the trees.

Then he's got a length ay rope and I'm thinkin *This cunt is gaun for a revenge hingin,* but he's winding it roond ays, securing me tae the chair. He heads tae the door. Ah'm about tae scream: *Get the fuckin bairns oot and run like fuck, now,* but he turns tae me, his eyes hidden in shadow. Under that slash ay darkness, ah see his lips, set tight. — Don't fucking move or shout out or you will hear gunshots. I guarantee it.

And he goes away. The bats are silent now. Amazing how they settle so quickly. This is the hardest bit. Every fuckin fibre ay ays wants tae roar oot a warning, but this cunt really does look ready tae start shootin. Ah think aboot they two wee lassies, lying dead, lifeless, in their ain blood, smashed by bullets. Mel the same wey. My knives are by my workbench, attached tae the waw by a magnetic strip. I start tae inch the chair back in that direction. Suddenly the sound ay tense whispering, and ah'm thinking: dinnae let the cunt get tae the point where he's left himself nae option but tae shoot ays. Save ays for the fuckin payback. Then, thank fuck, eh's back in wi Melanie. Her hands are cuffed behind her back, but she doesnae seem injured. Tears are running doon her cheeks as she looks at ays, imploring through her shock, but ah kin dae nowt, except concentrate like fuck on ma breathin, as she's pushed intae the identical chair next tae mine. It's aw ah can dae tae look at her, for the shame I feel aboot no being able tae protect her and the bairns.

This Hammy Hamster cunt stands in the doorway wi his gun pointed at us. Eyes focused but wi that glaze that aw men ready tae hurt need tae pit between them and their prey. Mel pleads softly with him, keeping her voice firm and professional. — Please don't hurt the children …

— That's down to you, he snaps, moving towards ays.

It's hard tae witness. Ah'm no keen tae stoap a bullet, but ah'll take yin for them. — Leave her and the kids out of this, I tell him, trying tae stand up in the chair. — This is between you and me.

It's funny, but ah hear Mel scream oot before ah feel any pain. — No, please! she yells as the cunt connects the butt ay the pistol wi the side ay my jaw, and pushes me doon.

— Don't wake your kids, the cunt goes, makin it sound like a threat. — Now you, he looks at me, — you tell this stupid fucking whore all about the man she married!

Ah keep quiet. Ah look up at the ceiling fan. Then doon at the concrete flair. Sensing the knives behind ays, wi the hammers, chisels, n aw the other sculpting stuff.

— Tell her!

— Harry, please, Mel begs, as ah'm lookin ower the other tools in view, like the gas canisters and the acetylene torch, off tae the side. — It doesn't have to be like this, she goes, aw breathless. — You say you care for me! How is this caring for anybody? And she's greetin, tryin tae keep control ay hersel. The fear is nearly overwhelming her.

— I thought you were strong, he sneers at her, pacin up n doon in front ay us, — with that proud, stuck-up-bitch way you had. But I was wrong. You're weak, soft in the head. Easy meat for evil bastards like this scumbag. He points at ays. — This asshole broke into my home! Tried to kill me! Tried to fucking well hang me with a noose! My own garden hose! Have you told her that? He bends doon and screams in ma face: — HAVE YOU?!

Ah feel his gob on ma cheek.

— What? You're fantasising, mate. Ah shake ma heid. — Auto-asphixiation, was it? Jerk off, did ye?

— TELL HER! And he batters me in the pus again with the gun. Ah feel ma cheekbone depress.

Breathe ...

Pain's never bothered ays much. It's jist a message. Ye kin put pain outside ay yirsel. The eyes, teeth n baws are hardest, but ye can dae it.

Mel screams out again. — No, Harry, please!

There are stars, aw different colours, dancing in front ay ma eyes. Ah tries tae blink them away as ah focus on this cunt. — Ever done DMT?

— You shut the fuck up!

— A mate gied ays it, ah explain. — Said it was the ultimate trip. Said that as an artist, ah should experience it.

He looks tae Mel, then back at me. — I'm fucking warning you ...

— Now ah nivir really liked drugs. A peeve, aye, sound, ah smile at him. — A wee bit ay ching. But this stuff, couldnae really caw it a drug as such –

— Harry! Please! Mel shouts. — This is lunacy! We have two little girls in their beds! We need to work this out!

This cop cunt laughs in her face. — What can *you* work out? You, who can't even see what you fucking married! I used to be in *love* with you. Wanted to be with you. He laughs in that daftie sneer again. — Now? Now I pity you. I pity the useless, pathetic cunt that you are!

Ah fuckin hate the way some American cunts call lassies cunts. Fuckin offensive, that shite. Ah'm tastin ma ain blood doon the back ay ma throat, as ah try tae breathe steadily in through ma neb. That sweet Pacific air comin through the metallic scent. Nowt like it. — That's a bit sad, mate.

— What?

— Ye cannae be in love wi somebody whae isnae in love wi you. It's no love, it's just a fucking noncey sickness in the

381

heid. You're no well, pal, I say. — Get treatment. Doesnae need to be this way.

— Jim, no, please … Mel's urgin ays tae be quiet, let her do the talkin.

— You?! You call *me* fuckin sick in the head! *You?!*

— Listen, ah tell him, no likin the wey Mel's lookin at ays, like she might half believe this radge, — do what you like with me but leave them out of it, Mel n the kids. They're not the issue. That's what ye always wanted, me out the road. Make it happen.

— Jim, no! Melanie squeals, drawin Hammy's attention back tae her.

— It's too late for that, the cunt tells her, then eh's back tae me. — You tell her. Tell her what you done! Coover! Santiago! Tell her about them! Tell her who you are!

Ah'd go tae the fuckin grave before ah'd grass masel up tae Mel aboot removing they two rapist trash. — Tell her what, ya fuckin bam?

He jumps forward and his pistol butt cracks down on my beak this time. A bolt ay searing pain shoots up tae the centre ay ma brain. It feels fuckin good. The sickness maist cunts would feel rising in their guts, ye just laugh at that shite n away it goes. Ye huv tae make friends wi pain. Ah see them aw in ma mind's eye again. Like they were in that DMT trip; Seeker, Donnelly, Chizzie, Coover, Santiago, Ponce, naebody really seeming that upset. Just enjoying the feast …

383

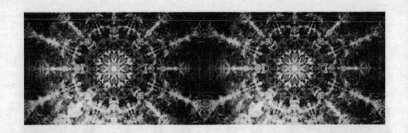

But the mood was sort ay … disorganised. It was like this grand stately dining room, but it felt like a bus terminal or railway station, somewhere that would take ye somewhere else. There wis this overriding idea that we needed tae just sit doon and get on wi the meal. Finish it, so we could move on, go somewhere else. Ah wonder where. Ah'm thinkin that it would be good tae try that DMT again, maybe see if we could take it tae the next fuckin level.

— Harry, stop, please, let us go! You're a police officer, Harry! Melanie's screams cut through ma thoughts.

— And what use was that? What respect did I ever get from you, from cunts like you, for that?

— I respect the police, I respect the law, Mel says, calm, reasonable, and finding strength again fae somewhere. — This isn't the law, Harry!

The cunt seems tae think aboot this for a second or two. — You go with this fucking murdering old jailbird, who's not even from here, he points at ays withoot looking at ays, which gits ma fuckin goat, — and you talk about the goddamn law. That is rich. You really are a piece of work.

I'm staring at him. The blood trickling slowly doon the back ay ma throat. I've never hated anything so much in ma life. Ah pull in a deep breath. — Uncuff ays, ah say, nearly in a whisper. — A fuckin square go then, ya shitein cunt.

384

The cop pervert looks at ays like ah'm a radge. He cannae understand a fuckin word. — What are you talking about, fool? Then he puts his gun tae Melanie's head.

— Noo ... Melanie shuts her eyes.

— Please ... I hear a small voice coming fae inside ays. It's no ma ain. It is ma ain. — Don't hurt her. If you loved her like ye say ye dae, you cannae hurt her. *Please* ...

— Tell her, Hammy screams at ays, his eyes doolally. — Tell her what you did or I'll pull the fucking trigger!

Ma heid is startin tae clear n ma eyes ur getting intae focus.

Hammy pivots n slowly points the gun at me. *At least it's away fae Mel.* — Now I'm gonna blow your fucking head off. You're too much of a selfish asshole to deserve to see your kids grow up ... or even your fucking wife grow up, you sorry old motherfucker, n eh turns tae Mel briefly before whip-lashing back tae me. — You will never know what is gonna happen next: to her, or your kids. Tell me, how does that feel? His face is grinning right at ays.

Nowt ah kin dae but spill n beg, and then ...

And then ah see him ...

Standing just behind the copper.

My old mate. In his hands, the baseball bat I got fae Karl Gibson. The ex-Dodgers boy who got ays tae make that mutilated heid ay his former coach. The story eh telt, how eh hit the home run tae win game one for the Dodgers in the World Series. And there the cunt is, half in shadow, the bat raised ...

RENTON ...

... He takes a swing and skelps Hammy right across the side ay his pus. The polis cunt goes doon and the gun fires off, a shot ringing oot. Renton is right on Hammy, on top ay him, battering the cunt. The most amazing thing is that it isnae even a fight. It's a fuckin massacre. Renton's heid smashes repeatedly into Hammy's nose. Then his elbays. He grabs the bat again n wedges it on Hammy's windpipe. *Renton.*

— THAT'S IT, RENTS! KILL THE CUNT! YLT!!

— I'M A CAW-CAW-CAWWP ... the dopey cunt gargles.

— I'm a fuckin social worker, ah think Renton sais, n he isnae letting up until the cunt's eyes roll right intae his heid. Even though Rents wisnae a fighter, ye kin see that schemie flint in they squirrelly, shifty, sunken eyes. That ruthless snide streak that would never hesitate and surrender any advantage life throws at ye by accident. This Hammy Hamster cunt is fuckin well out for the count! I'm trying tae git tae ma feet in this fuckin chair ...

— Stop, Mark, Mel begs, — he's done!

Renton eases the pressure and looks up at us, panic in his wide eyes. He's spooked himself now, at where he's taken this. The cop cunt is fuckin spangled, right enough. Renton takes the cunt's pulse oan his neck. — He's still here, he says in a gasping, euphoric chant ay excitement and relief.

— Thank God you came, Mark, thank God you came ... Mel blabbers, pale and disbelieving as she stares doon at Hammy, his face bloodied and pulped.

Rents's eyes are everywhere before they settle on me. — Where's the keys tae they cuffs?

— The cunt's poakits, ah tell him.

Renton goes back tae Hammy and fishes oot these keys on a chain. Tries a couple before they work. He frees Mel first. — Oh, bless you, Mark, she goes n flings her airms around him, then she turns tae me, and does the same, as Renton takes oaf ma cuffs n starts windin that rope oaf ay ays. Ah stand up too quick and feel like ah'm gaunny cowp ower n be seek, but ah fight the impulse doon. — Rents ... what the fuck are you daein here?

— Well, it looks like ah'm fuckin helpin you oot, bud, ay? Renton says, shaking, his teeth hammering thegither in shock. — What's gaun oan here?

Mel's still got a hud ay me, but suddenly ah see the blood. Ah wriggle oot her grip. His fuckin bullet caught her in the airm. — Ye okay?

— It's only a graze, she says, and wraps an auld rag roond it. She looks tae the door n goes, — The girls, n she runs through.

Ah picks up the shooter that Hammy cunt droaped when Rents tanned the fucker's pus. Ah'm careful no tae touch the handle. The barrel's still hoat in ma fingers.

Renton sees ays looking at the cop's body. He's still half oot, groanin oan the deck, baith eyes rollin n tryin tae focus, blood pishin oot ay his mooth.

Renton kens what I'm thinking. — He broke in, ah tell him. — He's been stalking Mel. Obsessed wi her, since school. A weirdo. He's a cop, an ex-cop, but an alkie.

— The polis'll do the cunt, Franco.

— One fuckin shot but, ay? Self-defence. Solve the whole fuckin problem!

— It's his shooter, Frank. He's fucked. Dinnae shoot the cunt, you'll jist fuck it aw up.

Ah thinks aboot this. Hauls in a deep breath. He's probably right. Ah pits the gun doon oan the bench. — AH'LL FUCKIN KILL THE CUNT! N ah step forward, ready tae stomp that heid intae that concrete flair, till the skull cracks n grey shite spills oot ay it, till ah kin smell the cunt's brains …

— JIM, STOP! Mel has come back through, and she's ower grabbing ays by the airm. — The girls are okay, she shrieks at ays. — They slept through it all! Just call the police!

— It's the way tae go, Franco, Rents smiles, like he's comin up oan a fuckin ecky.

— Aye, right … n ah pull in some mair gulps ay air.

— Honey, he's an ex-cop and a stalker. The trauma is back in Mel's eyes. — This is for the police! You must see that!

Ah'm lookin at Hammy Hamster, still tryin tae git ma breathin sorted oot. The rush ay blood tae the heid, like the tide comin in, the same sort ay sound ah heard when ah fucked they two wide cunts oan the beach, the ones the cop cunt wis talkin aboot … it slowly starts tae recede. Ah look at the cunt oan the deck. It wid be easy …

Naw … jist breathe …

— Mel's right, Franco, Rents says, bug-eyed n excited, makin a fist ay a scrapped and swollen mitt. — Think ay the life he'll have in prison as an ex-copper: ungreased butt-fuckings every day. He's gaun tae a place a lot worse than death, Franco!

Mel looks at Rents in a vaguely chastising way, as ah haul in another deep breath. — You eywis kent how tae get roond me, I say tae um, and I walk ower tae Hammy's groaning body, swing ma leg back and boot oot three ay the cunt's front teeth with one blow.

— JIM, NO! Mel screams.

— Sorry, doll. Ah move away, nodding tae her and then Renton. — Fuckin polis it is then, ay, n ah pits ma hands on her trembling shoodirs. — I know it's primitive, but there's no way he's touching you without me getting a lick in. Wis never gaunny happen.

— Enough now, she commands.

— Of course.

Renton is connected tae 911 right away. — Hello, I'd like to report a break-in, kidnapping, assault and possibly attempted murder.

Then Mel's calling the lawyer, the boy who has a copy ay the tape and whae's been pit in the picture. Wi Hammy bein filth it's the smart move. We sit there, Hammy shackled wi his ain cuffs, lying on the floor, face bleeding over the concrete. The visible side is misshapen and reddish black, both his eyes slits in swollen red bulbs. Aye, Renton fuckin well pummelled the cunt pretty good. Wisnae fuckin aboot wi they elbays. Could have done wi that style fae the shitein cunt up the toon in our youth, instead ay daftie here huvin tae sort everything oot. Still, fair play, better late than never. I envy the cunt every single fuckin lick he goat in. If it was doon tae me, ah'd set aboot the cunt wi the tools, n pit in a steady shift till thaire wis nowt left.

The lawyer gets here aboot a minute before the polis and the first thing he does is supervise them gettin that cunt oot ay the hoose. The Hammy Hamster fucker goes quietly, like he's in shock, mutterin tae ehsel. It's Mel whae's daein maist ay the talkin tae the polis. Ah just sits doon n speaks whin spoken tae. Ah tells them that he was obsessed wi her, and seemed tae think that ah wis some kind ay serial killer. — It's utterly bizarre stuff, ah tell them, thinking ay how Iain, the bad boy ay Scottish art, back in the New Town, would respond in such a situation. Ah'm sucking in ma breath at times, but ah'm as polite as fuck tae they cunts. If your instincts are bad, ye train yersel by acting counter-intuitive, daein the reverse ay what ye feel like daein. Mel and Rents are as plausible as fuck. He eywis wis a smart cunt. He's goat that managerial tone, that *in control* shite gaun oan. The lawyer sits thaire, looking intently, occasionally nodding but no really saying anything, but ye know that just wi him being there the polis play by Queensberry rules n dinnae overstep the mark. This is how coppers should be, but *ah've* never hud them like this before.

When the polis leave, the lawyer debriefs us before he goes n aw, and then Mel goes tae check oan the bairns, whae, eftir sleepin through aw the aggro, got woken up by the cop car sirens. Like there was any need for aw that fuckin fuss when the cunt had been taken care ay!

It leaves me and Renton in the front room. Ah take him tae the kitchen and make him a cup ay tea. — Dinnae keep peeve in the hoose, ah tell him when he pills a wee face. — So, what's aw this aboot?

— They cannae fuck aboot wi the YLT, mate, he sais, half laughin, the bones ay his face defined in the moonlight comin through the windae. Always was a skinny cunt.

Ah hus a wee giggle at that, as ah pours, intae they Hibs commemorative Scottish Cup mugs ah goat fae Terry. — I meant what brought ye here?

— You wouldnae believe this, he smiles, — but ah came here tae have a row wi ye aboot the money. Was even gaunny offer tae fight ye for it! Seems a bit pointless now.

— You'd huv fuckin done me now, mate, ah laughs, taking another sip ay tea. — Violence just isn't my bag any more. Never led me anywhere but jail. Ah looks him up and doon. — But when did you git tae be such a tidy cunt?

— That's thanks tae you as well, Renton sais, his sly eyes burning away. — Was practising for you coming for me. Then it happened and a car got in the way first. Just as well, cause I fuckin froze!

— Well, thank fuck ye never this time. Come wi me, ah tell him, and pick up the pot, milk n mugs, n stick them on a tray. We go back intae the studio, and tae my desk in the recess, where ah set it down. Ah pull an envelope out the drawer. It's his money, the fifteen grand, still in UK dosh. — Ah wis gaunny gie ye it back, ah tell um, although that's no exactly true. Fact is, it was gaunny sit in my desk forever, tae remind ays that there's other ways ay getting even wi a smart cunt. — Jist wanted tae hud oantae it for

390

a while, teach ye a wee lesson aboot rippin yir mates oaf. How it feels, ay?

— Thanks. He takes the envelope and slaps it against his thigh. — Helps me oot a bit. Means a lot. And, aye, lesson learned, he goes.

Ah sortay realise that ah've been a bit hard oan the cunt, cleaning him oot wi the *Leith Heads*, cause eh came through big time. And ah suppose eh really did just want tae make things right, even if ah wisnae struck oan the wey eh went aboot it. — Good, cause ah've found a buyer who's interested in the *Leith Heads*. If ye ever fancy sellin them, like.

— Seriously?

— One ay ma regular collectors. Boy named Villiers. Very wealthy. If you're of a mind to sell I'll get you what ye peyed plus twenty-five per cent on top.

— I'll sell, the cunt goes, a bit too fucking quickly, then adds, — … no offence tae the works, Frank, but I really do need the money. But ah don't get it, ah mean …

— Why is he peying that much for a pile a shite I've just cast, and huvnae even given ma signature mutilation?

Renton looks at me for a wee bit, raises the mug, takes a sip. — Well, aye.

Ah huv a wee laugh at that wi the cunt. — You dinnae get how art works, mate. It has zero value other than what people are prepared to pay for it. By paying what you did for it, you gied it that value. You also outbid a cunt whae doesnae like to be outbid. Ever.

— So why was he?

Ah pour us some mair tea fae the pot. — He instructed his agent tae go tae a certain price, thinking, like every cunt else, that the bidding would fall way, way under it. Then you come along and scooby every fucker. The agent, this boy Stroud, that cunt bidding against you, he was huvin kittens trying tae get the radge on the mobby before that hammer came doon.

— And he would have paid …

— Whatever it took. It fucks his heid that he didnae even ken who you were. Nae social media presence or nowt. Ah sits back oan the workbench. — He probably thought you were working on behalf ay some rival whae wis tryin tae stiff the cunt! But what ah want tae ken is, what the fuck was Mikey Forrester daein biddin it up?

Renton blows on the top ay his mug ay tea. — That was our auld buddy Sick Boy's doing. I think he felt I needed a bigger financial hit. He was daein you a favour and me a bad turn. And Mikey and I never got on since back in the day. I rode this bird fae Lochend he was intae. He smiles in memory.

It sounds plausible enough. Everything in life is distorted by wee irrational jealousies and daft impulses. Ye huv tae get control ay these cunts or they destroy ye. So best thing tae dae – n aw they politicians n business cunts get this – is fuck up people that have nae real connection tae ye.

Renton looks around the studio. — I'm in the wrong game. All those years fannying around in music wi nae talent for it.

— Talent is way, way overrated, mate. Timing is all. And that's maistly luck, and a wee bit ay intuition and savvy. I point tae him. — And thank fuck you've got that, bud. Ah owe ye big time. That cunt would have made ma bairns orphans.

— Ah'll settle for us being square. Finally, he smiles.

Ah extend ma hand. — Square it is.

He gies a cheeky wee smile, which reminds me ay the way he looked as a kid. — And you were always quite good at art, back at school, before ye got flung out the class!

— That was the only class ah minded getting bounced oot ay. Ah lower ma voice cause ah kin hear Mel talking tae the bairns. — The best rides were in the art class.

— They still comprise twenty-five per cent ay ma wanking material, he grins.

— That's quite low.

— I've been working in clubs for years. That's steadily reduced it.

We just laugh, the baith ay us, like we used tae dae comin hame fae school. Doon Duke Street, along Junction Street, towards the Fort, pishin ourselves, just talkin aboot some daft shite or other. — Ken the funniest thing? We're now both rich enough tae never let money come between us again.

It's probably the nerves but Renton starts laughing like a fucking loony. Ah join in. Then he suddenly goes aw serious. — Ah want ye tae come down tae LA sometime, tae meet somebody.

Fuck knows whae, but it's the least ah kin dae. — Sound.

40

SICK BOY – HUCKLED

The meal was eaten in stilted circumstances, but the job was done. Euan is, hopefully, once again isolated from Carlotta. That was just phase one: next that bastard is out of my family for good. This town ain't big enough for the both of us! Then Marianne and I head back to the hotel to celebrate, and I'm straight online.

I thought it might be a bitty unwise to get Jill along to the room tae help Marianne and me celebrate our love. That somewhat unedifying bit of history from Christmas. Best make those accessories purely business ones. Jasmine, sadly, seems to have vanished. I was almost even tempted to call Syme to pull a favour, but I'm staying away from that grotbag. Instead, I get on to a wannabe Colleagues agency, and I'm ogling their app. My preference is for an African princess, black as coal, or even a raven-haired, dusky-skinned Romany maiden, in order to provide a contrast to Marianne's Nordic Nazi. She looks over my shoulder and pulls a face. — Why can't we get a guy? I want to be done by you and another guy! I want an uncircumcised dick with a big fat cherry bursting onto the scene.

I feel my brow crinkle in distaste, and lower the phone. — But, darling, I hate men. I can't look at another man's naked body without feeling sick. I can barely talk to them, I insist, as I'm psychologically scythed by a horrible image of Renton, fucking her, my soon-to-be wife.

— Maybe you need desensitivity training. C'mon, let's get a guy!

I shake that Treacherous Ginger Bastard out of my head.

— It won't work, honey. I've tried to tell you that over the years. I once went to an orgy and got a sweaty bawbag and hairy arse-crack in my face. Way too traumatising, and I'm far from the squeamish sort, I explain, shuddering in recall of a terrible incident in Clerkenwell. — I envy the fuck out of you, as I've always aspired to be bisexual.

— I'm no bisexual, she protests.

— Well, if you prefer, 'a-woman-who-knows-how-to-pulverise-another-woman's-clitoris-until-she-explodes'?

— I dinnae like labels, she says, then commands, — Suck my clit.

— Try stopping me, babes, just you try stopping me, I grin, — but *only* after you've picked a lassie, I nod to the phone.

Tutting and rolling her eyes, Marianne takes the iPhone off me, scrolling the profiles. She settles on Lily, another blonde who looks like a younger version of her. Fucking narcissists everywhere. It's not a great contrast, and I stress the need for visual variety, but as she's getting a bit twitchy, I decide it's best not to push it. I call the agency and Lily will be at the hotel within the hour.

I get to work and multiple-orgasm Marianne, deploying fingers, tongue, cock and, most of all, speech play that would make a death-row sex offender blush. Fucking her down the years has been like reading that leather-bound *Collected Works of William Shakespeare* I ordered ages ago – you find something new each time you pick it up. She's a feisty opponent, but I've hammered her into a dopey state of lassitude by the time the hooker arrives. I've taken care not blow my own wad, this was just a starter before the main dish of the day.

Lily comes up and I'm a bit despondent as her shots flatter her. Like *extremely*, like in an Exercise-Bike's-Facebook-Page sort of way, where the posted snaps stop at around 1987, but no point in quibbling, as time is money. We go through only the rudimentary courtesies before getting down to business. Lily has a huge strap-on which she works into the arse of Marianne, who is crouched on the edge of the bed. I assume a similar position in front of Marianne, in order to take my fiancée's lubed dildo up my hole. It's going in with slow relief, like shitting in reverse, Marianne screaming as the base of the device is grinding against her clit like a demented Italian waiter on speed with a pepper cellar. I feel my soul being eye-wateringly spiked as Marianne gasps and shouts, — That's my boy, take it right up ye ... this is the faggot bitch I'm gaunny fuckin mairray ...

I'm moving my hips to try and accommodate more dildo, while watching all this in the mirror, drinking in Marianne's demented scowl and Lily's gum-chewing detachment (at my instigation, all part of the set-up). Meanwhile, I'm chugging at my lubed penis in long strokes, feeling the pressure steadfastly building, like Hibs on the Rangers goal in the closing phase of the Hampden final. I'm thinking *this is what married life will be like*, when the door opens and the fucking cleaner ...

Fuck me, it's no the fucking cleaners ...

The party literally crumbles as two men burst in, flashing IDs, wearing shite cop clothes and expressions of dumb, crass entitlement. They stop in their tracks as they take in the scene, speechless and bemused for a couple of seconds but not leaving. Then one says, — You've got two minutes to get dressed, we'll be waiting outside!

They depart, one saying something I don't catch and the other responding with a deep, throaty laugh, then slamming the door behind them.

— What the fuck, Lily squeals.

Marianne looks at me and haughtily says, — I dinnae mind ay ordering those boys ...

41

RENTON – SHEDDING KING LEARS

I'm so buzzed, shocked, tired, relieved and *fucking rich*, I shouldnae be driving back to Santa Monica. My knuckles are ripped and my hands are swollen on the wheel, stubbornly reminding me that it happened. That fucking weirdo was going to shoot Franco and Melanie! And I saved the cunt! Me!

I've strayed into the wrong fucking lane and a horn blares out, a trucker giving me the finger as he passes. I've just beaten a cop to a pulp with my bare hands, and now I would shite it from my own shadow. I can't concentrate; I'm wondering how much the *Leith Heads* will really fetch and whether I should play hardball with that collector cunt, as Conrad is going to jump ship and I'll make fuck all from Emily or Carl.

This isn't working. I pull off at some services and drink shit black coffee at Arby's. It only burns a volatile stomach that feels like a nest of squirming maggots. I eat half a burrito and throw the rest away. Begbie explained that I was just suffering an amateur's stress reaction to perpetrating violence. I'm beset with the idea that dark consequence and terrible reprisal lurk around every corner. In spite of the cops totally believing our story and the lawyer's assurances that I'm in the clear, the paranoia is ripping out of me. I consider turning on my phone, but I know that would be the worst thing to do right now, even if the urge is almost irresistible. It's always just bad news, anyway. Conrad is ramping to jump ship, just when I hear from the Wynn that he's got the big gig at XS, on the back of his latest big hit. Now some other cunt will reap the benefits. Fuck it.

I get back in the rental, driving like a learner, conscious of every move, never so relieved to get off the 101 onto the 405. The jammed city traffic slows things down, composing me, giving ays time to think. I decide it's good. I did a virtuous thing and got payback from it. I fantasise about the likely and unlikely rewards. A mystical healer or breakthrough wonderdrug for Alex, that miraculously connects him to the world. But no amount of money will make that happen. It will, however, get me an essential three-bedroomed apartment. Then I'm onto the 10 to Santa Monica, then coming off it, and parking in my underground lot. I get out the car and hold my hand in front of my face. It's shaking, but I'm home in one piece.

Then, from the periphery of my vision, I see a figure step out of a car. It moves between two parked vehicles, and starts walking towards me, still obscured by darkness and shadow. It's big, and powerful-looking, though, and I feel my pulse kick up and my sore fists ball. I'm ready to go again but, fuck me, it's Conrad, now lit from a yellow lamp in the roof above.

— You are okay! the fat bastard sings in delight, tears welling in his big eyes as he grabs me in an awkward embrace. I'm nervously patting his back, totally scoobied. I never expected this. — You should phone, text, email ... he gasps, — it is not like you not to return calls! For many days! I was worried, we all were!

— Thanks, pal ... Sorry about that, loads to sort out, congrats wi the track, I lamely hear myself say, as he releases me.

— I know there are money problems with you, Conrad whispers. — Anything you need, you must tell me, and I will give it to you. My money is your money. This you know, right?

Well, no, I never had a fucking inkling that he was anything other than a tight, selfish cunt. And I thought that this was the fucking bullet coming. That Conrad would surely be signing for a rival, moving tae Ivan's stable. I certainly never imagined we had this kind ay stuff going on. — That is incredibly generous of you, pal, but I've been out of the loop, attending tae this personal and financial stuff, I explain, adjoining, — to my extreme satisfaction, I might add.

— That is good. I am pleased to hear this. But we need to talk, there have been developments, he adds an ominous tone.

— Right, well, first I have to go upstairs and check on my dad and my boy. Meet me in the Speakeasy on Pico in twenty.

— Where is this? he asks.

— Wouldn't it be great if there was this device called the Internet, whereby you could type in *Speakeasy* and *Pico Boulevard*, and the directions would come up as if by magic?

Conrad looks at me, and laughs disparagingly. — I think I know this device. It is in something called a phone, which you can also talk into when it rings. But I'm not sure that my manager has a fucking clue as to what it is!

— Point taken, bud, see you in a bit.

So I go up to the apartment, a bit trepidatious at the reception I'll get from my dad, for taking off and leaving him and Alex, and now having to head straight back out. I've been leaning heavily on the poor old bastard. Since the two funerals, Vicky and I have been hanging out a lot, and I've stayed more than a few nights at hers down in Venice. Dad doesn't seem to mind, agreeing that the couch won't do my back any good, though I suppose I've been taking the piss a bit. But when

400

I get in he's sitting on the couch, playing video games with Alex. He points to the Xbox and the pile of games. — Just been stocking up, he says, neither one of them averting their eyes from the screen to me.

It's fairly obvious that they are both fine with me going right out again. I head to the Speakeasy and Conrad's parked up in the street outside, slumped over the dashboard like an activated airbag. I tap the window and he springs awake. We go into the bar and he orders a *Diet* Pepsi. Fuck me, the revolution has started. I order a nice bottle of California Pinot. The Speakeasy wine bar is almost empty tonight. Two young women sit at one table, and a group of executives at another, their loud chatter telling the world that they're in TV. Conrad declines a glass of my plonk, but then augments his soft drink with a beer, as we settle down at a corner table. — I thought you were here to sack me, I confide.

— No, and he looks shocked, — do not be stupid! You are family to me, he says, as I quickly work through a glass, then refill. — Sometimes it feels like you are the only one who has ever taken an interest in me.

Fuck sake, now it's me fighting back the King Lears here! This *has* been an emotional day. I rescue Begbie and Mel, and pummel some bent psycho copper half to death, get back the fortune I'd lost, and now this Dutch cunt is breaking my fucking heart! So I cope by letting the manager in ays kick in, the sudden intimacy between us giving me an opening. — The family thing, I look at him gravely, — I feel the same way about all you guys, mate ... and that's why it's killing me to see you letting yourself go.

— What ...?

— The timber, bro; it needs to be shed, and I punch his airm. — This weight is killing you, and it shouldn't be that way. You're a young guy, Conrad, it's not right.

There's a brief flash ay hostility in his eyes. Then they soften, moistening as he starts telling me about his old man. The dude is a classical musician with the Dutch National Orchestra, who has never respected his son's love of electronic dance music. This lack of acknowledgement and credibility in his dad's eyes depresses the fuck out of Conrad.

I suck in a long breath, and unload. — This maybe isnae what ye want tae hear, mate, but *fuck him*. He's respected by some stiff-arsed old cunts who go tae listen tae his fanny-baws orchestra playing the music ay deid fuckers. You're respected by teenage Lyrca-clad goddesses who want to suck your brains out through your dick and then fuck whatever's left out of your head. The old cunt is *jealous*, mate, it's as simple as that. If our one goal in life is to replace our fathers, and I think in guilt at the lovely old Weedgie boy down the street, — then job done, and at a precociously early age, and I raise my glass in a toast. — Nice one!

He looks at me with that same tremor of anger again, before it melts into considered deliberation, then enlightenment and finally, a hopeful, — You really think so?

— I know so, I tell him, as the two young women who have been looking over at us come across.

— It's you, isn't it? one of them says to Conrad. — You're Technonerd!

— Yes, Conrad says robotically as I look at him in affirmation. This woman has dramatically underscored my point.

— Oh my God!

They want selfies with him, and Conrad is happy enough to oblige. Afterwards, they have the grace to see that we're into something, and head back to the bar. I'm surprised Conrad didn't ask for a phone number, it's very unlike him.

— Now back tae this business ay the coral reef. I jab a finger at him. — I know a trainer in Miami Beach. You like it down there. She's as tough as fuck, but she will sort out your brain and body. I hand him the card of this woman Lucy, whom Jon, a flabby promoter at Ultra (at least until she got a hold of him), recommended tae ays.

Conrad takes it in his grubby fist, and slips it into his pocket. — Now that we are being frank, he says, — there are some things I need to tell you. The first one is that you are right about Emily. She is an amazing talent. Her new stuff is very, very good. I am remixing some of her tracks. We have been working in Amsterdam, but we need to find a new studio here for the Vegas season.

— Brilliant! That's great news! I'm totally on it with the studio. I have several options –

— The second is that we are having a relationship. Emily and myself.

— Well, that's your business, bud …

My face must be giving away that I believe they are probably the two most fundamentally unsuited people on the planet. But maybe not, as Conrad says, — She said that you guys had been fucking. So this thing with her and me, it is not a problem for you?

— No … why should it be? It was just once … I look at him. — She told you we had sex? What the fuck … what did she say?

— That you were good in bed – creative, was the word she used – but also that you do not have the stamina of a younger man. That you can no longer fuck all night, which is what she needs, and a trace of a smile spreads across the corners ay his chops.

I can't help but laugh at that. — Let's just leave it there and allow me to congratulate you both. I have a bit of news too. This will be your last season at Surrender.

403

— They cannot fire me, he fumes, then smashes his fist on the table and my wine glass wobbles, — you cannot let them do this!

I raise my hand to silence him and cut in, — Next season you'll be playing XS.

— Fuck! He jumps up, and shouts across to the bar, — Give me a bottle of your best champagne, then says to me, — I have the best manager in the world!

I can't resist it. — To quote Brian Clough, I'm certainly in the top one.

— Who is Brian Clough?

— Before your time, bud, I say depressingly.

For the first time, Vicky, with Willow and Matt, joins me in Vegas. We see Calvin Harris at the Hakkasan, Britney Spears at the Axis, and, of course, Conrad, Emily and Carl at Surrender.

While Conrad is on the decks, and Carl is explaining DMT to the others, I collar Emily. — Thanks for telling him about us. I nod to the box and Conrad's hulking back.

— Oh, it just slipped out. Sorry!

— I should think so.

— Don't take the hump. Emily raises a brow. — It was me who helped convince him, and Ivan, that you were the main man.

The fuck ... — Ivan? What about Ivan?

— Yes, Conrad and I have been hanging out with him in Amsterdam. I've been trying to get him back onside. It's only gone and worked, hasn't it? she grins. — He wants to come back to Citadel Productions. You should expect a call soon.

Fuck me. It's not Ivan who has been trying to poach them for the big boys! It's them who've been grooming

Ivan-the-treacherous-Belgian to return to the Citadel camp.

— Emily, I'm eternally grateful, but why are you doing this?

    — I feel a bit bad, because of all the aggro I caused you.

    — Look, it was just a daft wee shag and it shoul—

    — Not that, you fucking idiot, she laughs and leans into me. — This one you really need to keep to yourself …

    — Okay …

    — … the dickhead thing wasn't Carl, she confides, and we both start fitting with laughter.

42

INTERROGATION

The interview room is stark and bare. There is a Formica table, on which sits recording equipment. It's surrounded by hard plastic chairs. Simon David Williamson has regained his composure, and part of him, as it always does, is relishing the interpersonal challenges ahead. He grinds his teeth together in a move he considers galvanising. On his arrival at the police station and prior to his placement in a holding room, he immediately insisted on calling his brief. The lawyer instructed silence until he arrived. Williamson, though, has other ideas.

He looks aloofly at the two police officers who have taken him into the room. They have sat down, one of them placing a plastic folder on the table. Williamson opts to remain standing. — Take a seat, invites one of the cops, as he turns on the recorder. This officer has cropped fair hair in quite a dramatic receding 'V'. He has attempted to cover up an acne-ravaged chin with a beard that grows only wispy hair, therefore just emphasising the scarring more. *Married the first bird that opened her legs to him* is Williamson's pitiless evaluation. In his laughing eyes and incongruously crueller, tight mouth, he reads the classic tells of the bad cop.

— If it's all the same to you, I prefer to stand, Williamson declares. — Sitting down isn't good for you. In fifty years from now we'll laugh at old movies where we see people sitting at desks, in much the same way we do now when we see them smoking.

— Sit down, Bad Cop repeats, pointing to the seat.

Williamson crouches down on his hunkers. — If it's eyeline or microphone pickup you're concerned with, this should do it. It's the way the creature known as *Homo sapiens* naturally lowers itself; we do this instinctively as bairns, then we get told to –

— In the seat! Bad Cop snaps.

Simon Williamson looks at the officer, then the chair, as if it's an electric one, designated for his execution. — Have it on record that I was forced into sitting out of some anti-quated attachment to social convention, and against my personal choice, he says pompously, before lowering himself.

My hands are steady. My nerves are cool. Even rattling on ching and alcohol withdrawal, I can still man the fuck up and function. I'm just a higher form of evolution. If I'd had the education, I would have been a surgeon. And not fannying about with stinky wee feet either. I would be transplanting hearts, even fucking brains.

As Bad Cop makes the aggressive pitch, Williamson studies the reaction of his colleague, the ironic smile of slight disdain that says: *My-mate's-a-wanker-but-what-can-I-do? We understand each other.* It's a variation on the good cop/bad cop routine. Good Cop is a tubby, dark-haired man who looks permanently startled. The harsh lights above bounce un-flatteringly on his uneven, putty-like features. He keeps the grin on Williamson as Bad Cop continues. — So you were in London on the 23rd of June?

— Yes, I believe so. Easy to verify. There will be phone calls, probably a withdrawal from the NatWest cashpoint at King's Cross Station, which I visit regularly. And of course, there's the sandwich bar on Pentonville Road. Tell your colleagues at the Metropolitan Police to ask for Milos. I'm a *weel-kent* face there, as you like to say back up here, he smiles, starting to enjoy himself. — I always travel by tube, my Oyster card transactions should show a confirming pattern, and of course, my fiancée would be with me … So, what happened to Victor Syme?

— Friend of yours, was he? Bad Cop tugs at his ratty beard.

— I wouldn't say that.

— You're on his calls list enough.

— We explored the possibility of doing business together, Simon Williamson declares, voice now set in the authoritative cast of the tetchy businessman having his time wasted by incompetent public servants. — I run a reputable dating agency, and I was talking to him about the possibility of expanding into Edinburgh.

Bad Cop, aware that Williamson is pointedly examining his facial ministrations, lowers his hands. — So you didn't do business together?

Simon Williamson envisions him having eczema in his genital region and trying in vain to pass it off as an STD in the dressing room of the police football team. It amuses him to think of the flakes of skin nestling in the law enforcement officer's pubes, sticking with sweat to the face of his wife as she grimly performs fellatio duties. — No.

— Why?

— To be quite frank, Syme's operation struck me as very low-rent and sleazy, and the girls were obviously common prostitutes – not that I make moral judgements, he adds in haste, — just not what I was looking for as a business model. I'm focusing more on MBAs, the premium market.

Bad Cop says, — You do know that prostitution is illegal?

Williamson looks at Good Cop in faux amazement, then turns to his interrogator, speaking patiently to him as one would a child. — Of course. As I say, we're an escort agency.

Our girls, or partners as we call them, accompany executives to meetings and dinners, they host events and parties. This is the legal framework within which I operate.

— Since when? You've had two court appearances for living off immoral earnings.

— One was when I was a very young man, addicted to heroin. My girlfriend and I were extremely desperate, driven by the dictates of that horrible drug. The second one was related to an enterprise I had absolutely nothing to do with –

— The Skylark Hotel in Finsbury Park –

— The Skylark Hotel in Finsbury Park. I happened to be visiting those premises when they were being investigated by the Metropolitan Police vice squad. There was a lazy association and some nonsense, trumped-up charges, which I was proven innocent of. Totally exonerated. That was well over a decade ago.

— So you're Mr Snow White, Bad Cop scoffs.

Simon Williamson allows himself a highly audible exhalation. — Look, I'm not going to insult your intelligence and claim that sort of thing doesn't go on, but, as I say, we are an agency selling escort services. Prostitution is nothing to do with us, and if any of our partners get involved in that and we find out about it, they're off the books straight away.

— Us?

— My fiancée is now a company director.

Good Cop comes in with a complete change of emphasis. — Do you know Daniel Murphy?

To avoid seeming wrong-footed, Simon Williamson attempts to think of the great injustices Spud visited on him; concentrating on his snowdropping of a much loved Fair Isle jersey from the concrete drying greens of the Banana Flats. But all he sees in his mind's eye is the Oor Wullie smile on a younger Spud, and he feels something in his heart melt.

— Yes, and may his soul rest in peace. An old friend.

Bad Cop is back in the chair. — Do you know how he died?

Shaking his head, Williamson composes himself. *An expression of genuine grief would be a good reveal, don't panic. I tried to save him.* — Some sort of illness. Danny, God love him, well, he led a very marginal life, I'm afraid.

— Somebody ripped out his kidney. He died from complications resulting from that, Bad Cop snaps. The air in the room seems to lose half of its oxygen.

— I really think I need to wait till my lawyer gets here before answering any more questions, Williamson declares. — I've tried to cooperate as a concerned citizen, but –

— You can do that, Bad Cop cuts him off, — but you might find it's to your advantage to cooperate with us informally if you don't want to be charged with the murder of Victor Syme, and he takes a photo from the plastic file in front of him, throwing it under Simon Williamson's nose. He examines the picture in morbid fascination. It shows Syme lying in a pool of blood, which seems to have come from multiple wounds, most of it a gash in his stomach.

Then Bad Cop shows him a closer image, and two maroon bean-shaped things seem to be sticking out the sockets where Syme's eyes once were. It gives the impression of a comic Photoshopped set-up and Williamson laughs.

— Is this for real?

— Oh, it's real alright. Those are his kidneys, Bad Cop says.

Williamson lowers the photograph. Feels his hand tremble. Knows Bad Cop has noticed it. — This isnae fucking well on, I know my rights –

— Yes, so you say, Bad Cop mocks. — Okay, come with us.

The officers rise and take him next door into an adjoining anteroom. On one side, through a one-way plate glass,

Williamson can see the empty interview room they've just vacated. On the other side is an identical room. But there, at the table, sits his brother-in-law, Euan McCorkindale. The disgraced podiatrist seems beyond catatonic; it's as if he's been lobotomised.

— He's basically told us about your part in the removal of Daniel Murphy's kidney, Good Cop announces in sad compassion. He looks as if he's genuinely going to burst into tears on Williamson's behalf.

But Williamson remains composed. — Aw aye, he says disparagingly, — which was?

Good Cop nods in stagy reluctance to Bad Cop, who takes over. — That you removed it, under his supervision, with another man, in unsanitary conditions, at a location in Berlin.

Williamson hits back with a dismissive tirade so contemptuous, the police officers unprofessionally swither between visible anger and embarrassment. — Under *his supervision*? Williamson thumbs at the man through the mirror. — Is he on fucking drugs? I'm not qualified to remove a kidney! Wouldn't even know where to fucking find it! Do I look like a surgeon? Simon Williamson tosses his head back, openly revelling in his performance. Then he looks from one cop to the other, sensing their unease. He says softly, — He's the doctor, and he points back to the glass again, — that fucking balloon there. So work it out for yourselves.

Good Cop slips back into the driving seat. — He said he was being blackmailed by Victor Syme, over a sex tape, into performing this surgery –

— That I can believe –

— But couldn't go through with the removal of the kidney. He said that *you* took it out, assisted by a YouTube video and a man named Michael Forrester –

411

— Now we're delving into the realms of fantasy, Williamson snorts.

— Are we, Simon? Are we really? Good Cop pleads.

— Mikey Forrester? YouTube kidney-removal videos? What the fuck are youse boys on? Simon Williamson laughs loudly, shaking his head. — That one will amuse the fuck out of the magistrates when this goes to court!

The cops look at each other. To Williamson they now give off the underlying desperation that they are grown men playing a silly child's game they can no longer believe in. But then another sudden change of tack blindsides him, as Good Cop's face takes on a cuntish hue. — Can you explain a deposit of ninety-one thousand pounds in cash into your bank account on the 6th of January?

Williamson knows that his face will register little, but he feels something die inside of him. *Renton. I'm going to be done by fucking Renton.* — How do you know about that money?

— We contacted your bank. You're part of an investigation, so they were obligated to let us know any substantial recent deposits made.

— This is fucking outrageous, Williamson booms. — Since when did the fucking banks, who have ripped off and exploited every citizen in this country, become ... he blusters. — That was a payback from a business deal!

Good Cop delivers the line like a soap-opera actor. — The business of organ harvesting?

— No! It was ... Look, talk to Mikey Forrester. He's Syme's business partner. They had a bad falling-out.

Both police officers stare at him in silence.

Williamson wonders where the fuck his brief has got to, but in this anteroom no recording device is in evidence, so this is probably off the record. He glances again through the mirror, at the immobile and miserable Euan. He counts to ten slowly in his head, before speaking. — Okay, cards-on-the-table time. I was in Berlin, at Spud's request, to look after him. I learned that Euan was being blackmailed by Syme, he explains, wondering whether to throw Forrester under the bus, and deciding against it. Mikey would manage that easily enough himself, and it would be far more convincing coming from the horse's mouth. — I was there to make sure my old mate was okay. A hand-holding exercise. I obviously suspected it was a dodgy deal, but that wasn't my business. Ask Mikey!

Bad Cop looks to Good Cop. — Mr Forrester has gone to ground; he's not returning our calls. His phone is switched off, and we're trying to trace it. I would suspect that it isn't on his person.

Simon David Williamson decides it's time to stop busking it. — I'm saying nothing more till my lawyer gets here. He shakes his head. — I have to say I'm very disappointed in the attitude displayed by you officers today. There's nobody more pro-police and law and order than me. I try to cooperate and assist you and I'm treated like a common criminal, subjected to all sorts of snidey innuendo. So where's my brief?

— He's on his way, Good Cop says. — Tell us about Syme.

— No comment.

— You sure you want to do time? For these bams? Syme? Forrester? Not easy at your age, Bad Cop says, then leans forward and drops his voice to a whisper. — Somebody else will be drilling that hot bitch of a fiancée of yours soon, mate.

— Somebody probably already is, Williamson replies.

Good Cop seems to chastise Bad Cop's crassness with a disagreeable pout. — Go easy on yourself, Simon, he softly urges. — Just tell me, can you think of anybody, other than Forrester, who might have done this to Syme?

Sick Boy couldn't see Mikey perpetrating such violence on Victor Syme. But he can't think of anybody else other than diffuse and shadowy East Europeans who must have been his sauna and organ-harvesting associates. — No. I can't. But Syme was obviously mobbed up with some dodgy people, he states as Bad Cop opens the anteroom door. Williamson immediately sees what looks like a lawyer, coming down the corridor, trying to get his bearings. The man walks past the anteroom, then double-backs and looks in.

— I'm Colin McKerchar, from Donaldson, Farquhar, McKerchar, he says to Good Cop. Then he nods to his client. — Simon David Williamson?

— Yes, Williamson says and looks at the policemen. — So for any future questioning I will have a lawyer present. And I will fucking well exercise my human rights and stand on my feet. But right now, I think I want to leave.

— No charges? McKerchar fixes a searching, professional gaze on the cops. — Then let's do just that.

— Of course, says Good Cop. — Thank you so much for your assistance, Mr Williamson.

— The pleasure was all yours, Williamson snorts, turning on his heels and exiting, followed by his brief.

Epilogue

Summer 2016

I Met You in the Summertime

We make an odd quartet, me, Vicky, Alex and the old boy. Fishing off Santa Monica Pier, catching zero wi our solitary cheapo rod, compared tae the mair dedicated anglers with their specialist equipment and bait. But this is about nothing mair than being together. There will be a good eighteen months of fannying about with documentation for my father and son. Social services in Holland are being cunty, and lawyers will get richer, but we're no going anywhaire.

Alex obviously reminds the old man ay Wee Davie. He's indulgent with him, more than I am, certainly more than I ever was ay my wee brother. I hated all the gob, snot, shit, pish, sound and general radge behaviour that emanated from him; saw Davie as little mair than a human excrement factory, designed tae facilitate ma constant social embarrassment on the streets of Leith. Never got how the old man could stand it. Well, that's one ay the benefits ay developing a thick skin. I've learned to accept it all, even love it, in my own kid, not that he's as clarty or as full spectrum as my brother was. He's never gaunny play for Hibs, though, or front a happening band, or, saddest of all, know the rapture ay making love wi somebody. But he's never gaunny be a skagheid, or spend his adult life having tae babysit DJs. Most of all, he'll live wi the sun in his face as long as there's a breath in my body.

I catch Vicky correcting her hair, the Pacific breeze constantly whipping out strands across her face. She likes my

417

old boy, and seems fond ay Alex. Even when he looks at her and says for the zillionth time, — I asked for one, not two.

It's not all roses, though. She's made it very clear that she doesnae want kids, which I totally get and suits me tae fuck, but the idea of living wi somebody else's teenaged handicapped one is something she never considered signing up for. We're talking about how complicated our lives are and it's no the time tae discuss moving in together. But we're talking about no talking about it a lot. And will continue tae do so.

Life isnae so bad. Conrad has settled into the Vegas residency, with his eager eye on his forthcoming upgrade to XS, and has Emily and Carl as regular guests. No, it didn't last between Conrad and Emily, but they've stayed close, and their collaboration raised her status and profile. Maybe that was her plan all along. Conrad moved his permanent base to Miami, after I hooked him up with the personal trainer there. I thought he'd run like fuck, as she has a pretty fearsome rep, but they get on and he's stuck with the programme. The results have been spectacular. He's gone from 354 to 226 pounds and is still shedding. I don't have to help him get laid now. Post-Conrad, Emily has moved to New York. She's in the studio a lot more and the results have been highly encouraging. The Vegas residency will mean less travelling, and neither she nor Conrad is as clingy now. They're just growing up, I suppose, but a lot quicker than I ever did. And I have Ivan, the Belgian-formerly-known-as-treacherous, still tearing it up, back on my books.

Carl has moved tae LA; the cunt is in West Hollywood, but I don't think he's given up on Helena yet, and I sense that might only set him up for more hurt. However, ye never can tell a windae-licking Jambo cunt anything.

And here, walking through the hazy tendrils ay heat, under the pale blue sky, comes the other odd quartet, though the rest ay the world would see them as normality squared. Heading towards us, along the sand, is the artist-formerly-known-as-psychopathic, his wife and his two wee girls, one ay whom – the youngest yin – has a definite Daughter-ay-Begbie edge. At her urging, probably for the umpteenth time, he hoists her into air, to her rapture. The older one, Grace, a very bright kid, is chatting tae her mum, who embraces Vicky, as my dad shakes hands with Franco. Sauzee, their dog, bounds over tae Toto, and they sniff each other, deciding that they get along.

Of course, I had to take Spud's daft wee mutt. Alex loves him, sits with him across his knees, dispensing rhythmic strokes over his head and down his back. Neither of them tires of this. I sometimes watch tae see whae'll end it first, and they only stop when it's mealtimes. Even I've gotten attached tae Toto and I'm no really an animals guy, especially small dogs.

Franco takes advantage ay Eve charging after our canine pals, and comes over, playfully squeezing my bicep. — There's ma fuckin hero. He looks wistfully at the two girls, playing now with the pooches. — Could have lost it all.

— It's cool, bud, I whisper. I've got big money in the bank thanks tae him. He did sell the heads for me, at about forty per cent more than I paid for them. Franco, Melanie and I agreed tae play down that horrible incident with the rogue cop. The stalker is likely to get banged up for at least ten on abduction, assault and breaking and entering charges. I'll be in court soon as a witness. I've given Vicky and Dad a broad outline. Time enough to tell them all the details later.

I'm working out a lot, going for runs with Vicky. I'm eating well, and keeping off the drink and drugs. I occasionally dae NA as a lifebelt, like before I go travelling with the DJs, and have an app tae tell ays where the meetings are in each city I visit. I'm watching my weight, for the first time: I was always a thirty-two-inch waist. Now Billy's thirty-fours fit me just fine. My tribute tae him and Spud is tae wear them until they fall off.

But maybe we'll all have some ice cream. Just like when Franco and I first met back at that van, outside the Fort, him carrying the Tupperware bowl. This time he won't be chasing radges, and I won't be chasing drugs. My phone rings, and I step down the beach to take it. It's Gavin Gregson, the publisher in London. The one I sent Spud's manuscript tae, with just a few corrections. Well, two words mainly, both on the title page. He will reiterate to me about how excited they are to be publishing my book next spring. I think about Sick Boy's words, that you can only be a cunt or a mug, and you really can't be a mug. A thousand things go through my mind at once. Maybe atonement is about doing the right thing. But who for? I see Vicky smiling at me, as Alex does a wee dance on the spot. What do I do? What would you do? I let it ring another couple of times, then hit the green button. — Gavin, how goes?

ACKNOWLEDGEMENTS

Big shout out to all at my publishers, Jonathan Cape. Thanks again, people.

Special thanks to the magnificent Dan McDaid for his wonderful DMT illustrations.